Christian V

christian
VASSIE
beneath the
bittercrest
No rules. No safety net.

beneath the bittercrest

christian vassie

injini

Copyright © 2006 christian vassie

The right of christian vassie to be identified as the Author of
the Work has been asserted by him in accordance with
the Copyright, designs and Patents Act 1988

First published in Great Britain in 2006
by Injini Press

All rights reserved. No part of this publication may be reproduced,
stored in a retrieval system, or transmitted, in any form or by any
means without the prior written permission of the publisher, nor be
otherwise circulated in any form of binding or cover other than that
in which it is published and without a similar condition being
imposed on the subsequent publisher.

All characters in this publication are fictitious
and any resemblance to real persons, living or dead,
is purely coincidental.

ISBN 0 9552437 0 X
978 0 9552437 0 7

Injini Press
a division of Drink Me Productions Ltd.
10 Blake Court, Wheldrake
york YO19 6BT

www.injini.co.uk

For Mary, Jaz, Dominque & Roxanne
la vie est belle

For Françoise and Maurice
thank you

Prologue - January 2002

Set back a little from the road are tall iron gates, held in place by a heavy steel chain and a padlock the size of a boxer's fist. Cold dark rain clatters from a moonless sky.

Escape! The gates are all that stand between him and freedom.

Jumping on the spot and beating his thin arms against his chest, he considers his options. The gates are topped with ugly spikes. The fence to either side of the gates are crowned with barbed wire.

How long is it since he had seized the chance to slip away? Eight minutes? Ten? Is a search party out looking for him?

In normal circumstances scaling the gates would be easy but he is a thousand of miles away from normal circumstances, barefoot and in summer clothes. His lungs ache from the frostbitten air and he hasn't eaten for five days. He has no money and no idea of what town he is in. His only certainties are: one, that he has reached England, for the voices that ring in his ears day and night shout in English, and two, that he has to escape.

A car speeds past along the road beyond the gates. All at once the full glare of headlights finds his face. He throws himself to the ground.

As the motor roar fades, he hears a dull metal ringing coming from the darkness over his shoulder.

Barely visible against the night sky are two huge towers. He guesses they must store oil or gas. Is someone looking down on him? Has he been spotted? Another sound. This time there can be no doubt. Voices. Two men shouting. Their voices getting louder.

He spins away from the gates and crashes his way through the bushes, throwing himself back towards the wasteland. Failure is not an option, he has to go back the way he has come and find another avenue of escape.

There has to be a witness, the others are depending on him.

He stifles a scream as gorse spikes hammer into his heels and ankles, his bare toes jarring against rocks and stones, skin torn from the soles of his feet. Up ahead is the low building, backlit by light from the car park. He alters his course to avoid passing too close but, as he does so, the ground dips away. Staggering, desperate to stay upright, he trips and falls, smashing his head against a jagged outcrop of concrete.

one

November 2001

Jackpot day for the Big Issue seller who takes the seventy quid he's offered, dumps the entire pile of magazines he has been clutching for six hours in his benefactor's arms and hurries away before the eejot can change his mind. They say there's one born everyday and, for the first time in his life, Patrick 'Scuggs' Vern has been granted the privilege of meeting one. Who said there are no angels?

His Benefactor, a forty year old African, watches the scruffy tramp shuffle off towards the nearest off-licence, muttering away to himself.

An arctic cold prowls and probes every exposed surface, the few people there are on the platforms press against the walls as close as coats of paint. A festering monochrome sky sits heavily on Doncaster. Snow is forecast.

The new seller of Big Issues hovering just inside the station entrance is not much better off than his predecessor, no bank account, no national insurance number, no work permit, no proper home ... but he does now have a job. Two jobs. He adjusts his small brightly patterned African hat, stuffs his free hand into one of the voluminous pockets of his scruffy purple track suit, and waits.

He has sold three magazines and earned almost six pounds when he spots the target striding into the station. The description is good: mid thirties, white, above average height, blue eyes, sideburns, dark coat and, most usefully, carrying a black briefcase bearing a sticker of a cartoon dragon.

Still calling out Big Issue the African turns away to avoid eye contact with his quarry and is therefore completely unprepared when the man bumps into him from behind, sending thirty copies of the magazine spraying out in all directions across the station concourse. The African drops to his knees to pick up his magazines. Towering over him, the quarry mutters an apology and strides off towards the departures boards.

No sooner is the man out of eyeshot than the African drops the

BENEATH THE BITTERCREST

magazines he has retrieved, stands up and walks briskly out of the station, mobile phone in hand. In his wake loiter thirty scattered Big Issues, their pages flapping back and forth in the bitter wind. An hour later, a now drunk and confused Patrick 'Scuggs' Vern will stumble across them, mutter grateful thanks to the almighty, and stagger off into the night with the magazines tucked into the plastic bag he calls his designer hand luggage, along with his five remaining cans of Special Brew.

Roxanne Lepage steps out of the taxi and heads quickly into the station, barely exchanging glances with the African who has, finally, proved himself useful at something.

She heads straight for the ladies toilet where she finds a mop that she angles between the door and the wall in such a way that anyone else wishing to use the facilities will have to wait.

In front of the mirror she pauses briefly to take a good look at herself. Long blond hair, thick and wavy, brown eyes, a little too much makeup perhaps, dark blue trouser suit, oatmeal blouse. A career woman dressed for a business conference. She glances at the Rolex watch on her wrist, very elegant and very feminine. Very fake. She has less than four minutes.

She opens her case and takes off her hair.

It has begun to snow. Peering round the corner of the waiting room she spots him up ahead on platform five. In the distance down the tracks the GNER service to London Kings Cross has just appeared, its blunt nose inching forwards against the urban backdrop. A cardboard cup skids along the platform. Advertising boards in front of the snack stand come crashing down.

Roxanne makes an adjustment to the waistband of her skirt and shivers.

A few handfuls of snowflakes follow her onto carriage H but reach no further than the automatic door. The compartment is thankfully almost empty and she lingers just long enough to let him find his seat.

Moving in quickly while he is rummaging in his briefcase, with its cartoon sticker, she takes the table seat diagonally opposite him and opens her newspaper up in front of her, a barrier between them, to give herself time to think, to plan and control what happens next.

Her work at the conference earlier was straightforward: observe the three men, attend their presentations, talk to others in their field to gain an understanding of how they are regarded. Without getting too close, without introducing yourself or talking face to face. The Dome conference centre was perfect for that, nearly three hundred people, primarily software specialists working in the field of encryption and data security. God, how she was bored by them all, their acronym-filled chatter, the condescending way most of them expected the few women present to laugh appreciatively at their feeble jokes. From the back of the room she watched their presentations, observed how each of the men communicated, how they dealt with questions. All in all, the man she is now sitting opposite appears to be exactly what her employer is looking for.

Which is too bad.

Now she needs to push him a little further. She has ninety minutes, the time it takes to reach King's Cross, to provoke him into revealing other aspects of himself.

She is aware of movement in the periphery of her vision but ignores it.

It has taken many weeks to reach this point and while she doesn't hold out much hope, following what she has seen during the course of the day, the stakes are high. If there is a chance this man might be useful to her she needs to know about it, and then omit what she has learned from the report she presents her employer.

A finger is tapping on the top of her newspaper.

'Someone wants to speak to you. Out on the platform. Excuse me.'

Roxanne moves the paper forward to give herself a view of the window.

Why is it that some people seem incapable of carrying out instructions? She expressly told him 'no visible communication', he was to do his job and then disappear into the shadows. Instead of which there he is, in his brightly colour hat and purple track suit, bobbing up and down like an acidhead on a trampoline. She ignores him, praying everyone on the train assumes he is a deranged tramp making a spectacle of himself. The train must surely be leaving in a few seconds.

The performance at the window continues unabated. He is shouting the same word over and over. Through the thick glass she can barely hear him but his lips seem to be saying 'lying, lying, lying'. With her eyes she indicates to him the person sitting on the other side of her newspaper and silently mouths 'Piss off', her face as cold as the gale buffeting his track suit.

BENEATH THE BITTERCREST

The African hesitates momentarily, his expression one of confusion, then, changing tack, he rummages in his pockets, produces a scrap of paper and a pencil and begins writing or drawing.

The train starts to move. Roxanne sighs with relief.

But instead of giving up he walks, keeping up with the window, scribbling frantically. As the train picks up speed he breaks into a jog then, tossing the pencil aside, presses the paper against the window. He is mouthing the same word as before, 'lying, lying, lying'.

On the paper is the number 2 and a picture of what looks like a cat on a box.

He races along the platform as the train accelerates then suddenly he trips and is gone, his sheet of paper sucked away in the slipstream.

'Sad git,' says the voice behind her newspaper. 'I hope he hasn't broken a leg.'

Roxanne lowers the paper a few inches. They exchange glances, eyebrows raised, there are idiots everywhere. She raises the newspaper and turns her attention back to the view outside the window.

Doncaster is being airbrushed away, swirling snow busy like the eraser tool in Photoshop. Car parks cling to the twilight trackside for a while. Freight yards and industrial estates take their place, littering the edges of the track like flotsam gathered at the high tide mark on a beach. Street lights have come on and everything has that blue hue that photographers love in fashion shoots.

She slips off her shoes and puts her bare feet up on the chair opposite, gently pushing his briefcase back with her toes. Fine quality leather, soft and warm to the touch, not unlike the huge bag the doctor carried with him on his regular visits to see her grandmother when Roxanne was still a child.

'Welcome to the Edinburgh London express. This is Graham your onboard human resource strategist speaking. I'd like to draw your attention to the buffet car which is in ...'

Fed up with the Independent, Roxanne puts the paper down and retrieves her mobile and a punnet of strawberries from her case.

"... and passengers are reminded that carriage H is a mobile free zone."

Roxanne stands up to remove her jacket and places it, and her case, on the overhead rack, well aware of his eyes on her body as she does so. Sitting back down she prises open the plastic box restraining her strawberries, catching her own reflection momentarily in the window.

Short spiky black hair, silk blouse, a glint from the sapphire nose stud.

Her fingers reach into the punnet, pull out a strawberry and, cradling it, warming it between her fingers tips, she brings it to her nose, breathes it in with eyes closed, allowing the aroma to transport her to other places and times, before popping it in her mouth.

When her eyes open she finds herself looking directly into his, across the table. Her gaze flicks downwards an instant. Sometimes opportunities just fall out of the sky.

'Strawberry, Eliot?'

He seems confused at the unexpected intimacy. Her green eyes smile and gently guide his attention towards the badge on the lapel of his jacket.

Eliot Balkan, Office Solutions.
S N E European Conference
The Dome Centre, Doncaster.

'Business conference,' he explains.

She enjoys these moments, in control, orchestrating male attention as easily as positioning skittles in a bowling alley. Tell me something I don't know, Eliot, her eyes say.

He takes the strawberry, places it on the table in front of him, then stands to remove his jacket which he places with his coat on the back of the seat behind his briefcase. Sitting back down, he loosens his tie before picking up the strawberry and taking a bite. Mr Relaxed. Men are so transparent.

'So, you offer security?' Her voice is casual.

'What?' Taken aback a second time. 'Oh,' he laughs, remembering that the name of the conference is also on the badge. 'Sort of. Not physical security. Computers. Encryption, data protection, that sort of thing.'

'Must be very complicated,' she prompts, her voice as silk as her blouse.

'You're not going to flutter your eyelids as well, are you?' His gaze playful.

Her smile is tight lipped, like that of a tennis player acknowledging the skill of an opponent's passing shot. Whatever else Eliot Balkan is, he isn't a sucker.

'Must be like being a priest hearing confessions. Entrusted with other people's grubby little secrets,' she continues. 'How do you decide which to keep and which ones to sell?'

Her intense green eyes never leave his own, follow every incrimental flicker of his pupils, evaluating his response, judging him. He holds her gaze. For a second she worries he might be recognising her from the conference, seeing through her elaborate precautions. His eyes flick away towards the window.

'I only make the boxes,' he says eventually. 'I don't put the secrets inside.'

Exactly what her employer would want to hear, a mindless apparatnik who does his job and asks no questions. 'I don't kill people, I only make the tanks,' she goads him, prising him open.

'You've read too many thrillers,' he reposts. 'There are perfectly valid reasons for confidentiality. Why shouldn't a company keep the names of its suppliers, or the cost of its stock, private? Why should you have access to the names and addresses of, say, everyone in Doncaster on social security?'

'And if it was life and death?' She can't stand being patronised and struggles to keep the rising contempt out of her voice. 'Or slavery? You just do your bit and walk away?'

He is like the rest of them, head down, take the money, no questions asked. Another wasted journey. Another dead end. Her mobile phone rings.

'Yes? Oh, Pierre, hi.' Her mood suddenly bright and carefree. 'Yeah, sure, couldn't be better. I'm by the pool now actually. Suncream's on, Jacques has gone off to find some nibbles. Oh, you know what he's like ...' Her voice mimics a mutual friend's, 'Roxanne, Roxanne, ces olives sont magnifiques,' then back in her own voice, 'Anyway, what time is it in freezing England?'

She stares across the table as she speaks, watching Eliot Balkan leafing through a pile of brochures he has produced from his briefcase.

'Oh, stop, you're making me thirsty just thinking about it. Look, I've got to go, I want to get a swim in before lunch.'

A middle aged couple across the aisle are staring, the kind of outraged expressions that people with empty lives wear when witnessing minor deviations from normality. The man is indicating the quiet coach sign, a mobile phone behind a big red cross. Roxanne smiles blandly back as she speaks.

'Don't worry about the money. I've told you, everything's ... No, they've agreed, they can't pull out. You did organise the transfer? Good ... OK, OK. Yes. Ciao.' A moment's pause while she cuts the call then, under her breath, she mutters 'Useless shit.'

She puts her phone down on the table in front of her and sighs audibly.

'Another strawberry, Eliot?'

Outside, the snow has picked up again, lashing the side of the Edinburgh to London express which is still picking up speed. The orange glow of Doncaster has disappeared from the sky. About five hundred metres ahead, along the cold steel track, a carefully placed block of concrete crouches in the darkness.

In carriage S a youth listening to Atomic Kitten on his MP3 player notices the surface of his coffee start to tremble in its paper cup. The old lady in seat 29A is surprised by a suitcase falling over. Roxanne, curling her legs beneath her, remembers another strawberry eaten at another time, and Eliot Balkan stares across the table at Roxanne. In the buffet car a dozen packets of crisps rattle about then fall one by one to the floor. The Human Ingestion Resources Manager treads on a packet as he turns to feed the till and curses.

The first set of wheels leaves the track and, juddering gently, coaxes the rest of the engine out after it. The block of concrete comes to rest in a field fifty metres from the point of impact as the engine slowly edges left towards the embankment, at one hundred miles an hour. The carriages remain upright as one by one they jump the rails, following the engine on a heading one degree to the east of their projected course.

Staring through the windscreen at the tumbling tunnel of snow flakes, looking towards a south he will never reach, the driver tosses his thermos aside, crosses himself, and presses the intercom button, wondering what to say to the passengers and crew.

A headache the size of Doncaster. His feet are pinned beneath an obstruction beyond his eyeline. A deep, throbbing ache ferrets about in his chest like a vulture picking at a carcase. An ominous flashback of standing alone at one end of a terraced street watching a crowd of rival football supporters turn and spot him.

'Hi, yes. Oh, thank God you're in,' a voice says away to Eliot's left. 'Yes, I know I said four o'clock. No, listen ... just shut up and listen,

John ... John. There's been an accident. I'm in the train. I love you, don't forget that.'

A vague light kisses the edge of a mangled luggage rack. Someone screams and, suddenly, Eliot feels very cold. A bulky pair of trousers seem to be snared somewhere above his head. He reasons that the train must be lying on its side.

Blood drips slowly from the pair of trousers. They fall, crash against the window by Eliot's head. The smell, like a slap across the face with a brick wall. Entrails tumble casually about. The room is spinning in the stench of it. Eliot blacks out a second time.

two

Doctor Mary Anning smiled. 'Two cracked ribs. Extensive bruising. A few minor lacerations and a black eye. You're a very lucky man.'

'Care to swop places?' Eliot said.

'There are people here who have lost limbs, and people who never made it to hospital at all.'

'And people who weren't on the bloody train. I'd call them lucky.'

'You're a young man, Mr Balkan.' Dr Anning checked Eliot's chart to confirm his details. 'Yes ... thirty six. No age at all. Aside from your injuries, you're fit and healthy, so stop feeling sorry for yourself.' She handed the chart to the nurse and walked briskly away. 'I'll be round again at six to see how you are doing.'

'Can't wait.'

Nurse Riggs glared disapprovingly. Eliot glowered as Riggs fussed around him.

'Where are my things?

'On your bedside table, Eliot.'

'I don't mean my apples and my banana and my Lucozade. I mean my clothes and my briefcase.'

The nurse was clearly familiar with the thrust of this conversation, and spoke as if reading from a instruction manual. 'Your clothes were cut away to allow the medical team to treat you when you were brought in. Anything that is left will be in storage, along with your briefcase, and will be made available to you when you are discharged. And, in case you haven't noticed, we are very busy.'

'Great. OK. Well just get me some pills so I can sleep until you're ready to evict me. I need ... my ... briefcase.'

'Are you always such a pain in the backside?' the nurse asked.

'Sod's bloody Law, a hospital full of mouthwatering brunettes and blondes and my nurse is the rude bald headed git with a moustache.'

Nurse Riggs laughed. 'I'll see what I can do.'

Two days had passed since the crash, the first Eliot had spent unconscious, the second he had woken up to find his family around his bedside. In his book, trial separation meant just that, being

BENEATH THE BITTERCREST

allowed to recuperate in peace and, while he was thrilled to see his kids and appreciated that they were making a seven hour round trip to visit him, an hour discussing maintenance payments with his wife did not constitute 'getting plenty of rest.' Nor did he think a couple of bananas, a few apples and a fizzy drink was adequate compensation for the forty percent hike in the amount she had arbitrarily decided he would have to dole out every month in maintenance.

At least she knew where he was for a change she had said as she was leaving.

The children had turned their innocent confused faces back towards his bed as they were steered out of the ward and Eliot's physical injuries had all at once seemed slight and insignificant to him.

To numb the void Eliot watched television. Even after two days, images of the crashed train still dominated the news bulletins. The carriages sprawled out across a field, facing in all directions, like bone fragments in a multiple fracture. With the sound turned down, the images took on a curious distance; like images of the world seen from space. Early indications were that mindless vandalism lay behind the crash according to the banner headline at the bottom of the screen.

He had asked for the volume to be turned up only to be told that there were people sleeping. At four in the afternoon.

Playing paradiddles with his fingertips against the bedside table, he looked around the ward. More fun to be had in the reading room of a public library.

There were eight beds in ward H, all occupied. At least six of the patients, including himself, were survivors from the crash. All still in shock and all the others suffering worse injuries than Eliot's. The two remaining beds were occupied by men who had been unconscious since Eliot had himself woken up. No-one seemed to know if they had also been on the train.

On his bedside table were a collection of books Sue had brought with her. Gifts from Stephen, his business partner. In the three months since they had sold a majority interest in Office Solutions to a group of venture capitalists, Eliot had received many gifts from Stephen. 'The One Minute Manager', 'Getting People On Your Side', 'I'm the mouse. Where's the cheese?' and 'Leadership for Titans'. Stephen's subtle way of pushing Eliot into taking a more management orientated role in the company. Sue's subtle way of showing she agreed with Stephen. No bloody let up, even in hospital.

Just how small would a minute manager have to be, Eliot wondered briefly before turning back to the television - sound or no sound.

Snow was thick on the ground at the crash site. It was clear that a fire had broken out in several of the carriages. Eliot hadn't seen any burn victims, he imagined they would be in a special unit.

Of the disaster itself, he remembered nothing. He recalled purchasing a ticket at the station but couldn't even remember getting on the train. Had it been day or night? Had he been alone? He had to call the office.

'Here you go.'

The nurse was standing beside his bed with a large plastic box.

'Come here, Nurse Riggs, you deserve a huge smacker.'

'Yeah, sod off,' Riggs brushed him away, 'you're not my type, Eliot. Nineties rehash of the Sixties rockstar look, all blue eyed, pouting fringe and half-arsed sideburns - save it for Oasis groupies. You've two minutes to see if there's anything there you need, then I take the box back.'

Eliot rifled through his belongings. A tie, a watch, his wallet.

'You'll be safer leaving them in the box,' Riggs advised. 'This is a public ward.'

'There's confidence.'

'The boxes are all kept securely.'

Eliot stared at the lidless box. 'Yes, I can see that.'

He took his wallet, fumbled inside the briefcase. A squashed sandwich and the oily fragments of a plastic pot of olives. No phone. Then he spotted something tucked into his shoes.

'This phobile isn't mine. Where's mine?' Seeing Nurse Riggs' confusion, he explained, 'Phobile moan, mobile phone, get it?'

'Everything you had when you arrived went in that box. Except the stuff we threw away or handed over to the police.'

'The police?'

'Evidence,' Riggs explained. 'So, whose phone is it?'

Eliot turned the phone over in his hand. The room was spinning slowly. He let his head fall back slowly onto the pillow. 'I think I need a bit of shut eye.'

Riggs stepped forward and gently prised Eliot's fingers apart to release the grip on the phone, which he placed back in the box. With a tissue he removed the worst of the olive oil from Eliot's hand then, carrying the box, walked towards the door.

'Riggs. Thanks.'

Riggs turned. Eliot's eyes were closed.

As the room continued to roll about like a car ferry in a hurricane, Eliot felt the residual stickiness of the olive oil between his fingers.

three

They crouched at the back of the lorry, behind forty crates stuffed with clothes and trainers assembled by child labour in some nameless faraway place, the drone of the engine numbing their senses, the cold eating at their bones. The seven men had each sold everything they had for the chance to get away, to leave their war-ravaged homes and head for Europe. A last chance to do more than survive from one day to the next.

Left behind were dull-eyed children who ran without shoes, and wives too tired and hungry to breast feed babies who were too weak to smile. They had exchanged the rudimentary comfort of corrugated iron shacks, where pots were dotted about the earth floor to catch the fat rain drops that clattered down every time it rained, for the interminable vibration of a juggernaut journey across two continents. Stifling heat by day and bitter cold by night; the seven men alternately wrapped cardboard scraps around them and huddled together for warmth like rock hyrax or stripped down to their underwear and draped themselves over the crates.

Either way they avoided touching the metal sides of their moving jail, fearful of being burnt or frozen.

From time to time the shaking and the noise would stop as the lorry pulled up at a filling station and the men would gag as the smell of diesel fumes filled their tiny living space. Peering through holes where rivets or screws had fallen away, they absorbed fragmentary sights and sounds of yet another country never to be visited, praying that the doors of the lorry would remain shut, that no inspection would take place, that their escape would continue.

From being total strangers the seven men had, in just over a week, become as close as lovers. Enforced intimacy had robbed them of any personal space. Water, stale bread, tears, farts, hope, dispair, everything divided equally.

The weather turned colder as the lorry headed north, and they tucked the cardboard into their clothes and fought over scraps of fabric they found between the crates. They took to jumping up and down, singing and dancing to keep the numbing cold at arms' length. Then the driver of the lorry had stopped by the roadside and screamed at them in a language they did not know. But they had understood the sentiment behind the words, the dancing and jumping stopped.

Two hours later one of the men, who had been shaking with fever since daybreak, suddenly threw himself on one of the crates and began smashing it up with his fists. Before the others could summon the resolve to stop him, he had reached into the crate with bloodied hands and pulled out several brightly coloured garments and wrapped them around his head, and stuffed them into his shirt.

The others stared hopelessly at the broken crate and hesitated, aware of how precarious their existence was, aware of how little it would take for their driver to hand them over to the police or turf them out onto the roadside, abandoning them to their fate.

Half an hour later the crate was empty and six of the men sat huddled together, cocooned in pretty summer dresses and blouses, praying the journey would end and that their fates would be decided.

The seventh man, still shivering from a fever that no amount of extra clothing could contain, sat alone, ostracised and afraid.

The driver poured himself another cup of coffee from the flask on the seat beside him and checked his speed. It was almost eight pm, if he put his foot down he might still make the nine o'clock ferry across the channel.

four

He was sitting at a table out in the open air. Bells were tolling and, way up in the crisp blue sky, the silhouettes of a thousand starlings chattered and tumbled around a church steeple.

The plate was round and white and Eliot felt his nostrils flaring as he breathed in the time fracturing scent of the strawberries. Clock hands spinning round at dizzying speed; he was six and he had taken a strawberry from a market stall and his mother was snatching it and handing it back, half-eaten, to the stall holder; he was twelve and his dying grandfather slept quietly beside a bowl of strawberries in the geriatric ward; he was twenty one and at a friend's wedding eyeing up one of the bridesmaids who was wearing strawberry earrings ...

'Another strawberry, Eliot?'

He looked round but all the other tables were empty.

A Puma sat on a box and howled. Someone laughed.

He was a large house, with shutters on every window, all open, his south wall warm in the sun. A lizard darted under his eaves.

Out in the drive was a blue car with huge headlights. In the car were Stephen and Serina, his business partners.

'There's no rush. Take your time, Eliot,' said Serina.

'That's right, mate. We'll manage until you get back,' Stephen smiled.

A baby drifted in the breeze like a balloon and Eliot realised that they were planning to sell the company in his absence.

'Big Issue?'

Now a different woman was driving the car, a woman with short hair and a jewel in her nose. The car was on a beach being pulled down towards the sea by the tide. And they had to get out before the car disappeared beneath the waves. Eliot lashed out and heard the sound of breaking glass as darkness fell.

Ten minutes later he was at the reception desk. Hospital gown flapping behind him, bum visible to all, Eliot demanded to know which ward the woman with short spiky hair was in.

He allowed himself to be escorted back to his bed, cracked ribs shrieking and head spinning.

BENEATH THE BITTERCREST

Nurse Riggs appeared.

'We've been a naughty boy, I hear?' Riggs bent down to pick up the broken fragments of glass that had only recently been a vase on Eliot's beside table.

'Yeah, yeah.'

'What's her name?'

Eliot hesitated then thought what the hell. 'I need your help, Riggs. I need to speak with one of the crash survivors. Green eyes. spiky dark hair, a jewel in her nostril. Left nostril, I think. Beautiful. Blue jacket and ...'

Riggs' raised hand cut him off in midflow. 'If I do decide to go and ask some questions for you, will you promise me you'll stay in your bed and stop wandering about, flashing your ... stuff at all and sundry?'

'I'll keep myself for you alone. I won't look at another nurse as long as I live. Stay with me here forever.'

'I'm serious. If your wounds become infected you'll be here for weeks. Not that I need to worry, I'm out of here at the end of the month. Tata Doncaster. I'm going back down south. Or west. Wherever the fancy takes me.'

'I really have to speak with her.'

'Your wife know? Sorry, none of my business. Leave it with me. I'm off shift at ten, I'll ask then.'

There was no crash survivors in the hospital matching the description Eliot had given. St Mary's, Doncaster had received thirty people, fourteen male, sixteen female. Riggs had toured the wards and personally seen all of them.

The crash survivors had been taken to three different hospitals but the story was the same at each of them. Pontefract had twenty three, ten of whom were women. The county hospital had received forty two, including the twelve in the serious burns unit. It was possible that she might be one of the burns victims, in which case she might not have been identified yet, but the ward sister didn't think so.

Riggs passed by to see Eliot before leaving for home. The main lights had been turned off and Eliot seemed asleep. As he turned away, Eliot's eyes opened, saw the silhouette framed in the light spilling in from the corridor.

'Riggs.'

Riggs approached the bed and relayed the news.

'Did you check the description? spiky hair, nose stud.'

Riggs nodded. 'What makes you think this woman went to hospital at all?'

'I thought everyone did after this kind of thing?'

'Yes and no, and some are discharged in a matter of hours, if they've only bumps and bruises. It's a bit tricky without a name. Are you sure she survived? The dead aren't brought to hospital.'

'There would be a record though?'

'Not here, not if she walked away uninjured. Maybe the police ... Anyway, how's your head?'

After Riggs had gone, Eliot lay back in his bed, staring at the ceiling but seeing only junk tumbling in space, suitcases, books, cups, food. A baby. Oh God, there had been a baby, flying through the air as the impact stretched time to infinity.

Eliot sat up. His body was shaking and with the shaking came pain as the broken bones of his rib cage jarred against each other.

Another patient in the ward, muttering in his sleep 'No, no Kathleen'.

Heartbeat sloshing about in his ears, Eliot gripped the sides of the bed to steady himself. The ward was spinning, lights rushing past like cars on a motorway. A huge bruise was slowly crossing his chest from right to left, turning from blue to purple to black as it went. He looked like a map of the crash site, his skin revealing by degrees the path taken by the shockwaves that had passed through him at the moment of impact.

The train carriages had fought each other like hounds tearing at the flesh of a fox, a growling violence ripping them apart, tossing them up then smashing them down onto the cold snow. Everything in slo-mo, two thousand frames per second stretching time without end. Automatic doors dividing the carriages banging backwards and forwards, backwards and forwards. The noise so loud his head must explode.

Hands holding him.

Eliot opened his eyes. Two dark figures standing over him, pinning him down. He screamed.

'It's OK. It's OK. Mr Balkan.'

'Eliot, you are all right. You are in the hospital.' Then to the other figure. 'Shall I give him it now?'

'Yes. Yes!'

BENEATH THE BITTERCREST

A stab. In the arm? He wasn't sure. Gradually he noticed that he had stopped shouting, the air was returning to his lungs, deeper and longer breaths. Sweat was dripping down his back. The arms that held him were covered in freckles and thick as telegraph posts. He gazed up into the nurse's face and decided she was in her forties and the kind of woman who knocked back pints and enjoyed watching male strippers on a Friday night.

The grip was gentler now. He sagged into the sheets and became aware again of his tears, of an itch on his scalp.

The second nurse was taking his pulse, her lips silently counting off the seconds, her fingers pressed firmly on his wrist.

'That's better. You gave us quite a fright, Eliot, so you did.'

Eliot smiled weakly. "I gave you a fright?'

'Hush now, concentrate on breathing ... and relaxing.'

Eliot did as he was told and eventually the larger nurse released his arms and left. Tiredness surged in, wave over wave. The sea of his pain receded to a dull ache.

'Would you be wanting a drop of water?'

The nurse's eyes sparkled in the light of the bedside lamp. If Eliot hadn't been so consumed by years of cynicism he might almost have allowed himself the thought that this middle aged Irish woman with a face as plain as paper was the living embodiment of an angel. So she was.

He sipped the water.

'There,' she said and mopped his brow.

five

Six men took it in turns to stand up and stretch their legs. The lorry had now been stationary for seven hours. The air in the lorry was thick with the stench of human waste. All but one of the men had been sick during the sea crossing. The driver, having decided it would be too dangerous to have them wandering about on deck, had locked them in so they had been left to throw up over each other. None of them had ever been on so much as a dingy before, never mind a passage in the bowels of a car ferry crossing the Channel in a winter gale. They had been drained of all dignity and were now ready to accept their fate. No more dreams of work or asylum, of sending back for loved ones, of escaping the horrors of war. No money to take them home again. Nothing. Time would do with them as it pleased.

The seventh man had stopped coughing. In fact he had stopped doing anything at all and lay at the far end away from the others, a thin foetal figure curled on the cold metal floor.

A dull drone of traffic shook the air. The winter wind whistled through tiny holes in the lorry's flanks. A half-hearted attempt at dawn to return the garments they had taken from the crate was aborted when the biting cold had obliged them to reopen the crate to protect themselves against the cold.

While the lorry had been travelling across Europe the drivers, there had been a succession of them, had opened the doors three times a day to allow the men out to relieve themselves by the roadside. Two one litre bottles of water had been distributed at each stop, no food, the men had been expected to provide that for themselves. Aside from a brief stop outside Calais the previous night, they had been stuck in the lorry for over twenty four hours. After a few abortive attempts to relieve themselves through a group of holes between the lorry and the cab, the six men had resigned themselves to fouling the floor around them.

Footsteps outside brought an exchange of fearful glances. Large rusting bolts securing the back doors were worked back and forth. Padlocks were unlocked.

'Any trouble?'

BENEATH THE BITTERCREST

'At Dover? Nah. By midnight there's just four of them running the whole place. They're either asleep or Brahms and Liszt.'

Bolts were drawn back and the doors swung slowly open.

'How many have we got in there then?'

'I've seen seven.'

'All right you lot, let's have ... Phooah. Fuck me, what you got in there? Pigs?'

Only one man understood anything of what was being said. On his lead the others dropped the clothes they had taken from the crate and climbed out. They stood in a row in thin cotton shirts, trousers and sandals, gazing at the ground.

'Where's the other one?' the driver shouted at the men as he peered into the gloom of his lorry. 'Holy shit.'

The lorry was backed into a warehouse. The tallest of the six men looked up briefly. A fat ginger-haired man in a donkey jacket smacked the side of his head.

'Oi, do you fancy me or something? Well keep your bloody head down then.' Then, to the driver. 'I'll lock them up downstairs for the moment, then we can hose everything down.'

Without waiting for a reply, the fat man led the six travellers through a door and down a long flight of concrete stairs deep into the ground, across a large room and on through corridors, a kitchen, more steps, until finally they reached their destination, a large cellar. At one end was a dirty toilet and a sink, cracked blue porcelain thick with grime. A stack of old newspapers by the toilet. A single twenty watt light bulb hung in the middle of the room. The walls had been painted at one time but years of mould had reduced the paintwork to a series of ugly blotches.

'How many?' asked a voice outside the room.

The fat man turned.

Silhouetted in the doorway a tall figure used a torch to light the faces of each of the men from the lorry. Anxious faces squinted back. The flotsam of the earth.

'Six,' the fat man replied.

'I meant how many did they lose this time?' The voice taut as a bloodhound straining against its leash. 'In transit?'

The lorry driver appeared in the doorway, out of breath. He tugged uncomfortably at his collar. 'Just the one. The body's ...'

'That's thirty percent of your fee forfeited then,' the tall man said.

The driver bit his tongue until the tall man had walked out of earshot then muttered 'bastard' under his breath.

Joining the driver in the corridor, the fat man turned back to face his audience. 'There's a cup in the sink. No hot water. Home sweet home, eh?'

The heavy iron door slammed shut.

six

Three weeks later Eliot was heading back to work, Doncaster, the crash, Yorkshire accents, hospital food, mysterious spiky-haired women, and fourteen dull days lying in bed at home, a million miles behind him.

In stationary cars all around Shepherd's Bush Green a dozen radio stations did their best to keep drivers from taking the law into their own hands - soothing classical moods, friendly chat, hiphop, football gossip, boy bands, girl bands, boy/girl bands, brass bands, Bollywood anthems ...

Narrowly avoiding being mown down by a madman desperate to occupy the three metre stretch of tarmac that had suddenly appeared in front of Diapolou's Kebab House, Eliot made a mental note to contact Jazz FM. The rush hour playlist was probably not the best slot for 'Hit the Road, Jack'.

The office was a shrine to clutter. A maze of partitions concealed a dozen people, faces glued to computer monitors. Sheets of paper were stuck up on every free surface, detailing schedules, and extension numbers for the various departments that were in fact only a sheet of particle board apart. Long forgotten pot plants left by the previous tenants died slowly on various window sills. Some joker had wrapped crappy green tinsel around a bunch of twigs that had once been an exotic ficus, as part of the countdown to Christmas. A large inspirational poster of an orang utang surveying a distant golden sunset had been re-subtitled so that it now read 'pull your finger out, fuckface'. Under every desk were boxes of envelopes, rolls of fax paper, end of year accounts, boxes for coffee machines, microwaves, spare bottles for the water dispenser.

Office Solutions was a bespoke software design company on the way up, everyone in shirt sleeves, working like there was no tomorrow. A triumphant *Yes!* filled the air as someone reached their cold call target for the month.

'Wow, look, Eliot's arrived.'

'Put the coffee on, mate.'

'And for God's sake, if you're going to have a fag...' someone started in a sing-song voice.

'... go outside,' six voices chimed in together.

'Missed you too,' Eliot said. He tossed his coat over a partition and disappeared into his office.

His desk was cluttered with books. Another copy of 'The One Minute Manager', in case he hadn't read the copy sent to him in hospital. 'Making the Leap to Management', 'Small Elephants and Large Mice', and half a dozen other self- improvement publishing gems. It was as if he had never been away.

'Cathy.'

Cathy appeared at the door, carrying a huge stack of files. Her wavy auburn hair had fallen over her eyes and she was struggling to see anything.

'Eliot, Hi. How are you? We were all worried sick.'

'Yeah, sure. I need a coffee. Whose are these books?'

'Stephen thought you might find them useful.'

'I don't know how I could have survived this long without them.'

'Oh good.' The relief in Cathy's voice was palpable. 'I was worried you might not like them. Stephen said to keep lunchtime free. Serina wants a one o'clock.' She went to the door. 'By the way, you look tired. Oh, and I put a little present for you. There, by the computer. Welcome back.'

'Thanks Cathy.'

Eliot watched her leave, she might not be the brightest star in the heavens but she had real heart, the only human being left in the office. Besides himself.

He swept Stephen's books off the desktop and into his wastepaper basket and sat down. The ashtray also had to go. He pulled open a drawer and dropped it in and, among the clutter, found some peppermints and took two or three.

Cathy's present was a packet of his favourite sweets, pear drops, and a CD. Miles Davis, Bitches Brew. Anyone other than Cathy and he would have assumed there was a message in there somewhere. Anyone other than Cathy would have told him sweets were bad for his teeth.

There were only three of them left from the original company, Stephen, Cathy and Eliot. Stephen and Eliot had set Office Solutions up fresh out of college and within three years it had grown to employ twelve people, with Stephen as manager and Eliot as technical wizard. It had been a rollercoaster ride, repeated cycles of boom and bust as Stephen attempted to steer the company towards more lucrative contracts and away from servicing two bit employment agencies, small hotel chains and the occasional minor project for the local authority.

Eventually they had been forced to accept the validity of the maxim that it wasn't what you knew but who you knew. Stephen had pursuaded Eliot that they should relinquish half the company. A sell out. Retaining the role of managing director for himself and promoting Eliot to Technical Manager, Stephen and Eliot sold fifty one percent of the company to Serina Falcon, the high-flying ex-wife of an old college friend. Eliot and Stephen retained the remaining forty nine percent.

Over the previous four months Serina had turned the company on its head. Without doubt the balance sheet had benefitted. Four new clients, all bigger and more prestigious than any the company had dealt with before.

The downside. Within weeks motivational peptalks book-ended each working day. A strict dress code was introduced. Ignoring Stephen's pleas to stay and give the new setup a chance, six of the team walked away, leaving Serina free to wheel in a fresh group of lantern-jawed thrusters ready to take Office Solutions up into the big league, leaving Eliot a foreigner in his own office. It could only be a matter of time before the premises had a major makeover. Out with the clutter and in with minimalist furniture and café latté, WAP phones and beetroot juice.

'It's nearly midday.'

'And a good morning to you too, Steve.'

Stephen was standing in the doorway. Venture capitalism suited him. Stephen had always been a designer label victim, slick suits, fancy shirts and hair wax, which he now called pomade, having seen it called by that name in a movie.

Eliot offered him a pear drop. Stephen shook his head.

'Looks bad, that's all. Staff motivation. Corporate image. You look tired. Shame they don't do haircuts in hospitals. Anyway, I've booked a table at Enrico's. You, me, Serina. We've got a two thirty in the city. Did you bring a tie?'

Eliot pulled open a drawer. 'I can wear this,' he said, lifting a crumpled blue and green number blotched with what looked like ink.

'I'll send Cathy out for one.'

'She's bringing me a coffee first.'

'Shave before we go.' Stephen studied Eliot critically. 'Are you sure you're up to this?'

Eliot didn't bother to answer, back in the office ten minutes and already it was getting him down.

It was a basement wine bar, a pianist fiddling disinterestedly with Gershwin, a posse of noisy bankers showing off at the bar, a wine list that started at thirty quid a bottle.

'How's Chloe?' Eliot asked.

'The same,' Stephen toyed with his wine glass. 'They have to find a donor. Serina even offered one of her own kidneys but it has to be a match. Foster parents don't cut the mustard on that one. They were all on standby last week then, at the last minute ... Serina's got to the point where she just can't ...' His voice trailed off as he spotted Serina emerging from the ladies.

Serina crossed the restaurant and sat down. She was in an immaculate green trouser suit that offset her brown eyes and long red hair, which had been swept back into a french plait. The waiter brought them their pasta. While they ate, Stephen and Serina brought Eliot up to date.

'They'll be a major client.' Serina sipped sparkling Italian water. 'Bring in lots of other business.'

'And we have to take on how many people for this?'

'Two to write the code, working directly for you, a project assistant to help manage everything, install the software, teach the client how it works, etc.'

Serina looked to Stephen for support.

'Say four people,' Stephen said. 'Make sure we're covered. Temporary contracts. Plus new kit, of course.'

Stephen leant back and beckoned the waiter over.

'Which all means,' Serina continued. 'we have to raise about thirty grand this afternoon, to tide us over. Say forty - to keep things rolling.'

'The bill,' Stephen told the waiter

Eliot looked far from convinced.

'Trust me, Eliot, we've looked at everything,' Stephen said. 'This is the way it has to be. While you've been away ... All right. Look, we know you've been in hospital but, I'm not being funny, we had to move on this. Take a decision.'

'One that ties thirty grand's worth of debt around our necks,' Eliot retorted. 'For a project that hasn't even been green lit.'

BENEATH THE BITTERCREST

'Eighty grand. For one month, two maximum. We'll go for the Allstar Marketing account as well while we're at it.' Serina looked across at Stephen. 'Eight extra staff. We've just got enough desks. Time to expand, Eliot. No risks, no victories. Who dares wins. Think outside the box.'

Eliot had had enough of management guru bullshit. 'Yeah, right. Fuck it. Do what you want. As long as the loan isn't guaranteed or secured.'

Stephen and Serina exchanged glances. Eliot threw his hands in the air.

They got the loan in return for a percentage of the income from the deal and the money back, with interest. Eliot hoped it was worth it. When you sold your soul it had better be worth it.

While washing his hands Eliot studied his face in the mirror, he looked tired. He removed his tie, mauve with the small motif of a rabbit being pulled out of a hat.

'Am I expected to wear this?'

Anyone else would have told Eliot he could go to the meeting stark naked for all they cared, but not Cathy.

'Don't you like it?' Like she was really upset.

Pulling open the door, Eliot went back into the wine bar to join Stephen, Serina and a magnum of champagne.

'What do we know about BitterCrest Imports?' Eliot asked Serina, the following morning back at the office.

'No bad debts. Good payers. A turnover that can afford us.' Serina carried on reading the three month sales forecast figures.

'What do they import?'

'What's that got to do with anything, Eliot?'

'Well, what do they import? Chairs, groceries, football kits, endangered animals, beer, weapons? What?'

Serina looked up. 'Are you in the Trotskyist Alliance? Hello? Like who cares what they import? They have money, we need money, end of story.'

'Oh well, maybe the credit check will tell me.'

'What?'

'A credit check. P.S.Partners are doing it,' Eliot elaborated.

Stephen appeared in the doorway.

'It's what we usually do,' Eliot continued, looking to Stephen for support, 'when we're taking on a large debt to do business with ...'

'Fine,' Serina turned to Stephen. 'Are you going to let him run the company?'

'Who keeps sending me all those teach yourself management books?' Eliot said.

'That's different and you know it,' Stephen countered lamely.

Eliot shrugged and walked off.

'Planning to be there all day? Shall I bring you a chair?' It was Luther, one of Serina's new protégés in Sales, all sarcasm and gold-toothed smile.

An hour had passed and Eliot was standing by the photocopier watching it disgourge a productivity report.

'Yeah, OK. And a coffee as well. Thanks. No sugar.'

Luther stood there with the confused deflated look of a con artist who finds he has somehow been persuaded to invest in a time share on Mars.

Eliot's phone started ringing. He left Luther, and the copier, and went to his office.

'Neville Draper, BitterCrest.

'Mr Draper, hello.' Eliot sat on his desk.

'I obtained your private line from the receptionist. Lax security. Anyway, a quick call to check there won't be any problems for tomorrow.'

Not so much a question as a statement. Eliot was still wondering how to respond when the pause was quickly filled.

'Good. I'll see you at eleven, as agreed.'

'Yes ... I should point out that it is our business practice to ...' Eliot started.

'Eleven o'clock it is then. Goodbye.'

The line went dead. Eliot's fingers drummed the desk top. He still had no idea of the job requirement. How could he prepare a proposal in the absence of information?

He found Cathy busy texting, as usual, crunching away on her mobile. She had sent the fax as he had asked but, when he rang back to speak with Draper, a board meeting was in progress, so he had to leave it at that.

The phone rang.

Cathy took the call, listened, then cupped her hand over the receiver. 'Eliot. Peter Han from P. S. Partners. Are you in?'

BENEATH THE BITTERCREST

'Put him through.'

Eliot grabbed the nearest phone.

'Eliot, we need to talk.'

'Hang on, Peter.' Eliot craned his neck to see if Cathy had put the phone down. 'Call me on my mobile in a couple of minutes.'

He gave Han the number for his new mobile phone then went out onto the roof, sitting at one of the benches that looked out towards the tube line. Even with his coat on, the cold got to him in seconds. It would snow again tonight, he was sure of it. The mobile rang.

'Yes, we can talk.'

'What's this about, Eliot? You're not in business with this mob, are you?'

'What's your problem?'

'Not my problem, your problem. You're not in their league. These people have contacts in high places, protecting them. And, believe me, they need it.'

'I just need a credit rating. We're doing some work for them, import/export management software.'

'Don't. Just drop it and walk away.'

'Why? What's the problem?'

No answer. Had he hung up?

'Peter?'

'I can't. Not over the phone.'

The line went dead. A Police car, siren screaming, tore round the block, four floors below. A metropolitan line train clattered past, an explosion of sparks lighting up two youths who were spraying graffiti onto a junction box, just inches away from the track.

Ten minutes later Eliot left for the day. A gentle hour on the climbing wall at the gym would sort him out, stretch his limbs, free the tension in his shoulders. It was probably just nerves, dealing with office politics after being away.

Whilst not an athlete, Eliot was strong and climbed confidently. Only the easiest routes for the time being, while his body healed. Orange route followed by green, with a fifteen minute break between them. They had moved several of the footholds on green he realised as his foot came down on fresh air and his ribs whinced. His body ached and his muscles would be complaining in the morning but it felt good to be exercising again, the time lying about in the hospital and then at home had driven him to distraction.

Reaching the top of the wall the second time, Eliot paused to catch his breath and found himself mulling over what Peter Han had said. They had worked with clients they didn't particularly like in the past and it hadn't bothered Eliot. True, P. S. Partners had never actually advised against doing work for a particular organisation before but Peter did have a tendency to overdramatise. That was what they paid him for.

Checking and adjusting the ropes, Eliot glanced down at the floor fifteen metres below him. He pushed himself back and abseiled down.

seven

An endless series of roundabouts steered him round the town centre towards an industrial estate on the eastern side of Swindon. Cursing himself for have missed the first junction to Swindon off the M4 and trundling along with the last of the rush hour traffic, Eliot found himself wondering if it might not have been smarter to take the train, unpleasant memories or no.

It had been his night to look after the kids. He had put up a token protest, to focus Sue's mind on the fact that he was only a few days out of hospital but her angle was that she had been looking after them single-handedly for weeks and she wanted a break. She won, drove off for a night on the town, left him to it. And in truth it had done him a power of good. Bedtime stories, round sleepy faces giving him good night kisses ... peace at last. For a few hours.

And so, a brief sleep under his belt, he had got the kids up, fed and off to school before heading west in a car he no longer enjoyed driving, towards a town he had never visited, to a meeting he felt ill-prepared for.

And yet, now, under the bright blue sky, the sun bold and brash at his back, the world seemed OK. His anxieties of the previous day seemed misplaced. That was the trouble with employing investigators, they had an inbuilt incentive to scare the pants off you, make you spend more money, make you more reliant on them.

Maybe Stephen had a point. Daring to think the unthinkable, Eliot considered the suggestion that he should manage projects more and learn to delegate, instead of insisting on doing everything himself. It might even have the added benefit of improving his relationship with Sue.

Why was it that being called a manager carried more status than actually doing the real work? Even with your wife. A sudden vision of standing beside the marital bed barking instructions down to a man he had employed to give Sue a good rogering. Oh thank you, Eliot.

He reached instinctively for the glove compartment but, although the car still stunk of tobacco, there were no cigarettes. Yet another stick of chewing gum.

And another roundabout, this one a huge gaudy bed of bright pansies. It was as if winter had already given way to spring. Eliot took the exit for the Sopford industrial estate, slowing to negotiate a broken down van that had its axles up on bricks and all its glass gone.

Access to and from the estate was controlled by two barriers operated by a security guard seated in a cabin placed between them. Eliot stopped by the cabin, wound his window down and waited.

'You have to come inside,' crackled a loudspeaker mounted on the side of the cabin.

Eliot found his shoes and pushed his feet into them, and climbed out of the car.

A morning chatshow droned on a small television in the cabin. Nude women torn out of girlie magazines were plastered about like those charts showing cuts of meat that hung in butchers' shops.

'Can't you read?' The guard thrust a clipboard at Eliot. 'The sign outside clearly states ...'

'Where do I sign?'

'There and there. Time of arrival, person you're visiting.'

As he scribbled, Eliot wondered what the biplane emblem stitched on the guard's jacket pocket signified. He passed the clipboard back.

'Unit 6,' the guard mumbled, having checked to see who Eliot was visiting. 'It's right round the back.'

He followed the road round the main block of units, passing a squat single storey building on the edge of a patch of wasteland.

The industrial estate, built in the 1980's, was surrounded by a huge expanse of tarmac, scrubland, and an assortment of run down buildings, of which the low building was one example, that appeared to date from the Second World War. It was possible, Eliot thought, that the site had at one time been an airfield. Which would explain the biplane logo. Had there been a Sopford biplane?

Beyond the low building, in the distance, several gas towers rusted lazily in the winter sun. To his right were a row of parked lorries.

Working on the assumption that the initials 'B.I.', stamped in red letters across the rear doors of the nearest lorry, stood for BitterCrest Imports, Eliot pulled up and parked. He got out and stretched his legs. A smell in the air, faint but unpleasant, like raw sewage over the horizon. He pulled on his jacket and straightened his tie, a plain blue clip-on he had bought to irritate Stephen.

In fact, he was outside Unit 12. Rather than get back in the car, he walked, following the road round the corner in what he hoped would prove to be the right direction. It was.

The block was an ugly confection in yellow and brown, garish and yet drab, a monument to the decade that gave it birth. When he finally reached it he found that unlike the other units, which all had huge billboards and signs advertising their presence, Unit 6 was travelling incognito, not even a name plate by the door.

Reception was not exactly a temple to design. The furniture and fittings had obviously been assembled from an ancient cut price mail-order catalogue. A dozen plastic chairs, all different, all cracking with age, all pressed back against the wall. A row of dry unloved plants, very similar to the ones in Eliot's own office, occupied drab pots on the window sill. Below the window, with its dusty view of the car park, was a radiator from which patches of magnolia paint were slowly peeling away.

A middle-aged, underpaid and overweight receptionist, who gave the impression of having been purchased from the same company that had supplied the furniture, sat behind a mountain of paperwork, pink for in, yellow for out, green for pending, and red for overdue. The colour of her face suggested overdue.

To complete the period ambience was the wallpaper, a loud pink, orange and brown concoction, its large geometric pattern burning into the retina with all the subtlety of a migraine. Whatever else BitterCrest might be accused of, it certainly had not lavished resources on its reception area.

Having informed the receptionist of his arrival, Eliot picked a chair and sat down. No magazines to read, nothing to do but wait. Peter Han had it all wrong, Eliot decided. Far from being well connected, it was unlikely that BitterCrest Imports had any kind of reputation in north east Swindon, let alone in the wider world. Payment terms would have to be strict and rigorous.

He coughed loudly to attract attention.

'Excuse me. Mr. Draper is in, isn't he? Only it took two hours to get here and I do have other ...'

'I'll try again, Sir. I'm sure he won't be too long.'

From deep within his briefcase Eliot heard the cigarette calling him. Instinctively, he looked around for signs of an ashtray. Couldn't see one.

He hadn't been the first to crave nicotine while waiting in the reception area of BitterCrest Imports. Closer inspection of the potted plants revealed them all to be 'growing' in a mixture of compost, burnt matchsticks, ash and cigarette stubs.

'Mr. Balkan, you must forgive me.' More of an order than an entreaty.

Eliot turned.

'Neville Draper,' the man introduced himself.

Draper shook Eliot's hand with the grip of a monkey wrench. His eyes, the colour of which Eliot would later be unable to remember, stared with all the tenderness of a laser scanning a barcode.

Draper was tall, tanned, and in his early fifties. His white hair was cut in an army length crew cut. The beautifully tailored blue suit barely disguised a body still in excellent shape, the result either of years scrambling up and over assault courses in the employ of Her Majesty or dancing in a corps de ballet. The former seemed more likely, Eliot surmised. A darker blue handkerchief poked out over his breast pocket. Italian shoes, dark crocodile skin belt, bespoke shirt and tie from the Burlington Arcade.

'Time is money. Anna, send out for coffee and cakes.' Draper steered Eliot towards the door through which he had entered. 'There's only rubbish to drink and eat here,' he said.

Draper led the way down a beige corridor lit by bare fluorescent tubes. 'Never spend money on the appearance of things, Mr Balkan. Substance, that's what counts...' Eliot allowed himself a moment of reflection regarding Draper's professed disregard of appearances as they passed through another cheap door and into a warehouse stacked with crates. Two large men with upper arms the size of parma hams sat playing cards, using one of the crates as a table.

A staircase run up the far wall of the warehouse, and this they took, ending up on a walkway high above the crates. Draper opened a door and ushered Eliot into a sparsely furnished office, two desks, four chairs, one filing cabinet. The calendar on the wall was a year out of date.

'...and the substance behind this operation,' Draper continued, as if the sentence had not been interrupted, 'is worth a great deal of money. Sit down.' And, as an afterthought, as if he were making an effort. 'Please.'

The chair was comfortable enough but way down low, inches from the floor. Alarm bells sounded in Eliot's head as he sat down. Draper sat on the edge of a desk, towering over him.

Eliot stood up again. 'Not the low down chair trick, thank you.'

Draper smiled briefly, the appraisal had already begun. 'Please,' he said again, sitting on the other low chair.

With them both at the same height, the conversation began. It felt more like an interview than a presentation and Eliot found himself revealing far more than he intended. Questions about his education and background, questions about Office Solutions. How many staff? How were they vetted? How long had the company been trading? Who were their biggest clients? What did he think of his business partners? Who handled their accounts? Had they ever been involved in litigation?

Draper appeared to pay only scant attention to the answers and Eliot quickly formed the view that Draper already knew the answers to most of his questions and that he was more interested in the manner of Eliot's answers than in the substance. After a few minutes he tried turning the tables on his inquisitor but later, when he checked his notes, Eliot found that the information he had been given was, in every respect, too vague to form more than a cursory impression of the company's affairs. What he did learn was that a huge variety of products were imported from a dozen or more countries, that a dizzying array of permits and visas were required on a daily basis, and that encryption was a key feature of BitterCrest's requirement.

As the conversation continued, Draper's earlier aloofness softened and he became almost personable. He wanted complete control of what information was made available regarding the company's affairs. Even the company accountants were only to have limited access. Everything was ultimately to be controlled by Draper himself.

Coffee and cakes arrived. Eliot had a Danish pastry with his coffee. Draper left both cakes and coffee untouched.

Draper had a good basic understanding of encryption and database management, he would be a demanding customer.

'All this is going to cost.' Eliot brushed crumbs from his notepad and resumed his scribbling.

'Substance, Mr Balkan, substance. The cost doesn't interest me particularly. Now, what have you brought?'

They spent less than fifteen minutes on the evaluation. Eliot slipped the CD into the drive of the computer that had been set up in a corner of the office. He would have preferred to have used his laptop but Draper insisted on seeing the software running on one of his own machines.

Having installed the software, Eliot demonstrated the advantages of the approach Office Solutions had developed, the novel uses the software made of private key/ public key encryption and the ways in which the database could hide 'unnecessary' data from view.

'Of course, the system we would design for BitterCrest would be unique to yourselves. This is only a fairly basic demonstration of the ...'

'Quite so,' Draper cut him off with a sweep of his hand. 'Carry on.'

From time to time Draper would ask a technical question, listening intently to the answer and writing notes. He was after a system that gave him total flexibility with regard to information retrieval and secretion. He was aware of the encryption limitations imposed on private companies and individuals by the national governments, but a little hazy on the raw computing power available to government agencies.

'I want a system that works, is completely foolproof and secure. I want no unauthorised access. No business competitors, no snoopers, no Inland Revenue, no GCHQ, no-one. Is that understood?'

The intercom burst into life.

'Mr Draper, I have the hospital on the phone. When will you be ...'

'Tell them to wait, I'll deal with it later.' Draper cut the call.

'Just spent time in one of those myself,' Eliot sympathised. 'Nothing serious?'

Draper affected not to have heard him.

'You do understand that no system of encryption can properly be said to be one hundred percent secure?' Eliot changed the subject. 'What I can do for you, what Office Solutions can do, is to buy you time. We can design you an encryption algorithm that keeps out the little guys: hackers, your business competitors, private investigators, the police. A segmented pass key of maybe a thousand bits will do that. But that won't keep the big boys out for very long, not any more. In the seventies, a thousand bit key would have kept even national agencies, like GCHQ or the CIA, busy for twenty years or more. Today, for an outlay of a few hundred million, they can string a hundred thousand processors together, all working in tandem. For a thousand bit key, you can think in terms of days, if that.'

'Secondly,' Eliot continued, 'if you're interested in security, you need to ensure that any computer holding sensitive data is never connected to the internet or to any other machine that goes near the internet. You should also completely overhaul your firewall software while you're at it to prevent illegal access.'

'Thank you for being honest with me, Mr Balkan. I was told you were one of the best in your field and it would appear that my sources were correct.' Draper stood up. 'I have seen enough. You may remove the software from my computer.'

While Eliot did as he was told, Draper carried on. 'I want no broadcasting, no putting us on your client list, no features in trade magazines, etc. etc. I will require you to be personally responsible and answerable to me on an ongoing basis throughout the contractual period and for six months afterwards. I will require that you, and you alone, carry out all the work, from development to installation.'

'You're not planning to kill me at the end of it, like they did to the men who dug the tombs of the pharaohs?' Eliot quipped. 'So their secrets died with them,' he felt obliged to explain.

Draper crossed over to the window and stared outside for a moment.

'What I want in return for my money, Mr Balkan, is both your expertise and your silence.' He turned to face Eliot. 'A form of covenant perhaps. If you are confident that you can provide the level of service I am looking for, you will submit the proposal in the next forty eight hours. Thank you for your time.'

Draper held the door open. Eliot muttered his thanks and hurried for the stairs, glad to escape the pomposity that Draper wore as a halo. Thank God you didn't have to like your clients.

The sun had gone, he noticed, as he walked down the stairs towards the warehouse floor. He paused at the window. Overlooking the back of the industrial estate, the sky was a dull grey punctuated by a pack of darker storm clouds. Below the clouds, a wasteland of stunted trees and discarded oil drums, squat ugly buildings with plants sprouting from the gutters, barbed wire and rusting machinery. In the middle distance the lumpen mass of the gas towers.

'Everything all right, Mr Balkan?'

Eliot turned. Draper was at the top of the stairs.

'Swindon, international city of culture and beauty,' Eliot answered. 'I was admiring the view. The award can only be weeks away.'

Draper's mouth smiled. He came down and accompanied Eliot across the warehouse floor.

'Reception is over there. I do hope to hear from you soon.'

Eliot pushed open the swing doors and headed down the beige corridor.

Behind her reception desk, Anna quickly put away her vanity mirror and make-up.

'Everything all right?' she said, seeing his pale complexion.

Why did people keep asking him that?

'Yes.'

'And the cakes? I forgot to ask what you would like. Mr Draper can get a little tetchy if I forget sometimes.'

'A little tetchy?'

'Well, you know, he's a bit of a stickler.'

'I'll bear that in mind. Ah, well, time to go.'

'Looks like snow. Do you like snow, Mr Balkan?'

'Gotta go, sorry.' Snow talk had never been his forté.

Eliot walked back to his car. As he sat down, he reached for the glove compartment and found the chewing gum. His breath was steaming up the windscreen, the temperature must have dropped six or seven degrees in an hour.

A movement caught his eye. The single storey building he had passed on his way in stood maybe seventy metres away to his left. A large sliding door was partially open. A dog barked. Suddenly a figure dressed only in a t-shirt and baggy shorts rushed out from the darkness within, racing barefoot across the concrete towards Eliot.

From within the low building a transit van suddenly appeared, its doors still open, speeding after the running man. The van overtook its quarry, turned round in a wide arc and stopped. Like a stag caught in car headlights the running man stopped, hesitated, turned and ran in another direction. The van gave chase, this time passing so close that Eliot thought they would knock the man down. The van turned again, reminding Eliot of a bull rounding on a matador, pawing the ground before a charge. A huge bruiser in a black leather jacket leapt out of the van, long baton or stick in hand. The runner turned again. The van revved up and followed.

The runner was again heading directly towards Eliot's car. As he approached, Eliot could see how scrawny he was. Twenty metres away now. Eliot realised his own body was trembling, adrenaline pumping. The runner tumbled, picked himself up and rushed away to Eliot's right, disappearing from view with the van and the man with the stick in pursuit. A screeching of brakes accompanied by a

BENEATH THE BITTERCREST

thud. Eliot sat there for over a minute, his eyes on the wasteland and the squatting ugly enormity of the gas towers, his mind replaying what he had seen, his hands trembling as they gripped the steering wheel.

His ribs were aching again, the climbing wall visit had been premature.

He dropped the chewing gum on the floor, swallowed a painkiller and started the car, throwing it into reverse and mounting the kerb before speeding away.

Only when he was several miles away from the Sopford Industrial Estate did he reach into his briefcase. He smoked without pleasure and threw the cigarette out of the window after only a couple of drags.

eight

Ted 'Aura' Johnson was on a bit of a roll. Two Rolex watches, two girlfriends, and now two vans. True the watches were not your actual Rolex, the girlfriends were little more than an occasional drunken shag, but the vans were for real. Going up in the world. A blue Renault and now a yellow Citroën. Choice wheels. He ran his hands over the bristle of his number one haircut and put his foot down.

Whatever people said about the price of diesel and the over-strong pound or the over-weak pound, it just depended on what week it was, there was no stopping the entrepreneur. Beer and wine from France, sweets from England, tobacco from Italy, carpets, designer clothes, magazines, videos, computer games, motor parts, it made no difference to him, he was happy to smuggle anything in any direction. The hours were long but he was clearing almost a seventy grand a year and, since he was only twenty eight, he could expect to retire by the time he was forty. If he started saving. If he could stop himself from splashing out big time on clothes and bling. Yeah right, flying porkers.

The right windscreen wiper on the Citroën had a split in it. A greasy smear traced an arc at eye level, and the glare of approaching headlights on the other side of the motorway fractured into a thousand retina-burning torches on the filthy glass. Johnson alternately hunched down under, or craned his neck over, the smear in order to see the road ahead. Calais was still seven hundred and fifty kilometres away; he hoped he could stay awake that long. In the back he had a full load: fois gras, three hundred corn-fed chickens, and fifteen cases of cognac, bought for a song, and an assortment of other goodies that he was delivering to a mate with a market stall in east London. The trip was worth nearly a grand, after costs, and probably twice that to his mate who would sell as much as he could to the restaurant trade before taking what was left to the market. The chickens should be in a refrigerated lorry, since they had been frozen when he picked them up, but if he made good time they should still be pukka - it was December after all and they were all piled up on top of each other.

He picked up his mobile and dialled.

'Yeah, Luis, Aura. All right? Yeah, I'm six hours from the boat, by the time I've made the last pickup. I'll check with you half ten or eleven ... Nah, they didn't 'ave it. Yeah, got the fois grass. All right, see you later.'

He dialled another number.

'All right, babe? ... About midnight. I know ... well I'll meet you at the club then. At midnight ... Yeah, Belgian chockies ... You too, babe.'

He wound the window down and spat out his chewing gum and turned on the radio. A deafeningly loud garage beat pounded from large speakers set into the doors. A more muffled version of the music drifted up from the bass bin in the back, currently lost under the pile of chickens. Johnson pounded the steering wheel in time with the music, hitting the dashboard whenever he heard a cymbal crash. Life was sweet, man.

nine

'You know how beautiful a piece of code can be? Like a snowflake?'

Everyone nodded indulgently, he would get over it. It was always the same with kids fresh out of college.

'Welcome to reality.' Eliot steered him towards a pile of grey boxes.

'Wow, man, hardware. Wicked. '

Eliot smiled and watched the kid assemble the computer he was to use. Eliot had just been like Laurie when he had landed his first job. Joining a team that would 'make the future'. Describing lines of computer code as beautiful as poetry. With a bit of luck Laurie might stay like that for a few months and come up with a couple of great ideas before he succumbed to the boredom of the daily grind and the soul-sapping demands of compromise and commercial constraints. He left Laurie behind his partition and went to his office.

'Laurie seems nice,' Cathy said, looking up briefly from her text messaging.

'Yeah, if you like skinny good-looking guys with loads of hair, perfect teeth, a first in programming and a juvenile interest in computer viruses, then I suppose he might seem nice. Is Stephen about?'

Cathy shook her head.

'Serina?'

'They had a breakfast with Chatham Venture Holdings. How was your meeting this morning?'

'Bit of this, bit of that.'

'Coffee?'

'Go on then, twist my arm.'

He watched her leave, absent-mindedly admiring her curves.

Eliot realised he was being frozen out of the decision making process. Stephen and Serina were stacking up debts. Debts which, it turned out, were totally unnecessary as Neville Draper had said he wanted Eliot to work alone. Hiring Laurie might well be a mistake, unless they could use him on another contract.

Not for the first time, Eliot considered walking away. He would still have shares in the company, if they made a fortune he would get his cut. If they didn't, he would already be away, finding something better to do with his life. The trouble with being in business with a childhood friend was that the knots that bound you together were deep and murky. Loyalties that got in the way of business. Patterns of behaviour that owed more to the classroom than the office.

'Penny for your thoughts.'

Eliot looked up, took the mug, barely registering what Cathy had said.

'What's up? Are you OK?'

'Yeah.' He smiled. 'Yeah, I'm OK. Something I have to sort out, that's all.'

'Sue and the kids?'

'No. What makes you say that?' He stretched and yawned. 'Don't answer that, I don't want to know. Coffee smells good. And I like the blue top, suits you.'

Smiling happily, Cathy went off to see how Laurie was settling in.

He was trying to get through to Peter at P.S. Partners when Serina showed up.

'Eliot, you made it.'

'Serina.'

'Shall I tell you what we've decided.'

'What you've decided.'

'Well, what Stephen and I have ... Oh, I see. Do I have to spell out what ...'

'Spare me the mission statement,' Eliot said. 'Is Stephen here?'

'We came in together.'

'How about we all sit down and have a little chat?'

'There isn't time right now. We have to ...

'Well, fucking well make time. If not, you can kiss the Swindon job goodbye.'

'This is a team thing, Eliot. We can't just ...'

'Get Stephen ... Now,' he said and turned back to the computer screen.

She slammed the door. Which suited Eliot. He was checking the football results on the internet when the door reopened.

'I hope this is worth it.'

'Ah, Stephen. And Serina. How kind of you to drop in.'

'Cut the crap, Eliot,' Stephen said, closing the door. 'I'm busy, so get on with it.'

'OK.' Eliot put his hands behind his head and stretched his legs.

'Is it worth it if he's in this mood?' Serina said.

The three partners faced each other in silence. Eliot was in no hurry.

'Right, that's it.' Serina grabbed the door handle.

Stephen held the door closed. 'Eliot, you have to tell us what is going on. From where I am, Serina and I have been busting our balls to make this thing happen. Building the business up. For all of us. You were in hospital, what did you expect? An opportunity came up and we grabbed it. Look, put it this way, if we play it right, it could be worth millions in the medium term.'

'And that's it?'

'What does that mean?' Stephen said.

'I asked you what we knew about this company.'

'And I said why? Why should this contract be any different to any other contract we've taken in the past five years?'

'You're right,' Eliot said, cleaning his fingernails. 'Maybe it's me. Maybe we've always been this crass.'

Serina tried opening the door but Stephen held it shut and stared at Eliot. Eliot stared back, wondering what to say, how to say it.

'Today,' he said finally, 'at the meeting with BitterCrest Imports ...'

'No way,' Serina shouted. 'Don't even think about it. This started way before today. Ever since I bought into the company ...'

'Are you listening?' Eliot shouted back.

Stephen waved a calming hand. The other two shut up.

'All right, look,' Stephen said, collecting his thoughts. 'You're right ...'

Eliot glanced triumphantly at Serina.

'You're right about BitterCrest. This is a bit different...' Stephen cleared his throat. '... to what we've done before. The import/export business plays to different rules. It's not so black and white. Just the way it is. Global markets. International trade agreements. Every country has its own laws. Companies like BitterCrest have to walk a tightrope. What is completely legal in one country is a grey area in another. Most of the time you know where you are but sometimes ... sometimes you play the percentages. Take your chances.'

'Are you talking about BitterCrest Imports or about us?' Eliot asked.

'I don't know exactly what their business is, but ...'

'They're a reputable company,' Serina interjected. 'Very well connected.'

Wasn't that exactly what Peter had said?

BENEATH THE BITTERCREST

'Tell me,' Eliot asked Serina. 'Are they well connected because they are reputable, or reputable because they are well connected?

'Whatever,' Serina snorted contemptuously. 'This is pointless.'

Facing off like gladiators in a Roman arena.

'All right, let's put it another way, how did this all start? Did they contact us or did we contact them? Is this another of your brother's helpful nudges?' Eliot directed this last question at Serina.

Serina's brother worked in one of the government ministries. Eliot had been unable to discover which one. It was an official secret apparently.

Serina gave Eliot a look that would have stapled a job application to the boards at the Employment Centre. She transferred the same look to Stephen, who acquiesced and released his grip on the door. Serina left. Eliot stared at Stephen, who glared back.

'This isn't really working out,' Eliot said.

'Correct,' Stephen replied.

Stephen waited for Eliot to continue.

'OK. Say I go along with you. What if, a few weeks down the track, we find this company is up to its neck in ... in whatever, criminal activity, VAT evasion, smuggling. We'll be accessories. Draper all but admitted that he ...'

'Were they showing back to back Bond movies at the hospital?' Stephen asked.

'I saw a man being hunted like a dog ...'

'Where?'

'In Swindon. On the same industrial estate that BitterCrest ...'

'Don't be ridiculous. How many different companies operate from that estate? In any event, what you say you saw might simply have been a company protecting itself against a trespasser or a thief. Completely reasonable measures that any organisation would take. '

'Maybe,' Eliot conceded. 'But if we find ...'

'Give me a break. I've put my neck on the line for you, Eliot.'

The two men stared at each other.

'For us,' Stephen continued in a gentler tone. 'We need her, Eliot. She can turn this company into a real player. We couldn't go on the way we were. Like she says, it's a vision thing. Look, something comes up, we'll talk about it. As and when. In the meantime, let's make money.'

Eliot shrugged. He turned to stare out of the window at a passing train.

'If I say yes, Draper wants me to work on it alone. No team, just me.'

'Fine. What's the problem?'

Stephen stared blandly at Eliot.

'Well what about Laurie and the forty grand debt?'

'Eighty grand. And we'll use him, and the money, for something else.'

ten

The bar was moving about more than usual. Bottles sliding this way and that, people lurching about like total piss heads. Cheesy music trickled out from the speakers embedded in the ceiling, jazzy christmas carols. The Winter Wonderland Big Band with Cheeseman Dribble and the Kaks. Made you sick. Still, if it made people spend their dosh, hand over the spondoolies, who was he to moan? Aura Johnson downed his lager and cast a bleary eye towards the clock. Christ, another hour of this. Why had he been such a berk? He could have taken the Tunnel.

Once a month he crossed the Channel by boat, for variety, for a lark. Occasionally he went by Seacat, faster than the ferry but since it rocked like the helter-skelter at Broadstairs, you had to be in the mood. Still, unlike the tunnel, you could always go outside and freeze your balls off clinging to the handrails and throwing up over the side.

Boats were romantic.

And, last but not least, varying your route kept Customs off your case.

Aura headed for the amusement arcade. By the door he had to side-step a pavement pizza and round the corner he bumped into its source, a middle-aged old tosser with bits of diced carrot on his chin and eyes like a haddock's.

'You're a bloody liability,' he said, leaning to shout in the man's ear. 'Go to the gents and clean yerself up.'

The man groaned and clutched the wall. Laughing out loud, Aura sauntered off down the corridor, jingling the change in his pockets, he couldn't remember if the boat took euros, or only pounds.

It was a joke. The pinball machine had some crap written on it about not nudging. In a force ten gale? Were they completely mental? The boat was rolling about so much he could barely put his money in. He decided instead to waste his change in the fruit machines, maybe the pitching of the boat would bring him luck.

It didn't.

Out of nowhere Aura remembered the cricket. How could he have forgotten? Jesus, he was thick some days. England were playing a test series in India and the West Indies were doing something somewhere else. He had put money on them both, he was sure. Trouble was his radio was down in the van. He looked at his watch. Ten past seven. The summary of the day's play would have started already. Giving the fruit machine a hefty kick, for good luck, he went off to find the stairs down to red deck.

There was something soothing about cricket. He'd never actually been to a match, but driving about all over Europe as he did, the matches made him feel like he'd taken part of home with him. Especially the five day games. They could accompany him all the way to Turkey and back, if the reception was any bloody good. Which it wasn't.

I say, Aggers, that's an awfully nice cake you've got there. Here's Pillock coming into bowl. Yes, a Mrs Loftus from Wolverhampton sent it in. And, oh dear, bit of a bouncer there, his head has a second parting now. Chocolate and cherries. A black forest gateau, I believe. I think you maybe be right, Rupert, isn't that the twenty third time Rhodes has played silly mid off at a home international? I was just thinking the very same, Howard.

And so on, and on, and on. Pitch reports, luncheon, afternoon tea, luncheon, dark clouds gathering over the Smithers memorial stand, disagreements over the night watchman, luncheon. Meaningless drivel, like the shipping forecast, a slow special world measured in furlongs, slices of cake and bloody luncheon. And you could make a few bob on it, if you were lucky. Perfect.

Aura found the stairs past the bureau de change and descended past the posters that advised how much of this and that you could carry. He sniggered, having enough cognac in the van to have a bath in the stuff.

The heavy iron door was closed, to seal off the deck if the sea broke in. Aura pulled back the levers, pushed the door open and stepped onto red deck.

The deck was deserted. Lorries, vans and a few cars stretched from one end of the deck to the other but all the occupants, drivers and passengers, were upstairs in the bars, lounges and toilets. The ship's engines rumbled. Chains clanged against metal walls which creaked and groaned. A distant and muffled roar of the sea. It was as cold as a morgue. Aura zipped up his leather jacket and looked up and down, trying to spot his van. Two juggernauts blocked off any view to his left; to his right were a short row of family cars, a minibus and several camper vans. That had to be dodgy, who went camping in December?

The van must be behind the juggernauts or on the other side of the deck. He squeezed between two cars and walked round the back of the lorries.

It was a good job he'd come back down, he had left his lights on. The headlights looked dim, he hoped he hadn't completely drained the battery.

As he approached his van he heard a crash. A door closing? He stopped in his tracks. The noise had come from up ahead, beyond and behind the van. He opened the driver's door and climbed in to retrieve his radio. Switching off the headlights he climbed out, slammed the door shut and locked it.

The sound again. Closer this time. Shit, not my van. He ran round to the back but everything appeared to be in order. He tried the handle, it didn't budge. A movement in the periphery of his vision spun him round to face the second of the two lorries in the adjoining lane of parked vehicles and, for a split second, he thought he detected a movement, a buckling of the side of the lorry.

Pocketing his keys, he approached slowly. The lorry was in worse condition than he had at first thought. There were dents, scuff marks, and stress fractures or tears along the forward corner, immediately behind the cab. One gash was over ten centimetres long. Standing on tiptoes, not being particularly tall, he peered through the gash into the lorry. It was pitch dark and he could see nothing. But his nose was working. There was a strange warm sweet smell, as if the lorry were full of livestock. But that would be illegal, certainly in a closed vehicle. How would the animals breathe? He was as up for a bit of smuggling as the next man, but not if it caused animal suffering. He imagined the grief his mum would give him if she heard he was carrying live animals, it didn't bear thinking about. He made a mental note to keep one of the chickens back for her, assuming they hadn't defrosted too badly. Casting a last quick eye around the deck, he went back to the exit and headed for the bar upstairs.

The muffled sea wash swept along the hull. Chains rattled and clanged. Shallow pools of water trickled back and forth between the tyres of the vehicles.

The inside handle on the back door of Aura's van was wedged shut with an iron bar. A man sat in the back, in almost total darkness. Violent shivering shook his body as he struggled to stifle yet another bout of coughing so painful he thought his lungs would burst.

Fearing he was contagious, the other men being smuggled with him into Britain had ordered him to get out of the lorry. Too tired to fight back, the man had climbed out and found the nearest refuge to rest his aching bones. The floor of the van was a puddle of thawing chicken juices. The man curled into a foetal position and tried to sleep.

eleven

The following day Eliot rang BitterCrest and said yes. It was agreed that the contract would start the second week of January.

In the meantime, two projects gave him a perfect opportunity to put Laurie through his paces. Keen to clear his desk before starting at BitterCrest, Eliot pursuaded Laurie to do overtime four nights a week. Computer code as beautiful as snowflakes became 'this stuff's a bitch' as the graduate grappled with applying pure science to the nitty gritty of commercial constraints. The nights grew colder as the weeks tumbled towards the end of the year.

'How's it hanging for Christmas?' Laurie asked one evening while the computer did an autosave and backup. 'Oh, by the way, I got you this.' He handed Eliot a package the size of a matchbox wrapped in festive paper.

'What?'

Christmas ambushed Eliot every year, a flurry of missed shopping days, sudden requests to buy decorations or turkeys, drunken attempts to hail cabs after office parties held in basement winebars disguised as hawaian beach huts, hangovers, mooning bums on photocopiers. I'm dreaming of a white cliché.

'It's a sort of game,' Laurie explained. 'You know, like brainfood for programmers.'

Eliot leapt to his feet and grabbed his coat. 'Keep working on the interface.'

'Something I said?'

'Do you drink lager?' Eliot called over his shoulder as he rushed out.

'Only with chicken masala,' Laurie shouted down the stairwell.

Eliot's coat flapped into view briefly, two floors below, as his boots hammered noisily down the steps. 'Done,' he shouted back.

It was after ten when he returned. He raced upstairs, pushed open the office door, and found Laurie slumped and snoring in front of his computer.

'No stamina,' Eliot wafted the metal container under Laurie's nose.

'What happened?' Laurie rubbed his eyes. He grabbed a fork and shovelled curry while Eliot found a bottle opener.

'You don't want to know. Trust me, you don't want to know.'

Laurie took the bottle of beer Eliot was offering him. 'Try me.'

'Chicken masala, naan, veg korma, rice, prawn malayan. This beer's not bad.'

'Sweet, man,' Laurie agreed, his mouth full of Indian bread. 'So?'

'If you ever have kids, set an alarm clock for the week before Christmas.'

Eliot was absent from work the last two days before Christmas but he was on time on Christmas morning. Sue opened the door to let him in, they had agreed a truce for the children's sake.

'Good God, Eliot what the hell is that?'

Eliot struggled past her.

'Mind the walls.' She followed him into the dining room.

'It's a present for Alexandra.'

'What is it? A sofa?'

'Something I made.'

'Oh right, you forgot to buy them presents so you cobbled something together hoping she won't notice.'

'Daddy!' Alexandra rushed in and threw herself at Eliot.

Eliot placed the package on the dining room table before sweeping his daughter up in his arms.

'I need to lay the table,' Sue said, heading for the kitchen.

'My turn,' Toby shrieked. 'Let me hold it. Let me.'

'Daddy, it's the loveliest present in the whole world.'

Alexandra looked up at her father with eyes that made his heart ache. She clutched the giant papier maché dolphin as if her life depended on it.

'Can I go swimming with dolphins one day?' she begged. 'Please. In Florida ...'

'She's not going to the States, before you even think about it,' Sue said, re-entering the lounge. 'Not while that bastard's president.'

Eliot exchanged a smile with his daughter. 'Do you want to see some magic?'

'I want magic.' Toby pushed his sister aside. 'Me magic.'

Eliot fished the juggling balls from his jacket pocket.

'I'm glad someone has time to learn silly tricks,' Sue said, clearing the table.

BENEATH THE BITTERCREST

He didn't respond, he wasn't going to let her get to him.

'Watch this, kids. Oops.'

The children howled with laughter as Eliot dropped all the juggling balls.

'Do you want a cup of coffee before you go?' Sue asked.

'It's only six o'clock.'

'The children need to be in bed.'

Back at home, on the sofa in front of meaningless festive drivel on television, and tucking into a box of mince pies and a can of Guinness, Eliot remembered he had a present to open.

He had bought a small Christmas tree, knowing the children would be spending the day after Boxing Day with him. Around the foot of the tree were a few small presents for the kids, and Laurie's present to him.

It wasn't a cigarette lighter, which was a relief.

Laurie had given him a flash drive, a tiny memory storage device less than four centimetres long and designed to slip onto a key ring. Emerald green in colour, and the last word in gadgets, the flash drive plugged directly into the USB port on a computer, allowing files to be downloaded and transported from location to location. There was also a hand written note.

Eliot hi,

Thought you might find this useful. Careful what you plug it into though - there's a few 'extras' on it !!! Found this dread group on the net who swop beasties. The game is to see how long it takes to find the killer code and zap it. If your hard drive goes down, you're out.

Back everything up before you start - these babies are the bling!

Have fun, Happy Crimbo.

Laurie

At Laurie's age, Eliot too had been full of passion and curiosity, only kids fresh out of college would waste their evenings playing with viruses. Fifteen years older, Eliot was more careful, more aware of how such a hobby might be perceived by others, by the police for example.

Search programmes existed designed specifically to hunt out rogue code, maybe Laurie was creating or using something similar. Even so, without knowing whether he was dealing with trojan horses or worms, or worse, there was no way Eliot would risk damaging a computer by plugging a bucket load of viruses into it. The flash drive itself might be useful, once he'd worked out how to remove the files without infecting anything. Eliot threaded the gadget onto his key fob. He should ring Laurie and arrange to go out for a drink.

twelve

Three weeks after Christmas, Eliot was sitting in a dreary office in Swindon with fake wood furniture, not even crappy veneer but plastic, a desk, a socket to plug his laptop into, a polythene chair, and a shelf that was barely clinging to the wall. High up on one corner of the ceiling a camera lens stared down at him and, directly above his head, a light bulb had committed suicide, hanging sadly from its noose in the middle of the ceiling.

Draper, having insisted that Eliot work three days a week at Bittercrest, had not visited him once in two weeks. Every evening, before he left, Eliot was required to produce a progress report which was to be left in a case with Anna at reception. The first time he had asked, Anna had told him that Draper was at the hospital, though what was wrong with him she could not, or did not want to, say. Thereafter, she had said she didn't know where he was.

Every morning a thickset Latvian, who had no doubt worked in a gulag somewhere in Siberia, would deliver Eliot a letter detailing Draper's responses to the previous night's report and adding such information as Draper saw fit to enable further development of the software.

Eliot's work was done on a laptop and a PC purchased for the job. The computers had no connection, internet or ethernet, with any other computers other than to each other and, at the end of each day, both machines would be stored in a safe overnight, carried away by the sullen Latvian, from whom Eliot had been unable to ellicit any information other than his nationality and his first name, Sten. Eliot was not allowed to produce hard copy other than the daily reports for Draper.

When he had requested permission to complete his work in London, agreement had been given on the condition that Sten accompany Eliot, that the laptop be in a secure case, keys held by Sten, and that the laptop always be in Sten's line of sight. Secrecy verging on paranoia. Just the thought of Sten occupying a corner of his London office, his vast grey-suited presence like an ugly KGB building, and Eliot realised his mistake. Even commuting was preferable. And that was without considering the grief he would get from everyone else at Office Solutions.

He stayed in Swindon.

It occurred to Eliot that he might have brought the excessive zeal for secrecy on his own head by alarming Draper about the security risks at his interview. Next time he would not try so hard to impress.

A knock at the door.

'Yes,' Eliot called out.

'Gustave Brown, head of accounts.'

A tall, skinny man in a nylon shirt and dark suit stood in the doorway, hand outstretched. The limp and clammy handshake was accompanied by a cloying sour odour, as if Gustave Brown suffered from rising damp. Beneath a dyed mop of lank ginger hair his face displayed a permanent air of mild disappointment, an expression only enhanced by the heavy dark frames of his glasses. Behind Brown stood the ever-present Sten.

'I have been asked to come and observe,' Brown offered by way of explanation.

'Number one, it's lunchtime. Number two, Mr Draper made it very plain that I was answerable to him and to no-one else.'

Brown smiled understandingly. 'Indeed. Unfortunately, he has been called away at short notice. He gave me this letter.'

Eliot tore open the envelope. Barely eight lines long, to the effect that Draper was pleased that Eliot was taking his terms and conditions seriously, and that Gustave Brown was to be trusted with assisting in the installation of the software and shown how to operate it. He was not, however, to be given access to any passwords or to the protocols surrounding access to the passwords. Eliot cross-checked the signature against the one Draper had made on his contract of engagement, which he still had in his briefcase. It matched.

'Fine.' Eliot folded the letter and put it in his jacket pocket. 'Welcome to the house of fun.' He turned to Sten. 'We'll need another chair, mate.'

For an hour, with Brown peering at the computer screen, Eliot explained how the database operated whilst trying to keep his nose facing away towards the window; it was clear the head of accounts had a passion for all things garlic. Brown had several ideas of his own and Eliot agreed to make some modifications.

'Please, claim these little enhancements as your own. I am already in good odour with Neville.'

Eliot didn't venture an opinion on either Brown's suggestions or on his odour.

The encounter did little to change his impression that the operation at BitterCrest was fairly pedestrian stuff. If there was a reason for the extraordinary level of security Draper wished to see implemented, Eliot could not see it. The trade in carpets, foodstuffs, perfumes, porcelain, white goods, and clothes seemed of little consequence. True, there was to be provision in the software's design for the cataloguing of fine art objects and jewelry, the provenance of which was to be concealed within the encrypted areas of the database but, given the state of BitterCrest's headquarters, Eliot decided they must simply be trying to avoid taxes, VAT or import duties rather than criminally masterminding thefts of priceless works of art. Could Office Solutions be accessories to a crime for providing software? Eliot didn't think so.

'Thank you, Mr Balkan. Most illuminating. Mr Draper has chosen wisely and the Institute are to be commended for the recommendation.'

Who the hell were 'the Institute' Eliot thought to himself as Brown stood up, nodded his thanks and left. Out in the corridor, Sten was still on sentry duty.

'I'm desperate for some fresh air. I'll leave you to lock away the family jewels.'

Sten started unplugging the computers and Eliot left him to it.

'They keeping you busy today?' Anna asked at reception.

Eliot nodded and stepped out into the bright chill air. He crossed the car park towards his car but, at the last moment, decided that he needed a walk.

It had snowed in the night, a couple of centimetres of snow hid the tarmac from view, charting the comings and goings in a latticework of tyre tracks. The shiny leather soles of his new shoes slipped about on the packed snow and he had forgotten his jacket, having initially planned to drive to lunch, but by the time Eliot noticed, he had already gone through the main gates and couldn't be bothered to go back. The barrier was up, the security guard was watching European football on television and, for the wages they paid, Eliot would have done the same.

It took fifteen minutes, traffic roaring past, sludge spraying his shoes, to reach the arcade of shops and takeaways beyond the roundabout on the Oxford Road. He was no longer sure a greasy doner kebab would actually hit the spot, no matter how much salad was heaped in. It was always a mistake to visit fast food joints after hours, when the food was tepid and tired. He ordered felafel. The chef, working on Greek time, placed individual leaves of salad carefully into the pitta bread as if time were a currency and he a generous millionaire. Eliot hugged the radiator.

By the time he stepped outside again, the sun had vanished behind dark clouds straddling the gas towers and the wind had picked up and was practically scraping paint off the cars parked outside the betting shop. The industrial estate was just visible through the bars of the fence on the other side of the road. He would save ten minutes if he could cut across the wasteland. Clutching the soft warmth of the plastic bag containing his felafel, Eliot crossed the road to take a closer look.

Set back from the road were two tall iron gates. The gates were padlocked but, just to the left of them, Eliot noticed that one of the vertical metal slats of the fence was hanging loose. The industrial estate could be seen through a gap between the large bushes that flanked the service road. As a large flake of snow settled on his shirt sleeve, Eliot nudged the slat aside and stepped through.

Beyond the gates the road led towards the gas towers. After some thirty metres Eliot left the road, squeezing through the bushes onto the wasteland. The going was rougher than he had imagined. Gorse and bramble clawed at his clothes. Beneath this matted undergrowth lurked huge fractured slabs of concrete and, within minutes, Eliot had twisted his ankle, torn a hole in his trousers and dropped his felafel. Behind him loomed the grey rusting bulk of the gas towers, gangways running around their girths in a series of thick belts.

Eliot staggered forwards, thinking of gangster flicks, drug runners, shootouts, bodies tipping over handrails like toppling dominoes silhouetted against the falling sky, until a dull ringing sound brought him to a stop. He looked back at the gas towers expecting to see someone running high on a gantry, and suddenly felt vulnerable, as if a camera somewhere were following his every move.

'Don't be ridiculous,' he said out loud.

But the feeling didn't go away. Snow swirled as the wind wrapped a large plastic sack round his legs. The sack flew away as suddenly as it had arrived and Eliot set off again towards the industrial estate. The large back doors of BitterCrest's warehouse loading bay were briefly visible in the distance before the land dipped away at his feet and he found himself sliding into a hollow.

'Shit, shit, shit.'

All for a frigging felafel he hadn't even had a chance to eat. Sod fresh air. In future, exercise would be restricted to the gym, you couldn't tear your clothes to shreds on a bloody climbing wall. He scrambled out of the hollow and started to run. Less than a hundred metres from a main road and yet, shivering in his shirt sleeves, he might as well be on a one man expedition to the north bloody pole.

Abruptly the weather worsened and he was in a blizzard. The units were away to his left, still two hundred metres away, barely visible through the snow. Ahead, to his right, was the silhouette of a single storey building. A door was opening.

At that moment Eliot's left foot was brought to an abrupt halt by an obstruction hidden in the undergrowth and he fell headlong. His last thought was that he had tripped over a tree trunk. He was wrong.

thirteen

The towpath was a rough mess of frozen mud and stones hidden beneath a layer of snow. The three girls, in grey uniforms and black bomber jackets, had continued to take the towpath to go home from school, in spite of the protests from their parents, because it offered a chance to have a lark and a fag.

Tiffany had her bike, as usual, and the other two were on foot. For the most part, they walked three abreast, Tiffany dropping back behind where bushes or trees encroached on the path. The canal was black, shiny as Whitby jet. The usual assortment of debris poked out of the water: supermarket trolleys, binliners of garden refuse, mounds of dumped commercial waste, the odd bicycle wheel ...

A couple of barges were tied up by the bridge, coils of smoke, thin as drainpipes, reaching up into the sky. Emily had befriended one of the old couples who lived on the canal and been invited on board. It was like a house where all the rooms had been shrunk to a tenth of their normal size, then lined up end to end. Naff, and freezing too.

From under the bridge the water beyond shone like mercury. They shouted and shrieked, like they always did, their noise drowned in the hum of the traffic above.

On the far side of the bridge, the path turned up away from the canal briefly to avoid a muddy quagmire that had developed as a result of water dripping down from the girders higher up. Emily and Charly linked arms for support, with Tiffany pushing her bike up the outside, trying to squeeze in alongside the other two. A dead bramble snagged her tights. She pushed harder to get away and stumbled, falling into the bushes along the path. The bicycle toppled on top of her.

'Oh, what?' Emily laughed.

'Yeah, nice, Tiffany.'

Tiffany, flat on her back, 'Pull the bloody bike off of me, you cow.'

She had fallen on a pile of old clothes and something else, something lumpy. She pushed herself up as the bike was lifted from her. Her hand slipped on a plastic bag and back down she went.

'Shit!' Emily was looking down at her.

'What?'

BENEATH THE BITTERCREST

'It's chickens, a pile of dead chickens. Oh, rank!'

Tiffany sat up and looked around her, chickens everywhere, hidden away under the bushes. Most were in plastic bags, frozen solid. Emily and Charly helped her up.

'There's hundreds of them.'

'I wonder how long they've been there.'

'Why? You want to take one home? Like, I'm so poor I eat chickens off the canal?'

'Shut up, Charly, you're sick, man.'

'How many do you think there are?'

'Fifty. Sixty,' Emily suggested.

'Maybe there's more under here,' Tiffany said. She reached down to pull at the dirty coat she had landed on.

'You're disgusting,' Charly said.

The coat clung to the frozen ground and the brambles . The others joined in, pulling and shouting. Suddenly the fabric gave, the coat ripped down the middle throwing the girls backwards onto the path. Still laughing, they helped each other up and looked at what they had revealed. Screaming, they raced back towards the bridge, without looking back, without a word being exchanged, without Tiffany's bike.

A crow flew down from a nearby roof to look around. It tilted its head from side to side as it weighed up the situation. Very gingerly it half-flew half-hopped across the scattered chickens then stopped. Again it tilted its head.

Among the chicken corpses were two black canvas shoes. One stood upright, its worn sole visible. The other lay on the ground beside a broken foot that was bent at a very unnatural angle and, beyond the foot, a leg.

Hesitantly at first, then with growing confidence, the crow began to peck at the foot, tearing strips of skin and flesh to reveal the bones beneath. By the time the scissor beak had reached the meat just above the ankle, the cold air carried the sound of distant sirens.

fourteen

It was dark and his body seemed absent. He wanted to sleep, to sleep and drift away. Behind the numb comfort of the enveloping dark a distant voice was calling out in a language he did not understand. A rough repeating phrase, a monotone that grew neither closer nor further away. He tried opening his eyes but could hardly be bothered; better to lie there, resting in the cold crystalline cocoon, light as the air, at peace with the world.

From nowhere a coughing sound. Ugly rasping, hacking. Close by, someone was close by.

A hazy out of focus tangle of horizontal lines brushing up against his face. More coughing. Someone was pushing him. Pushing him behind his head, bending him up. They had to stop, leave him alone. He didn't want someone else's germs. Sleep and they will go away. But the coughing wouldn't stop.

The repeating foreign monotone started up again and with a shock he realised what it was. Not a human voice at all. A dog was barking.

Pushing himself up on his elbow, then on his hands and knees, he found the wasteland crowding in around him, thick with snow. Through torpid veins a lazy blood struggled to remain liquid as adrenaline began to pump in a last desperate attempt to save his life.

Carefully, painfully, Eliot got to his feet. A chain of lights up ahead seemed familiar or significant but his mind was on a go slow, barely processing the input from his senses. At some level he realised he had fallen and that he was suffering from exposure, but the reason for his predicament eluded him completely. His muscles went into involuntary spasm as his body attempted to raise its core temperature above critical. A headache was welling up, he must move towards the lights.

His foot thumped against an object sending a sharp jarring pain up his leg and almost toppling him. Eliot went back down on his hands and knees and felt the ground around him. He recalled falling over a tree trunk before ... before he had woken up.

But this was no tree trunk.

A fabric concealing something hard, a pipe perhaps? His frozen hands patted the pipe, following it to his right where it met another pipe running parallel to the first and joined up with it to form a larger pipe around which was some kind of strapping. His fingers followed the strapping.

A join or buckle, it was too dark to see which, on top of the larger pipe. Eliot reached out to the right of the strapping. The fabric continued. His fingertips scuffed against a small round obstacle that seemed embedded in the fabric. A dull sickening sensation was growing in the pit of his stomach. Beside the small round object was a second identical object.

The dog was barking again, a cold angry noise that tore at the throat of the enveloping gloom. Like an alarm or the flashing light on a fire engine. Eliot felt a third lump, round and thin as a coin. He tried to pick it up but it was stuck to the fabric that surrounded the pipe in some way and his cold hands could not prise it loose. His fingertips brushed against leaves and something sharp. Howling with pain, Eliot withdrew his hands and inspected them. A thorn was embedded deep in the pad of his thumb. He pulled it out and watched the blood well up and drip, black and glistening in the faint light from the orange night sky.

Reaching out again he found that the pipe continued beneath the leaves. He was feeling slightly less confused now, aware of his surroundings, aware of the need to find shelter, to get warm, to eat. But still something propelled him on and his hands fumbled along the pipe, brushing aside the blanket of leaves.

Quite abruptly he understood. He leapt backwards, mouth open to scream, but vocal chords only capable of a stuttering moan. He strained in the faint light to make sense of what he now saw; the frozen body of a man laid out, his chest and head partially covered in leaves and sticks.

He ran.

The running seemed to wake him up and, as he ran, Eliot found his memory returning. He recognised the buildings up ahead, knew that he should be heading towards the larger buildings to his left, knew his car was parked there somewhere. He made for the low building seventy or so metres ahead of him where the wasteland became tarmac and the going would be easier. He was within fifty metres of the tarmac when the first man emerged from round the left hand side of the low building, torch in one hand, a lead in the other, at the end of which a large dog strained to get away. Eliot carried on running towards the building, lifting his hands to show he did not present a threat. A second man appeared on Eliot's right. Eliot came to a stand-still, hands on his knees, gasping for air, head spinning.

'Who the fuck is this?'

A stick crashed down on Eliot's back, flooring him.

'Just throw him back in with the others. You've given us the right run around, you little shit.'

This last remark was accompanied by a hefty blow to the shoulder blades.

'No, it's a mistake,' Eliot grimaced from the pain rippling across his back.

'Bill, this one speaks English. Like a fucking local.'

A blow to the thighs this time. Eliot lifted his head enough to see the man holding the dog, which was salivating and growling menacingly. A blue uniform with the image of a biplane stitched onto the breast pocket. The estate security guards. In an instant Eliot remembered who he was and where he was.

'Call Draper.'

'What?'

'You little shit,' said Bill, the stick man

Another huge blow rained down on Eliot's back.

'Listen to me. I work over there at Bittercrest Imports. Unit six. Call Draper, the boss, or Brown, or Brown.'

The dog strained forward, its jaws brushing against Eliot's trousers.

'And get that fucking dog off me,' Eliot shouted, his voice suddenly thick with rage. 'or I'll sue your arse so hard you'll never work again.'

Eliot's anger brought the first signs of hesitancy in his assailants. The dog handler hauled his hound back and the stick man dropped his arms.

'I've cut myself,' Eliot said calmly. 'I need first aid. Is there a toilet in there?' Eliot stood up and turned towards the low building.

The man with the dog stepped in front of Eliot, blocking his path. The dog perked up.

'Great. Well, if you two gentlemen don't mind, I'll just stagger off in that direction, to my office.'

Eliot hobbled off towards the BitterCrest building. He could feel eyes on his back and, as he put distance between himself and them, he picked up his pace until he was almost running.

BENEATH THE BITTERCREST

Up until that day Eliot had never understood why it was that some businesses had showers installed. Allowing staff to have relaxing showers while paying them fifteen, thirty, or fifty pounds an hour seemed to be as close a definition as one could hope for of total insanity. Stephen, no doubt trying to impress upon Serina that he had the 'vision thing', had suggested they fit one at Office Solutions. To her credit, Serina had been as appalled as Eliot and the idea had been quietly dropped.

Now however, as he incrementally raised the temperature from lukecold to lukewarm, Eliot was counting his blessings. He stood beneath the soothing stream and felt his life returning to him.

A multitude of cuts and scratches covered his calves and ankles. He had scratched his face and could feel that his back would soon be a mass of bruises. This wasn't the Middle Ages. Industrial estates weren't allowed to have private militias running about, beating the hell out of people. Anyone would think nothing had moved on since the Peterloo massacre. He wondered who his assailants were. Were they the same men who had attacked the barefooted running man Eliot had seen from the window on his first visit? He tried to remember but everything had happened too quickly, his memory only served up screeching tyres, slamming doors and the haunted look on a hunted face.

He stepped out of the shower and back into his dirty clothes, hoping to God his jogging gear was still in the back of his car. Having smoothed down his hair, Eliot followed the beige corridor back to his office. It was eight pm.

The office still carried a rank and fusty echo of Gustave Brown's visit earlier in the day. The computers had been cleared away. There was no sign of Sten, the Latvian, which was just as well. Eliot collected his belongings, pens, a calculator, a handful of manuals and academic reference books and dropped them into his holdall.

Although deliveries occasionally carried on through the night, reception closed at six o'clock so Eliot headed back towards the warehouse to make his exit.

It was only the third time he had been in the warehouse, the first occasion being on his initial visit to meet Draper, and the second having taken place just some thirty minutes previously when he had staggered in after his meeting with Sopford Industrial Estate armed assault squad. While he was grateful that the warehouse door had been left unlocked, Eliot knew Draper appreciated neither spontaneous visits nor unsupervised wandering about. Eliot had learned that, in five years, Anna at reception hadn't even gone as far as the beige corridor.

The deliveries area was quiet, no sign of the warehousemen. Eliot had made his way down the aisles of packing cases, reached the side door and grabbed the handle when he heard voices outside.

'While we're at it, we can tell him that not only is security as flabby as a fag's arse but we're letting blokes wonder in off the street and ...'

Eliot recognised the voice of the man who had beaten him with a stick.

'I didn't mean like that,' a second voice answered.

His assailants were back.

'Hang on, I haven't finished yet. We've only let the bugger walk away and disappear into thin air.'

'Doesn't look great, I admit.'

'Yeah. Right, Chris.'

Eliot very slowly released his grip on the door handle, praying the movement wouldn't be spotted from the outside.

'So, do you think he actually went in there?'

'How the hell should I know? What do you want me to do? Sprout a bleeding periscope? Where's the dog?'

'Should we search the place? Is it open?'

'Tell you what, you fetch the dog and I'll ring the bell, see if anyone's in.'

The sound of departing footsteps.

'And get Stan to give you the phone number for Reception while you're about it,' Bill shouted after the departing Chris.

Eliot listened to the shuffling footsteps on the other side of the door. All at once the doorbell rang out next to Eliot's ear, and insanely loud. Now the warehousemen would appear and he would have a load of explaining to do. Trouble on either side of the door. In the distance a dog was barking. The whole thing was a bloody nightmare.

'Stop the bloody dog, you tosser,' screamed Bill on the other side of the door. 'Oh, for fuck's sake.'

Suddenly the handle jerked downwards and the door was pushed violently from the other side. Eliot steeled himself for confrontation.

fifteen

It turned out the door was locked. The sounds of cursing and a succession of keys being rattled about pointlessly in the lock was followed by the sound of receding footsteps.

And where were the warehousemen? Had everyone gone home? They must have shut up shop and left while he was showering.

Whichever way he looked at it, Eliot was right royally shafted. In the space of an afternoon he had gone from respectable technical manager, doing a few days consultancy, to prospective cat burglar, or whatever it was that the two monkeys outside thought they could pin on him.

He walked back down the beige corridor to reception, there was just a chance the door might be open.

The door was, of course, not open. Which left only one option. Well two, but Eliot didn't fancy waiting around till the morning to be let out. He went back to his office, picked up his crappy plastic chair and hurled it at the window.

The chair broke in three places.

Eliot ripped the shelf from the wall and smashed it against the glass. This time the glass shattered. Eliot dropped his holdall outside and clambered out. The dog was still barking. Eliot raced round the back of the building and on to the car park.

The barrier was up. As Eliot sped through, he saw the guard was still glued to his television.

As far as Eliot was concerned, Draper could stuff his job up his pompous arse. Aside from arranging compensation for his injuries from the company that ran the estate, Eliot wanted nothing more to do with Swindon or the Sopford industrial Estate or BitterCrest Imports.

'Can we tell how long he had been there?'

'A matter of hours, no more than that. Twelve hours, sixteen ... less than a day anyway.'

PC Tom Hampton stood as close to the steel table as he felt was necessary; wishing he had a cold and a blocked nose. The clothes, such as they were, had been removed and dropped in a plastic bucket.

He watched quietly as the forensic pathologist made his way across the surface of the dead man's skin, inspecting everything carefully and methodically, leaving no blemish unexplored. A strong cold light shone down onto the steel table lighting the body like forked lightning exposing a landscape. Every now and then the pathologist, a Dr Stoneman, took a photo, then moved on.

He had started at the head and face, using a swab to collect samples of residues on the man's face, in the nose, behind the ears. The face had several days' growth of beard and between the hair was a great deal of what appeared to Hampton to be grease or fat mixed in with traces of blood. Stoneman took samples which he put in sample bottles, labelling them as to content and location as he went. He opened the mouth with a spatula, swabbed the tongue.

The neck and shoulders next. The dead man was painfully thin, every bone visible and hard against the grey dead skin. Hampton wondered if all dead bodies looked this way.

A name tag was tied around the dead man's left ankle. Only the gender and approximate age had been filled in, male about thirty five years.

'Did he die where we found him?'

Stoneman did not answer him. He was turning the dead man's hands over, inspecting the wrists, the fingers, the nails.

'What exactly are you looking for?'

'Fingernails, PC Hampton.' Stoneman looked up at the young police constable, why had they sent him to see this? To break him in probably. Throw them in the deep end. See who sinks and who swims. 'Fingernails are like the notebook of the crime scene. Fibres, fluids, skin, dust.'

He found what he was looking for and reached across for the scissors. He clipped the nails one by one into marked envelopes taking care to catch the reside under each nail. Wood fibres and grease, the rest would become evident under the microscope. He placed the envelopes on the nearby shelf beside the other evidence he had collected, bottles and bags that had already been filled and tagged.

'Did you say the chickens were piled up over him?'

'No. The photos should arrive any minute. They were more scattered around the body rather than piled up in any way. Is that important?'

'If we are trying to establish whether this man is a victim of fowl play, it might,' Stoneman said, grinning at his own joke.

An assistant entered the room, a young woman, hair pulled back under a hat. Like Stoneman she wore a surgical gown, gloves, and boots. Even Hampton had been obliged to kit up. Stoneman looked up long enough to register the woman's arrival, then returned to his inspection. He swabbed an area on the left upper thigh, carefully studying a large bruise.

' I would hazard a guess at this stage that our man died before he reached the canal. We will know more in a few hours but the situation as I see it for now is this. There is no evidence of violent death. No stabs wounds, no evidence of a struggle, no signs of his having been tied up and so on.'

The pathologist turned to check that he had the policeman's attention. Hampton, who had been looking at the female assistant, trying to work out why she had chosen such a grisly career, turned quickly to face the pathologist.

'No evidence of a struggle.'

'Exactly,' Stoneman replied. 'Now this is where it gets interesting. Because of the temperature outside, things are not as clear cut as they might be, but I believe that this man died of cold. Not of exposure but of frostbite. Furthermore, I am of the opinion that the cause of death was probably due to frostbite brought about by being buried under a pile of frozen objects, quite possibly frozen chickens. His skin is covered in localised areas of frostbite and his skin is thick with animal grease. The question is this: if he was not out by the canal when he died in this way, where was he?' He paused to see if Hampton was following his drift. 'Some sort of store, a commercial freezer perhaps.'

Hampton was writing in his notebook. He looked up. 'How certain are you of all this?'

'Early days, PC Hampton. Early days.'

The pathologist stepped back from the body and smiled at his assistant. 'Victoria, we will leave you to swing the blades in peace.' He told her briefly what he had found and what he wanted doing, then took PC Hampton's arm and steered him away towards the door.

As they crossed the autopsy room, Hampton heard the assistant pathologist turn on the taps. The sound of running water muffled the other sound but he recognised it all the same, the sharpening of a long knife.

They went out through the pair of swing doors just as a loud buzzing started up behind them. Hampton had seen the saw hanging on the wall and was grateful to Stoneman for sparing him the worst of the autopsy. Stoneman suddenly stopped and stroked his chin.

'I have to join Victoria now, but here's something else to think about. Why would a man allow himself to be buried under a pile of frozen poultry without putting up a fight?' He raised one eyebrow. 'A group of them playing Chicken?'

Hampton couldn't even raise a fake smile for Stoneman's benefit, he was beginning to feel very queasy, probably as a result of the cloying deodorant smell in the corridor. It had been a mistake to have a fry up for lunch. As Stoneman disappeared back into the autopsy room and the swing doors swung back, a blanket of foul-smelling air flooded Hampton's nose and lungs. He clutched at the wall and just made it to the fire bucket before throwing up.

Hampton fiddled with his tie and stared at his notes for the tenth time. Had he remembered everything? Probably not. There would surely be something the D.I. would pick up on and give him a bollocking for, there always was.

'The Baker wants to know if you've finished pansying about with that report. It's half past bloody ten and the Premiership highlights are on in half an hour.'

Hampton looked towards the door. It was Walsh. She smiled sweetly.

'His words, not mine.' Then, more gently, 'Shall I put him off a bit longer?'

Hampton took a deep breath and stared into her blue eyes, one day he would ask her out. 'No, go on, tell him I'm coming.'

She nodded.

'Thanks .'

She smiled again.

Hampton watched her leave before standing and collecting the papers together into the blue card folder.

Hampton sat and waited as the Detective Inspector leafed through his report. Detective Inspector Machin, alias The Baker, alias Pasty, no-one could quite remember why. Way before Hampton's time anyhow.

'Fine,' Machin looked up at the new boy. 'You can leave this with me.'

Machin slid the papers together. He looked up again, surprised to see Hampton still sitting there.

'I said you can leave this with me, Hampton.' He looked towards the door, showing Hampton that the meeting was over.

'What's going to happen, Sir?'

'I'm sorry.'

'What's going to happen about this case? What should I do next?'

'Nothing, Hampton, you're going to do nothing. That shouldn't be too difficult, now should it?'

'But the man? Who's investigating the murder? Sir.'

'No one is.'

Hampton could not conceal his disapproval.

The detective inspector cupped his hand to his ear 'Well, I can't hear anyone clamouring to protest, can you, Hampton?' He spat out the word Hampton like a gobbit of phlegm. 'I don't think anyone gives a toss about some nameless arab who died under a pile of chickens.'

'But the murder.'

'What murder? Some greedy towelhead bought himself a big box of poultry for Christmas, got drunk, and died by the canal before he could wolf them down.'

Machin's look probed the younger man, dared him to challenge his authority. Hampton wrestled with the desire to point out that Christmas was unlikely to be on the dead man's list of religious festivals. He stared down at the carpet and fiddled with his ear then looked up at the Detective Inspector, the fight gone from his eyes.

'Well done, Hampton. Good boy.' Machin beamed a patronising smile and shoved Hampton's report along his desk, out of Hampton's reach. 'Now sod off.'

sixteen

Eliot rang from a call box. Kept the message brief, said he had been walking his dog and come across a body. Declined to give a name. A squad car was on its way they told him.

By the time he reached home it was gone eleven o'clock. The stop at his local pub had seen to that. The long drive, the day's events, the need to relax, thirst - a few pints had done him the power of good. He knew two or three of the other regulars and had ended up playing several games of pool.

The motorway had only provided a burger and a limp sac of pre-digested potato flour sticks with the texture of congealed glue and the taste of beef crisps. French fries? The French weren't usually reticent in taking on the Yanks. Any nation had the right to defend itself against being associated with that kind of shit.

Home was a Victorian terraced house, with stripped pine floors, minimalist Swedish furniture and the pervading smell of takeaway curries. The dining room and lounge had been knocked through to create the illusion of space.

It was many months since the dining room had played host to a meal of any kind. When Sue had moved out, taking the kids with her, Eliot had immediately seized the opportunity to move the dining table and replace it with his practice drum kit, which had been festering in the attic. Though he only sat down to play once a fortnight, the kit had more than repaid the effort of setting it up.

He had splashed out on a drum kit within the proceeds of his first summer job and for seven years had played in bands, firstly at college and thereafter in pubs and clubs. Mustang Sally, Brown Sugar, R & B, Blues, jazz and bit of Brit Pop. He hadn't ever really believed in the fame and the money, that was for singers and guitarists, but he had always loved the workout, loved the feeling he got when he was 'in the pocket', sticks flying, hats clapping, drum pedal thumping. Like dancing, only better. And the great thing with a practice kit was that he could just plug the headphones in and go. All the neighbours might hear through the walls would be a faint ticking, like someone tapping the sole of their shoe with a pencil.

Trouble was Sue hadn't seen it that way. She had accepted the presence of the drum kit in the back bedroom until Alexandra was born then BANG, parenthood slapped a stop sign on music making. Same thing had happened to his music posters, all replaced with Matisse collages and giant photos of pebbles from Ikea.

After a brief detour to the kitchen for paracetemol, food and drink, in that order, and an even briefer detour on the drum stool, Eliot collapsed on the sofa. The answerphone was bleeping irritatingly to let him know there were messages. Eliot reached for the remote control on the coffee table, and switched on the television. Another late-night celebrity love in where three presenters traded 'amusing' anecdotes about other interviews on previous occasions at different times for other channels. Eliot closed his eyes and let the meaningless waffle sedate him.

He awoke many hours later to the sound of banging on the front door. The letterbox was pushed open.

'Mr Balkan. Mr Eliot Balkan.'

Eliot stood up and grabbed the sofa until the room stopped swinging about.

'Mr Balkan.'

'Yes, all right,' he shouted. He stepped into the hall and pulled open the front door. The noise of birdsong savaged his eardrums. Bright sunlight reduced everything to silhouette. 'What time is it?

'It's eight am, Sir.'

'And?'

'I'm here to accompany you to the station, Sir.'

'I didn't order a taxi.'

'The police station, Sir. We'd like to ask you a few questions. All very routine.'

'No, it's not. Nobody ever comes by to take me to the police station. It's not routine at all.'

'If you would please accompany us, Sir,' said a second voice. 'It won't take much of your time.'

'I need to wash my face and ... and stuff,' Eliot said to the second silhouette.

'We'll wait in the car, Sir. You have five minutes.'

'Well, thank you very much,' Eliot said, closing the door. He trudged upstairs to the bathroom, took his time, showered and shaved.

They took him to a station in North London. He had known where he was until they passed through Harrow, at which point his guts began to protest violently about something he had eaten the previous night. It was all he could do to keep his eyes closed and his buttocks clenched, praying he wouldn't add soiling a police car to whatever list of misdemeanours he was going to be cautioned about.

The interview room was a tip, more routinely used as a store cupboard: stacks of chairs, two tables, one upturned on the other, and a filing cabinet, all crammed into one corner of a room that even an estate agent would have called compact.

Eliot sat and waited. He mulled over the previous day's events, the walk across the wasteland, the falling over - he still had a headache and a tingling in his fingers and should go to a doctor - the behaviour of the security guards. The broken window to his office. Was that it? Had BitterCrest filed charges for the damage? Office Solutions could lose the contract. Eliot had to speak with Stephen, to find out if there had been any calls from BitterCrest.

It was still only half past eight, unlikely anyone had yet spotted the broken window. Then he remembered the alarm and his speeding through the gates. He would be on camera. The whole thing was a bloody nightmare.

All he had to do was to explain the situation, he had been attacked and assaulted and feared for his safety. But asked why he had been attacked, he would have to explain that he had been on the wasteland, that he had fallen. They would put two and two together, realise he had made the phone call about the body in the snow and ask why he had not given his name. He would then be obliged to voice his concerns about... About what exactly? What would his employer make of his smashing a window? The door opened and two police officers, one of whom had driven Eliot to the police station, looked in.

'Mr Balkan. Tummy settling? Have we had a cup of tea yet?'

Eliot shook his head.

'Can we have three teas in room 4?' one of the men shouted down the corridor. Looking back into the room at Eliot, he added, 'We may even get biscuits. You live in hope, don't you?'

The two men grabbed chairs from one of the stacks and sat down facing Eliot. One man, the fatter of the two and with greasy lank hair, opened a notebook and made a show of flicking through the pages while the other man, balding and with a boxer's nose, the shape of a segment of Toblerone, made the introductions.

'Mr Balkan, good morning. I am Detective Sergeant Store from Swindon police and my colleague here is Detective Sergeant Miles.

Thank you for agreeing to come in for a chat.'

Eliot raised an eyebrow. The faintest hint of a sneer crossed Store's lips.

'We understand that you were in Swindon yesterday and the day before, Mr Balkan,' Store said.

'Yes.'

'You were in Swindon?' Miles this time.

'Yes.' Eliot stared straight back at him.

'Between what times?'

'Between the time I arrived for work and when I left. Both days. '

Miles looked up from his notebook and stared thoughtfully at Eliot.

'Is this one of those meetings where I have to ask for my lawyer to be present?'

'Oh?' Store this time.

The three men sat in silence for over a minute. The door opened. The duty officer Eliot had seen at the desk on his way in poked her head into the room.

'They're ready for you now,' she said.

Store addressed Eliot. 'We'd like to do a test. If you've no objections?'

'Testing what exactly?'

'A blood test. And a swab.'

'A blood test? And if I refuse?'

'It will be noted that you refused. And we may well return to the matter more formally in a few days, Sir.' Store said.

'It's all a matter of routine,' Miles said reassuringly.

'I keep hearing that this morning.'

'We're simply eliminating people from our enquiry, Sir.'

'And this enquiry is?'

'I'm not at liberty to divulge those details at this time, Sir. As Store said, you are entitled to decline the invitation to provide samples, if you prefer.'

What could his blood have to do with anything? All eyes were on him. He couldn't see what they could possibly have on him. The seconds ticked away.

'OK, let's get on with it. I have to go to work.'

'You did what?' Stephen was incandescent.

'I was locked in the building and it was the only way out.'

'You could have phoned someone,' Stephen yelled.

Cathy appeared in the doorway, carrying a stack of files and the morning's post. She glanced briefly into the room and turned tail.

'I was feeling confused,' Eliot said eventually.

'Understatement of the bloody year. You smash a client's windows and throw yourself out. You've blown us a hundred grand's worth of work, probably more. What the hell am I going to say to Draper?'

'Window, singular,' Eliot corrected him. 'I was concussed. These men, security guards I think, beat me with a stick.'

'What? They just waltzed into your office and set about you?'

' I was outside, passing a warehouse and ...'

'Oh God, you weren't snooping, were you?'

'No, I was not bloody snooping,' Eliot shouted. 'I was walking back from buying my bloody lunch when two neanderthals beat the crap out me. I told you before this all started that BitterCrest were a bunch of crooks. Peter Han warned me but you and Serina wouldn't listen. Too keen to get your fat noses in the trough.'

'What have BitterCrest got to do with this? Are you saying the men who attacked you are employees?'

'Yes, that's exactly what ...' Eliot stopped, then backpedalled. 'Well, no. Actually I think they're employed by the industrial estate.'

Stephen stared out of the window at a passing train.

Eliot remembered the body on the wasteland. Had there really been a body? He briefly considered, then dismissed, the idea of mentioning it. The situation was already complicated enough. Besides the body would be a police matter, completely unrelated to anything. 'Anyway, I'm through with it. I'm not going back to Swindon. I've got a bloody headache and I need to see a doctor.'

Serina appeared in the doorway. Stephen turned, saw her, waved her away.

'Right,' Stephen said, 'why don't you go home, see a doctor, visit a psychoanalyst, whatever. I'll ring Draper, see if I can retrieve the situation.'

'Fine.'

Moments after Stephen had left, Cathy stuck her head round the door.

'Are you all right?'

Eliot smiled and drew a deep breath. 'Nothing a short holiday wouldn't put right.' He grabbed his jacket. 'Fancy coming with me?'

'What? Now?'

'Why not? It's Wednesday. Bit of sun. A day on a beach. Back Friday night?'

Cathy laughed.

'Italy, Brazil. You name it.'

Cathy hesitated. 'My mother's staying with me and ...'

'She can come too.'

'Really?'

Eliot gave her the look he reserved for Alexandra when she asked questions like 'Does money really grow on trees, Dad?'

'I'm going for a walk, to clear my head,' he said. 'Might take the afternoon off.'

'Laurie was hoping ...'

'I'll ring him later.'

Eliot walked home. A headache was sloshing about between his ears, and his hands and feet were throbbing. He remembered stories of frostbite in Antarctica, fingers and toes falling off, blackened stumps snapping like twigs, while men in thick pullovers nursed stiff upper lips and pretended they weren't slowly starving to death. Having turned the heating up, Eliot sat on the sofa flexing the muscles in his hands and feet, wishing it was summer.

By mid-afternoon he had had enough. No news from Stephen. No call from Draper. No explanation from the police.

He had done nothing wrong. Stephen would have to vouch for him. They went back a long way. Stephen wouldn't abandon him, even over forty or fifty grand.

But Serina might.

Why did women like Cathy always wear their mothers like mill-stones?

The journey to the airport dragged on interminably. He rang the office to let Stephen know he was taking the afternoon off. Cathy took the call.

'I'll be back Monday. Saturday morning if it's urgent. You'll tell Stephen?'

'Where are you going?'

'It's only for two days. Tenerife, Cairo, Nice ... I don't know. Sun and sand. Come along, you can choose.'

'I'd love to Eliot but ...'

'It's OK. No worries, I'll send you a postcard.'

The Piccadilly Line had reached South Ealing. By the time he had visited the bank then popped home to stuff a few things in a bag nearly two hours had past and it was almost dark. A message for Sue telling her he'd pick the kids up Saturday morning, as agreed. Sent them his love. Made a mental note to buy them presents whenever he arrived wherever he was going.

The doors were closing when a man leapt on board. As the train started to move Eliot noticed the man was clutching a strap, his bag on the other side of the doors. The man was black, with pronounced cheek bones and dull yellow eyes, a maroon woollen hat pulled tightly over his ears. The other passengers behaved as if nothing were happening and the man did not exist. The man alternated between peering at his bag through the glass and looking up and down the carriage.

'What you want, Whitey?' the man said, catching Eliot's glance.

Nervous glances from the other passengers, all in Eliot's direction. The bag started banging against the glass. The man rubbed his brow nervously. His trousers and shoes were covered in mud. Eliot knew a few people like him. People like Felix and Philippe, a couple of regulars in Eliot's local who did building work, refugees from Ghana. Refugee was probably not the word. Illegal immigrants was closer to the truth. Good pool players though, both of them.

'You know what hurts the most?' Philippe had said to Eliot one evening over a game of pool. 'Being stuck here.'

'You could always go home,' Eliot said.

'You do not understand,' Philippe said. 'It is not that I do not like your country. My family is poor. I have many brothers and sisters. It is a game. You make it difficult for us to come but we are hungry. We do what we have to do to find work.'

'Have elections then and get rid of corruption. Less corruption, less poverty.'

Philippe smiled. 'Do you know that we are not even allowed to grow our own food anymore? America has decided that we have to buy American rice instead of buying our own. You call it free trade. So now my village plants no rice, the WTO has said it's illegal, and we starve while the US feels happy. It takes more than elections to bring freedom, my friend.'

It was the kind of thing Sue would say. Eliot watched as Philippe, his sleek head as smooth as the balls on the table, potted three spots at once, the white ball bouncing from cushion to cushion with perfectly executed precision.

'You're better off here then, aren't you?' Eliot missed an easy ball.

'Last week, my brother died in an accident at home. And I have to sit here. No funeral. No wake. I cannot do my duty or help my parents. I just sit in my room and think about him. I have another brother in Holland. I can not visit him either. No crossing frontiers. I cry alone. I'm stuck here.'

Eliot finished his pint. 'Something to drown your sorrows, Philippe?' he offered.

The train was slowing for the next station. Eliot's eyes zigzagged as he tried to read the station signs rushing past the window. Northfields. The doors hissed apart. The man reclaimed his bag, sighed with relief, glanced at Eliot.

Out of nowhere two burly men in raincoats leapt into view in the doorway, grabbed the black man and pulled him violently off the train. In seconds they had him in a headlock and were wrestling him to the ground.

'Help me,' the man shouted desperately. 'I am refugee. They will kill me.'

The middle aged woman opposite Eliot briefly lowered her Daily Mail, turned towards the commotion and snorted contemptuously.

Eliot stood up and moved towards the open doors.

'Police officers. Stay where you are. '

While the African continued shouting, handcuffs were produced and snapped on the man's wrists and the doors closed and the train began to move. The African stared at Eliot, his eyes saying 'you are the witness, you are the witness'.

Like the last reel of a film, the scene was lost as the train left the station and darkness replaced light. Eliot sat down. The other passengers continued reading, listening to music, picking their noses, ringing home to explain why they were late, as if nothing had occurred, as if violence were a dream one could awake from, or a story that never happened.

Destination Florence - he'd never been there, the tickets were cheap, and the flight was leaving in an hour. His ticket was checked, his bag x-rayed, his pockets scanned, his passport gawped at. He bought a newspaper, a pack of chewing gum, and a sandwich. Removing his raincoat and folding it over his bag, he sat down in a ridiculously low chair in a viewing area that afforded the glorious vista of millions of litres of aviation fuel going up in smoke over Runway One as planes left London like bullets from a machine gun.

People wearing clothes for all seasons meandered aimlessly about as if their shoes were in charge and their brains were already far away, summer frocks mingling with ski jackets and great coats and safari shorts.

He couldn't be bothered with the newspaper so he read the sandwich box, and learned that within its plastic contours were almost a hundred ingredients. He read the label on the back of the cover on the chair he was sitting on and learned that it shouldn't be washed in hot water. He read the instructions on the fire hydrant by the wall and learned that pointing the jet directly into someone's eyes was a bad idea. The minutes simply flew by.

Finally his flight was called. Eliot grabbed his bag and coat, made his way to the gate and stood in line waiting to board, checking his passport photo to see if he had aged. As he stepped forward a hand touched his shoulder.

'Mr Balkan?'

He turned round.

'Mr Eliot Balkan?' A female police officer, her eyes hidden beneath her hat. 'You're under arrest, Sir.'

The other passengers melted away, they couldn't have gone faster if someone had announced that Eliot had the bubonic plague.

'This is a joke, right?'

The police woman shook her head. Eliot noticed a second police officer to his right, closing fast.

'What are you arresting me for?' Eliot said, his voice rising. 'Come on, I demand an explanation. '

'It's nothing personal, Sir.'

'Oh, that's OK then.' Eliot said sarcastically. 'As you were.'

'If you'll just step over here to allow the other passengers through.' Her voice was calm and unhurried, as if she were a shop assistant steering a customer towards the menswear department.

'This is police harrassment.'

'We're simply following orders.' Her hand indicating where Eliot should go.

'You're under arrest on suspicion of murder,' said a voice behind Eliot.

Strong arms helped him to step aside. They took his bag, left him his coat.

The police van sped away from the airport and into dense traffic. Eliot, wedged between two officers, felt lost and numb. Who did they think he had murdered? His thoughts raced so furiously he could barely hold on to any of them. Was it something to do with the train crash? It had started to rain and the van's wipers thudded back and forth. No. It must simply be a case of mistaken identity. They were looking for a different Eliot Balkan and had simply messed up. He tried to imagine a world full of people called Eliot Balkan. Failed.

Of course, somewhere in his head Eliot knew instantly what he was being accused of. It had to do with the frozen body lying in wasteland by a gas tower. A body Eliot had practically fallen over in the darkness. But it was insane. The most perfunctory of autopsies would show he was innocent, that the man had been long dead by the time Eliot fell over him. The corpse had been rock solid for God's sake. What evidence could the police possibly have? There wasn't any. They were stitching him up. But why? What had he done?

Eliot suddenly realised the van had stopped. He was escorted into the police station, a seventies-built concrete box that simply plugged the gap between the two equally dull buildings to either side of it. Heavy doors shut behind them as they made their way into the heart of the building. Along one corridor and then a second. Up ahead was a bench. A man was already sitting there, head bowed.

'My bag?' Eliot asked.

'Mr Balkan, we can't keep you away,' said a voice over his shoulder.

Eliot turned to find Detective Sergeant Miles standing in a doorway, grinning.

'Ha ha, I'll die laughing.

'Wait there,' Miles indicated the bench, then disappeared from view.

The seated man looked up. Eliot sat down. Beneath the maroon woollen hat were the haunted yellow eyes from the train. Eliot stared back, raised his eyebrows, that's the way it goes. The African laughed and laughed, a deep rolling wave of sound, rocking from side to side, the tears bouncing off his cheeks.

Some two hours later, a policeman made his way down the corridor towards where Eliot and the African sat, awaiting their fates.

'Ah, we have a visitor,' said Rufus Dibango.

Rufus, a Cameroonian, appeared far less anxious than Eliot. It was a matter of survival, he explained. Rufus had long experience of having his motives questioned, his movements constrained, his freedom curtailed. Since childhood he had learned that he was low down on everyone's list of priorities. He had spent many hours waiting patiently for others to decide his fate. In his home village, where there were no telephones, it was normal when visiting friends to find them not at home. The choice was simple, walk home or wait. Two or three hours sometimes, in the shade of a tree or in an armchair on a balcony overlooking the comings and goings.

They knew how to wait in West Africa. They gave good waiting.

The English also knew how to wait, but here they did it standing up, queueing for hours to buy things, see things ... Even in their cars they would spend hours in line, long after drivers in Douala would have abandoned the roads and driven up onto the pavements. It was all a question of climate, the temperature in England was suited to queueing, comfortable and gentle. When it wasn't snowing.

Whatever fate awaited Rufus Dibango, he would accept it calmly and quietly, unless he had an audience, while calculating his escape to fight another day. He was a stoic, he had to be. He smiled pleasantly at the approaching policeman.

Eliot, on the other hand, was a tangled mess of knotted muscles and burning stomach, a boiling crucible of anxieties, suspicions and confusions.

'Eliot Balkan.'

'Just when I thought things couldn't get any worse.'

'A pleasure to see you too.' DS Store looked tired. 'Caught trying to leave the country, I hear?'

'Why shouldn't I leave the country?'

'Indeed, why shouldn't you?'

'Nobody told me I had to stay in London.'

Store raised his eyebrows but said nothing.

'You, they won't allow to leave the country,' Rufus said, 'And me, they won't let me stay. Maybe we could do a deal?' He looked up at Store.

'Is this bunny with you?' Store said.

'Do they pay you to be an ignorant shit or do they breed you like that in Swindon?' Eliot was rewarded with a view of Store's jaw clenching angrily. He'd got under the man's skin. You took your victories where you found them.

Store indicated with his thumb the direction Eliot was to go. As Eliot stood up Rufus grabbed his hand and shook it.

'Same shit, different day,' Rufus said.

Eliot nodded and patted Rufus on the shoulder before following Store down the corridor to whatever lay beyond.

What lay beyond was another interminable van journey through the capital's gridlocked streets. It was still raining, dark cold bullets strafing the windscreen and rattling the roof. No-one paid attention to Eliot. He half-listened as Store argued with the other two about the Premiership and Manchester United's chances of turning things round before the end of the season.

Eliot had been allowed one phone call. He had rung the office but found only the answerphone. What the hell could he say? Help, I've been arrested on suspicion of murder, send me a lawyer? Actually, on reflection, that might have been exactly what he ought to have done.

Traffic inched along. Eliot pillowed his coat, put it between his head and the window and, closing his eyes, imagined a beige corridor that went on and on, the doors all locked, the light dimming with every step as if he were slowly descending into the earth.

seventeen

'Oi. Rumple Stiltskin.'

Eliot was roughly shaken from his dreams. Rain was still pouring. The van was in a courtyard surrounded by various police vehicles. It was bitterly cold.

They frog-marched him into the red-brick building and found him a bench. Eliot readied himself for another two hours of heady excitement. Becket hadn't understood a thing about boredom, Waiting for Godot was way too interesting.

The height of the ceilings, the pelmets and architrave suggested that he was in a building of a certain age. Late Victorian perhaps? Not the seventies chic of the London cop shop anyway. Large rooms had been butchered to create the dingy cubicles modern people preferred to live and work in; the mouldings along the walls would stop abruptly as they hit a blank wall thrusting out at ninety degrees. A triumph of philistinism over form. Eliot continued his amateur musings on the architectural value of shoddy conversion jobs, for lack of anything better to do, for what seemed like an hour. Long enough to worry that he might be turning into his uncle, with his half-baked prejudices and overpolished cynicism.

He was again given the opportunity to make a phone call and this time rang a lawyer. The lawyer in question, a Mr Burling, specialised in divorce settlements and was representing Eliot in his battle with Sue over custody of the children. Not exactly suited to helping a client on a suspicion of murder charge, but Eliot had never previously had reason to develop a relationship with lawyers who specialised in murder cases. Mr Burling, in any event, was not in his office. It being half past ten at night. Eliot left a message.

As he sat waiting, Eliot thought of Florence. He'd have been in his hotel by now, or in a café watching passers-by coming out of cinemas or theatres. A mandolin strumming to the flickering water of a fountain seen through an arch. The fleeting glimpse of a malignant dwarf in a red coat ... or was that Venice?

'Mr Balkan.'

Eliot looked up. 'Mr Store.'

'Detective Superintendent Store. Follow me.'

BENEATH THE BITTERCREST
85

Eliot followed Store to a cell with a bench and a blanket. Eliot entered and sat down. The door slammed shut behind him.

For the first time in his adult life Eliot was deprived of his liberty. The door slam had a finality he could never have imagined, a metallic crash reverberating in his head with the power of a judge's gavel. Guilty. Guilty. Guilty. Of what, exactly? He was being set up but who by? It didn't matter; without a defense he could be spending twenty years in the cells.

Who could provide him with an alibi? He knew no-one in Swindon, except Draper, Sten the Latvian minder, Anna the receptionist, and the malodorous Gustave Brown. He could hardly call on his assailants to act as character witnesses. Whoever had set him up must know that, must know that he could not defend himself. On the other hand, there could be no incriminating evidence. He had killed no-one, so how could there be proof of his having done so?

He lay back on the bench. Metal cages cradled bulbs recessed into the ceiling from which a harsh white light burned his retinas, even when he closed his eyes. A sudden insight - Rothko painted what people saw with their eyes closed, the after images that slowly faded on the backs of your eyelids.

Eliot turned this way and that, trying to make himself comfortable. A commotion started outside. Several very drunk men were being marched down the corridor. Eliot sat up.

Screaming, swearing, shouting abuse, kicking of doors. A door flung open, smashing against the wall. More shouting. Kicking or beating. A door slammed shut with such force that the walls in Eliot's cell shook. Shiny black footsteps led away down the corridor to the accompaniment of shouting and door rattling.

Lying down again, Eliot covered his ears and eyes with the blanket.

'Mr Balkan has been advised of his rights and the interview is commencing at,' Store checked his watch, 'ten minutes past eleven.'

They were in one of the interview rooms. DS Store and a woman officer sat across a table from Eliot and Anthony Burling, who had received Eliot's message and turned up to represent him. Store checked the tape was rolling and, with obvious relish, turned his attention to Eliot.

'Sleep well, did we?'

Eliot stared back, saying nothing.

86 christian vassie

Store turned to his colleague, a woman officer, and gave her a smile that suggested he was looking forward to a bit of fun. PC Winters pursed her lips slightly, she had never liked Store, but knew better than to show it openly. Her antipathy did nothing to upset Store, he quite liked the sullen resentful type, especially when it came with red hair and a turned up nose, and large knockers. Still staring blandly at Winters, he picked his nose while addressing Eliot.

'So, let's start at the beginning. What brings you to Swindon?'

Silence. Store shifted his gaze towards Eliot.

'I already gave a statement.'

'No, Mr Balkan, an informal chat is not a statement. *This* is a statement.'

'I have been working for a company based in Swindon.'

'Yes? Go on.'

'And that is why I have been in Swindon.'

Store liked the sarcastic bastards, the cocky ones who thought they were so smart. They were the most fun of all. Watching them snivel. He slowly produced a pen and a small notebook from within his jacket.

'This process can take an hour or so. Or it can go on for days,' Store said. 'What company were you working for?'

'BitterCrest Imports. On the Sopford Industrial Estate.'

'And what was the nature of your employment?'

Eliot glanced across at his solicitor. Anthony Burling seemed more tense than Eliot, police interview rooms were not on his usual itinerary. He was also overdressed, heavy blue woollen suit, burgundy waistcoat, thick woollen shirt, and no doubt a vest beneath that. His forehead looked clammy and he dabbed at it with a large hankerchief.

'I've been doing consultancy work there.' Eliot's voice a dull monotone.

'Care to be a little more specific?'

'It's confidential.'

Store turned towards Burling. 'Could you advise your client as to the merits of making a full and frank disclosure?'

The wait was agonising. Eliot found himself wondering if Burling still had the power of speech. Store tapped with his pen on the folder that was resting on the table between them..

'My client is ... er ... within,' Burling began. 'As far as I can see, he is ... er... within, within his rights to protect the confidentiality of his ... er ... business arrangements.' Burling stared at his shoes.

BENEATH THE BITTERCREST

Store smiled, this was going to be fun.

'OK then,' Store turned to Eliot, 'now you have had the benefit of your lawyer's wisdom, let me tell you what you were doing, Mr Balkan. You have been installing a security system for Mr Draper of BitterCrest Imports. You work for a company called Office Solutions, based in West London. As a senior partner, your expertise and personal touch was a prerequisite to your company's successful bid for Mr Draper's business. You have been working from an office within BitterCrest Import's Swindon headquarters for four or five days. How am I doing?'

'It hardly seems necessary me staying,' Eliot said, standing up. 'Why don't you finish the interview without me?'

PC Hampton sat in his car across the road from the entrance and waited, his mind a torment of divided loyalties and ambitions. If he did as he was told, his silence would make him a team player, one of the boys. If, on the other hand, he actually found out how it was that a man had ended up dead under a pile of chickens by a canal, he might fall out with his boss but his abilities would be recognised and he would surely get promotion. Promotion for achieving something, rather than promotion for turning away and leaving a man's death ignored.

Every ten minutes or so, he started the engine and revved her up to get some heat into the car. Good car the Volvo, solid, reliable. Bloody good heater. Not exactly sexy, but looks weren't everything. Besides he liked red. He'd been there an hour when he saw a car approach and slow down. It wasn't Stoneman but a young woman, a secretary probably. The car went through the open gates into the car park. Suddenly, he remembered. He leapt out of the car and gave chase, reaching the woman as she rummaged in the boot of her car. She spun round to face him.

'Oh, PC Hampton, isn't it? You gave me quite a shock.'

He hadn't expected the long dark curls.

'Almost didn't recognise you without the gown and mask,' he explained.'

'What can we do for you? Stoneman's away in court today.' She reached into the boot and collected a huge stack of files, which Hampton dutifully accepted to carry. Next she pulled out a large briefcase, closed the boot, and turned toward the entrance to the pathology wing.

'It's Victoria, isn't it? Call me Tom. I had a few quick questions about the man you autopsied the other day.'

'You'll have to remind me, I'm afraid. It's been chaos this week.'

'Chickens. Frozen chickens.'

'Oh yes, I remember. Do you mind if we go inside? It's freezing out here.'

Hampton nodded his assent. They walked towards the doors, Hampton all but hidden behind the stack of files.

'Can this conversation remain confidential? Off the record?'

Victoria stopped and faced him, arching an eyebrow.

The test match was slowly drifting towards yet another draw and the radio commentators were shifting their attention away from the pitch and towards a marvellous battenburg sent in by a Mrs Larkin from Solihul.

The jet hose seemed to have done its job on the chicken fat. The yellow Citroën van stood dripping but gleaming outside Aura's dad's lockup. It had cost him, maybe dumping the chickens had been unnecessary, but with any luck that would be an end to it. Life could be a bitch sometimes.

'All right then, you tell me, why I would pop out for a bite to eat and suddenly feel the urge to murder someone? In my lunch hour?'

'Is that what happened, Mr Balkan?' Store's voice had a conspiratorial edge.

'Oh yeah. And on my way home I blew up the Twin Towers and sank the Titanic. The answer is NO,' Eliot shouted. 'Who's setting me up?'

'Mr Balkan,' Burling interjected. 'It might be better if ...'

Eliot glared at Burling but got the message and shut up.

Store opened the folder that had been sitting between them and produced a sheet of paper. He made a show of reading it although he knew exactly what it said. A quick glance at P.C. Winters who, in turn, looked over at Eliot. Store pushed the sheet of paper across the table towards Burling.

'Your client agreed to a blood test this morning. The result matches blood samples found on the clothing of the deceased.'

'That's ridiculous,' Eliot protested.

Burling pulled the sheet towards him. Store scratched his ear casually. Winters took a sip from her now cold mug of tea. Burling's chair creaked as he leant forward and slid the sheet of paper across to Eliot.

'We had it rushed through,' Store said quietly. 'Amazing technology. Of course, you can contest it. The odds are about fifteen million to one, I believe. Better than the lottery.'

Eliot finished reading and shot a glance over at Burling who stared back impassively. A memory of something stabbing his thumb slid over a second memory of his hands pushing undergrowth aside to reveal a corpse, a kaleidoscope of hazy fragments, of running, of a dog barking. A splinter embedded in his thumb.

'This I can explain,' Eliot said, to Burling as much as to Store.

'Wonderful.' Store turned to Winters. 'Isn't that wonderful?'

'We don't process the material here, you'd have to contact the labs directly.'

'I'm simply asking if there's anything you can give me, any information at all.' Hampton leant back against the wall, her office was as small as his own, though she didn't have to share with three colleagues. A pigeon fluttered briefly against the window, scratching and squawking, confused by its own reflection.

'There appeared to be a huge assortment of different materials, fibres, and so on mixed in with the fat that was all over him,' Victoria said eventually.

'Go on.'

'Well.' She hesitated. 'This is all very preliminary.'

'I understand. Please.'

Victoria sat down and made a show of looking for something in the drawers of her desk. 'Stoneman was of the opinion that death had not occurred by the canal, and that the fibres and other residues found about the deceased's clothes and person were probably from the vehicle that carried the body to the canal. It was quite possible that the poultry and the body were in the vehicle together.'

Hampton muttered his thanks and left. He was almost at the stairs when he heard footsteps running after him.

'Here.' She pressed a scrap of paper into his hand. ''He's a friend of mine. Works in the labs. That's his direct line.'

'So, you fell over the body whilst returning to your office from a visit to a takeaway on the Oxford Road?' Store's tone was sceptical and sarcastic.

'Exactly.'

'Does this kind of thing happen often, Mr Balkan?'

'What?'

'Stumbling across stiffs on your way to and from the shops?'

'If I may be allowed to interject?' Burling said.

All heads turned wearily towards him.

'It might be construed that ... er ... that you were perhaps bullying my client.'

'We will bear that in mind,' Stored sneered and turned back towards Eliot. 'It didn't occur to you that you had a duty to report this alleged discovery of a body?'

'I did report it.'

'Oh?'

'I rang in on my way home. After I had left work.'

'And no-one here answered the telephone. How unfortunate.'

'No, they did answer and I told them about the body and where it was located.'

'From the office? From BitterCrest?'

'I told you, after I left work.'

'You do realise that this interview is being recorded, Mr Balkan?' Store waved his hand in the direction of the video recorder. 'Good. In which case I would ask you to supply us with the number of your mobile phone.'

'I rang from a call box.'

If Store was taken aback he didn't show it.

'Why not your mobile phone?'

Eliot hesitated. He had begun to think that maybe he had given his name inadvertently but, if the police didn't know that he had made the call, how on earth had they thought to associate him with the body by the gas towers? Who could have known that he had come into contact with the body? He had been alone. They couldn't have carried out a DNA test of everyone living or working within miles of the corpse.'

'Mr Balkan?'

Eliot re-ran the events of the day. Sneaking through the gap in the slats by the gates. Walking past the gas towers. A dog barking. A metal clanging that he had thought might have come from one of the gas towers. Maybe there had been someone up there. Or a camera.

'Mr Balkan, why did you not use your mobile phone.'

Eliot was snapped from his introspection. 'I rang from a call box.'

'You have already told us that. Which call box and at what time?'

BENEATH THE BITTERCREST

'It was about eight thirty, maybe a few minutes later. The phone was outside a pub. If you get a map, I'll show you.'

'The interview pauses at five minutes past twelve while PC Winters goes to find a map of the Swindon area.'

Store clicked the recorder off and nodded at Winters who stood up and left the room. The three men sat in silence awaiting her return. The half-smile stayed pasted across Store's large face as he stared smugly at Eliot.

'Can I have a glass of water?' Eliot asked.

'Off the record?'

'Yeah, OK.'

'Off the record you can fucking wait, you piece of shit.'

Store folded his arms and leant back in his chair. Eliot did the same. Winters arrived with the map. Store restarted the recorder.

'The interview recommences at 12.07. Present are Eliot Balkan, Mr. Burling, PC Winters and myself, DS Store. Mr Balkan will now show us on the map where the alleged phone call took place.'

He spread the map out on the table and spun it round to face Eliot.

Pubs weren't marked on the map, just streets and roundabouts. Thousands of bloody roundabouts - the map looked like a cross section of an Aero bar, bubbles everywhere. Eliot thought he recognised the curve in the road, about a mile from the Industrial Estate. It was after that but how far after? He felt Store staring at him. Burling cleared his throat and shifted his weight on his chair causing it to creak loudly.

'Here,' Eliot said finally, prodding the map. 'Just off Dorcan Way. That's where I rang from. Edison Road.'

He only hoped he'd got it right.

'Get them to check the records.' Store folded the map and handed it back to Winters. 'PC Winters leaves the room at 12.10.' For the benefit of the machine.

'Could I have a glass of water now?' Eliot asked. 'On the record.'

Store stood up, his hands bunched into fists. He had enough of playing police cat to Eliot's mouse. Burling looked up anxiously. Eliot savoured again the pleasure of the boot being, even momentarily, on the other foot.

'The water? he said.

'Do you know the minimum stretch for murder?' Store said finally.

'Is this a quiz. Right answer and I get my water?'

'Can I have a ... a .. a word with my client?'

Store waved his hand towards Eliot, 'be my guest.'

'In p ... private perhaps?'

Store looked from Burling to Eliot then back to Burling. He turned towards the camera. 'Interview stops at 12.11 to allow Mr Balkan to confer with his solicitor.' He switched off the machine. 'You'll have food sent to you. Don't make any plans for this evening, boys, the speed we're going this may take a few days.'

eighteen

There was no making any sense of any of it. Eliot and Burling had just finished two rather unimpressive cups of coffee, and two equally dull pastries, when PC Winters came into the interview room.

'You're free to leave. I must advise you to stay in the country, however, as further attempts to leave will result in your being incarcerated pending the completion of our enquiries. Your personal effects are at the main desk.'

And with that she left.

'Can they do that?'

'Your phonebox must have turned up trumps.' Burling lit a cigarette and shoved his phone and notebook back into his briefcase. The two men stepped out into the corridor. Burling indicated the way he had come in. Eliot followed him.

'I meant can they stop me leaving the bloody country?' Eliot was shouting. 'A cross-eyed dog could see I had nothing to do with this ...'

Burling, purple with anger, grabbed Eliot's sleeve and spun him round.

'Mr Balkan, I may be unfamiliar with police interviews but I do know a little about human nature. I suggest you wait until after you have left the police station before commencing your tirade.'

Burling stormed off. No chance of a lift then. Eliot made his way to the reception desk where, eventually, the duty officer handed him his coat and bag.

The air outside was cold and damp. Eliot pulled on his raincoat. He needed to find the railway station and head back to London, he had had a bellyful of Swindon. Traffic on the high street was nose to tail, a taxi to the station might take longer than the journey to London. The walk would do him good. He headed down the high street without looking back.

A few minutes later Store stepped out into the open air, mobile phone to his ear. He pressed a hand over his free ear to block out the traffic noise.

'What was that? Oh. Yes, We shook him up a little. ... No, no, of course not, but if he has any sense he won't be returning to work.

You'll be ... Yeah, out of your hair. Exactly ... I understand. By the way, I ...'

Store found he was listening to a dialing tone. He pocketed his phone, looked around warily then, satisfied that he had not been overheard, he shrugged his shoulders and went back inside.

It was a nightmare in technicolour. Up was down, left was right, right was wrong, and nothing made any sense. In a matter of hours he had gone from semi-respectable citizen to murderer, in the police's eyes at least. Eliot's world was collapsing like a house of cards.

His mood found its match negotiating a route round the town's notorious and incomprehensible 'magic roundabout', a collection of mini roundabouts clustered round a larger one like Saturn haloed by its many moons. A city engineer's wet dream, with dazed drivers tentatively lurching from mini-moon to mini-moon like drunk bees hopping from bloom to bloom in a municipal flowerbed.

Eliot stopped at an old fashioned newsagents, bought a local paper, a quarter of pear drops, real ones out of a glass jar, and some cigarettes. Told himself it was really the paper he wanted.

Wandering into a park, he found a bench in front of a statue of a man on a horse and sat down, putting the newspaper to one side and the fags to the other. The sugared surface of a pear drop felt rough against his tongue as he pulled out his mobile and dialled the office number for Han, the private investigator.

The acid tang of the boiled sweet reminded Eliot of his gran. Or, more truthfully, his grandad. His gran had had a furious temper, which subsided as quickly as it appeared. Pear drops were grandad's way of smoothing the waters, taking the heat out of the moment, reassuring the grandson that everything was alright. They still worked their magic thirty years later.

'I'm afraid he is not available.'

'What's his mobile number?'

'I'm afraid I cannot give that kind of ...'

'I'm a client, for God's sake. Office Solutions, we've been dealing with P.S. Partners for three years.'

'I'm sorry, Sir.'

'Fine. Is he in the office?'

In the background, Eliot could hear a second voice, talking to the receptionist.

'Eliot, hello.'

BENEATH THE BITTERCREST

'David, hi. I'm trying to reach Peter. It's worse than ringing the bloody bank.'

'New receptionist. Very keen. Look, I'm afraid Peter isn't here. Didn't show up. I imagine he's got that flu bug that's doing the rounds. Back on Monday, I'm sure. Could try him at home if you want. He's probably sleeping it off.'

'OK. Listen, what's his mobile number?'

'I'm not sure, Eliot. He's very ...'

'Don't you start, I've already had that from the receptionist.'

'I'm sorry, it's just that he ...'

'Just give me the number. If he throws a fit, I'll buy him a new phone. OK?'

David gave in.

'Thanks, David.' Eliot hung up.

A seagull veered away in the stiffening breeze. The sky was very dark, there were lights on in several windows beyond the park. Eliot stood up, looked at the newspaper, and at the fags. Clenching his jaw, he took the newspaper, thrust it deep into his jacket pocket, and strode away from the bench without looking back, feeling the cigarettes calling out to him, seagulls shrieking in the wake of a fishing boat. He wandered towards the railway station, barely noticing the icy wind.

What had precipitated the interrogation? Who was the dead man by the gas towers? Why did the police suspect him?

The only people who knew that Eliot had been on the wasteland were the two security guards who had roughed him up. Why would they seek to throw suspicion on Eliot? What were they covering up? Were they acting on their own initiative or had someone put them up to it?

Fresh out of school, Eliot had worked in a chocolate factory for a few months and had seen the way very tidy sums of money could be made stealing from an employer. Thousands of chocolate bars stuffed into sports bags hidden away beneath work benches, smuggled out to sell on markets stalls at weekends. Was that it? Two security guards stealing from the low building, covering their tracks? Had they killed the tramp? Or ... or what? What wasn't he seeing?

Reaching the station, Eliot discovered he had an hour's wait for the next train to London so he crossed the road to an Italian restaurant. While he waited for his pizza, he downed a bottle of Nastro Azzuro. And then another. The tension started to slip from his neck and shoulders. He returned to the events on the wasteland. The answers were there somewhere.

If the guards weren't acting on their own account, then ...

Who owned the low building? Might the dead man on the wasteland simply have been a snooper, poking his nose in where it wasn't appreciated? What could he have seen?

Eliot cast his mind back.

The first man had emerged from round the left hand side of a low building, with a large dog. At that point Eliot had carried on running towards the building. Then the second man had appeared from the right, shouting. Eliot had then stopped and they had attacked. Suddenly he understood, it wasn't his presence on the wasteland that had triggered the attack. The two guards had positioned themselves between him and the low building. That was it. They had thought he was heading towards it and they protected it. What could there be in that building that was important enough for the police to pull him in on a bogus murder charge?

He looked at his watch. Twenty minutes waiting for a bloody pizza. It was worse than waiting for his felafel. The Italians made the Greeks seem like the Germans. He caught the waiter's eye.

'Look, forget the pizza. How about a salad?'

'Yes, Sir.'

As the swing door to the kitchen swung and the waiter went through to change the order, Eliot briefly glimpsed the chef, feet up on the sink, leafing through a magazine. The door swung shut.

Eliot gave up and left, but instead of crossing the road to the station, he headed in the opposite direction.

The day had finally collapsed under the weight of its gathering black clouds. A few snowflakes tumbled in the darkness.

Eliot stood on rough ground about a hundred metres from the low building on the Sopford Industrial Estate. With the help of a bus shelter he had scaled the fence on the Oxford Road and approached from the north west. Some distance away to his left was the BitterCrest building. To his right was the wasteland that had nearly cost him his life.

He had purchased a nightscope from a small camera shop. Adjusting the focus, he could see that there were two windows set into the north wall, both fairly small and both protected by heavy iron bars. He moved round carefully to his right. A gathering mist hung over the wasteland. Behind him, the tail end of the rush hour traffic rumbled homewards along the Oxford Road.

There was no moon. With the naked eye he could see nothing but the vaguest of silhouettes against the background gloom. With the nightscope the view was altogether different. The west wall had only the one window, a little larger than those in the north wall, but with same heavy iron bars.

Eliot remembered that from where he had parked his car on his first visit he had seen a large sliding door, in what would be the eastern elevation, but from that direction he would be close to the main car parks and no doubt visible to CCTV cameras and maybe even the guard's cabin at the estate entrance.

He continued southwards, to the fringe of the wasteland. It took him several minutes to cover the ground, stopping frequently to check the terrain and look for signs of danger. The frozen grass crunched beneath his boots.

From the south, he could see a couple of windows, one secured with iron bars, the other with what seemed like a heavy grill. There were lights on in both windows. Eliot lowered the scope. How solid would the grill be? He took another look. While the scope gave a good sense of shape and form it wasn't possible, at distance, to see what condition the grill was in. He would have to get closer.

He went cautiously, first retracing his steps so as to approach from the west, where the windows were unlit and shadows hugged the landscape. A vague orange glow, reflected back from the clouds, threw into dull silhouette the trees and buildings along the edges of the wasteland. Eliot felt the dark bulk of the gas towers crouched like sumo wrestlers in the gathering mist.

About thirty metres from the low building he stopped again and checked his watch, the last train back to London left just before ten and he intended to be on it. Reaching the west wall, he pressed himself against it, pocketting the scope, calming himself down, taking his time. He felt excited, adrenalin pumping.

A car sped down the Oxford Road, tyres screaming as it braked for the traffic lights. The distant whine of a police siren. With his back against the wall, Eliot edged to his left until he reached the end of the wall. Having first glanced to check the coast was clear, he turned the corner and continued along, stopping only when his shoulder brushed the corner of the window sill. He stopped. Listened.

He leant round to peer through the glass. Frosted glass. The bars were completely solid, not a millimetre of give in them.

Inching along again, he reached the second window, the one with the grill. This time he heard muffled voices. A radio? He turned to peer into the window then stopped. What if he was spotted?

Pulling the scope out of his pocket, he took the front cap off and, facing the scope towards him, slowly lifted it up towards the window. A mirror image of the room through the window appeared on the surface of the lens.

People seated around a table. Two in dark blue. Behind them two dark-haired people standing, in their shirt sleeves. It was hard to make sense of the tiny inverted image but abruptly Eliot recognised the figure nearest the window. Beside someone in a white jacket, like a doctor's housecoat, and across the table from a shorter person with long blond hair was a third figure. Gustave Brown, the malodorous head of accounts at BitterCrest. Eliot recalled Brown's handshake, the limp cold fingers, like carrots that had spent too long in the fridge.

One of the faces appeared to turn towards the window. Eliot flinched involuntarily, banging his head against the sill.

And in that fraction of a second, everything changed.

In the room all faces turned to the window. Someone grabbed a phone and started shouting into it.

Eliot threw himself away from the building towards the mist enveloped wasteland. Behind him lights were coming on. Voices shouting. He was forty metres away now. Forty five. Fifty. His ankles jarred as he hurled himself across the difficult terrain. Manic barking throbbed in the night air, muffling the sound of orders being shouted.

Gasping for air, his ribs straining like hoops round a beer barrel, Eliot propelled himself forwards. The mist grew thicker with every step. The ground beneath him suddenly dropped away and he found himself flying through the air. Only a few milliseconds, long enough to wonder what would lie beneath him when he landed - gorse, bramble, concrete, bricks, mud, water.

Gorse or bramble. The thorns snatched at his clothes. Pinned him down. The barking getting louder. He couldn't outrun a dog. He scrambled to his feet still clutching the night scope and was turning to face the dog as it grabbed his left arm. The pain was excruciating, teeth scraping bone. Eliot screamed. The dog clung on, its muffled feral growls buried in Eliot's flesh. In the violence of the moment Eliot was aware of approaching voices.

BENEATH THE BITTERCREST

He remembered something from his school days. Boy talk behind the bike sheds. No occipital orbit, dogs. Nothing to prevent their lower jaw from pushing their eyes out if you hit them hard enough. Was it true? He brought the scope up hard. The teeth bit deeper into his wrist. Eliot yelled, lashed out again, even harder this time. Whether or not its eyes had left their sockets he didn't see but it was enough that the dog let go of his wrist. Eliot turned heel and ran. Behind him the dog's howls swam in a sea of shouting voices.

Eliot faced a dilemma. His pursuers were not gaining on him, the terrain was as difficult for them as for him. He would soon reach the gas towers and the service road that led to the gates and the Oxford Road, but what if the loose slat, through which he had gained access two days previously, had been bolted back into place? He would be a cornered rat.

The service road rang out beneath his feet. His legs threatened to buckle and give away, his lungs wheezing in and out like a broken accordion. Bent over double, clutching his knees, head spinning, Eliot closed his eyes and threw up. Behind him the shouts drew nearer. He glanced right. The road curved away into the mist. At a jog he disappeared into the darkness between the gas towers.

Moments later a barrel chested giant of a man staggered onto the service road and sank to his hands and knees. A second man caught up with the first. Almost as heavily built but in much better shape. He shook the first man roughly.

'Get up.'

The first man got up and the pair of them ran off towards the gates, their footsteps echoing in their wake. The mist hung like a shroud and the men quickly disappeared into the freezing gloom. An owl shrieked briefly. A muffled metallic thumping sound carried briefly in the air. A handful of snowflakes danced lazily.

In the vague darkness that enveloped the structures, the bolted iron surfaces of the gas towers might have been the flanks of a allied warship looming out of the frozen waters of the North Atlantic. Raindrops fumbled along the rusty surfaces, met up to form larger drops, the seeds of icicles gathered in swelling clumps on the lower rims of the massive bolts that held the structures together. Water glistened slowly before tumbling towards the frozen earth below.

The footsteps clanging against the metalled road grew louder. Vague shadows assumed solidity, the two men had returned from the gate.

The gap between the towers was four metres at its narrowest point. The men moved cautiously, if someone were plotting an ambush, this is where it would take place. Beyond them the perimetre fence appeared, crowned by brutal looking spikes. Wherever their quarry had gone, he had certainly not slipped over the fence. They bore left, round the taller of the towers and away from the Oxford Road. The towers creaked and groaned like huge beasts turning in their sleep.

The gap between gas tower and fence grew narrower, further restricted by a heavy metal gate at the side of the gas tower, blocking access to steps that curved up and away. The gate didn't give an inch, two huge padlocks held it firmly in place. Neither man noticed the drops of blood glistening on the top bar of the gate.

'Without the dog to sniff him out we're stuffed. Might as well go home.'

'You'd like that, Chris, wouldn't you?'

Fifteen metres up on a gantry, high above their heads, Eliot waited for them to pass. Slowly he stood up. Somewhere beneath his feet a bolt snapped, the sound distorted and amplified by the vast hollow centre of the tower.

'Over there' a voice shouted down below.

Eliot pressed himself back against the tower wall, not even daring to breathe. Below him the thick sea of mist hid the ground from view but up where he stood the air was clear, affording him a good view of the Oxford Road and leaving him feeling very vulnerable.

A heavy thud caused the tower to resonate like a gong.

'See what I mean?' said a voice down in the fog. 'The whole fucking thing is rotten.'

A second thud, louder than the first. A shower of rust fell onto the gantry.

'Could collapse any moment.'

Footsteps receding, they were giving up.

Eliot waited five minutes, all the while fighting an increasing urge to explore the sound of the structure by tapping out a rhythm against the rough metal. He would simply have to take it out on his drums when he got home.

Cramp in his leg, left wrist throbbing, body shaking, counting the seconds off in his head, finally he shuffled slowly back the way he had come. The tower groaned and sighed as rusting bolts strained against ageing sockets.

About halfway round he stopped and looked over towards the

industrial estate. Lights on everywhere. The mist was thinner away from the wasteland. He could just make out figures on the tarmac by the low building. He hauled the night scope out his pocket. The dog's jawbone hadn't done it any favours, the focusing ring had jammed, but it was better than nothing.

His two pursuers emerged from the mist, one of the men carrying a large dark lump that Eliot guessed was the dog. He swept the scope back across the low building one last time and finally he found what he was looking for.

There was a way of sneaking inside.

nineteen

He reached the station two minutes before the train was due to depart. The platform was deserted and, when it arrived, the train was practically empty.

Four paracetemol washed down with bottled water and then a check of the torniquet he had applied to his damaged wrist. He had torn his handkerchief into a long strip. It was bloody, but well hidden under his sleeve. Eliot felt nauseous but focused on remaining calm. His heartbeat slowed, unless the dog had rabies he would be fine.

The soft clicking rhythm of train and track was soothing. Tapping the seat along to the beat with the fingers of his good hand, he put his feet up on the chair opposite and closed his eyes. An hour and ten minutes to London. His eyelids drifted slowly down towards a dreamless sleep.

Vigorous shaking woke him. The cleaner, having roused him and explained the train had reached its terminus, smiled and continued down the train.

Outside Paddington station, Eliot climbed into a taxi and asked to be taken to the nearest hospital's accident and emergency unit.

He could see that they didn't exactly buy his story about the neighbour's dog getting a little too playful but they seemed content to treat the injury and leave it at that. X-rays, the wound cleaned and dressed, a prescription for painkillers and he was on his way home, all in less than four hours. Incredible. Who'd think to live anywhere else in the world?

Four in the morning he reached his front door, left arm bandaged up. No broken bones. No lasting damage.

But not night for sitting at the drum kit.

While the coffee was brewing he downed a couple of painkillers, found a glass and a half empty bottle of whisky. He had never liked the drink and had no idea how long it had been sitting in the cupboard but ... in the circumstances.

The fridge was empty, not even ice cubes. He carried the coffee and the whisky through to the lounge and sofa slumped. Something dug into his back. Cursing aloud, he rolled aside to retrieve the object, one of Toby's plastic trains.

The kids.

It was Friday morning. Sue had said Thursday to Saturday not the weekend. She was taking the kids to her parents over the weekend. How could he have forgotten? He should have picked the kids up early evening. Overwhelmed with guilt and fatigue, Eliot knew nothing could be done until the morning.

When he awoke four hours later, Eliot was still on the sofa, and still clutching the plastic train. He awoke on the sofa most mornings, unless the kids were staying over. In fact, though he had not yet admitted it to himself, he hardly ever ventured upstairs except to collect things, not wanting to confront empty bedrooms, toys nobody played with, chairs nobody sat at, and a double bed where only a single was needed.

Pain consumed him, as if his whole body had vanished except for his wrist, as if someone was slamming a door against it repeatedly. His right hand flayed about for the pain killers. The whisky bottle fell off the coffee table, whisky pissing out over the carpet, the multipack strips of pills falling onto the expanding puddle. The only liquid to hand, the dregs in the coffee pot. He drank it cold straight from the pot with two of the pills. After five minutes he was sorely tempted to take another two pills but a small sane voice held him back. He cold-turkeyed until, finally, the waves of pain went out on a retreating tide.

He had to ring Sue. But what could he tell her? What could he say that wouldn't be used against him to prove what a crap dad he was, a man who deserved only the privilege of paying for the upkeep of children he would no longer be allowed to see. Sorry I couldn't pick the kids up yesterday, I was in a police station being interviewed about a murder. Sorry I was late, I was busy snooping with a view to carrying out a break in. Oh and by the way, I ended up in hospital after a dog savaged me while I was trespassing. Everyway you looked at it, he was upcreek minus paddle.

Whatever story he came up with would also have to work with his business partners. Trouble was people didn't like victims, they assumed you had to have done something to fall in the hole you found yourself in. The bitch was that Eliot was far from sure himself that he understood what was going on.

The low building at the Sopford Industrial Estate was clearly at the heart of things. Or was it? The estate's security guards were clearly implicated in everything. Or were they? True, he had seen them chasing the running man on his first visit to Swindon. And it was they who had attacked him, not once but twice. But then, when he had looked through the window into the low building, he had seen Gustave Brown, BitterCrest Import's accountant. What the hell was Brown doing there? Who did the building belong to? What was happening in it?

And that was without even beginning to consider what the police were up to.

One way or other, Stephen and Serina had to be persuaded to drop the BitterCrest contract. Or leave Eliot out of it. The trouble was, he had no proof of anything, only hunches.

He paced the room considering his options. Peter at P.S. Partners, he could try him again. There had to be something behind his coded warnings; a starting point, a clue as to what was going on.

The number rang and rang. Eliot left a message and checked his watch, eight fifteen. Where the hell was the bugger? He was meant to be ill, at home with flu, that's what they had said. Eliot slammed the phone back down into its cradle.

Food. He seriously needed to eat. His jacket was hanging over the back of a chair. As he pulled, the chair fell back, the jacket fell from his grasp, and a newspaper fell from one of the pockets onto the wet carpet.

The Swindon Post he had bought the previous afternoon. He started separating the pages and using them to mop up the spilt whisky. On the fourth page he stopped. Halfway down the page, beneath an article about the dangers of children skating on Shaftesbury Lake, was a photograph. Over a caption reading 'Swindon businesses celebrate success' a dozen smiling people in tuxedos or evening dress, champagne flutes in hand, were standing in the lobby of a hotel.

Two of the faces leapt out at him. In the foreground stood Gustave Brown, smile flushed with alcohol, a mesh of hair tumbled untidily across his face. But what really startled Eliot was the young woman standing beside Brown. A woman with long and thick blond hair, dressed in a sharp suit. Something about the eyes and lips. And nose. It was like seeing a face through a kaleidoscope, a disassembled face he recognised but couldn't place.

Tom Hampton had just buttered a teacake when the phone rang. 'Hello,' he said, picking up.
'PC Hampton?'

'Yes?'

'I understand you've been trying to reach me. I'm a colleague of Victoria's.'

'Oh, from the lab.'

'That's right.'

'Good. I wanted to ask you ...'

'Victoria has explained. Where would you like to meet?'

'I'm just off to work. How about this evening?'

The front door flew open and Eliot rushed in, his breakfast in a carrier bag. He ran into the front room, grabbed the paper and stared at the photo a second time. Who was she? Why did she interest him? How could you recognise someone and not recognise them at the same time? His mind was itching with impatience. The face was like a lost word on the edge of the lips. Had she worn glasses? Maybe that was it. Maybe her hair had been in a pony tail or tied up somehow. He placed the newpaper on the back of the sofa and, with his fingers, covered up the woman's hair. Now only the face was visible. Still he struggled to identify ...

... suddenly the fog had gone. It was the woman on the train, with the strawberries, and all the questions about his work. It was so clear to him that Eliot could no longer understand how he could ever have been confused. It was her with Brown. But why the change of hair? The woman he had met had had short dark hair. Was it an old photograph? The caption under the photo did not give that impression. A wig perhaps? What was her name? And, more to the point, what the hell was her link to BitterCrest?

Charging upstairs he disappeared into the spare bedroom where he kept all those belongings he pretended might one day be useful again: trousers too tight to put on, shirts too flagrantly early Nineties to be worn during the hours of daylight, old tomtoms, a bent cymbal, books he would never read, possessions Sue had left, computer hard drives the size of dustbins.

A pile of junk grew behind him in the doorway, as he tossed stuff aside. It had to be in here somewhere, there was nowhere else he would have put it.

'Where are you, for God's sake?'

'Are you listening?' Eliot was irritated, it was always the same with Stephen, always asking questions never answering them.

'Yes, I am listening.' Stephen articulated each word slowly as if talking to a foreigner. 'You believe the whole of Swindon is infiltrated by, or run by, the mafia. We can't go to the police because of a conspiracy that you alone ...'

'OK.'

'... are capable of ...'

'OK. Shut up,' Eliot shouted, bashing the receiver against the wall. 'What about what Peter Han said? About BitterCrest? He warned us that ...'

'Peter Han was thrown out of the police force for getting too excited, for running personal vendettas. In case you didn't know.'

There was a pause.

'Eliot, we're really worried,' the tone more gentle, more conciliatory. 'Why don't I come round and pick you up? We can have a proper chat, face to face, mano a mano. What do you say? I've had a chat with Neville ... Draper. Let's meet up. And sort it all out. I understand where you're coming from. And if there really is something dodgy then ... you know. How about it?'

Another pause.

'Yeah, all right. Just you though.'

'Have you eaten?'

'A sandwich from the service station round the corner. I'm at home.'

'Well, put the kettle on. I'll buy some croissants and see you in fifteen.'

'Right. And Stephen?'

'Yes?'

'Thanks, mate.'

'What are friends for?'

Eliot put the phone back in its cradle, at least Stephen was seeing sense, things were looking up.

He went back upstairs to the spare room, moved boxes, tried to think back to the night he had returned from Doncaster. They had given him everything in a box, a brown cardboard box. He had dumped it on the floor. Unopened. There had seemed no reason to open it. Torn clothes, dirty hankerchief, sodden briefcase, nothing he needed or wished to look at.

Under the window was a quilt, hauled out on those rare occasions when a friend came back from the pub, and shared a spliff, and decided to stay the night on the sofa. How long was it since that had

BENEATH THE BITTERCREST 107

happened? Eliot tossed the quilt aside. More books. A plastic toddler truck.

And the box.

He picked it up. A faint odour emanated, vaguely sulphurous. Eliot pulled his swiss army knife from his jacket and sliced along the tape. The odour escalated exponentially. He gagged and threw open the window. The sound of traffic wafted in, a child shouting, a bird lost on a rooftop.

His briefcase was thick with green hair, mould rising up from the remains of olives and a sandwich that hadn't seen the light of day for the best part of two months.

In the distance, a police siren was wailing.

Shoes. His tie and watch. Various bits of paper. The badge he had worn to the Doncaster conference. A fragmented memory of a mobile phone bleeping Agadoo in a dark, acrid silence.

The police siren had stopped, replaced by the sound of a vehicle speeding down the street. Eliot, his eyes staring blankly out of the window, fumbled in the box, his fingers on autopilot. Two cars screeched to a halt nearby as Eliot's fingers found what he was looking for, a thin metal case nestling inside one of the shoes.

In the back of the second car was a face in partial profile, facing away from the house. A face out of context but crying to be recognised, downcast, the shoulders hunched, as if sadness weighed heavily or an onerous responsibility were being discharged. A Grand Inquisitor feigning immense sadness while sentencing an innocent to burn at the stake.

Adrenalin tumbled out, hitting the ground running, barking out a million microscopic warnings to Eliot's organs and limbs as it went.

All at once car doors started to open and the figure in the back of the second car was turning his head towards the window. Eliot leapt back from the window his senses on fire, his mind feral. Time around him had slowed to a crawl.

Out on the street, people were climbing out of their vehicles. Police officers. Bright black shoes clattered across the tarmac. A cat squealed.

Eliot crossed the landing, found the back bedroom. The window wouldn't open, hadn't done so since he had painted the room four months previously for when the children came to stay. He slammed the catch. Nothing. Pushing the object he had retrieved from the box deep into his pocket, he picked up a chair and threw it through the window. Remembered the same action from two days previously. The bright song of shattering glass mingled with hammering on the front door. Eliot pushed the shards of glass out of the frame with his sleeve.

By the time the six policemen were all in the house the kettle had finally started to boil.

'He's jumped out of the upstairs window and legged it,' said one of the officers running down the stairs.

'Send Brian and HRH after him.' DS Miles turned towards the open front door. 'It would appear that your friend has done a runner. I'd like you to hang around.' He nodded his head in the direction of the yelling kettle. 'Would you be mother?'

'All right.'

Stephen crossed the threshold into Eliot's house. As the police began a more detailed room by room examination, Stephen removed the kettle from the cooker and found the teacups, his mood sombre, his eyes thoughtful.

twenty

'Do you feel that you're paranoid?'
Eliot didn't know how to answer that one.

The directions hadn't been all they might have, particularly with regard to distance. Total rubbish in fact. He had walked well over five miles since leaving the small country station with its five trains a day service and its vending machine stuffed full of fifteen year old kitkats sagging in their foil wraps.

There seemed to be more hills here on the Welsh border than in the Swiss alps and Eliot was cursing every last one of them.

The town was from a bygone age. Yellow cellophane blinds protected shop window displays from discolouration. A funeral parlour had caught his eye. It specialised in 'natural' coffins and eco-aware burials, which no doubt meant bunging the deceased in a cardboard box prior to shovelling them under the compost heap at the end of the garden.

The hill appeared to end some forty metres ahead of him, but Eliot had already faced disappointment. At least it wasn't snowing. Overcast but not too cold, and a good half hour before nightfall. He looked over his shoulder for the hundredth time, no sign of anyone following him.

The cottage, when he finally reached it some twenty minutes later, turned out to be surrounded by trees on three sides and invisible from the single track road. The path from the road to the cottage climbed through a meadow. After a dozen very slippery stone steps, the visitor was faced with a long walk in full view of the cottage, a hundred metres or so, no cover, no trees, no shrubs, nothing. Within seconds Eliot's trousers were soaked to the knees.

The windows of the cottage were deep sullen pools, reflecting the dark cloudscape, revealing nothing. Eliot became aware of the squelching of his boots in the damp silence of the meadow, and of the total absence of birdsong. With thick pine forest hugging the edges of the meadow, Eliot walked the last thirty metres to the cottage. Dew hung from the densely packed trees. No wind, no movement of branches. Some ten metres to his right a track came into view, just wide enough for a car.

The cottage was surrounded by a three metre wide moat of gravel. He crunched his way to the front door and knocked.

'So, do you feel that you are paranoid?'

Eliot cradled the mug of coffee, feeling the warmth flow into his hands. 'About Stephen setting the police on me? No,' he said finally. 'I feel I'm on the edge of a precipice clutching at straws.'

'Never been particularly keen on mixed metaphors. Kind of thing footballers use. You're not about to tell me you're over the moon to be sick as a parrot?'

'What made you buy a place like this, Peter?' Eliot changed the subject. 'I took you for the sophisticated urbanite, it's not exactly opera and gentleman's clubs out here, is it?'

Peter Han crossed the sitting room and poked at the fire, moving a couple of logs into the flames before skewering a crumpet on a toasting fork. 'Are you sure I can't tempt you?'

Eliot shook his head. He had met Peter twice before, three years previously. Peter didn't encourage face to face meetings, claimed it was safer to conduct business at a distance. He had aged in the intervening period and looked all of his fifty seven years. Slightly stooped, as if he had decided six foot four no longer suited him, his moustache completely white, his hair thin and lank, his pale eyes jaded and tired. Gone were the dandy suits, the silk hankerchiefs. Instead he was sporting a shapeless brown cardigan, bespeckled with a peppering of dandruff.

Eliot watched Peter with his crumpet, if he didn't move the bloody thing closer to the flames it would still be raw at breakfast.

'Let's talk about BitterCrest Imports,' Eliot suggested.

'Are you sure no-one followed you? From the station?'

'Oh, for God's sake Peter, if we just ask each other questions all night neither of us is going to be any the bloody wiser. Can we just get on with it?'

Peter looked up briefly then turned back to his crumpet.

'The dossier is on the kitchen table.'

Eliot walked through to the tiny kitchen, coffee in hand, taking care not to crack his head open on the low door frame. The kitchen was like the sitting room, off-white walls, black beams across the ceiling, small windows, tassels on the lamp shades, flower printed curtains.

BENEATH THE BITTERCREST

A collection of old teapots on a shelf running round the room at head height. Very cottage. The table was covered in clutter, crockery, books, newspapers, various bottles of alcohol, a pack of vacuum cleaner bags, and a large brown envelope. He pulled a chair out, put his mug on the table beside him, sat down and tipped the contents of the envelope onto his lap.

There wasn't much there. Dates mainly, dates of incorporation, dates of accounts filed with the Inland Revenue, dates of applications for importation/exportation licences, and so on. It appeared that at one time BitterCrest Imports had applied for a licence to export small arms and anti-personnel devices to the middle east. A licence had been granted in 1995. It had lapsed a year later and the company had not reapplied. The company's turnover for the most recent accounting period had been £4,000,000. This figure seemed totally out of sync with the scale of operation Eliot had seen in Swindon, but maybe the company had recently hit on hard times.

'What I really detest is the way companies such as yours pretend to be interested in security and probity and ethics operating within the law when, in fact, you couldn't care less,' Peter said from the doorway. 'When, in fact, all you care about is the bottom line.'

'What?'

'You know exactly what I'm talking about.' Peter leant back against the sink, took a bite of his crumpet, and brandished his toasting fork at the younger man. 'I deal with a dozen companies as smug and self-serving as yours, all run by up-and-coming johnny-come-latelies whose only ambition is to make a million and retire by the time they're forty. Any job undertaken, no questions asked.'

'I didn't come here to be insulted.'

'Why did you come, Eliot?'

Eliot made a show of leafing through the papers on his lap before replying.

'I had hoped you might find it in you to help me see why I've been set up on a charge of murder.'

Peter filled a pan of water and placed it on the Aga. He stood, with his back to Eliot, watching the water slowly coming to the boil.

'Before I joined P.S. Partners I was with the Met,' he said eventually.

'I heard.' Eliot suddenly had the vague feeling he had missed a detail, that he had failed to pick up on something someone had said.

'Gustave Brown. Form as long as your arm. Embezzling, false accounting, fraud, handling counterfeit goods, affray, you name it. I almost nailed him eight or nine years ago on a charge of gun smuggling. Uzis and other toys sneaking in from Yugoslavia. Or whatever they're calling it this week. He got off on a technicality.'

'And Draper?'

Peter moved the pan to a hotter part of the Aga.

'Small potatoes,' he said, shaking his head. 'Arrived in the country four years ago. Bought BitterCrest from an acquaintance a year later. Before that he was in the Middle East and Africa. Typical ex-pat, friends all diplomats, bored embassy secretaries and the like. Probably earned his keep procuring whisky for homesick Brits stuck in some godforsaken desert surrounded by a sea of over zealous towelheads. Then suddenly he's over here, shiny new British passport and safely tucked up in bed with the Establishment's finest.'

'It's a good thing you're not the type to get bitter.'

'His biggest mistake,' Peter continued, ignoring the interruption, 'was recruiting Brown. If he had kept his head down, limited himself to smuggling booze out to Oman, or avoiding the odd thousand on import duty, we would probably never have heard of Neville Draper. My guess is he wants to play on the wild side. With the big boys. Like they said of Sinatra and the mafia. Draper probably misses the excitement of Ougadougou or whatever hole he crept out of.'

'Why did they sack you?' Eliot said.

Peter stood a moment in thought before answering.

'An earlier investigation into a company Brown was involved with, in the mid-nineties. Put a few noses out of joint. The ministry were very polite. Lack of evidence, poor chance of a successful prosecution, etc. So we had to drop it. Then I had another go, shortly after Draper had bought BitterCrest and headhunted Brown. This time the gloves were off. National security, and immunity from prosecution.'

'So someone was feeling embarassed ...'

'Who knows? The bottom line is I overstepped the mark, someone took offence and twenty years with the Met went down the chute. End of story.'

Eliot reflected that Han appeared very selective about the information he was prepared to divulge.

'What does any of that have to do with Office Solutions? With me?'

'Your company pays me for my advice. I gave it.'

'But who set the police on me? Why would they ... '

'I don't know if you know anything about power, Eliot. I suspect not. You think you know. Everyone thinks they know. They buy

BENEATH THE BITTERCREST

celebrity comics, read the captions beneath the photos of partying z-list fame seekers and think they understand power. Do you read Hello magazine?'

'Your point being?' Eliot was tiring of the older man's barbs.

Peter changed tack. 'So, you've been working at BitterCrest. Doing what? What have you learnt? What do you think you've seen?'

'This would all be a whole lot easier if you weren't quite so friendly and enthusiastic.'

Peter continued to gaze down on Eliot, a surly headmaster about to administer punishment.

'We've been sorting out security for their computers, encryption of data that sort of thing. Draper wants a system that no-one can access apart from himself. Not even the CIA.'

'And out of the kindness of your heart, you decided to help him out. I hope the money brings you happiness.'

'It wasn't my decision. Anyway, there's nothing necessarily wrong with a company wanting high levels of security. Is there?'

Peter looked unimpressed. Which didn't surprise Eliot, he wasn't entirely convinced himself. I only make the boxes, I don't put the secrets inside.

'Were you ever a team player?' Eliot asked defensively. 'If I walked out everytime I disagreed with my partners, and if they did the same, there would be no company. In fact ...'

'What have you actually seen?' Peter interjected.

Eliot, caught in mid-flow, paused to collect his thoughts. Peter rinsed out the coffee percolator.

'I'm not sure. No company records, if that's what you mean. More a question of hunches. I can't even prove BitterCrest are involved though I'm sure Brown is. I saw a man beaten.'

'What man?'

'A trespasser. Two security guards laid into him with sticks.'

'What did this man look like? The one they were beating.'

Eliot thought back. 'Thin, dark hair, foreign possibly. He was running from a warehouse on the industrial estate.'

'When did this happen?' Peter, trained to keep his emotions out of interviews, ensured his tone remained flat, barely interested.

'Just before Christmas.'

'How was the person dressed?'

'No idea.'

'Think. Think back.'

Eliot remembered the sun shining, cold but bright. Crossing the car park after the interview. Hearing a shout and looking through the car window.

'Summer clothes. T-shirt and trousers. I remember thinking he was underdressed. No shoes.'

'What gave you the impression he might be a trespasser?'

'I saw him run out of a building. Across the tarmac from where I was parked, maybe forty, fifty metres away. He didn't look like an employee.'

'Why did the police arrest you?'

Eliot told Peter about the body by the gas towers while the older man brewed another pot of coffee. Peter asked whether the body had resembled the trespasser Eliot had seen. Forced to consider the matter, Eliot realised that it did.

'Could it have been the same man?'

'No.' Eliot hesitated. 'Maybe ... I don't know. They were similarly dressed.'

'Same race? Same features?'

'Don't know. I guess so. I'm not very familiar with the colour of frozen bodies in the dark.'

'European features? African? Middle Eastern?'

'Could have been from anywhere. Greece, Egypt, Iran, Romania. Anywhere.'

'And the other man?'

Eliot threw up his hands. 'The same. Look, I don't know.'

Peter looked thoughtful. 'What have you seen that you should not have seen?'

The question hung in the air. The gentle liquid pouring of coffee into two tin mugs. Peter fetched a fresh bottle of milk from the fridge.

'Cream?'

Eliot shook his head.

'Me neither. No good for the arteries.' Peter poured the top of the milk down the sink then added milk to the coffees. 'Or this,' he patted his belly. He passed Eliot a mug. 'A tot of whisky in that?'

Eliot declined.

'So, now or tomorrow night?' Peter asked.

'What?'

Peter didn't bother to answer. He gulped his coffee down and disappeared, returning a few minutes later with two rucksacks, one of which he tossed at Eliot. Gone was the cardigan, replaced by a fleece

BENEATH THE BITTERCREST

and a jacket. Gone too was the stoop, as if he had suddenly been revitalised.

'Shit. What have you put in this? Lead weights?'

'You're going to take me on a tour.'

PC Hampton took another sip of coffee from his flask, ten miles from Dover. Time to have the meeting, slip in for a pint before the pubs closed, and grab some fish and chips. Back home by one a.m. It was leaving things a bit late but then he knew he was making a career move - if he made a hash of things he could be kissing goodbye to his job - if he did well ... even if he did well there was every chance he would still end up on his arse.

The Baker, DI Machin, saw no value in investigating the death of a foreign-looking vagrant found beneath a pile of chickens by a canal. Hampton, however, couldn't let go. Wasn't entirely sure why. The pathologist's tone perhaps; patronising sod, assuming the police would make a total balls up of everything.

Anyway what was done was done. Hampton had met up with Victoria's friend in the labs, and what he had learnt had intrigued him. A proper detective job waiting to be done, worth using up his remaining leave.

He followed the signs to the ferry terminal, parked his car and headed into the main terminal building to find John Frisk.

'Sit down. Sit down. Pleasant drive?'

'Oh, you know.'

'So, what can we do you for?' Frisk sat down behind his desk, toying with his moustache. 'Only kidding. Got the paperwork ready for you.' He leant out of sight behind the desk. 'Should warn you, there's a lot of it.' He dumped a mountain of paper on the desk.

'Don't you use computers?' Hampton said dejectedly.

'It's not as bad as it looks. This pile here represents all vehicles coming into the country over the past week. You just want Tuesday, eh?'

'Tuesday,' Hampton agreed.

'Well, there you go.' He pushed a pile of paper half an inch thick across the table. 'Codes are there, left hand column; lorries, cars, vans, caravans, motorbikes, don't suppose you'll be interested in them. There another list ...'

'This is all I need.'

'... detailing the vehicles we stopped and searched,' Frisk completed his sentence.

'I'll start with this lot,' Hampton said, flicking through the pages. 'How many vehicles are we talking about?'

'Tens of thousands,' Frisk deadpanned. 'Only kidding. No, you're in luck. Bad weather on Tuesday, well over half the boats were cancelled. A dodgy Tuesday in January. Three or four hundred, maybe five at a pinch.'

'And what's the favourite time of day for smuggling?'

Frisk hesitated just long enough for Hampton to find himself wondering whether Frisk was squeaky clean or whether he might occasionally turn a blind eye, if the price was right.

'We shift our resources. To keep them on their toes. Can't check every vehicle.'

'Of course not.'

'At the moment we're concentrating on the early morning runs. Word gets out though, loose tongues, rotten apples.' Frisk smiled conspiratorially, the police knew all about rotten apples didn't they?

'So the smart operators would be coming through in the afternoon or evening?'

Frisk looked uncertain of himself, Hampton wasn't playing the game. 'That's right.'

'Good. Can I work in here?'

'Why not? I'll have someone bring you up a drink.' Frisk stood up to leave. 'By the way, what branch did you say you were from?'

'The Metropolitan police, Mr Frisk.'

'Ah, yes. Do I know your boss?'

'Shouldn't think so,' Hampton said easily, producing a notepad and a pen and getting to work.'

Frisk loitered by his desk for a few seconds more. He scribbled a number on the corner of Hampton's pad. 'I'll leave you to it then. That's my number, if you need me.'

Hampton watched him leave then turned his attention back to the stack of paper in front of him.

A yellow Citroën according to the forensic lab. The poultry fat had proved very useful, all sorts of stuff stuck to it, including flecks of car paint, a yellow paint only found on three and four year old Citroëns.

Bob in forensics had provided a very detailed list. The chickens were probably from France, corn fed, yellow fat. Chickens and corpse had travelled together in a yellow Citroën. This same vehicle had also

BENEATH THE BITTERCREST   117

contained, either on the same occasion or at different times, video tapes, CDs, and a wide range of clothes or fabrics. There were traces of many different tobaccos and a variety of cardboards and plastics. In short, the vehicle carried goods between the UK and the continent. The information seemed to point at a van or a lorry rather than a car. So, a yellow Citroën van.

He got to work.

Peter Han lowered his binoculars.

'Right, lead on.'

They crossed the wasteland towards the low building. A whisker of moon was visible behind thin cloud. On the horizon, behind the gas towers, a vast cloud bank was gathering.

'There are two guards. And maybe a dog.'

'I'm sure there are.'

'All the windows have bars or grills. The door faces ...'

'We won't be availing ourselves of the door.'

As they approached, Eliot allowed himself a sideways glance at Peter. What did he know about him? Next to nothing. An ex-copper now private investigator, who collected teapots, had a foul temper and harboured grudges against the establishment. Not compelling grounds for following the man into an illegal act of breaking and entering. He felt growing concern that Peter Han's judgement might be impaired by the history there was between him and BitterCrest, whatever that history was. The fierce intensity in the older man's face didn't bode well.

'You're not going to let this get personal? Because if ...'

'You listen to me,' Peter hissed. 'You called me. You got yourself into this. I've waited years for this. This bugger cost me my career. Get that rucksack off your back, we've work to do.'

'I was some distance away when I saw it, you can't see it from close up ...'

'Just open the rucksack.'

If Eliot had ever harboured fantasies of appearing in the Great Escape he now had the opportunity to live them out. His rucksack turned out to contain a rope ladder with lightweight metal rungs and some sort of grappling hook at one end. There were also two balaclavas, one of which Peter pulled over his head, the other he passed to Eliot.

The two men moved forwards towards the low building. The cold was making Eliot's wrist throb. He munched a couple of painkillers.

Peter took the rope ladder and, with one deft movement, threw the grappling hook end of it up onto the roof. Having tested that it would bear his weight, he started climbing. Eliot grabbed the rope ladder and, ignoring the pain in his wrist, followed Peter up. At the top Peter grabbed his shoulder and hauled him onto the flat roof. They crossed the roof on their hands and knees.

The records didn't list models but after an hour Hampton had extracted the cars and motorcycles and was left with a list of a hundred vehicles. He rang Frisk.

'Do you have details of who travelled?'

The background roar suggested Frisk was outside. 'Of course, but it'll have to wait till the morning.'

'Last minute tickets. People who just turned up, without booking. Will the records show that?'

'The French will have those records.'

'How about video footage? Does the port authority film the vehicles as they leave the boat? At this end?'

'Since last October. The videos are kept for sixty days then destroyed.'

'Good. I need to see the tapes for Tuesday afternoon and evening.'

'I can have copies sent to you tomorrow.' Frisk's voice was cooling fast.

'Not tomorrow.'

'It's the middle of the night,' Frisk protested. 'The office is closed. There aren't enough of us to ...'

'I need to see the tapes now,' Hampton cut him off.

A moment's silence. 'All right, but I'll be reporting this back to your boss. It's regular procedure.'

'You do that.'

Ten minutes later Frisk arrived with three tapes and slammed them down on the desk. Hostility burning in his eyes.

'There's a VHS player down the hall.'

'Great.' Hampton stood up. 'I won't keep you. You must be very busy.'

He found the room without much difficulty and settled down in front of the video machine. It would take a while, separating out the vans and lorries from the cars, freeze framing to check number plates.

BENEATH THE BITTERCREST

The cameras only recorded a black and white image so pin-pointing yellow vehicles was not going to be easy.

Eliot had been right. There was no visible protection to the sky-lights, no bars, no grills. They peered through the frosted glass into the blurred gloom below.

'Do you think there will be motion sensors or CCTV?'

Peter produced a roll of sticky-backed plastic. He tore off a strip and fixed it to one of the glass panels. 'Hold it here.'

Using a glass cutter, Peter etched a circle round the perimeter of the sticky-backed plastic. There was a sharp crack as he punched the circle of glass free from its pane. Eliot started to lift the glass away from the frame but Peter grabbed his arm and held it in place. For thirty seconds they waited, barely breathing.

Finally, Peter let go of Eliot's arm. Eliot placed the glass beside him on the roof. Han lowered his face towards the hole and surveyed the room below.

It was a large room, dimly lit by weak flickering light. Packing cases were scattered about the floor. Shelves, laden with boxes of various sizes, ran the length of one wall. Peter produced a piece of paper from his rucksack, rolled it into a ball and dropped it into the room. Still no sound, no alarm.

They set about removing the rest of the pane of glass. A large metal bar ran the length of the window. Peter attached the rope ladder to the bar and let the other end fall into the room. Having removed his thick jacket, he manoeuvred himself into position over the hole and set off down the ladder.

Eliot stared about him. A car sped down the Oxford Road closely followed by a motorcycle, their headlights strobing through the empty branches of the trees that lined the edge of the wasteland. Eliot felt the warm air drifting up through the gap in the glass. He dropped the rucksacks through to Peter, took off his jacket and, squeezing through the window, descended into the heart of the low building.

Hampton paused the video. The freeze frame showed a light coloured van climbing the ramp to leave the ship. Twin chevrons on the grill. A Citroën. The driver's face was indistinct. White, bald or with a crew cut, clean shaven. Dark jacket. Hampton made a note of the number plate and pressed play. The van slowly climbed up the ramp and out of view.

Two cars followed, then two lorries. A movement caught his eye. The side of the second lorry. A panel seemed to move as the lorry climbed the ramp.

Hampton stopped the tape, wound it back in slo-mo. The panel moved back to its starting position. Backwards and forwards. Was it a natural movement, a loose panel rocking on its rivets? The image was very dark and the contrast was appalling. He ran the footage at normal speed. It was impossible to be sure.

What was certain was that lorries were meant to be secure. The fines the government were imposing were meant to have put paid to smuggling people. So what was causing the panel to move? Hampton fiddled with the contrast and the brightness. He pressed his face up against the screen and set the video into forward play mode, one frame per second.

The lorry was barely visible behind the cars. It came down into view from within the bowels of the ship. The estate car ahead of the lorry revved up and moved up the ramp, frame by frame. The lorry's grill came into view. Reflections on the windscreen made it impossible to see into the cab.

The panel was halfway down the side of the lorry. The adjustments he had made to contrast and brightness had changed the dark paintwork to a charcoal grey. He could almost make out the darkness within the lorry through the crack in the panel. Was the panel rotating on a rivet or was it pulled back, prized back somehow? For what purpose? To let air in? To allow someone inside to see out? The frames ticked away in slo-mo.

There. He saw it. A face perhaps? The lorry moved out from under the shadow of the ship's bay doors and into the glare of the ferry terminal's lights. The panel became lost in a sea of dancing white pixels. Hampton moved his hand to pause the video, fingers fumbling with the buttons. Suddenly he noticed something else. It hadn't been visible before but now, with the image enhanced, he could just make out two letters on the side of the lorry, the letters 'B.I.' and underneath them, in much smaller letters a single word 'Swallow'. Swanley. Swinton?

Eliot let out a low whistle.

There was enough space to park eight or nine cars. A solitary failing fluorescent tube flickered at one end of the room, lighting up a treasure trove of luxury bathroom fittings from Italy, fabrics from

BENEATH THE BITTERCREST 121

around Europe, carpets from Afghanistan, quality watches from Switzerland, cases of champagne, and racks of designer clothes. The key words was quality. The shelves were stacked with goodies. Of course it might all be fake, Eliot wasn't qualified to judge, but, even then, it was quality fake. He meandered about, reading labels, guessing how much the contents of the room might be worth, wondering who owned it all. He reached out to touch a vase.

'No fingerprints. Here, wear these.' Han handed Eliot a pair of gloves.

Eliot donned the gloves and rolled his balaclava up off his face.

Across the tarmac in the estate office, Bill Tyson checked his watch. Five to midnight. Almost time to do their round. In his hand he had two kings, a ten, a seven and a four.

'Pull your finger out. What are you on? Tamazepan?'

'Fuck off.' Chris wasn't about to be hustled, he'd lost too much money already. The two men faced each other across the table.

'Come on,' Bill whined, his voice all singsong, needling Chris as only he knew how.

'Fuck off.'

Ace, queen, jack, and six and a four. All clubs. Chris flicked the cards backwards and forwards. He glanced up at Bill.

Bill was all smiles, thirty quid up and coasting.

'Where's the dog?'

'Where do you think?'

'I'll go and get her.' Bill tucked his cards into his jacket pocket.

'No, you won't. Sit down.'

'Well, get a fucking move on then.'

They sat there for another minute, Chris hesitating, Bill jiggling his heels.

'Right, that's it.' Bill sprung to his feet, throwing his cards down onto the packing crate and taking back his money. He headed for the door.

Chris flipped Bill's cards over. 'You bastard, I'd have won that.'

'Twat,' Bill laughed and headed outside.

There were three doors. The first opened onto an office containing a table and chairs, a desk, a row of files, and a computer.

'I can smell him in the room. This is where I saw them. Brown and the others. Garlic and rancid sweat, like he never changes his shirts.'

'You finally gave up smoking then?'

It was true, Eliot hadn't thought about it until then but his nose was definitely working more efficiently. He sat down at the desk and attempted to power up the computer.

Peter had pulled open the drawers of the desk. He peered inside each one in turn, then put his arm in and felt the bottom of each drawer from underneath.

'No cables,' Eliot announced having rummaged round the back of the machine. 'No cables, no juice.'

Peter's fingertips found what he was looking for. There was a ripping sound of Selotape being prised away from plastic. 'Looks like someone has a little secret,' he said triumphantly, holding up a Zip disc. 'Here, you're the computer wizkid.'

Peter passed Eliot the disc and turned his attention to the shelves.

'What do you think this is?' Eliot asked, turning the disc over in his hand.

'I take it back, you obviously don't know a computer from a hole in the head.'

'I mean what do you think is on it?'

Peter raised his eyebrows pityingly. Like he should know. 'Come on, there's nothing else. Or if there is, we don't have time to find it.'

They walked back out into the larger room. The second door opened onto a darkened corridor. Peter flicked his torch on and set off, Eliot tagging along behind.

'How did you get involved in all this?' Eliot said.

Peter ignored the question.

'I'm serious, this whole private eye thing?'

The corridor led round to the right.

'It's a job.'

'That's it?'

'I needed money, I joined the police. That didn't work out. I still needed money, I set up an investigation company.'

'It must be interesting though.'

Peter stopped and faced Eliot. 'It's crap. That's what it is. Total crap.'

Ahead of them was another door. As Peter pushed the door open, Eliot saw into the room beyond. A window at the far end looked out towards the car parks and the entrance to the industrial estate. Very suddenly, visible through the window, two silhouettes appeared. Eliot grabbed Peter's arm and hauled him back. The beam from the

BENEATH THE BITTERCREST

torch in Peter's hand threw a wild arc across the ceiling as he fell back through the doorway.

They ran back along the corridor. In the large store room the ailing fluorescent tube was moments away from failing altogether, strobing nauseatingly. Outside, the weather had changed and a hard rain was hammering the skylight, a damp patch forming on the concrete beneath the missing pane of glass. Eliot ran to the third door, threw it open and charged through.

The room beyond the third door was large and damp. Cold as a morgue. Water was dripping somewhere, a metallic ringing beat. Peter, coming up behind Eliot, swung his torch about, revealing a large lorry and a large sliding door. Eliot guessed the door faced east. It must be the door the running man had come out of.

A small mound of rubbish had been swept to one end of the room: cardboard, bits of wood, and polystyrene chips. Shelves ran the entire length of the wall opposite the door. Eliot took the rucksack off his back and fished out the torch he had spotted earlier. To his left, a couple of girlie calendars hung on the whitewashed wall. Someone had scrawled over one of the girl's faces. August 2001 wore a thong, a moustache, a pair of glasses and nothing else. Eliot wondered what kind of a person wanted to see facial hair perched over a perfect pair of breasts.

Next to the calendars was an old black and white photo in a thin wooden frame, glass covered in years of dust and fly shit. Eliot brushed the dirt away with the back of his hand. Twenty men in white coats posed for a group photo.

'Over here,' Peter hissed from over by the lorry.

Eliot hurried across. 'What have we got?'

'You have to stop fannying about. This isn't one of your reality television shows, son.'

Noise outside emphasised the point as a stone hit against the sliding door, followed by a bark or growl. Muffled voices, torchlight appearing in the gap beneath the door. Eliot and Peter smothered their torches and froze, scarcely daring to breathe. Eliot thought he heard a dog sniffing on the other side of the door. He flashed a glance at Peter but the older man's eyes were focused on the door. Eliot noticed Peter had one hand buried deep inside his rucksack.

The passing seconds clung to each other stickily. Eliot became aware of a source of light at his feet. Without moving his head he slowly looked down. The light was spilling from his smothered torch.

At his feet was a small puddle of what seemed like oil, a black glistening surface. A metre ahead was a second puddle. Ahead of that tyre tracks in the dust. Scuff marks too, and footprints, all leading to or from his left, where the shelves hugged the wall.

Voices talking on the other side of the sliding door, too low to make out what they were saying but loud enough to tell that an argument was in full swing.

Footprints as ancient hieroglyphs, a language waiting to be deciphered. Still rooted to the spot, Eliot very cautiously moved the torch beam away from the sliding door and towards the shelves. Why so many movements to and from a set of empty shelves? What could have been stored on them?

A sudden noise by the door. Eliot waited, became a tremor in his leg, an ache in his neck, the dull throb in his wrist. He needed another painkiller. He needed a cigarette. Sod his sense of smell.

And still the muffled sounds of an argument outside went on. Was Gustave Brown outside, beyond the door? Eliot thought he caught the word 'clubs'. He remembered the beating he had received, the barking of the dog.

The words 'four of fucking hearts' were clearly audible through the door. A bloody card game. They were talking cards. A rhythmic metallic tapping sound started, Eliot guessed one of the men was punching the door with a key. Or a gun?

Still the seconds walked in slo-mo, mourners in a funeral procession. The waiting was unbearable, the tension burning at his insides. He heard himself make a small involuntary grunt, became aware of Peter staring at him. Turning a fraction, he saw the whites of Peter's eyes just visible in the gloom. In a confrontation between Peter and Brown, Eliot suspected he would be plankton, disregarded in a blood feud that went back years.

The tapping stopped. Silence clung to the dark air like fog. Eliot could not bring himself to look at the sliding door. His ears were full of the wooshing sound of blood pumping. Another involuntary grunt. He had to look.

A whisker of light ran the length of the underside of the sliding door. Shadows broke the light in four places: four boots, two guards. What were they doing? The shadows moved, closer to the door or further away? Another shadow, broader and moving fast. The dog? Yes, there could be no mistake, the sniffing was clearly audible. Peter heard it too, Eliot could see it in the older man's narrowing eyes.

BENEATH THE BITTERCREST

Then, just as abruptly as the crisis had started, the footsteps moved away and the shadows moved on, and it was all over. The dog lingered a moment longer, a liquid trickling against the sliding door then it ran off. In the silence that followed, a thin waft of steam appeared in the light under the door.

Eliot exhaled loudly, took in a huge lungful of air, breathed as if it would soon be unfashionable. Peter removed his hand from his rucksack, hooked the sack over his shoulder and walked quietly across to the sliding door.

Eliot shifted his attention to the footprints at his feet.

And the empty shelves.

Approaching them, he ran his finger along a couple, they were thick with dust. It was curious; there had clearly not been anything on the shelves for months, years even. So why did all the footsteps clearly led towards the shelves?

There were two different types of shelving unit. The first were simply made from lengths of wood that had been bolted together to make frames, upon which the shelves rested at fifty centimetre intervals. The second type were cheap bookcases you could buy at discount furniture warehouses, veneered chipboard with patterned cardboard backs. It was to this second type of shelving unit that the footsteps all led. Even more curious was the fact that while most of the footprints had been made by boots or shoes, a few seemed to have been made by bare feet.

Suddenly he understood.

'Over here.'

Peter joined him by the shelves.

'Look, the units over here. And over here. These shelving units have got back boards.'

'Amazing. What will they think of next?'

'No, can't you see? They're different.'

Han turned away but Eliot grabbed his arm and pulled him back.

'Just help me move it.'

Eliot grabbed at the middle shelf and started to pull. Peter took hold of the other side. The unit moved an inch at a time, the wood squealing against the concrete floor as it came.

'There, look.'

Set in the wall, behind the shelving unit they had pulled out, was the edge of a door frame. They pulled another unit aside to reveal a heavy steel door.

'Well done, son.'

Peter was puffing a little from the exertion. Nevertheless, he looked like he had just found the Holy Grail.

'What do you think?'

'I think we may have struck gold.' Peter said, trying the door handle. 'And it opens. Even better.'

Peter very seldom smiled and, when he did, the muscles of his face didn't seem entirely comfortable.

'What about the guards?'

'Sod them.'

The two men crossed the threshold and down concrete steps that led steeply into the ground.

twenty one

A smell loitered on the horizon of the senses, distant, dank, cloying, almost fetid.

The sound of their boots echoed against the concrete floor, walls and ceiling, recalling for Eliot a recurring childhood nightmare. At home, in his bedroom, when he heard a call from downstairs. Leaving his comic open on the bed he ran down the stairs. Only the stairs didn't end. One flight. Two. Three. Four. The ground floor never arrived, the stairs just kept on going. A grim understanding that he was running towards a place he would rather not visit. And his treacherous feet kept on. Down and down. His back was tingling. He was shouting but no-one heard. Pairs of eyes hidden behind the wallpaper were following his progress as claws were unsheathed and rows of sharp teeth glinted in a purple light.

Thirty nine steps. Forty. Peter Han just ahead of him, silhouetted in the torch light. And still the steps went down. Eliot remembered the dusty black and white photo in the room above, the men in white coats posing for a group photo. What was this place? If the wasteland had been an airfield, and the large expanse of concrete and tarmac once a runway, then this building might date from the last war and the steps might lead to a bunker. His only reference points were old war films, which always seemed to have a scene set deep underground where military types with clipped moustaches and handlebar accents pushed toy ships and tanks across huge tables upon which, spread about like soup stains, were countries and seas, territories possessed or desired.

As if confirming Eliot's suspicions, they reached a second steel door, three inches thick this time and with huge bolts operated by spinning a large wheel located in its centre. The door was open. The steps continued downwards.

Almost immediately they turned a corner and found themselves in a large room. Like potholers discovering a new cave, the two men wandered about, casting their torch beams around, getting a sense of their surroundings. Peter produced a camera from his pocket and clicked away, each camera flash lighting up the whole space for an instant like lightning.

The ceiling must be four or five metres above them, the space almost large enough to house a tennis court. The walls were of unplastered brick. In a distant past a coat of whitewash had been applied but time had taken its toll and the paint was a mess of peeling flakes and cracks. The smell was still there, a little stronger now. Eliot had a sudden memory of his uncle's greenhouse, a humid vegetable sweet smell blending with the unpleasant odour of blood meal and dried manure.

A large cupboard stood in the middle of the far wall. Eliot walked over and pulled at one of the doors. Neat stacks of teacups, plates and saucers in cheap light blue china. Beside the cupboard some trestles and, propped against the wall, a collection of tatty table tops, everything thick with dust.

There was one door in the room and two corridors leading off, one of the corridors being the one by which they had entered. Eliot went to the door. The rusty handle shrieked as he turned it. Beyond the door was another corridor. The smell was immediately more intense, more acrid.

'I'm just going to have a look down here.'

Peter, busy at the other end of the large room, grunted in response.

Torch trembling slightly in his hand, Eliot stepped into the corridor. Almost immediately there was a door to his right. He pushed it open.

Whatever he had been expecting this was not it. He backed out of the room, his hand against the wall to hold himself steady. A bead of sweat flicked from side to side as it trickled down his back. He stepped backwards into the large subterranean hall.

'Peter. Peter?'

A torch beam turned towards him.

'Found something?'

'Through here,' his throat dry, the words barely audible.

Peter ran across and grabbed Eliot's arm. 'Are you OK?'

Eliot nodded unconvincingly. Peter stepped through the doorway.

'First door on the right,' Eliot called after him.

Han's footsteps rang out briefly then stopped. The seconds ticked away.

'It's just a pile of clothes, Eliot.'

'No,' Eliot said, joining Peter in the doorway. 'It's not just a pile of clothes. They're the same kind of clothes as the men were wearing. The trespasser and the dead man. Shorts, t-shirts, summer shoes, short sleeved shirts, sandals.'

BENEATH THE BITTERCREST

'And?'

'Have you never seen those films of genocides? Pol Pot, Rwanda, Dachau, Yugoslavia? There's always a pile of unclaimed clothes. Sometimes it's rags in a ditch, with bones tucked between the layers of fabric. Or a room, like this one, with piles of shoes, stacks of hats, dresses ...' Eliot's voice rose another notch. 'Something's happened here, I can feel it.'

'Calm down.' Peter took a couple of photos. 'It's a pile of laundry.'

'Don't patronise me.'

Peter left the room.

Eliot stood there staring at the dirty shirts and shorts. 'Someone has to check the pockets,' he said finally. 'Look for anything personal, anything that might identify the owners. '

'You do that,' from down the corridor.

'What do you think?' Eliot shouted. 'Peter?

The answer was clouded in echos.

'You don't want to know what I think.'

Eliot started shuffling the clothes about with his feet, reluctant to touch anything with his hands, even with gloves on. Shoes to the left, shirts to the right, trousers in the middle.

There were fewer clothes than he had at first thought, maybe ten sets in all. He took a deep breath and started on the trousers. He got lucky with the fifth pair, a couple of receipts and a small tight wad of paper which, once he had unfolded it, revealed several hand written sheets, scribbled in a foreign script. Searching his rucksack Eliot found Han had included a set of plastic bags, must be the retired cop in him, planning for every eventuality. Eliot slipped the receipts and the papers into one of the bags, sealed the bag and shoved it in his pocket.

There was nothing else. He dropped the last pair of trousers and stared at the pile at his feet. Who had worn these clothes? How had they got here? A small voice in his head cautioned against over-reaction. He wasn't in a war zone. Han was right. Keep an open mind. Maybe the clothes were used for packing. Maybe they had been collected to take to a recycling bank.

Yes, maybe, but how likely was that?

It could be that the people who had stepped out of these clothes had stepped into fresh clothes, newer clothes. Immigrants perhaps, being supplied with new identities. The question was whether two security guards could, by themselves, organise such a venture. It seemed unlikely. Could Peter Han be right? Was Gustave Brown behind it all? Or whoever owned the industrial estate? He ran out of the room to find Peter.

The next door led into a small kitchen. The light was on, a bare bulb hanging over the table. Peter had obviously decided to throw caution to the winds; ten metres underground in a room with no windows, turning on the lights didn't seem too much of a risk.

The walls were painted in a bland magnolia. Two chairs with tubular frames and canvas seats and backs were stacked against the far wall besides an archway. A worn dartboard hung on one wall, six darts clustered in the bullseye, the dart flights depicting naked women in saucy poses. Running along the walls, and warm to the touch, were thick pipes that must carry either waste or water. A 1950's kitchen unit that had, in its time, been painted in at least six different colours stood next to an old enamelled sink, worn with age. Dirty tin plates, a large kitchen knife and an assortment of mugs were stacked up on the draining board. A pile of spoons, a kettle, a microwave, and a Baby Belling cooker.

But the smell of fry-ups and cheap coffee couldn't conceal the foul odour.

The cupboard doors were open, revealing salt, sugar, and whole-sale-sized tins of beans, jam, coffee, and tuna fish. At the bottom of the cupboard were sacks of rice and several large pans. Various keys hung on the inside of one of the doors.

A scratching sound made Eliot leap back, just in time to avoid being hit in the chest by a rat that rushed between his legs and out of the door.

Through the archway, Eliot found a set of wooden steps leading steeply down into darkness. A narrow wooden handrail was all that stood between him and a drop of three or four metres.

For some inexplicable reason, Eliot suddenly recalled that he hadn't mentioned the woman on the train to Han, nor her presence in the newspaper photograph with Gustave Brown.

'Han. Peter?'

Eliot shouted a second time. Holding the handrail and peering down, he became aware of faint torchlight, Peter must be out of earshot, the deaf old tosser.

As he started to descend, Eliot immediately noticed the drop in temperature. The twisting and turning from ground level down to where he now stood had left Eliot feeling disorientated and edgy.

BENEATH THE BITTERCREST

Surely they had enough now, the receipts, the photos, the disc? Even if the local police weren't interested, someone somewhere would be prepared to pursue an investigation.

He stepped down from the last step onto a dirt floor.

The walls and ceiling were carved out of the solid rock. Set into the walls were several doors, each secured with padlocks and chains wrapped round metal posts embedded in the rock itself. The furthest door was ajar and the beam from what must be Peter's torch was visible. Eliot walked towards the door, his torch sweeping back and forth. Another rat, eyes bright as headlamps, reflecting back the light from Eliot's torch, scurried past him towards the steps, and the kitchen beyond.

The smell which had hit him way further up on the steps leading down from ground level was now intense and ugly. Something was rotting.

Eliot stopped and listened. The patient trickling of dripping water and a faint electrical hum, as if from a generator. Ahead of him in the darkness, the sound of an animal scratching, presumably another rat. And then a faint groan. Peter? Eliot hurried forward, his heart in his mouth.

The chain and padlock lay on the floor and Eliot stumbled as his foot slid over the surface of the chain causing the torch to fly from his hand, smack into the stone wall. A splintering of glass and a sudden drop in light.

'Shit, shit, shit,' he cursed under his breath and rubbed his knee.

But the tunnel was not in darkness. From behind the open door a weak haze of light brushed the far wall at the end of the tunnel. Eliot stood up.

Peter's torch was in the doorway, its front end hard up against the wall. The void beyond the doorway was black as interstellar space. Eliot picked up the torch, pointed the beam up at the ceiling and started to cross the threshold.

'No!'

In mid-step, Eliot fell backwards, keeping a tight grip on the torch this time. His rucksack bore the brunt of the fall. He lay there, catching his breath, then carefully sat up and shone the torch about. The floor was missing. Or, more accurately, it was one metre lower than might have been expected. There were no steps down.

Han was in a foetal position just beyond the doorway. Eliot eased himself down into the room.

'Bloody ankle. Wasn't looking. I've broken the bugger.'

'It's OK. I'll carry you out if I have to, Peter. Can you stand on it?'

Eliot's eyes were stinging, the smell was overpowering.

'Over there,' Peter said. 'Those crates in the corner.'

Eliot's torch swept across the room, leaving Peter in deep shadow. Two large buckets stuffed full of torn strips of shit-covered newspaper were bad enough, but there was worse. Beside the buckets was a pile of dirty plates, mouldy food refuse, liquid sickly sweet vegetable decomposition.

What Han had called crates were in fact a trunk and what looked like a casket. Eliot approached with trepidation. He had spent days worrying about what was happening in the low building and now he decided he no longer wanted to know.

'Here, take the camera. Get a couple of good shots then we can leave.'

Eliot took the camera and approached the casket.

It was a cross between a flight case and a metal sarcophagus. Eliot thought back to the coffins on display in the hippy funeral parlour's window. The catches were open. Dizzy from the smell, Eliot lifted the lid.

As he did so a slip of paper slid from the top of the lid to the floor. The casket was empty, no body, no padding, no silk, nothing. He picked up the slip of paper. Torn from the corner of a newspaper, it had a phone number scribbled in the margin of the page. Eliot put it in his jacket pocket, turned towards the trunk and lifted the lid. And found the body.

Blurred through several layers of plastic were the grotesquely distorted features of a face, bloated by putrefaction. Eliot reeled back and threw up over his shoes, his stomach contracting violently again and again until there was only harsh painful bile left to burn his mouth and throat.

'Take a photo, you have to take a photo,' Peter whispered urgently.

Eliot's eyes were stinging. The stench was worse than anything he had ever encountered. He knew Peter was right but didn't know if he was capable of looking into the trunk a second time. Finally he raised the camera to his eye. Even as he took the photographs he knew they would be useless. The flash was reflecting back off the plastic.

'I need a knife. To split the plastic sheet.'

'In your rucksack.'

Eliot took the rucksack off his back, found the knife. He leant over the trunk and slit the plastic from end to end and pulled the two sides apart.

Another ugly surging wash of the smell of death.

The purple bloated features stared up at him with sad disintegrating brown eyes. Skin and flesh had fallen from the cheeks like flaking pastry to reveal the teeth and blackened gums. The hands were clenched as if reaching out to grab an assailant, a last desperate and futile bid for life.

Take the pictures and get out.

Eliot put the camera's viewfinder between him and the corpse and steadied himself. He took a picture and changed position to get a better shot of the ... of the what? How could he be thinking about framing the shot? Eliot was as revolted by his own behaviour as by the stench; the ultimate betrayal of privacy, intruding into the decomposition of another human being. He guessed his subconscious was trying to detach itself, to run from reality and lose itself in abstraction, in the spatial orientation of shapes.

Overwhelmed by sensory overload, Eliot didn't notice the soft footfalls as a figure appeared in the doorway behind him.

But he heard the shot.

He threw himself back, away from the trunk and into the wall to his left, smashing his cheek against the stone. Pain sparked like firecrackers but even before he had fully finished falling he was starting to turn towards the new threat. There was a grunt from the other end of the room. Eliot was vaguely aware of the camera tumbling from his grasp.

Peter had disappeared from view beneath a second man who was struggling to get to his feet while punching and kicking. A torchbeam flashed sporadically, trapped beneath the struggling men. A bright glint of a blade. A scream. Was it Peter? More scuffling. Peter's assailant was up on his knees, the blade clearly visible in his hand. He plunged it down into Peter's torso.

Eliot threw himself forwards, grabbed the assailant by the shoulder to pull him off Peter. With one swift continuous movement the hand that held the knife flew back, the heel of the knife catching Eliot hard in the genitals. Eliot gasped and fell back clutching his groin and howling with pain.

Peter's hand was scrabbling in the dirt beside him, clenching and unclenching, with the primal urgency of a crab crossing the sea floor to escape a predator. Again the knife attacked Peter's torso. The hand was reaching behind Peter's head and suddenly found what it was looking for. It gripped and pulled back towards the carnage. Eliot caught sight of the gun just before the second shot was fired. Peter's assailant hung in the air over Peter for a moment as if time itself had stopped in the sound of a bullet. The knife gleamed its malevolent intent. The rattling gasps of the two injured men mingled like the sighs of lovers then, all at once, the attacker fell forwards, knife in front of him. He slumped down, the knife diving into Peter's chest as effortlessly as a spoon sinking into jelly. Peter twitched and pushed against the body lying on top of him, trying to lift the man away from him, his arms shaking with exertion.

Then, abruptly, the struggle was over. Peter's arms collapsed like a house of cards. The assailant's body obeyed the law of gravity. The remnants of air in two sets of lungs were gasped away and there was silence.

Eliot was left alone in the room.

Alone with three corpses.

PC Hampton, video tapes and papers in hand, closed the door and headed down the corridor. With luck a petrol station would still be open and he could buy a cup of strong coffee, two or three bars of chocolate for the journey home. Two o'clock. He might even have a couple of hours sleep. Alison would cover for him.

He tossed everything onto the passenger seat, started the Volvo up and headed out of the port towards the motorway. A dark saloon car followed in his wake. As Hampton pulled in to the petrol station the car carried on past without slowing down.

Fifty metres back on the slip road a second car inched forwards then stopped, engine idling, waiting for Hampton to rejoin the motorway.

twenty two

Eliot approached the bodies warily, half-expecting them to burst back to life. His feet slipped about in the viscous dark red puddle that was spreading across the floor. Without a solid foothold, he simply couldn't find a good enough grip of the guard's blood-soaked clothes to pull him off.

He reached out for Peter Han's wrist and felt for a pulse. There wasn't one.

The gun must be trapped between the two bodies. Eliot wasn't sure he wanted the gun anyway. He stuffed his hand in Peter's trouser pockets and found the car keys.

Without warning Eliot's stomach turned and he found himself vomiting again. Gastric acid and bile, there was nothing else left. Doubled over, eyes screwed up in pain, until a rasping sound from the tunnel alerted him to the fact that there had been two guards. It was only a matter of time before the second guard came in search of his colleague. Eliot grabbed both rucksacks and Peter's torch. The beam from the torch reflected off the lens of the camera he had dropped, drawing his eye to it. Grabbing the camera Eliot reeled off a couple of shots of the two bodies as evidence before climbing up and out of the room. Racing away he thought he heard a groan, but decided it was impossible and that he was mistaken.

He hurried along the tunnel, fearful of the dead darkness dogging his heels, back to the steep steps that led up to the kitchen. A dim glow was filtering down from above. Eliot took the steps two at a time and was through the archway to the kitchen when he heard the sound of someone approaching in the opposite direction.

He threw himself back under the archway and into the partial gloom. Should he stay put or go back into the tunnel to hide? He peered down into the darkness and knew he couldn't do it.

A sudden movement in the periphery of his vision caused Eliot to press himself back against the wall. A faint scratching noise from beyond the wooden steps drew his eye to a huge rat staring straight back at him.

Footsteps getting closer now, almost at the kitchen door.

Eliot waved a foot at the rat. The rat responded with a quizzical tilt of the head. A rodent with attitude.

The footsteps were in the kitchen now. A subtle variation in the light, and the fleeting shadow that grazed the wall beyond the sink, suggested the guard had crossed beyond the light bulb that dangled over the table. Pressed up against the wall behind the arch, Eliot suddenly caught sight of the long knife, bright on the draining board, and, as he noticed it, a hand reached out and grabbed it. Four more steps and the guard would have reached the archway.

The rat was still eyeballing Eliot, its whiskers twitching inquisitively. It started to edge towards him, teeth bared.

'Come on, Chris. Only worm food down there, Mate,' the guard called out as he passed under the archway.

Eliot braced himself for impact, while at the same time making a mental note that the guard knew what was down the steps. The rat, suddenly outnumbered, leapt back, distracting the guard.

It was now or never.

It was now.

Eliot threw himself forwards, hitting the guard from the side and causing him to fall forwards towards the gap. The knife fell from the guard's hand as he spun round, lunging at Eliot with his bare hands, at first to strike him and then to grasp hold of him. Eliot shrank back away from the clenching fingers. For an instant their eyes met. It was one of the two men who had assaulted him days earlier as he had made his way from the wasteland. The same large thickset neck, bulldog shoulders, and bad haircut.

Finding his footing, the guard smiled maliciously.

'You again,' he sneered. 'I'm going to enjoy this.'

He was fast on his feet, throwing his arm round Eliot's ankles and pulling his legs away from under him before Eliot had a chance to react. Eliot slammed down hard onto his coxyx and the thug was all over him, lashing out in a fury of fists and boots. The blows hailed down, a wall of pain enveloped Eliot who curled over in a foetal position to protect himself.

Somehow, in the midst of the attack, Eliot heard a scratching and, opening his eyes, saw the rat baring its teeth, black eyes glistening with cold calculation.

To Eliot's right, just beyond reach, was the kitchen knife. Searing pain as a boot connected a glancing blow to his ear. Eliot's fingers reached towards the blade. Catching sight of the movement, the guard stepped back and to his left to step on Eliot's hand. It was the

BENEATH THE BITTERCREST

opportunity Eliot needed. As the boot crunched down on his knuckles, Eliot twisted his body round and, with all the energy he could muster, kicked out at the man's knees.

A bone-jarring crunch of tendon and kneecap accompanied the guard's yelp as he whipped back against the wooden rail, which splintered under his weight. The guard disappeared into the void of the stairwell. A brief shout was followed by a brutal thud and heavy snapping of bones.

Then silence.

The rat was still there, back on its haunches, sniffing the air. It moved away from the wall and peered down into the gloom of the stairwell, its long yellow teeth bright in the light spilling from the kitchen. With the briefest of glances towards Eliot, it leapt down into the darkness. There was a dull thud as the rodent landed not on the hard stone of the floor below but on a surface altogether softer and more yielding. The muffled padding of its feet on the fallen man's chest was joined by the sounds of other feet scurrying forwards towards the body.

Nursing his hand, Eliot lingered just long enough to shine a torch down into the gloom. He had killed a man. He had become what the police had accused him of.

Grabbing the knife, he hauled himself to his feet and hurried away.

Stepping out into the large room, Eliot immediately felt the quality of the air change, the smell of death and damp hung less heavily. The lights were on, a series of fluorescent tubes in two rows high above his head, switched on no doubt by the security guards. Eliot's footsteps resonated loudly as he ran across the room towards the exit. He noticed a video camera high up on a wall and realised that whatever else happened that night, his visit would not pass unnoticed.

Limbs aching from exertion, and the kicking he had received, Eliot left the large room, heading up the steps that led towards the surface. He took the steps two at a time, no longer caring about who might hear him, he simply wanted out, wanted to be above ground. His heartbeat pounded in his ears, a heavy procession of muffled drumbeats like those that emanated from cars waiting outside nightclubs on Friday nights. Upon reaching ground level, Eliot grabbed the door frame and clung to it while his lungs worked overtime. His head was spinning and he feared he might pass out. He kept his eyes closed and concentrated on a day spent fishing by a pond when he had been just twelve. Lost in a memory of concentric circles drifting and expanding across a surface of quicksilver everytime he cast his line, he imagined sunshine and the buzzing stillness by a water's edge; and eventually his head stopped spinning, and the piston of his heartbeat slowed.

The sliding door at the far end of the room had been pulled back to leave a gap just wide enough for a person to slip through. The room was still in darkness. Eliot walked towards the open door, the quicker he was away from Swindon the better. The fresh cool air felt like stepping into a shower, cleansing him, washing away the subterranean stench that clung to him. He let go of the knife, was dimly aware of it clattering at his feet.

A trapezoidal wedge of light spilling in from outside lay across the floor. Eliot switched off his torch and slipped it into one of the rucksacks before stepping to the edge of the light, pausing to listen. The sounds of the urban night drifted in the air, a car accelerating away from a junction, the jumbled hum of distant traffic, the wind's muffled whine. Boring normal sounds that knew nothing of the enormity of murder. The rain had all but stopped, all that remained was the click of occasional large fat drops splashing down onto the concrete. It was clear the sliding door had been open for some time, a dark patch revealed the rain had swept into the building.

A brief scuffing sound. Even having heard it, he might so easily have disregarded it. As it was, he immediately knew it for what it was, the contact of a shoe against a rough surface. Eliot stepped quickly back into the shadows, it wasn't over yet.

'Fair point, fair point, but I still say we leave them to it.'

Moments later three men passed, one at a time, through into the building. A boot kicked the knife Eliot had dropped, sending it spinning into a dark corner. The last man in began to push at the sliding door, forcing it back on its overhead track, the door's mechanism shrieking as rust and bare metal ground against each other.

The other two stood idly by; the smaller one playing with a goatee beard he had recently grown to help cultivate an intellectual air, and the taller one, who had a weak chin and large ears that protruded like satellite dishes, staring into space. When the door was finally open, the third man, puffing from his exertions, turned to face them.

'Thanks, lads,' laced with heavy irony. 'So you two want to play cowboys and indians?'

'I was merely advancing a hypothesis, Simon. Trying to ...' The smaller man, pulled at his goatee beard, searching for the mot juste.

'I don't want to hear it, Einstein.'

The smaller man shrugged and walked over to the lorry. Pulling open a box behind the cab, he produced a couple of ugly tyre wrenches.

'And take Tonto with you,' Simon said. 'Don't forget, you have to head them off at the pass.'

The smaller man and 'Tonto' who, along with his other physical attributes, was as thin as a chopstick, passed through the doorway that led to the subterranean levels. Their footsteps echoed briefly on the concrete steps.

Simon turned his attention to the lorry. If the younger men wanted to risk life and limb, so be it, for his part he had long ago learned to mind his own business, do what he was paid to do, ask no questions, and enjoy the money. He climbed up into the cab and started her up. A brief splutter and she was purring like a three ton kitten. He tapped the fuel gauge to make sure it hadn't stuck again, checked the lights then, satisfied that everything was in order, switched the engine off and tuned the radio to his favourite country music station. Sometimes it's hard to be a woman. Indeed it was.

He was halfway through a heart-rending ballad of hungry children, lurching stetson-slinging drunks and empty homesteads, when a shout rang out. Simon threw open the door of the cab and leapt down.

'There's been a demisement,' Goatee said.

'Now there's a pretty word for it,' Simon commented.

'No, he's wrong. They're both dead. Bill and Chris,' said Tonto. 'He's only gone and killed Bill and Chris.'

'Who has?'

'Poor sod. Shot him just as Chris was ...'

'Several demisements in fact. A fracas resulting ...'

'Don't talk shit. If Chris was ...

'Are you two on speed?' Simon shouted above them.

In the silence that followed, Tonto scowled at Goatee who, in turn, looked sullenly at Simon.

'Right, let's start again.' Simon said. 'Where are Bill and Chris?'

'Down there.'

'Great,' Simon smiled. 'And you two geniuses are of the opinion that the men are deceased.'

'I never said they were diseased.'

'Dead,' Goatee explained.

'I knew that,' Tonto said, after a moment's hesitation.

'And the third man?' Simon said.

'If I may,' Goatee said, looking at Tonto. He turned back to Simon, 'He's dead too.'

Simon was unsure the subject would benefit from further discussion. 'Is our package down there?'

'Yeah, but first ...'

'No.' Simon looked from one man to the other, it was a wonder either of them had ever mastered walking on hind legs. 'This is what we do. You two are going down to collect the package, then we are going to leave. If any questions are asked, we were here two hours ago, before any of this happened.'

'But how will we know when this happened if we weren't here?'

'Leave the thinking to me, birdbrains.'

'The package,' Tonto said suddenly as if he had just woken from a deep sleep. 'It's in the wrong box.'

Simon spoke with measured calm. 'Then put it in the right box and bring it up here.' Then, shouting in their faces. 'Before I blow your fucking heads off.'

Simon watched them shuffle off before checking his watch. Twelve minutes past one. If they hadn't stopped off for a drink ... Well, it was too late to start worrying about that. He lit a fag and waited by the open door staring at the rain that had started up again with a vengeance.

Five minutes later, Tonto and Goatee staggered back, carrying the large metal casket between them. Simon stubbed his fag out with the sole of his cowboy boot and crossed the room towards the back of the lorry.

The back doors were partially open. Simon pulled them back and used the tail lift to take him up.

'Right, boys,' he said, sending the tail-lift back down. 'Load her up.'

The two men lowered the casket onto the tail-lift and hopped on.

'Shit, the stink's as bad in here as it is downstairs,' Tonto said, walking backwards into the lorry with one end of the casket.

They waited while Simon kicked various empty crates out of the way to make space for the casket.

'Maybe we should take the other three with us,' Goatee volunteered, wiping his brow on a rag he had found.

They secured the casket with a rope and climbed out.

BENEATH THE BITTERCREST   141

'You did bring the tyre wrenches back?' Simon asked, while sliding the bolts into place.

'Do popes shit in the woods?' Tonto said with the expression he believed made him look intelligent. He offered Simon the wrenches as if he were giving him a bunch of flowers.

'And you can both sod off and have a wash before you get in the cab,' Simon said. 'You'd turn noses in an abattoir.'

The lorry came slowly out into the rainswept night. It paused, engine revving hard, while Goatee pulled the sliding door shut then ran and climbed into the cab beside the other two.

Rain hammered on the roof of the lorry in an ear-splitting cacophony. A dull glow from passing street lights filtered through the transluscent plastic roof, illuminating the casket, the empty crates, and a pile of rags and boxes in the space over the cab. As the vehicle raced through the streets of Swindon the rags started to slide back and tumble down onto the crates below. Several cardboard boxes slid sideways as the lorry made a sharp turn, then crashed down on top of the rags. Tonto looked nervously towards the other two.

'If what we put in the back of the lorry is trying to escape then I say we let it.' Tonto said. 'Know what I mean?'

Simon just shook his head and put his foot down and turned the radio up. *Boom boom shake, you know I love it when you boom boom shake.*

In the rumbling gloom another box tumbled down. Eliot sat up and looked about him.

Aside from the flashing orange glow of street lights passing over-head, Eliot saw small pinpricks of light set into the sides of the lorry. From his position up above the cab he was close to three such holes. The first faced forwards, in the direction of travel. Through this hole nothing was visible other than water dripping towards his eye. There were other holes looking out to the left and right. Pressing his eye against one of these, Eliot was able to see the streets of Swindon flashing past in a haze of near horizontal rain.

The holes appeared to have been gouged through the metal with a blunt instrument. Who else could have been in the lorry, eager to see out?

Eliot set about discovering what Peter Han had put in the two rucksacks.

In Peter's rucksack were: a length of rope, a hunting knife, a compass, paper, the camera, the glass cutter, various items of clothing, a box containing amunition that was presumably intended for the pistol Peter had been holding when he died, pens, and a pair of binoculars. The second rucksack, which had been Eliot's and had contained the rope ladder, had fewer items in it. There was a camera, this one digital; a first aid kit; a compact box of lightweight tools; the computer disc Han had found stuck to the underside of the desk in the low building, and a can of pepper spray.

The lorry braked suddenly, and Eliot all but fell from his perch. The second rucksack, the one Peter had given him, tumbled away and crashed onto the packing crates below. The road noise changed as the lorry slowed and Eliot guessed the tyres were running on gravel. He leaned over to see where the rucksack had fallen and spotted it balancing on the edge of a crate to his left. Twisting round carefully to avoid making a noise, he turned until he was lying on his front. His fingers came within a whisker of touching the strap of the rucksack but closed only on thin air. He had to retrieve it, the computer disc might well have the answers they were looking for. Bracing himself as best he could, Eliot tried a second time, hoping desperately that his movements would not attract attention. Again his fingers missed the strap. The lorry came to a halt and Eliot watched in horror as the rucksack slipped away onto the rubbish beside the crate.

They had stopped in front of a pair of large wrought iron gates. Tonto and Goatee climbed out and opened them, holding them open as the lorry drove through and on, along a road that led about a hundred metres uphill to a single storey building with a tall chimney. The lorry continued round to the back of the building, pulling up close to a set of double doors. Simon cut the engine.

Above Simon's head, Eliot listened to the muffled country guitars as he did his best to cover himself with what was left of the rubbish. The music stopped and the cab door opened and someone jumped down. Footsteps across the gravel. A sudden clang at the far end of the lorry followed by a mechanical winding sound, Eliot guessed the tailgate was being operated. The grinding sound of rusty sliding bolts reverberated inside the lorry.

It was still raining, no longer the hammering barrage but a slower heavier pattern. Eliot guessed the lorry was parked under a tree. He pulled a foul smelling vest over his head and pressed himself flat against the walls of the lorry.

Simon was pulling open the doors as the other two men, who had

BENEATH THE BITTERCREST

walked from the gates, caught up.

'Do you think burns victims get a discount at this establishment?' Goatee said, provoking a bout of sniggering from Tonto.

'Will you two fairies hurry up?' Simon stepped onto the lorry and pressed the button to send the tailgate back down.

'Bugger me,' Tonto said, looking in on the chaos in the back of the lorry.

'It's the middle of the bloody night, just get on with it.' Simon said, bending over to pick up a shoe he had spotted.

Goatee and Tonto exchanged looks and set about clearing away the rubbish to get at the casket.

'I warned you last time about this,' hissed a voice .

A man in a dark suit stood behind the lorry, his face hidden beneath a large black umbrella.

'Total silence or the deal is off,' the voice continued. 'Do you have any idea ...'

'... of the risk you're taking letting us in here at this time of night?' Simon finished the sentence for him, mimicking the other man's furious whisper. 'Just go and put the kettle on, Timothy, there's a good lad.'

The umbrella shook as Timothy Wesley considered his options before walking lamely back to the double doors and disappearing into the building.

'Wanker,' Tonto said.

More sniggering.

Simon allowed himself a smile. He wandered about, poking at the rubbish, while Goatee and Tonto manoeuvred the casket towards the tailgate.

'Well, look at this.' Simon picked up a rucksack that had fallen between two crates. 'This is almost new. And they come here pleading poverty. It's a bleeding disgrace. Here, either of you two need a rucksack? I might keep it for the old girl.'

He made his way towards the ledge above the cab and reached out towards one of the large boxes; who knew what else he might find?

Without warning the crate under his right boot slipped away and he fell heavily onto the second crate. He howled as his knee smashed against the rough wood.

'Yeah, all right, all right. Have a cheap laugh.' Simon rubbed his knee. Slinging the rucksack over his shoulder, he hobbled back down the lorry.

Timothy Wesley stood in the small office, dropping teabags into four chipped mugs, wondering what he had done to deserve the life he was having. Due to squabbling, he and his two colleagues kept their teabags in separate tins and had individual cartons of milk in the tiny fridge under the sink. To the public they were a self-effacing and harmonious team, their faces only ever displaying quiet concern or professional sadness. In the privacy of their office, they were a nest of acrimonious vipers, hurling barbed comments about like harpoons.

Timothy Wesley was sixty years old, only a handful from retirement, and everything had been going swimmingly until three years earlier when his son had fallen ill. Well, maybe not swimmingly; his life had in fact been largely a disappointment, a monotonous procession of days without excitement, tenderness, or variety. But he had, at least, been able to count on stability and a sense of order. He lined the mugs up in a straight row and took the milk carton marked 'David's - do not steal' from the fridge.

His wife, Gwen, had never loved him, nor he her in truth, but she had cooked and he had worked, and their son had never lacked for anything, except a wife and a mind of his own. He blamed Gwen for that, a grown man of thirty four with a mother still happy to do his laundry and water his houseplants .

'Is that kettle on then?'

Wesley jumped and turned. Simon stood smirking in the doorway.

'You did that on purpose,' Wesley accused. He poured hot water into the cups while Simon watched.

'This one's a bit of a stinker, you won't want to let it hang around. Though I suppose in your line of trade ...'

'You know absolutely nothing about my line of trade, Mr Stroud, and your two monkeys know even less.'

'Steady on, all I was saying was ...'

'No, you steady on.' Wesley could feel his temples throbbing, could hear his wife's voice warning him about his blood pressure, but he was past caring. 'Just because I have to deal with you does not mean I have any interest in sharing the time of day with you. Take your tea and go.'

'Want us to teach him some manners, Boss?'

Simon made a show of considering Tonto's offer to let Wesley sweat for a moment.

'Nah, he's just a little upset, that's all. Isn't that so, Mr Wesley?'

BENEATH THE BITTERCREST 145

Wesley looked away. He flinched as Tonto brushed past him on his way to collect the mugs of tea.

'Nice tea,' Simon said. 'And how's the lovely wife? And that son of yours?'

'Please, just drink the tea and go,' Wesley whispered.

'Oops,' said Tonto, pouring half his tea on the carpet.

'Do you think his wife no longer attends to his conjugal needs?' Goatee said. 'Is that why he prefers to stay here all night?'

'All right, that's enough.' Simon put his empty mug down on the window sill. 'We'll pick the casket up on our next visit.'

Wesley nodded his agreement and watched them leave.

Eliot, having watched the lorry leave from the safety of a clump of laurel bushes, crossed the road back towards the building. He tried the double doors but found them locked. Stepping back he spotted a light coming on in a window some three metres up, partially concealed behind a line of conifers.

The trees were too densely packed to climb but a drainpipe at one end of the wall looked promising. Eliot tested it and, satisfied it would bear his weight, clambered up.

It was a large room. On an oak table near the door were a variety of floral displays of differing sizes. The twin doors of a tall cupboard stood open. Within it were several mops, buckets and brooms and, hanging on the right hand door, a row of pegs, upon one of which hung a dark mackintosh.

The casket lay open beside a trolley in the centre of the room. A man dressed from head to toe in white overalls, gloves, hat, and face mask, was pulling at the body, lifting it out of the casket and onto the trolley. Eliot shuddered as he saw the corpse for the second time, the bloated face in its grimace of death, the blackened gums, the broken eyes.

When the body was on the trolley the man stepped back and bent over as if steadying himself, regaining his composure or maybe offering a prayer. Presently, he took hold of one end of the trolley and wheeled it over towards the far end of the room. In the far wall was a metal door or hatch and, in front of it, a surface projecting horizontally from it. The trolley must have had a tray of some kind on top of it, for the man simply slid the body, and whatever it was resting on, forwards onto the other surface. He then walked to his right, out of sight. Eliot craned his neck to see further into the room but his view was blocked by a pillar.

All at once the body began to move towards the hatch which, in turn, lifted to reveal a sea of flame. Behind the body, the white overalls, shoe covers, gloves, mask and hat were dropped onto the moving carpet to join the body in the incinerator.

twenty three

The miles were slipping away in the rear view mirror. Eliot was dog tired and tempted to stop and grab a few hours sleep in a service station car park.

Having crossed through woodland to the west of the crematorium to make his way to the road, it had taken him the best part of an hour to get back across town to where Peter Han had parked the car hours earlier. A mile jog in the freezing rain before he came across a cab hire firm. The rain had at least had the beneficial effect of washing away the dirt and stench of death and the bloodstains on his trousers. Even so the cab driver had refused to take him until a plastic sheet had been found to cover the back seat.

With dank fingers the cold had burrowed through to Eliot's bones. The heater was on full and every few minutes he had to wipe the inside of the windscreen to remove the condensation. The weather grew steadily worse. Combined with the white noise of the rain, the monotonous futility of the wiper blades threatened to send him into a deep sleep.

There was no traffic except for the occasional juggernaut slicing its weary groove in the slow lane, curtains of spray chasing along in its wake.

While he was grateful to have a set of wheels, Han's dark blue Astra wasn't really Eliot's style, all the charisma of a Shopping Channel presenter. The radio was broken and Han's CDs were at best irritating and at worst pretty scary.

Passing under a bridge the windscreen became silent for a few milliseconds, sheltered from the rain then, bang, the full force of the downpour smacked back in as if it had never stopped. A juggernaut about three hundred metres ahead, barely visible in a cloud of spray. He leant over and opened the glove box, half hoping he would find a cigarette, half hoping he wouldn't. He didn't.

A sudden flashback. Footsteps running in the dark. Water dripping. The bloated face. Up on the roof looking down at Han and the rope ladder he had to descend. And that smell that clung to the skin like leeches.

The blast of a horn.

Eliot opened his eyes. The car was adrift in a tunnel of spray and noise. His eyes flicked down to the speedo. Ninety five miles per hour. The left hand side of the car became an ear splitting grinding of metal. He threw the steering wheel to the right. The car juddered violently, threatening to spin out of control. The windscreen wipers were having no effect whatsoever, he might as well be driving underwater. He jumped the brakes, praying the ABS system worked.

He emerged backwards out of the tunnel of spray. For a moment the juggernaut's rear lights were visible then they were swallowed up in the torrents of water lashing the road. Down to fifty miles per hour, Eliot tucked into the slow lane.

Soon he had passed under Birmingham and left the motorway towards Bewdley, Ludlow and a succession of minor C roads. An hour later he pulled up outside Han's cottage, killed the engine and lay back in his seat, too tired to move.

The temperature dropped rapidly and Eliot realised he should get indoors. Without a key, he was obliged to smash a window. He chose the downstairs toilet, blocking the hole he had made with tape and a framed picture he found in the hall.

And there he was, in his new country residence, not so much losing a life as gaining an Aga. It was still dark, would be for two or three hours yet. The only sounds were the muffled whine of the wind, the rain licking the windows and the slow click of a grandfather clock. He boiled a kettle and made himself some toast and a mug of soup; Han had quite a stash of soup tins in his cupboards.

The fire in the lounge was still just alive. Eliot threw some coal on it and poured himself a large tumbler full of Han's Glenfiddich. And then another. Settling in one of the armchairs he wondered how long he would be safe, how long it would be before they put two and two together and came to find him. How many people knew about Han's country retreat? No-one at his office seemed to have known. No land line; other than ringing his mobile no way of contacting Han.

That thought triggered another that lingered on the edges of Eliot's consciousness just beyond reach, like a swimmer occasionally glimpsed in a rough sea some distance from the beach.

The fire and the whisky were doing their stuff and Eliot found his thoughts becoming jumbled. He leapt up to check that the kids were asleep then sat down again. He thought about betrayal, why had Stephen come with the police? It didn't make sense, except that Stephen always had been a pompous twat and had probably convinced himself that he was saving Eliot from himself. It's for your own good. He could hear the words as clearly as if Stephen had been in the room.

And what about Serina? Why had she bought into Office Solutions?

He realised he had never properly asked himself that question. He hadn't really known her at college. She had been student liaison spokesperson of some sort, never missing an opportunity to go to the big dinners. For a while, he saw her once a week when she arrived in a covertible to collect his room mate Bruce after rugby sevens on a Saturday, but Eliot hadn't been invited to the wedding in Henley. Once she appeared on the scene, Eliot's friendship with Bruce Roberts had declined as Serina had steered Bruce away from beer fuelled revelries in local pubs to soirées in swanky clubs. She had kept Bruce just long enough to enjoy his boyish good looks and his broad shoulders, then shelved him for a thinner hipped Italian footballer.

What struck Eliot as odd, in his whisky induced haze, was that she should want to have a part in Office Solutions. She had always seemed destined for the top. Like her brother. Whatever Office Solutions was or would become, it wasn't 'The Top'. Had her ambition faded or was Eliot missing something?

Another finger of Han's Glenfiddich. He thought of the stupid things he had done with his life. Surely the night's events ranked right up there with the best of them. He had dug himself a hole so big that he could no longer see the other side. There was no possibility of turning back, he simply had to go on, reach the end of whatever road it was he had to travel and hope he came out of it alive. As the shock and adrenalin faded and tiredness and alcohol kicked in, the events of the previous few hours were riding back into town, five abreast, meaning business.

He saw the rucksack tumbling away from him as he sat in the lorry. The rucksack containing the computer disc Han had found. All that effort for sod all.

Han's death finally hit home. In all its stupid futility. Eliot sank back in the armchair realising, with a suddenness that overwhelmed him, that in his mind he had already distanced himself from the man. Peter had become Han, familiarity depersonalised, a surname marking the spot where once there had been a first name. If Eliot hadn't pestered him, Han would still have been alive, sitting in his kitchen or sleeping in his bed. Instead of which it was Eliot sitting by the fire, drinking the dead man's whisky. Unexpectedly, from depths Eliot could not hope to fathom, Han felt like the father Eliot had never had; a father who actually gave a toss about things, a father who didn't hide in the bottom of a bottle whenever trouble came knocking, the person who had been there when he was needed.

Eliot, tired and drunk, threw coal on the fire and headed upstairs to find a bed to lie on, preferably one with at least two quilts.

The following morning began at midday, breakfast sizzling in the pan, eggs, tomatoes and bacon. Eliot, nursing a fragile head, moved methodically like a condemned man who has just been reprieved and can't quite believe his good fortune. He eventually found the plates, heavily patterned with bright flowers and butterflies. The more he saw the more he realised how little he had known Han.

Out of nowhere, Eliot remembered the item he had retrieved from the spare room before fleeing his house twenty seven hours previously. He charged out into the small hall and retrieved the bag he had arrived with the previous afternoon.

Han's office was on the first floor, Eliot had discovered it in the night while looking for a bed to collapse on. Like all the upstairs rooms, the office smelt a little musty. A threadbare beige carpet almost covered the floor, leaving a few exposed floorboards under the mahogany desk. Tassels hung from the red lamp shades and fussy floral curtains over the windows. Eliot wondered whether any of the decor represented Han's taste or whether he had inherited the furnishings when he bought the cottage.

A trawl through the desk drawers produced what he was looking for, a phone charger. It wasn't a Philips but it didn't matter, it plugged into the mobile phone he had in his hand, the phone that had been in the box containing his possessions retrieved at the scene of the train crash. It seemed to be charging.

The kitchen was at the side of the house and, as he sat down to eat his breakfast he was drawn to the view through the window. The edge of the forest seemed close enough to touch, a dark green back-drop against which snowflakes tumbled. The ground was still wet from the night's rain but soon the snow would start to settle. How long then before he was completely cut off? Would it matter? After all, if he couldn't get down off the hill then, presumably, others would not be able to climb up it.

Flash cut, Eliot saw himself playing in the snow with the children.

BENEATH THE BITTERCREST

Building a snowman, pulling them both along on a sled, Toby squeaking with pleasure while his elder sister held him tightly and giggled.

He stood up and went to the fridge, hesitated, left the beer and grabbed the orange juice. He sat there, his head in his hands, the orange juice on the table in front of him, untouched.

An hour later he remembered the phone again and went upstairs to fetch it.

He felt its weight in his hand, remembering the woman on the train, she had been talking into a mobile phone prior to placing it on the table in front of her. It had to be the same phone. The crash, the moment of impact, must have sent it flying across the table to become lodged in his clothing or behind his briefcase. A quirk of fate had led to the phone being placed together with Eliot's property, his shoes, coat, jacket, briefcase, all gathered up at the crash scene and placed in a box to be taken away and safely stored until their owner had recovered sufficiently to leave hospital.

The dam of forgetfulness that had shielded him from the horrors of the crash had been breeched and memories began trickling back. It was not just her face he saw now, fragments of conversation floated towards him.

Strawberry, Eliot?

She had known who he was. Said something about him being like a priest keeping grubby secrets. The name tag, she had read his name on the conference badge he had on the lapel of his jacket.

But now he thought about it, doubts were beginning to surface. Her observations had seemed casual but how casual had they really been?

Upon being discharged from the hospital, Eliot had forgotten all about the mobile phone the nurse had brought him. Arriving back at home he had dumped the box containing his personal effects in the spare room expecting that, at some point, he would go through it, find his watch, check there hadn't been anything of importance in his briefcase, throw out his torn clothes. But that moment had not come and, had it not been for the photograph in the Swindon newspaper, the box would probably have stayed where it was for years, like a time capsule buried in a wall.

Eliot wrestled with a growing feeling that he wasn't in control, that he was being used, a pawn in a game that was larger than he could understand. Who was she? What did she know? What did the photograph signify? Were recent events all interconnected in a way he did not understand?

There was something else loitering on the edge of his subconscious, gnawing at him. Something the woman had said, or not said. An assumption he had made, a detail he was overlooking.

She had quizzed him about his work, implied that the person who made it possible for secrets to be encrypted was as guilty as the person keeping the secrets. And yet, for all her posturing, within minutes she had used the mobile phone to tell blatant lies to whoever was at the other end. The contradictions meant something, he was sure of it, but what?

Roxanne, ces olives sont magnifiques.

The whole phrase popped back into his head, something she had said into her mobile. Although he couldn't explain to himself why he thought so, Eliot was convinced that Roxanne was her name, that she had been referring to herself.

He recalled her eyes, the sapphire glinting in her nostril, the nonchalant smile challenging him to mention the lies she had just uttered on the phone. Which was the disguise, the fiesty hippy with spiky hair or the polished blond in the press photo?

It arrived so quietly, he almost missed it. He had made a false assumption. The badge on his lapel had not in fact said anything about security, there had only been an accronym.

Eliot Balkan, Office Solutions.
S N E European conference
The Dome Centre, Doncaster.

Security for a New Era. But the badge hadn't said that. How had she known what the letters meant? It was suddenly very clear that the encounter had not been an accident at all. She had deliberately sought him out and sat down opposite him in a carriage that had been practically empty.

He turned the mobile over in his hand, deep in thought.

Who had she been working for? Had she been at the Dome Centre? He might simply not have noticed her. But, in that case, why hadn't she spoken to him at the conference instead of following him to the train? Why had she seemed so antagonistic? How was it that she had disappeared after the crash?

For reasons he couldn't properly explain to himself, Eliot was convinced that Roxanne, if that was her name, held vital answers to his own predicament. He couldn't begin to make sense of her presence in the photograph with Brown, but he knew he must find her somehow and speak with her. And maybe her phone would be the key to doing just that.

There were four numbers stored on the phone, identified not by name but by initials: D, ZC, BI, MOB.

But no signal.

He moved about the room, then from room to room. It soon became clear that there was no signal anywhere in the house. How then had he contacted Han?

He must have tried Han's mobile twenty times before finally getting through. He cast his mind back. Han had seemed surprised. And out of breath. It had been a bad line. Heavy static hissing in the background. Or maybe rain?

It had been raining. Han had been outside.

The snow had started to settle. High overhead a crow struggled to hold its course against a stiff breeze that whistled through the chimney pots. Wearing wellingtons and a jacket he had found by the front door, Eliot followed the gravel path round to the back of the cottage and on, passing between two rows of tall shrubs before reaching the top of the garden where he found a gate that opened onto a narrow path leading off between the trees. Turning briefly to look back, Eliot noticed a large shed towards the top of the garden, hidden from the cottage by a rocky outcrop.

The forest path was muffled and quiet. An occasional call from a bird that seemed to have learnt its song from a digital alarm clock. Eliot's footfalls rustled gently on the carpet of pine needles. Water droplets gathered like miniature balloons on the ends of the branches before collapsing under their own weight and splashing down onto the leaf litter. Strange place for a city boy but it made a change.

He pulled the mobile from his pocket and instantly felt more at ease. The liquid crystal display brought him the comfort of technology, civilisation and the city. There were the beginnings of a signal as the ariel icon flickered briefly. Eliot kept climbing. A hundred metres further on and the signal appeared to be holding. He called up the stored numbers again and dialled each of them in turn. No answer from D or ZC. He tried BI. This time he let it ring, ten, eleven times. Just as he was giving up, BI answered.

He recognised the voice immediately, it was Anna, the receptionist at BitterCrest. Eliot cut the call without saying anything. At least it proved the photo wasn't an accident.

He tried MOB. No answer.

He sat on a fallen tree trunk and fiddled with the phone. Calls next. There were twenty stored. Five were to ZC, two to D, three to MOB. Of the other ten, eight were to overseas, France or Germany he thought from the code. The other two were to a London number.

Eliot scrolled through the menu pages - extras, settings, security, forwarding, messages. He didn't bother with security, Roxanne hadn't so why should he? The phone had just switched on and worked without PIN numbers or any type of code.

There were just six messages. The first one was dated 15oct 16:45 and read:

recu cou 2fil 2
max. OK ce soir

French. Great. All that time spent learning about monsieur Dupont and his bicycles was going to come in very handy. Did that mean that Roxanne was French he thought to himself as he fished about in the pockets of the jacket he had taken from the cottage, in the hope of finding pen and paper. A grubby looking hankerchief and a packet of Fishermans Friends. He would have to go back.

Jogging back through the trees towards the cottage was doing him good, relaxing his body and clearing his head. He started ordering his thoughts, attempting a reconstruction of the sequence of events.

Fact. The train crash. In the minutes before the crash he had been talking with a woman, possibly called Roxanne. A woman who had known who he was and what he did. A woman with probing, taunting questions.

Fact. Weeks later, he had seen her again, this time in a newspaper photograph standing beside Gustave Brown and Neville Draper of BitterCrest Imports, the very company Eliot was working for. Only this time the woman had long blond hair, the spiky girl who walked in the Out Door had been replaced by a cool professional business woman.

Eliot opened the gate and stepped back into the garden behind the cottage. Half an inch of snow now, the path would soon be invisible.

Fact. Something odd was happening on the Sopford Industrial

Estate. God, that was the understatement of the year. Corpses littering the place like a low budget horror film, guards administering beatings, a hotline through to the police. Gustave Brown, the accountant, as Count Dracula and ... Eliot stopped. Facts, he was trying to stick with the facts. Who owned the industrial estate?

A movement to his left stopped him in his tracks. The lower branches of a conifer on the edge of the garden were trembling. A cloud of snow fell to the ground. The gate was some five metres behind him, the shed to his left, the cottage maybe twenty metres ahead. How had they found him so quickly? He had to run but in which direction? Towards the house and he was a sitting duck all the way. Towards the woods and he would reach safety sooner but where would he go?

Another movement behind the tree. Eliot charged towards the cottage. As he ran, feet slipping on the path, he heard the sound of someone emerging from the trees. His peripheral vision told him it was someone big moving quickly, covering the ground twice as fast as he was. He had just reached the shrubs as he was hit from the side. The impact hurled him into a large bush that broke his fall and scratched his face. His assailant fell heavily on top of him. Everything became a confusion of movement during which Eliot felt hard feet kicking him and hair brushing his face.

And then it was over.

Not a person at all but a large red deer scrambling to its feet in a flurry of hooves before racing away towards the trees, snow kicking up in all directions. Having hurled colourful abuse at the animal's back, Eliot hauled himself out of the bush and continued down to the cottage.

He scribbled each of the phone messages onto a separate piece of paper then spread them out in front of him on the kitchen table. They were either in code or text message French. He looked at the first message again.

recu cou 2fil 2
max. OK ce soir

... OK this evening, that much he could read, but what did the rest mean? Cou was the French for neck. 2, deux, two. If texting worked the same way in French as in English there would be contractions, puns and graphic elements to the messages. He scribbled down the phone number from which the message had been sent. The phone code was 33, somewhere in France.

The second message was dated 23oct 12:12, eight days after the first.

26 57 93 PL WER
3 77 THIM SO

On the whole, Eliot preferred the French. The next two messages were also in code. He put them aside and moved on to the fifth piece of paper. The message was dated 05nov 00:56 and read:

ou ete tu? c pa
drole. a 2main.
jaq

The last message was in code. Eliot drummed his fingers on the desk, so much for the mobile phone.

If only her name had been in the newspaper beneath the photo, but that would have been too bloody easy, wouldn't it? As it was he had only a first name, and even that might be wrong.

As he had her phone in his hand, it was blindingly obvious that he couldn't ring her on it but there had to be some way of reaching her through her contacts, through the calls she had made or the messages she had received. He put the kettle on and paced up and down the kitchen, pausing from time to time to move the messages about, hoping inspiration would leap out at him. He had always got by on a mixture of raw intelligence and a sense of humour. Those two attributes had usually done the trick, made friends of enemies, and made difficult situations seem less difficult or less important.

But what he needed now was a degree in French. He made himself a cup of coffee, sat down and scribbled the message on a piece of paper.

ou ete tu? c pa drole. a 2main. jaq

Eliot wished that instead of mocking Cathy at the office he had spent more time watching what she was doing when she sat for hours texting her friends.

If French texting was similar to the little he knew of its English cousin, then could jaq be short for Jack? Hadn't she said Jack on the train? How was Jack spelt in French? Frère Jacques, dormez-vous, dormez-vous. With a 'c' and a 'q'? So Jacques could become Jaq.

He checked where the call had originated, another call from France.

Suddenly inspiration arrived in a flurry of car horns, flags flying. Eliot started scribbling, composing a message to Jacques. He worked in English, the translation could come later. He would pretend to be Roxanne. The key thing would be to provoke a response, to oblige him to reply. As he worked he realised that texting might work to his advantage, forget accurate spelling, just get into role and send Jacques a message so hot his phone would melt.

The words of the text began to unveil. '2main' became deux main, demain, tomorrow.

When he was happy with his message, he went upstairs in search of a French/English dictionary. Han didn't disappoint, there were dictionaries in Spanish, Italian and French. He flicked through the pages, scribbling ideas and translations as he went. Finally, having compressed and abbreviated the words into a form he hoped Jacques would understand, he keyed in the number and began crunching the letters into the mobile. It was a long shot but it was the best he had. He finished the text with a heart and a smiley face and pressed OK.

After a few seconds the phone beeped, no signal.

The path under the trees was still clear of snow but back at the cottage it was a different story, a thick white fleece hid the ground and the valley below had completely disappeared in the swirling snow.

When he reached the point where he had previously got a signal, he stopped and checked the phone. Nothing. He carried on walking. Twenty minutes later he came out the other side of the forest. The ground fell away steeply on two sides. Ahead of him was the top of the hill. He waded through the long matted grass and drifting snow. The wind had died down and the world was silent. Huge flakes of snow, without the wind to direct them, hung in the air like ash above a bonfire.

Finally the ariel icon lit up, the phone was working. He stood there, a fool on a frozen mountain in the middle of bloody nowhere, typing a sexy text message he wasn't sure made any sense into a phone belonging to someone he barely knew to a man he had never met. Did life get more surreal?

> ou e tu? tes
> olives e ton q
> me manq. Rox

Where are you? I miss your olives, and your bum. Rox.

Calculated to provoke a response. He learned that the French for bum was cul at secondary school, and the fact that it was pronounced 'q'. Eliot hoped Jacques would understand, and like the reference to the olives. Roxanne had said he was fetching olives as she sat by the pool. Of course, she had been lying through her teeth, sitting on a train in a wintery northern England, but Eliot was gambling everything on the hope that she had been drawing on a recollection of a real event.

Smiley face, heart. Send Message? OK.

The phone bleeped. It was done.

With near zero visibility it was quite impossible to say where the telephone mast must be but it didn't matter. Eliot headed back towards the shelter of the forest. A hundred metres down the path he realised his mistake and went back up the hill, that was where the signal was, so that was where he would have to wait.

So he stood in the snow, beating his arms against his chest, waiting for the phone to ring.

With time to kill, Eliot returned to facts. He tried to remember how she had looked on the train, the way her lips had formed the words 'Strawberry, Eliot?' Her bare toes brushing up against his case while she explained to someone somewhere that she was lying by a pool waiting for Jack or Jacques. He wanted to recall the shape of her eyes but couldn't even remember their colour. Green? Blue? She had smelt the strawberry before offering it, as if wishing to know its source, to know precisely where it had grown, under what sky, in what field? And, as her nostrils had flared to let in the strawberry's scent, the sapphire stud had caught the light and glinted.

Out of nowhere came an image of someone running alongside the train holding something against the window. At Doncaster station. Eliot struggled to bring the memory to the surface but it remained beyond his reach. A sixth sense told him the incident was significant, but where did it fit in?

BENEATH THE BITTERCREST

Unable to retrieve a coherent memory of the incident he returned to his facts. What was it that he knew but did not know he knew?

Facts. His business partners had taken on work with BitterCrest, and a substantial debt, without consulting him. So what? It wasn't the first time it had happened. Maybe it was Serina who ... No, stick to the facts.

Facts. He had asked Peter Han at P.S.Partners to conduct a basic search - did BitterCrest have any large debts, were they good for the money, were they on the edge of bankrupcy? Han had warned him off. Gustave Brown was a criminal. Draper had friends in high places.

Fact. Draper wanted his business dealings hidden from everyone, even the CIA. Why? Commercially available encryption software, particularly that from the States, was phenomenonly difficult to crack. True, anything available commercially would have been cleared with the national security services and they would feel confident of being able to gain access, 128 bit encryption or not.

Customising an off-the-shelf encryption package, which was more or less what Eliot had done, wouldn't create a system that was a hundred percent safe, but it would buy more time. Which was what it was all about. Encryption was a game of cat and mouse where the cat and the mouse would change sides periodically. A technical advance would occur. Suddenly an unbreakable code would exist. Mice on top. All messages secure. All cats in the dark. The cats would then wrestle with the problem against overwhelming odds while the mice basked in the certainty that the code could never be compromised. Then, a blinding moment of insight. The code was not infallible after all. It had a fatal flaw. The cat would become the mouse, the mouse the cat, and the whole game would start afresh.

Draper and Brown must know that.

What had Han said? Something about Draper wanting to play with the big boys. A fantasist who got his kicks pretending to be on the wild frontier, mixing with toffs and ex-pats one minute, employing a crook like Gustave Brown the next. Such a man might pay for encryption software for no reason other than to make himself look interesting, to impress his society friends. Eliot had seen for himself how vain and pompous he was. Aside from the initial interview, Eliot hadn't seen anything of Draper. He wasn't exactly hands on. Probably working on his golf handicap at a resort in Dubai.

Ten minutes became half an hour, became two hours. Eliot ran up and down cutting a groove in the snow, trying to keep warm. What had he been thinking? Why assume Jacques would collect his text messages immediately? And even if he did, he might not ring Roxanne for days. He might text her. He might be an ex with no desire to reopen old wounds. There might not even be a Jacques. She might have been making him up to impress the person she'd been talking to on the train. In which case who was the message on her mobile from?

His mind tumbled and turned as his body temperature dipped. Come to think of it, his assuption that the woman on the train was called Roxanne might be complete crap. Jacques might already have replied and a woman somewhere in Europe might be reading a message on a different mobile phone, wondering what on earth was going on.

He began to see how misguided he had been to come up with so crass a plan, trying to contact a woman who might or might not be called Roxanne because he couldn't think of anything else. This wasn't a game of Monopoly, there were no 'get out of jail free' cards.

He returned to his facts, the bodies stacking up. The body on wasteland. The corpse in the trunk. Han. The crematorium. The dead guards. Why had the police been so quick to threaten him? They must have known he had nothing to do with anything. Who had set him up?

The top of the hill again, for what felt like the hundredth time. He checked the phone. Clear signal, no message. The snow was almost twenty centimetres deep. Another ten minutes and he would have to admit defeat.

PC Alison Walsh looked across at the empty desk. Her shift had started at eleven with the usual ribbing from Dalton, the duty sergeant. Today it was 'you need a boyfriend' day.

'See lover boy's off. Tire him out last night, did you?'

Low level sexual harassment from dickheads like Dalton was part of the job. Walsh pretended not to hear. She carried on through to her office, the one she shared with Hampton and two other junior officers.

Hampton should have been in at eight and it was now twelve forty seven. Curiously enough, the Baker hadn't yet said a word, which was unusual, he had never previously missed an opportunity to lay into Hampton. It was also unusual for Hampton to be late, in fact she couldn't remember it ever happening before.

She took her third digestive from the box, definitely her last until five o'clock. Dipping the biscuit in her lukewarm mug of coffee, she

BENEATH THE BITTERCREST

wondered whether she should try to ring him, find out what had happened.

It was problematic because he had been courting her ever since he had arrived at the station. It wasn't that she didn't like him, he was a nice enough chap, she just wasn't ready to jump onto the relationship merry-go-round thing at the moment. It was the thought of having someone in her flat all the time, though of course, it wouldn't be her flat anymore.

Maybe her mum was right, maybe she was doomed to being a spinster. Still, she could try ringing him from the sandwich bar when she stopped for lunch.

'That report ready, Walsh?' from the open doorway.

'Almost ready, Sir.'

'On my desk by three, understood?'

'Yes, Sir.'

The phone didn't ring, it vibrated against his chest. Scared the hell out of him. Hand shaking, Eliot pulled the phone out from his jacket, pressed the green icon and put the phone to his ear.

twenty four

'Who is this?' A woman's voice thick with anger, the slightest whisper of a French accent.

'Roxanne?'

'Who the fuck are you and what are you doing with my phone?'

'It's Eliot. The train crash. Remember?'

A long silence. Has she hung up? He pictures her answering Jacques's phonecall. Jacques coming on to her, Roxanne wondering what is going on, learning about the text message, knowing she hasn't sent it. It's the logical thing do to, ring your mobile and find out who has sent the message in your name. He has been counting on it.

'What do you want, Eliot?'

'I thought you might want to join me in the pool.' Eliot brushes snow from his shoulder. 'I want to see you.'

'Not interested.'

'I think you should be. It's about Swindon.'

'A place or a person?'

'Nice try. I've a pretty photo of you with Gustave Brown. And Neville Draper. From the newspapers.'

More silence.

'It's not a good time. I'm a little tied up right now.'

'I'm sure you are. You need information. Shall we say ... five o'clock?'

He thinks he hears a conversation taking place in the background.

'Where are you?' she says eventually.

'The British Museum.'

'In the pool?' contempt in her voice.

Silence again. The temperature is dropping rapidly, Eliot is almost lost in the fog of his own breath. He clutches the phone as if his life depends on it.

'You know the Easter Island statue in the Great Court?' she asks.

'Where's that?'

'In the British Museum.' She is tiring of their game.

'I'll find it.'

Maybe Eliot has watched too many detective films. Maybe he has watched too few. In the monochrome splendour of the Great Court, with its whispering echoes, its stone facades, its massive sculptures, he imagines himself in a Hitchcock film. Every passerby a potential enemy, every passing minute taut with the ponticello scratching of melodramatic violins.

Night has fallen. He came in through the back entrance to the museum, having parked Han's car in the long stay car park beneath the YMCA building off Tottenham Court Road.

He sits on a bench, beneath the orange glow of the night sky, looking towards the Easter Island statue and the tourists drifting through the gift shops. How different this space must be in daylight, the sun pouring through the vaulted glass canopy, geometric shadows crawling slowly over stone surfaces.

Why does it feel safer to be in a crowd?

Suddenly she is there. But blond, like in the newspaper photo. Court shoes, dark blue trouser suit, white blouse with top two buttons undone, and a cashmere coat. Eliot is conscious of his tatty appearance, his lived-in look.

'Eliot, you look ...'

'Yeah, I know. The Armani Indiana Jones collection. Rough sleeper chic.'

She smiles. He is surprised how tall she is, five ten or eleven. He has previously only seen her seated on the train. Have her eyes always been blue?

'You, on the other hand,' he adds, 'look very professional. Not at all how I remember you. Your hair must grow very fast.'

She gives nothing away, makes no response.

'Are you hungry?' he asks.

'Oh, is this a date?'

Their eyes lock briefly.

'Only joking,' she says. 'I'd love a drink.'

She has a small mole, just beneath her left ear, makes her look cute.

'So which is your favourite collection?' She sips her expresso.

'My what?'

'Presumably this isn't your first visit to the British Museum?'

'No, of course not,' he answers, playing for time, struggling to remember anything the museum contains, beyond the rooms he has crossed to reach the Great Court. That would be too obvious.

'I love the African section,' she lets him off the hook for the moment. 'In the basement.'

164   christian vassie

'Right.'

'The masks. They make Picasso look like Rembrandt. Which is why he stole their ideas, I suppose.'

'Or maybe he was big enough to be influenced by them and respond to them,' Eliot replies. 'Maybe he saw the masks for what they were, great art, when everyone else still saw them as primitive.'

Roxanne looks up from her coffee, as if discovering something in Eliot she hasn't expected.

'I had a flatmate at University who studied art,' Eliot continues. 'Envied him at first. While I was hauling computer programming books around, he was visiting galleries and debating colour theory. One Sunday afternoon, he asked me to read an essay he had written on primitive art. All about how primitive people only make things in order to have a magical effect on the world. You know, prehistoric men painting animals on cave walls because they want to catch and eat whatever they have painted. His course was no freer than mine, just a different set of half-baked preconceptions.'

'Maybe there is magic to art,' she says gently.

'Sure, but this idea that people who are different to ourselves are governed by superstition, that they are incapable of seeing ... I suggested that he consider the possibility that prehistoric artists might actually have enjoyed beautiful things. Simply for being beautiful. Like us.'

Eliot stops self-consciously. Roxanne is staring at him.

'I know, I'm not an artist,' he back-peddles.

'I agree with you,' she smiles. 'About beauty.'

A man sits down nearby with his two children, one of whom promptly dives under the table and starts blowing bubbles while his dad tries catching the waiter's attention.

Eliot's heart flicks momentarily to a memory of his kids playing. 'Anyway,' he says. 'I want to tell you about Swindon, Brown and BitterCrest.'

'Sounds like a group of solicitors. I'm hungry. Let's find something to eat.'

Roxanne takes him to a small Indian restaurant in a side street off Shaftesbury Avenue, where she is on friendly terms with the management.

'Yes, of course I understand, I'll find out how much he knows.'

Eliot emerges at the far end of the restaurant, drying his hands on the back of his trousers, not having half an hour to spare waiting for the machine to dry his hands.

'Leave it with me.' Roxanne drops the mobile in her bag.

'Don't let me interrupt.' Eliot says, arriving at the table.

'An ex-boyfriend.'

'Oh.'

Eliot sits down and grabs a poppadom. His eyes light up, 'Not Max, Matt, Jack ... that's it. Not Jacques?'

Roxanne nods, disguising her relief as embarrassment.

'I haven't apologised yet. It was the only way I could think of ...'

'It doesn't matter,' she says.

'And Jacques?'

'He still has his pool. And the olives.'

They both laugh.

He lets her order, or rather he allows her to allow the chef to choose the food. A short round man who obviously enjoys his own cooking, the chef exchanges pleasantries with Roxanne. Eliot notices how easily Roxanne becomes a different person, now a considerate daughter imparting the latest news about her family, attentive, appreciative, quiet.

'So your family are all in Dorset?' Eliot says when the chef has gone.

The look she gives him is curious, weighing him up perhaps, her eyes cold and hard as flints. 'I have no family. I was just ... oh, I don't know, you work it out.'

She looks away, at people passing by outside on the street.

Eliot can't work it out. Why would a person make up stories and seemingly not mind that she is seen doing it by a third party?

The meal arrives and they eat. When Roxanne next looks at Eliot she has regained her composure.

'So tell me about your group of solicitors.'

As Eliot recounts what has happened over the past few days he is aware that he is sanitising his story. He is too traumatised to question why this might be or, indeed, what the events are that he is choosing to omit. For his benefit? For hers?

Roxanne appears preoccupied, not at all as he remembers her. Her blue eyes, which saw right through him on the train, seem somehow not as he remembers them, constantly shifting as if expecting trouble.

She pays great attention to what he and Peter Han found in the lower levels beneath the single storey building, asking him numerous questions about the layout of the place, the security, and how they gained access.

'So, enough about me,' Eliot sips what is left of his Chianti. 'What about you? What is your involvement with Gustave Brown? Are you in business with him? Is it love? Shall I get another bottle?'

Roxanne nods. Eliot catches the waiter's eye and waves the empy bottle.

'Tell me first about these men you found,' she says. 'On the wasteland and in the crate. How were they dressed?'

'In light summer clothing. Like the man I saw the guards beating up. That's why I thought they might be immigrants.'

'Where from?'

'Han asked me the same question. I don't know. Mediterranean? Middle East? North Africa? I don't know.'

Again that look in her eyes. Sorrow perhaps? Regret? She smiles.

'There's someone I'd like you to meet,' she says.

'When?'

'Now.'

'Yes, why not?'

The waiter arrives with the Chianti.

'We'll take it with us,' Eliot says, offering his credit card.

Roxanne gives him a look.

He leaves the Chianti on the table.

'Tell Kuldip the food was excellent,' Roxanne says to the waiter at the door.

Her car is parked at a meter in one of the side streets just south of the Museum, a dark Saab convertible. She presses her keys, the doors click. She pulls open the passenger door.

'There you go.' That smile again.

Eliot bends his head to climb into the car, doesn't notice the two men approaching quickly from the shadows nor Roxanne's nervous glance in their direction. But he does feel the cosh that kisses the back of his head goodnight and he falls into the car like skittles tumbling in a bowling alley.

'Sorry, Eliot,' she says.

His head feels like it has gone ten rounds with Iron Mike Tyson. A lump the size of the St Paul's dome throbs on the back of his head, and his ears are ringing the changes like for a royal wedding. Eliot, eyes still closed, senses that he is slumped over in a chair and that his limbs are uncomfortable. He tries opening an eye. A harsh white light slashes at his retina with all the finesse of a pickaxe.

'I don't think so. He told me everything.' A woman's voice.

'I didn't ask you to think.'

'I'm simply saying ...'

'Get her out of here.'

The voices drift in and out of focus, Eliot's head is swimming, rolling over and over. He doesn't get drunk very often but, when he does, he does so properly. For a moment he thinks he recognises the woman's voice. It can only be a matter of seconds before he falls off the chair, the rate the room is spinning. Male voices only now, low and conniving.

'She's a liability. We can't risk everything for the sake of some flash ... totty.'

'And you yourself are an exemplar of probity?'

The voice continues less confidently than before. 'But someone has to tell ...'

'Spare me.'

A liquid banging sound drowns out the conversation. Something is bobbing up and down. Eliot's nose is itching but his hands don't work.

Alarm bells start ringing in Eliot's head. He opens his mouth to speak but instead of words he hears only a distant moan. A trickle of saliva dribbles down his chin. If only he wasn't so tired, he might somehow find the energy to stand up. Stand and be counted, his old headmaster used to say.

His bum won't leave the seat, like he is stuck to it. He becomes aware of other sounds below the arguing voices. Water gently lapping. An engine humming. Through his closed eyelids he senses the direction of the light. He turns away from the light and squints. The image is blurred and distorted but he understands that he is looking towards an open window through which the bare branches of tall trees are silhouetted against the night sky. The window frame is of metal and has rounded corners. His head is swimming again and he has to close his eyes.

They have windows like that in caravans. And on boats.

He is on a boat.

What is he doing on a boat? He tries to think back, to retrace his steps, to access a decision, but finds he can not. There is only the boat, the lapping water, the engine purring. And the voices. He drifts unhappily into unconsciousness.

When he next comes round, the boat is rocking from side to side. The engine is straining, its note lost in the sound of the water lapping against the sides. Presently the engine throb dies down to be replaced by the sound of someone exerting themselves, followed by the sound of something heavy hitting something hollow. The boat starts to judder. The boat is being pulled towards the shore. Which shore? Where?

A door opens and he is lifted into the air, still on his chair. The air out on deck is cold. Footsteps clatter on a wooden deck. Eliot loses consciousness again.

Carrying Eliot, gagged and bound to his chair, the two men descend the gangplank to the jetty and, from there, up towards the house. Gravel crunches underfoot as they make their way up the winding path towards a pair of French windows that open as they draw close.

'Over there.'

Eliot is carried inside and lowered, none too gently.

'Remove the gag, and revive him a little.'

Fade out, fade in. A slight prick in his arm, maybe an insect has bitten him. His face is wet and his wrists ache. He was on a train when everything started to shake and cases flew past his head. And a baby. Oh shit, the baby ...

'Slap his face.'

Eliot tries opening his eyes. The light is too bright.

'Shut eye,' he drawls. 'Just let me sleep.'

'You have been in the wars, Balkan.' The voice is soft but hard, whatever that means.

'Ha ha. Very funny.' Eliot mumbles.

'Is he capable of opening his eyes?'

'Oh yes,' answers another voice. 'And quite capable of speaking. He simply needs a little encouragement.'

'Fine. Offer him encouragement.'

Eliot recognises the voice though he cannot place it. A slap hard across the face, followed by another.

'Wakey, wakey.'

Footsteps retreating. Eliot lifts his eyelids. Everything is blurred, like a Cubist vision of movement, sight splintered by a dozen perspectives.

'Ah, at last.'

Does he recognise the voice?

'I'm sorry it has come to this,' the voice says. 'But you don't know when to stop. You've been a great disappointment.'

'Goodnight,' Eliot says, smiling to himself.

'I don't have time for the pantomime villain routine so you'll forgive me for getting to the point. You poked your snout about yesterday, damaging two of the staff and causing serious mishap to your accomplice. Who have you spoken to today?'

'That woman.'

'Who else?'

'Who else?'

Eliot seems to have little control over the words he is uttering. But, in spite of his condition, or maybe because of it, he feels alert now. An out of body experience. As a student he took LSD a couple of times and now, deep within himself, he understands that he is experiencing a drug induced state. While it is frightening to hear words coming out of his mouth and to have little control of them, Eliot draws comfort from the knowledge that his current state is almost certainly temporary and that, sooner or later, he will regain control, if he stays alive long enough.

'I asked you who else you spoke to today?'

'No-one. I spoke to no-one.'

'Who else knows about what you saw?'

'Han does.'

'Han is dead.'

'Yes, Han is dead.' Eliot hears himself agreeing.

His eyes are still drifting in and out of focus. A grandfather clock ticks languidly. Two light coloured sofas leer at each other across a low table. A painting slouches against the wall. Bright colours with lots of lines and blobs. A vase with flowers perhaps? Or maybe something abstract? On a sofa is a blond. A woman with breasts?

'Listen to me, Eliot,' the voice peers into Eliot's eyes.

Eliot rests his head against the back of the chair. Concentrate, concentrate. Don't talk to him. Don't answer him. Who is he? Who is that woman?

'Where were you last night?'

'Swindon.'

No, don't answer him. Too late. It's Roxanne. My love. Sitting. Over there.

'After you broke in. Where were you then?' the voice urging, coaxing.

'Bitch.' Eliot says, keeping his gaze on the woman.

That's it, keep your mind on her. Tell him nothing. Fight him.

'Where were you? Who were you with?'

'Car. I was a car. And you're shit.' He laughs, very pleased with his wit.

His reward a slap across the head. He has got under the voice's skin and it feels good. A damp smell lingers in the air.

'He's resisting me,' the voice yells.

'No, he can't,' someone replies. 'He's confused. You simply have to ...'

'Shut up.' Screaming now.

There is a slight pause. The second voice starts again, hesitantly.

'It is possible that ... '

'I don't want possibilities. I want results.'

Another injection. Eliot feels himself fading away. How long his mind drifts in and out of consciousness he has no idea, only the vaguest feeling that people are talking behind his back, and that one of those people is possibly himself.

The sound of a door opening rouses him.

'Yes?'

'We have to go.' A new, male voice.

'Right.'

Eliot opens his eyes and sees a hand reaching out towards Roxanne. Like in a dream. Is it her?

'Take care of that for me,' the voice demands.

A number of people leave. As 'Roxanne' passes by him, Eliot lifts his head.

'I hope ... you're so ... bloody ...,' he drawls.

Her eyes are cold, a predator's eyes. Then, for a brief instant, Eliot fancies the glare softens, a flicker of compassion, before she shakes her head disdainfully and turns away.

Eliot remains with those who stay behind. He is carried back onto the boat still tied to his chair. Eyes open this time, Eliot notices two monkey puzzle trees, on either side of the garden just before the jetty. The cold air revives him. He takes in the two men carrying him, dark suits, cropped hair, moustaches, like Basingstoke bouncers. They probably wear trainers, he guesses.

BENEATH THE BITTERCREST   171

As they put him down in the back of the boat, Eliot sees they do indeed wear trainers. White trainers, dark suits. Says it all.

A small rowing boat dangles in the air behind the boat. Eliot knows nothing about river boats, beyond watching them pass the riverside pubs at Barnes and Sheen of a summer evening. He knows you have to steer them with one hand on the wheel, the other round a glass of bubbly, and that you have to talk very loudly so that those without boats can turn their heads and appreciate your passing. He cannot imagine what a small boat might be for.

The boat heads for the middle of the river. After maybe four or five minutes one of the men comes aft and starts to winch the small boat down towards the water. The gentle lapping of the water merges with the quiet throb of the engine.

It is disorientating in the middle of a river at night. Lights on the river bank are the only clue as to where the river is. The river is where the lights are not or, rather, where the lights are liquid reflections writhing like snakes on oil. Eliot's eyes are focusing now and he is aware that the boat is turning, slipping and sliding, fighting the current. A couple of minutes pass and the riverbanks are back on either side of the boat. As they should be. A splash as the small boat hits the water. The driver, pilot, captain whatever he is, cuts the engine and Eliot hears a new sound, a rushing of water, a wall of white noise on the edge of hearing.

Suddenly two sets of hands are on him, loosening the ropes that tie him to the chair. They are letting him go. Waves of euphoria sweep through him.

'Thank you,' he mutters.

One of the men laughs.

Eliot tries to stand up but his body is still numb, or paralysed, or whatever. Just as well he doesn't have to walk. They will help him.

They lift him up and lower him into the small boat. One of the men tosses in a couple of oars.

'So long, sailor.'

They loosen the rope securing the small boat to the larger one and push. Lying in the bottom of the rowing boat, Eliot watches the gap grow between the two vessels. Gratitude mingles with confusion. The larger boat's engine starts up again. The gap grows wider.

As the engine noise fades, Eliot becomes aware again of the white noise sound. Confusion mingles with fear. He has to get his arms and legs working.

Sitting down in front of the telly with favourite house makeover programme, PC Alison Walsh is still thinking about Hampton. A ping from the microwave. She pauses the video and slippers out to the kitchen to fetch her meal, thai curry with sticky rice.

By the time she returns with her tray, the local news has started. Walsh sits on the sofa, her food on her knees. The sound is off but the image is clear enough. A mangled red Volvo on its roof at the foot of an embankment. She knows instantly that it isn't any old red Volvo, it is Hampton's red Volvo. She grabs the phone and rings the station.

The boat is moving more quickly now. Eliot can just make out the silhouettes of the trees against the slightly lighter black of the sky. The noise is increasing exponentially. There is no mistaking the source of the noise, even in his drugged out state Eliot knows where he is heading. A weir, a waterfall, a drop of some sort or another, and it is getting closer all the time. Eliot tries sitting up, he can't. He tries rolling over, he manages that. He is on his side now. He tries reaching out with his free hand towards the side of the boat, if he can grab the boat somehow he might be able to pull himself up. His arm moves but nowhere near far enough. What have they given him?

Concentrate.

The noise of falling water is beginning to drown out all other sounds. Time is against him. Maybe the boat will simply jam up against a barrier and he will stay there, ears drowning in the noise, until he freezes to death. That or fly over the edge and crash down onto whatever lies below. Desperately he focuses his energy on just moving one hand. Surely, one hand cannot be too much to ask.

But it is. It is as if his skeleton has been extracted, leaving his limbs as limp as jellyfish. He cannot even lift his head to see what is coming.

That's it then. He has trusted his instincts, invested his hopes in a woman he met on a train, and this is his reward. Death on the Thames. It's not a mistake he'll be repeating.

The boat hits something. Hard. The cacophony of the water is deafening. A grinding splintering of wood. The boat starts to list and turn, pulling further and further onto its side. Eliot can see the oily black surface of the river, deeply furrowed where the undercurrent sucks the water down into itself. Still, at least he won't be freezing to death, he will be drowning, which is less time consuming generally.

BENEATH THE BITTERCREST

As the boat continues to tip onto its side, Eliot finds himself beginning to slide down towards the water, helpless to prevent it. A steady trickle of water coming over the bow. The smell of weed and silt fills his nostrils.

'Just get it bloody over with,' he shouts at the night.

He wonders if the fact that his limbs are beyond his control is removing the fear of death. Separated from his body, he is only a few short steps from joining the angels, just the formalities to complete. His only real regret at that moment is that he still does not know what is going on and that his pathetic efforts to make sense of his situation, and Han's death, have been such a total bloody waste of time.

The freezing water is sloshing against his ear. In his frustration, he kicks his leg out. It smashes against the bow, jarring his leg and splashing water about.

His leg has moved! Maybe the drug is wearing off. He tries kicking again. More controlled movement this time. The water is over his ear and brushing up against his eye. But it is too little too late, by the time his body is free of the drug there will be no-one there to use it.

'I tell you, it's Hampton's car.'

'Do I have to tell you how many red Volvos there are out there?' Dalton says.

Alison hears another voice, sniggering, in the background. It sounds like Rutland.

'All right, how about sending a squad car to see if his car is outside his house?'

'There's only two of us on tonight. I understand you are very familiar with the drive to his house of an evening.'

'Ha bloody ha.'

Alison cuts the call and counts to ten. How can an entire police station be left in the hands of such talent?

Maybe her mum is right on both counts; she will end up a spinster, and policing is no job for a lady. She puts her tray back in the kitchen, food untouched, grabs her keys and heads for the front door.

Eyes closed, Eliot submits to the moment. So this is what death feels like, peaceful and serene, light as air. As if carried by strong arms and lifted away from the noise and pain of life. Freed from suffering and fear. He relaxes and slips from consciousness.

twenty five

Eliot clamps his hand over his eyes and waits for the coloured sparks dancing on the backs of his eyelids to fade. His head throbs painfully and every muscle in his body aches. When finally he opens his eyes again, it is with his hand shielding them, spreading his fingers just wide enough to form an impression of his surroundings.

The room is off-white bare walls. For furniture, a bed and a chair, over which hang several articles of clothing, presumably his. He looks down and finds that he is wrapped in a nondescript grey blanket. The memory of an ill-advised last minute package holiday in Buccarest comes to mind.

Intriguingly, there are iron bars on the window, Romanian city break it is then. Eliot lifts his head to look at the door. His body feels like it has done service as a dummy in a crash test. When eventually his eyes focus on the door, he sees that it too is heavily reinforced. Before he can dwell on this, a key rattles in the lock. The door swings open and Eliot finds himself face to face with yet another British bobby. What is it with him and the police?

'How are we feeling?'

'We feel crap. What are we doing here?'

'We were hoping you might tell us.' A large chubby man in his late fifties, with a full moustache, the policeman's relaxed demeanour gives the impression that most of his career has been spent in sleepy shires villages following up missing bottles of milk and cats stuck in lilac trees.

'Where am I?'

'Ah, now that one is more my cup of tea. This is Guildford police station and you are a very lucky man, Mr ...?'

'I've found recently that when I'm told I'm very lucky the reverse is usually true. Eliot Balkan.'

'DI Havering,' the policeman identifies himself. 'Well, Mr Balkan. You were brought in on a drunk and disorderly. Appears you chose last night for a little pleasure boating. Unusual weather for it, especially for a man who's had a good night out, if you follow my drift. Lucky for you, two lads out walking the dog spotted you about to go over the weir, or your little escapade might have ended very

BENEATH THE BITTERCREST
175

badly.' He claps his hands together, as if keen to put the unpleasantness behind him. 'Anyway. Cup of tea? Then we can deal with the formalities. Before we go to church, eh?' Havering winks.

'Milk, no sugar. Thanks.'

The door closes. Church? Is it Sunday? Has he been drunk?

Slowly fragments of the previous night begin to jigsaw together, the betrayal, the house, the interrogation, the boat.

The formalities, which take place in Havering's small but very tidy office, involve Eliot giving his home address and telephone number, proof of identification, and proof of ownership of the boat he has been found in.

His recent experience of the police, this being his second night in a cell in just a few days, suggests extreme caution but Eliot feels at ease with Havering's friendly village bobby persona. He has given his real name already and now he adds his real address. He cannot however provide even the most rudimentary description of the boat he was found in.

'No problem, Mr Balkan,' says Havering, stroking his moustache in a manner that suggests otherwise. 'I'll give you one of these chits. You'll need to visit the police station you nominate, within four days, and supply the relevant paperwork.'

Eliot has almost no memories of his father, barely knew him but, if he had, he would like those memories to be of a man like Havering. Which explains why, in spite of everything, he is comfortable telling Havering what has happened. Not the whole story but starting from being carried into the house on the chair.

Havering listens patiently and politely.

'Tell me, would you recognise the house if you saw it again?'

'In the back garden, near the jetty, there were two monkey puzzle trees. You know the tall spindly ...'

'I am familiar with araucaria.' Havering taps his finger on the desk. 'Yes.' More moustache tugging. 'Righty ho. Oh, I almost forgot.' He pulls a box towards him. 'Your property. Had to check your pockets last night when they brought you in.'

Havering passes Eliot's keys and his sodden wallet across the desk.

'I was a little intrigued by this.'

In his hands Havering holds a plastic bag containing several sheets of paper. He waits for Eliot to speak.

'Something I found,' Eliot says eventually.

'Mind if I take photocopies? For the record.'

Eliot shrugs his assent.

The riverside houses stop about half a kilometre from the weir. Havering has called in a favour, and a boat has been made available. A couple of junior officers have been left at the station 'holding the fort'.

The sun is out, for the first time in more than two weeks. A crisp light blue sky reflects back off the rippling water as they make their way upstream. Eliot, Havering and another policeman with curly blond hair and an irritating habit of sniffing every few seconds, sit at the back of the boat, legs stretched out.

Each house has its own jetty and the morning sunshine has brought the river folk out. Navy jumpers, up on the decks of their boats, polishing, preening, giving their sunglasses an airing. Monaco sur Thames. Every now and then Havering waves at one of the middle-aged Captain Nemos, exchanging a few words across the water until they move out of earshot.

One elderly boatman is even wearing a nautical hat.

'Ahoy there,' the old boy shouts cheerily from what is, objectively, a fairly tatty craft not much bigger than a dingy.

'Morning,' Havering answers, waving genially. He turns towards Eliot. 'No idea who he is, but best stay on good terms with the admiralty, eh.' He winks.

The sun, the gentle lapping of the water against the bows, and the good humour around him, lull Eliot to the point at which he almost fails to recognise the house as they pass it.

'There. The trees.'

'Got you,' Havering turns to his friend. 'Could we turn her round and pull up at that jetty over there, Stanley?'

Stanley does as he is asked.

They are in the act of tying the boat up when a man in his late sixties, wearing beige trousers, a checked shirt, cravatte and cardigan, appears on the path from the house.

'This is private property.'

'Quite so.' Havering says, stepping from the boat. He walks briskly towards the man, hand out to shake hands. 'A few quick questions. D.I. Havering, Guildford police.'

'Has there been another break in?'

'Break in?'

BENEATH THE BITTERCREST   177

'Two boats last week. They took everything that wasn't nailed down.'

'No, no, nothing like that,' Havering reassures him. 'Might we go inside?'

The man raises his eyebrows, weighing up the consequences of a refusal, then, thinking better of it, turns and leads them in, past the monkey puzzle trees and up the path to the house. One of a pair of French windows is ajar. They troop inside to find themselves in a pub lounge bar.

'Ah,' Havering looks at Eliot. 'I had understood this to be a private residence.'

'It is. This is the boys' room. Come back here after golf for a bit of peace and quiet. No girls allowed. Care for a tipple?'

Over the bar, among the pewter tankards, is a page from the Guildford Echo, framed in gold. The photo at the top of the page shows a man in his early fifties, wearing waders and clutching a large salmon. 'Brian Eastfield shows off winning fish', the caption reads.

'That was a fish and a half, I can tell you,' Eastfield says, pouring himself a double measure of whisky from one of the upturned bottled behind the bar. 'Any other takers?'

Eliot shakes his head, as does Havering. The other policeman stands sniffing by the window.

'So, what's up?' Eastfield settles on one of his bar stools.

'Do you have a grandfather clock?' Havering asks, reading from his notebook.

'Why? Has it been caught chasing women on the high street?' Eastfield laughs at his own wit, laughs alone.

'Might we see it?' Havering continues.

'Of course.' Eastfield leads them through into a large lounge.

'Very nice.' Havering looks about him at the lavish furniture and soft furnishings. 'Very nice indeed, Mr Eastfield.'

'The product of hard graft,' Eastfield says defensively.

'This is it,' Eliot interrupts. 'This is where they interrogated me. Look the two sofas, the clock, everything.'

'You're sure?' Havering pressed him.

'Do you mind telling me what this is about?'

'And you said they brought you in straight from the garden?' Havering continues, ignoring Eastfield.

'I'm not sure, I was barely conscious, but I left through there,' Eliot answers, pointing at a sliding door that led out onto the patio.'

'I demand to know what is going on. And if I don't get an answer, I shall be obliged to ask you to leave,' bellows Eastfield.

Havering turns to face him. 'Would you care to tell us what you were doing last night?' he speaks calmly. 'Between the hours of, say, eight pm and one am?'

'What is this about?'

'Last night?' Havering prompts.

'We were out. With friends.'

'Until what time?'

'Two or three in the morning.'

'He must be a friend of Brown's, or someone else,' Eliot interjects.

'Mr Balkan, please.'

'Well, ask him.'

'I will conduct this interview, if you don't mind.' Havering turns back towards Eastfield. 'Can you prove your whereabouts last night? Where were you exactly, Sir?'

Eastfield hesitates. 'At the dogs,' he says eventually, looking at the floor. 'The wife enjoys a flutter. Nothing wrong with that.' He looks up defiantly.

'Indeed, nothing at all. We can't go to the opera every night, can we?' Havering says effortlessly. 'And, when you drove home ...'

'I didn't drive. We took a taxi.'

'Very commendable. As I was saying, when you came home, did you find everything in order?'

Again Eastfield hesitates, removes his glasses, makes a show of cleaning them.

'Do you or your wife smoke Gitanes?' says the curly haired policeman.

They all turn towards the sliding doors.

'Found these dog ends in the plant pot. Looks like someone has been doing a spot of cleaning by the door. I'll bag them for Forensics.'

'All right, look,' Eastfield decides to switch stories.

Smiling, Havering produces his notebook.

'We forgot to put the alarm on when we left last night. A few drinks too many perhaps. When we came back we found a broken vase and mud on the floor. By the window. She thought the dog must have done it. The insurance for this place is a bloody fortune and the vase was only a cheap bit of tat. No other damage, so I cleaned up this morning. If we tell the insurers, our premium will ...'

'Say no more, Mr Eastfield, we quite understand. So, it is possible

BENEATH THE BITTERCREST

that a person or persons might have had access to your house during the course of the evening?'

'Yes, I suppose it is.'

'Fine.' Havering closes the notebook. 'That will be all then ...'

Eastfield brightens.

'What about Brown?' Eliot protests.

'... for the moment,' Havering continues, ignoring Eliot.

Eastfield's gloom returns. Havering hands him a slip of paper.

'If you could arrange for these to reach me at the station: proof of your whereabouts yesterday evening, names of those who can vouch for you, and confirmation from the taxi company that you didn't drive yourself, to or from the dogs.' He made a meal of the last two words, smiling pleasantly all the while.

Eastfield stuffs the slip of paper in one of the pockets of his cardigan.

'We'll see ourselves out. Enjoy the sunshine, Mr Eastfield.'

They troop back down the path, Eastfield watching them go, tumbler of whisky in hand.

'Haul anchor, lower the topsail,' Havering shouts happily once they are all aboard.

The boat pulls away from the jetty.

'Turn her about, Skipper,' Havering orders, plainly enjoying his day out.

They head back downstream.

'I want you to organise a little phone tap and some surveillance, Andrew,' he says to the curly haired policeman. 'If Eastfield so much as farts, I want a written report.'

Andrew wanders down the other end of the boat, mobile phone pressed to his ear. Eliot and Havering sit down on the bench at the back of the boat.

'So, Lad, I need to understand more about why you were abducted. How did you get that damage to your wrist? What did you see in Swindon that might have provoked this response? By the way, here's my card, if you should want to get in touch.'

Eliot takes Havering's business card and trousers it. An alarm bell sounds in his head, he can't recall saying anything to Havering about Swindon. Did he say something the last night when he was brought in to the police station?

'I've no idea. I met this woman in London. We went for a meal and she set me up. I was suckered, that's all.'

'Are you married?'

'Why? Oh, I see.'

Eliot studies the other man's face. Havering stares back, his eyes showing only concern, one man to another.

In other circumstances, Eliot might either volunteer further information, or tell Havering his sex life is none of his business, or make a wisecrack, but recents events have finally begun to erode Eliot's sense of the order of things. The memory of the dark freezing waters of the weir rising up about his face is too fresh in his mind.

Aside from his current domestic situation life has, in truth, pampered Eliot. It hasn't all been laughs and bunjee jumps but, on the other hand, there has been no famine, war, plague, rape or destitution. Now everything is in flux. The stonework is crumbling and behind the facade is a dirtier, less scrupulous world, one that thinks nothing of breaking laws, terror, even murder.

Who are the good guys and who the bad?

In this new world Eliot no longer has confidence in his ability to make the kind of judgements his situation demands. He needs time to collect his thoughts, adjust to the new rules, work out a game plan, a survival plan.

Eliot smiles at Havering and says nothing. Let him think whatever he wants.

The two men sit in silence watching the riverside houses slowly drifting by.

PC Alison Walsh sits in bed with her breakfast tray on her knees. Some cartoon featuring martians is playing on the television across the room but her attention lies elsewhere. In her mind's eye she sees only the empty space in front of Hampton's flat. She has checked every vehicle in the carpark. No red Volvo.

Maybe he has gone off for the weekend. Maybe he has found some woman and gone off to Margate, or similar, for a dirty weekend. The chances are that, if she makes another fuss at the station, she will end up a bloody laughing stock. He isn't worth it, none of them is.

twenty six

'A last word of advice, Lad. You'd be well advised to stay low, out of the public gaze for the moment. Is there somewhere ...' Havering rubs his nose.

'I'll be the needle in the haystack,' Eliot reassures him.

Two hours later, heading west along the M40, having picked up Han's car in London, Eliot is in altogether better spirits. Detective Inspector Havering appears to have accepted Eliot's story, and has contented himself with a request that Eliot return to Guildford in three days time to give a fuller statement. The afternoon's crucial FA Cup tie has been the clinching factor, no-one seems overly interested in spending the afternoon at the station doing overtime .

The day has run it course and, above the embers of a cold sunset, a thin fistful of clouds skids in a whisper across the moon's path, concealing it, revealing it. Mist clings to the low lying fields. As Eliot drives, the night thickens and the beam from his headlamps grows brighter. Stopping to fill up on diesel, he draws a few hundred pounds from a cash machine, no point leaving a transaction trail too close to where he is planning to spend the night.

Promising to stay out of the limelight doesn't necessarily mean sitting on his hands and Eliot has come to the conclusion that Han was very selective in what he told him about BitterCrest, Brown and Draper. The dossier Han showed him, with its handful of Inland Revenue forms and import/export licences, can only be a fraction of the evidence Han collected. Han, by his own admission, spent years tracking Brown, surely somewhere in the cottage Eliot will find further incriminating evidence.

It is as cold inside the cottage as out, his breath fogging the chill air. Eliot finds a few carrots and a loaf of bread in the fridge. Having eaten, he changes the dressing on his wrist and swallows a few painkillers.

He trudges upstairs and sits down in front of Han's desk, ducking to avoid the low beam. The computer boots up noisily and for fifteen minutes Eliot searches through files and folders, without any success. No passwords, no secrets, just a fairly ordinary collection of letters to friends, various solitaire card games, and a folder full of stuff to do with astronomy, apparently Han was an amateur star gazer.

Another hour passes as Eliot goes from room to room, opening every cupboard, every drawer, searching for Han's work files.

Nothing.

And yet when he first arrived at the cottage Han had a dossier waiting for him.

Shaking from cold and exhaustion, Eliot finds a bed. He lies there, too tired to sleep, his mind racing back and forth, police cells, bodies, shouting dogs, dank rooms and an Easter Island statue. Has he told the Guildford police too much or too little? What will happen when Havering discovers Eliot has links to a murder enquiry? How long will it be before Han's body is found? How has he so totally misread Roxanne?

A woman who changes skin as effortlessly as a chameleon, who lies as effortlessly as others breathe, how has he convinced himself that she would be on his side? Just like he convinced himself that Sue loved him and that he and she, and the kids, would always be together.

One born every day.

No, it might take weeks, months, but it will happen. The key is to ride the flow and not fight it. He will send the kids cards. Not presents. How he hated the presents his father sent when he was a child. Never a word or a visit, just the occasional lavish present from an exotic country where he was stationed. Even at the age of five Eliot saw through that one. Buying love. All he ever wanted were words, words he could hide under his pillow and read over and over, to pretend his dad was coming home. He remembers afternoons, after school, spent writing 'mum, I love you so much' on dozens of bits of paper, littering the house with them, everyone worth a hug or a smile. As precious as jewels. He would have given up all his toys for a note like that from his dad.

Rain. Eliot lies there in the dark, listening to the rain peppering the window pane, hearing rhythms in the raindrops. In the morning he will have another go on the computer, work through all the evidence he and Han accumulated; the photos, addresses, receipts taken from the discarded clothes. He will write down what he knows, then send a copy of everything to the Guildford police before ...

BENEATH THE BITTERCREST

Detective Inspector Havering removes his reading glasses and rubs his temples.

'Cup of tea, David?'

'Thank you, Darling.'

'Everything all right?'

Havering looks up at his wife. Niveen is a good woman. He toys momentarily with the idea of discussing his anxieties with her, then thinks better of it. She accepts his tired smile and heads off towards the boiling kettle.

Has he made a mistake? Rather than letting Eliot Balkan go, should he have kept him in his cell until he was prepared to speak? On what charge? They have enough to do without locking up each and every passing drunk. On the other hand, what was the man doing with a plastic bag containing papers detailing the activites of a human smuggling ring? Written in Arabic, if you please.

Memories of a different time trouble the surface of his thoughts. Appearances are deceptive and, far from always having been a village bobby, the now rotund Havering remembers his military service in the Gulf in the late sixties and early seventies. A cacophony of memories he has fought so hard to banish from his conscious mind.

Going 'up country' in the British Protectorates, sniping, blowing up civilians, arson, torture. Both sides as bad as each other. Of course, it did not seem quite like that at the time. Shoot the wogs first before they shoot you. Plots, counter plots, dirty tactics, dirty war. Grenades, bullets and bombs. And a defining moment, when he saw a child run over by a Landrover, heard the drink-addled cheering of his countrymen, saw the tatty dogs emerge from the shadows and tear the dead infant limb from limb.

That was when he learnt to doubt the easy truths of those in power.

So he learnt Arabic, learnt to speak with the people who ironed his shirts and brought him tea, and later, when he visited Egypt towards the end of his time in the middle east, Havering fell in love with a Coptic Christian girl in Cairo. Brought her to a new life in England. Over twenty five years ago.

'Don't wait till it gets cold.' Niveen puts the tea on the occasional table beside his armchair.

Only when she has left the room does Havering reread the handwritten pages in which a man asks for forgiveness from his family for leaving them, promises to find work and send money, pledges to do all in his power to bring them safely to Europe. A letter that has never been sent, all detailed in a crisp neat hand. Who is the author? How have the papers come into Eliot Balkan's possession?

On the back of one of the photocopied sheets, Havering has scribbled down the text written in ball point pen onto the plastic bag.

phangbrown-23526102

Has Eliot Balkan written this? If not, then who has?

Havering is no fool. He knows that Eliot's story of finding the bag is cock and bull. The key is concealed in the text itself, either the marks on the bag are incidental to the contents or they in some way identify the contents.

He starts on the numbers. If the writer intended to identify the contents it is resonable to assume that the date or the time or both are labelled.

Working backwards there seems to be a date, 26th January 2002, which would be two days previously.

235. Is that the time at which the label was written? Half past eleven? 11.05 pm?

Or maybe nothing to do with the time at all.

It occurs to Havering that the text also shows something else. He wonders why he hasn't thought of it sooner. Whoever wrote the text is plainly organised and used to organising information. The plastic bag is in all probability an evidence bag produced by someone who is used to using or creating such items.

A policeman? A detective?

Havering sips at his now lukewarm cup of tea. He hears Niveen heading up to bed.

p hang brown. Could that be it? He scribbles the words that can be found within the letters. Hang. An. Brown. Own. If he were writing the text it would list either a place or a person or both, either identifying who has done the finding or the owner of the item. The only obvious name he can see is Brown.

It comes to him in a flash, a mixture of intuition, insight and memory. Surnames and first name initials. G. Brown and P. Han.

Havering knows a P. Han, not as a personal acquaintance, but by reputation.

The chap caused many ripples in the force, his sacking did not pass unnoticed. Peter Han played a prominent role in exposing the failings of the Fraud Squad in the Eighties and as a result made friends and

BENEATH THE BITTERCREST

enemies for himself in equal measure.

An abrasive man with a skin thicker than a rhinoceros.

He needed one. It took balls to take on the Fraud Squad. Not a job calculated to lead to a comfortable pension. Notorious investigations, into profiteering, pornography, smuggling, protection rackets and money laundering. Han in the thick of it, painting a picture of corruption on such a vast scale that it was hard for the public to believe there was a single copper who wasn't on the take.

That was his mistake, he alienated the good along with the bad. Many coppers, Havering counts himself among them, initially saw a great deal to be commended in Han's persistence even if he did, occasionally, bend noses out of joint or make a fool of himself but, by the time Han was transferred back to normal duties, everyone had tired of the pleasure he seemed to take from giving the press ammunition to throw at the force. Demoralising was the word.

So what is Han doing now?

As far as Havering remembers Peter Han spent the Nineties in one of the county forces, tilting at windmills, trying to regain his reputation for big stories, with less and less success. Even the press have abandoned him. Han is rumoured to have left the force and done what many ex policemen do in his situation, go private. Join a parkering agency or set one up.

Havering slips the papers into his briefcase. In the morning he will make a few calls.

It takes an age to realise that the noise belongs beyond his dream. Having woken up and made sense of where he is, it takes another age to understand the source of the buzzing vibration. A mobile phone is rattling against a torch at the bottom of the rucksack propped up against the bed.

'Sweet dreams?'

'What?'

'I hope you've had breakfast.'

'Roxanne. Listen, next time you want to kiss me good night, I prefer the lips to the leather cosh.'

'I'm sorry.'

'Great, let's both be sorry then. What's the time?'

'That's why I rang, you have to leave right away.'

She sounds genuinely anxious, it is a good performance.

'You almost had me there.'

'I'm serious,' she insists. 'They know where you are.'

'Who they?'

'Never mind who. They know you survived the river.'

'I didn't just survive, I now have my hundred metres freestyle certificate. Anyway, what's with the tip off?'

'Let's just say I owe you one.'

'OK. So tell me, why would ...'

'There isn't time. Just hurry and get away.'

The line goes dead.

Eliot listens to the sounds of the cottage, the hairs on the back of his neck bristling. Nothing but the slow hollow ticking of the grandfather clock below.

Parting the bedroom curtains a little, he peers out. The snow has gone. A thin cold rain falls, blurring the valleys, clinging to the lank grass, soaking the stone walls. A robin hops along the path that leads back down towards the road. In the middle distance a tractor hauls a trailer of huge round straw bales towards a cowshed. The dark clouds seem so low as to be resting on the treetops.

He crosses to the second window, looking through the narrow gap in the curtains down onto Han's parked car and the track that leads down to the road. The only movement is that of slow fat water droplets crashing down from the blocked guttering onto the gravel. How on earth can anyone know where he is?

A movement in the periphery of his vision. The track seems empty but there is a dip, maybe twenty metres from the road.

The roof becomes visible first, maybe sixty metres away, bright red, a car perhaps? As the vehicle comes into view, Eliot lets go of the curtain. Not a car, a van. The postman. Major bloody panic over nothing. He drops the phone in the rucksack which he slings over his shoulder and heads downstairs to find breakfast.

The kitchen window looks out onto the end of the drive. Eliot hopes he hasn't parked so badly that the postman has difficulty turning round. He finds cereals and a bowl. There is milk in the fridge. He sniffs to check it is OK then pours it over his cereals. A clock chimes.

He is wolfing his second bowl when he realises the post van hasn't reached the house. Dropping the bowl, he races to the window.

Han's car is there, but no sign of the post man.

The drive is single track he realises as he runs out of the kitchen towards the front door, a car could not turn round without coming all the way up to the cottage. Pulling open the letterbox, Eliot peers out.

The van has stopped, almost where he last saw it, some fifty metres from the cottage. Maybe the postman is sorting the mail, removing rubber bands, checking he hasn't dropped anything. Maybe he has broken down. The driver's door opens and the postman steps out into the rain, a large package in his hand. Eliot notices the wipers are still working, the engine is running. The postman adjusts his hat, which has slipped over his eyes, then turns away from the cottage, leaning towards the van as if speaking with someone. With animal intuition Eliot moves his head slowly back, away from the light and back into the shadow of the hall. A dark shape moves behind the reflection of the sky in the windscreen, there is someone else in the van. The passenger door opens and a second man, dressed in black and wearing a balaclava, steps out. Carefully Eliot lets the letterbox shut.

A third man, kitted out as the second, emerges from the back of the van. They exchange words briefly then approach the cottage in silence. It is eight fifteen. One man, the taller of the three, splits off from the other two and heads round towards the back of the cottage. The other two continue to the front door. It is clearer, in close up, why the postman's cap is causing problems. The cap is plainly several sizes too large, ditto the uniform.

Reaching the front door, the postman hunts for the doorbell and, not finding it, bangs the door with the package under his arm. The second man presses himself against the wall, out of sight. The cold rain drizzles softly.

The postman hammers on the door a second time. The sound reverberates inside the cottage. The men exchange glances and the postman takes a step back, points his package at the door, and pulls the trigger. The lock shatters. Further shots smash the bolts top and bottom of the door. The door swings slowly open. They step inside, the postman pausing briefly to look over his shoulder before crossing the threshold.

They proceed methodically. The dining room gives the impression of never being used, all the chairs in place around the polished mahogany table that has the beginnings of a layer of dust.

The curtain are closed in the sitting room, a cold charcoal black crumpet is impaled on the end of a toasting fork over the dead embers in the inglenook fireplace.

The sound of smashing glass rings out. The two men run towards the noise and end up in the kitchen, where they find the third man.

Behind him the side door to the garden stands open. The window beside the door is a mess of hanging shards of glass. The third man holds his hands up, admitting responsibility.

The 'postman' goes back into the hall, kicks open the door to the downstairs toilet and peers inside. Rising damp eats into the wall paint and the fittings look all of fifty years old. One of the window panes is boarded up. The postman wrinkles his nose and withdraws, pulling the door closed behind him. The three men head towards the stairs and the first floor.

The act of pulling the door to causes air to move in the downstairs toilet. The window drifts open silently, sucked into the room by the closing of the door. Almost immediately the rain starts to fall onto the sill, a spattering of tiny hemispherical bubbles, each containing an inverted image of the world through the window against the darkness within the room.

From the safety of the forest, Eliot sits among the pine needles, binoculars to his eyes, watching events unfold in the cottage. When the downstairs toilet window swings open he stands, ready to run for his life but the moment passes.

Someone shouts.

Through his binoculars Eliot sees into Han's office on the first floor. One of the men rubs his head and curses, presumably having walked into one of the low beams. The man pulls off his balaclava to reveal a shaved head, his thick neck almost as wide as his head, his skin the colour of chocolate. Rubbing his temples, the man turns towards the window, looking directly towards Eliot. Eliot lowers the binoculars very slowly, praying they don't reflect the light and give away his position.

An itch tickles his leg. Eliot wants to scratch but dare not move. The itch is joined by a second, and a third, moving up his trouser leg. He is being invaded. Ants? Wood lice? His feet are deep in leaf litter. Spiders? Wasps? City boy that he is, Eliot has no idea of what might or might not be hidden beneath the trees in mid-winter.

Raised voices coming from the cottage. The assault on Eliot's legs is almost at the back of his knees. Will the folds of his trousers prevent the invasion carrying on up his legs? Eliot stares down at his legs, glances up at the cottage. The thick-necked man is still at the window, haranguing his colleagues.

The scratching is unbearable, whatever they are up his trousers

BENEATH THE BITTERCREST 189

they are gnawing at his flesh. Eliot is convinced they are burying themselves deep in his muscles. Eliot shuffles backwards, an inch at a time. Finally, when he can no longer see the cottage for trees, he leaps up, slaps his legs furiously to kill whatever is crawling up his trousers. He feels the crunching of small exoskeletons and the smearing of insect body juices against his calves. In the cottage, a door slams. Eliot turns and runs off towards the path that leads up the hill through the forest.

Coming out from under the trees Eliot feels the rain on his back. He has a stitch from bolting his breakfast, and three killers on his tail.

The ridge to the top of the hill is exposed. To his left and right the ground falls away steeply. With a rucksack on his back and the heavy rain to contend with the slopes will be treacherous and he will be out in the open.

He races on to the top of the hill, where he throws himself to the ground, turns and raises his head to look back the way he has come. There is no sign of pursuit but, beyond the trees, a thick cloud of dark smoke billows into the damp air.

Have they set fire to the house?

Eliot lies in the grass, face down in the damp leaves, catching his breath.

Why has she rung him? One minute she is coshing him and turning him over, the next she is saving his skin. It makes no sense. Unless ... maybe the three at the cottage have nothing to do with Brown or Eliot? Maybe they are after Han and unaware he was dead.

But that simply adds to the confusion. How could Roxanne have known about the raid on the cottage if it has nothing to do with Brown? Who is she working for?

Eliot stands up and looks about.

There are two paths, one leading on towards the next high point along the ridge, the other leading down in the direction of a valley where, if the plumes of smoke are anything to go by, there is a village or at least a collection of houses.

The path leads down steeply toward a dry stone wall. Dead bracken and bramble from the previous summer snag his trousers and tear at his ankles. On reaching the wall the path follows alongside it, heading towards the smoke in the valley. The vegetation is very overgrown and progress is slow. Needing a vantage point, Eliot clambers up the wall. Beyond is a tarred single track road. He is swinging a leg over and about to drop down onto the other side when he hears the roar of an engine. The red top of a vehicle heading up the hill towards him becomes visible. Eliot throws himself backward, falling hard onto his rucksack.

The post van rattles past, changing gears heavily as the road levels out. For several minutes Eliot lies there, winded by the fall. Should he go back up and head along the ridge? Will his pursuers be waiting for him in the village? It seems unlikely. Unless they know the area they will have no particular reason to believe that Eliot will be heading in that direction. There isn't even proof that Eliot has ever been in the cottage.

How can anyone have found out about the cottage? He remembers the interrogation, or rather he remembers that he can't remember the interrogation; he may very well have revealed his whereabouts himself.

Having waited half an hour, Eliot climbs over the wall and takes the road down into the valley.

PC Walsh sits at her desk fiddling with a pencil. There have been a few glances in her direction, and the odd mumbled remark.

She has been to see Detective Inspector Machin, 'the Baker', after Dover police confirmed that the dead man found in the red Volvo was indeed Tom Hampton. Walsh, unable to contain her anger any longer, burst into Machin's office and screamed at him about the appalling behaviour of her colleagues.

The Baker coldly informed her that early tests show that Hampton was drunk at the wheel, that he died on impact, and that there was nothing anyone could have done. He further told her that in the circumstances he will, in respect for her dead colleague, not be revealing to the press that Hampton had been absent without leave, nor the fact that he was seen emerging from a brothel in the harbour area earlier in the evening.

'Here, have a coffee.'

Dalton, the duty sergeant places the plastic cup beside her and carries on his way. They are all giving her a wide berth. The general concensus is that Hampton had gone on a dirty weekend and that Walsh is an embittered cow. Sod the lot of them.

'You're telling me you haven't heard from him for days?'

'Mr Han is very particular about not being disturbed when he is away from the office.' The receptionist's mechanical tone suggest the

BENEATH THE BITTERCREST

words are trotted out several times a day. Havering drums his fingers on the desk. Almost an hour wasted already. 'Righty ho. Let's try a different approach. Has Peter Han ever been in contact with a Mr Balkan? An Eliot Balkan?'

'I'm afraid I am not allowed to divulge any ...'

'Well find some idiot who can,' Havering barks, finally losing his temper.

A brief wait then a new voice on the line, male this time, cautious. 'I understand that ...'

'Sod all that. DI Havering, Guildford police. Does Peter Han know of an Eliot Balkan?'

'Our confidentiality ...'

'If I have to send someone round ...'

A sigh at the other end of the line. 'Yes.'

'Yes, he does know an Eliot Balkan?'

'Correct.'

Havering cuts the call. The next step is to find Peter Han.

Eliot walks all the way back to town, passes the eco-friendly funeral parlour and is almost in sight of the station when a car draws up alongside him. There are plenty of people about and the station can only be a hundred or so metres away. One of the car's windows slides down.

'Eliot, stop.'

Eliot walks more briskly.

'Get in the car.'

Behind the wheel of a dull grey Saab is Roxanne. Distracted, Eliot narrowly avoids crashing into a large woman backing out of the dry cleaners with a pushcair.

'Slow down, there'll be an accident,' Roxanne pleads with him. 'Trust me.'

The Saab continues crawling along the kerb.

'I'm serious, they're waiting at the station.'

'Trust me? Do you have an idea how crap that sounds?'

'Forget how it sounds. Get in the car.'

He reaches the end of the road and turns the corner. Fifty yards ahead, and across the street, is the station. Eliot carries on walking.

'Oh, Eliot, grow up.'

Halfway across the street he sees the red roof of the post van over the parked cars on the station forecourt. It starts to move.

'OK, I'm sorry,' she is saying as he pulls open the passenger door and falls in beside her.

'Don't sit there being sorry, get us out of here.'

Roxanne throws the car in an arc, crashing up onto the pavement and speeding away with the red post van in pursuit.

Two pedestrians throw themselves backwards as the Saab roars down the high street. A Ford Fiesta coming out of a side road thinks better of it and reverses manically, crashing into the wall of a pub.

At the first major junction Roxanne turns left, crashing the gears, heading downhill. Eliot looks back over his shoulder. The post van is still behind them, gaining.

'Do you have a fourth gear?' he shouts.

'Do you have a problem with third?'

'No, even third would be fine.'

The road levelled out, veers right and then splits in two directions. Roxanne steers right and they find themselves on a narrow terraced street leading steeply downhill. Parked cars on both sides, as the Saab shoots past, ripping the wing mirrors from a couple of them. In their wake the post van lurches into view, its wheels leaving the ground momentarily before thumping back to earth.

In a flash the blur of terraced houses is behind them and instead of bricks, doors and windows, the roadside is all grass verge and footpath. They are almost out of town.

Suddenly the rear window shatters, spraying glass all over the back seat, the bullet ricochetting off the rear view mirror and burying itself in the floor at Eliot's feet.

As Roxanne points the Saab round the next corner, the bottom of the hill becomes visible. The road appears to disappear into a river before emerging on the other bank as a narrow country road flanked by high hedges, rising steeply.

'We're finished. Look.'

Eliot follows Roxanne's line of sight. Above them on the other side of the valley, where the narrow road curves and disappears behind the hedgerows, a tractor with massive wheels is slowly ambling along, taking up the entire width of the road.

They reach the bottom of the hill and are almost at the ford when Eliot has an idea. As the spray smacks against the windscreen, Eliot grabs the steering wheel and spins it hard to the left. With a violent scraping of the exhaust, and God knows what else, the Saab abandons the road and joins the bed of the stream that feeds the ford.

BENEATH THE BITTERCREST

'What the ...?'

'Shut up and drive, they're practically on top of us.'

The post van reaches the ford, juddering to a halt, engine revving wildly.

Fortunately, there seems to be no more than eight to ten inches of water and the stream bed is not mud but rocks and stones. The Saab ploughs through a tunnel of spray, caught in the deafening racket of rocks smashing against the underside of the car.

Another shot, glancing off the roof this time. Eliot looks back. The post van is turning off the road into the water, the chase isn't over.

Roxanne and Eliot are thrown from side to side as the car continues downstream. About forty metres between them and the post van.

'You're buying me another car.'

'Get us out of this alive and I'll buy you a boat.'

On one side of the stream the ground rises sharply, thick with bushes and dead brambles.

'Do you think you could get up onto that path?'

'Would I be driving along a river if I could get up on the path?'

The water must be getting deeper because the car is harder to control, sliding about and rocking from side to side. The wheels are no longer in continuous contact with the bed of the stream. Behind them the post van is gaining and, without the traction of the wheels, Eliot and Roxanne are at the mercy of the currents. They just have to go with the flow Eliot thinks to himself, smiling grimly.

'Keep with it, you're doing OK,' he tells Roxanne.

'This is the last time I rescue you.'

'It's the last time you'll have to,' he answers, as the Saab cleared a clump of overhanging vegetation.

The banks of the stream have risen on both sides. Up ahead, maybe twenty metres away, is a low bridge. Roxanne puts her foot down.

'What the hell are you doing?' Eliot shouts.

The car lurches forwards faster and faster. Spinning out of control, they clip the right hand side of the bridge, ricochet off the other wall, then spin again. Eliot is suddenly aware that his feet are wet, water is seeping into the car. Even Swedish car manufacturers cannot hold back the inevitable indefinitely. The headlamps pop and the bonnet buckles as bridge and car make contact a third time.

Then the bridge is behind them. Eliot turns to see how close the post van is. One of the pursuers is leaning out of the window, rifle in hand, taking aim as they reach the bridge.

In an instant it is all over. The top of the post van, which is considerably higher than the Saab, smashes into the arch of the bridge, stopping it dead in its tracks. The man leaning out of the window seems to snap in half like a twig as the rifle he is holding flies from his arms and sails out from under the bridge, splashing into the stream behind the Saab.

'Yes. Yes. Bloody Yes,' Eliot punches the air like a tennis player on heat.

As Roxanne takes her foot off the accelerator, Eliot grabs hold of her and they hug, a little self-consciously.

'Brilliant,' Eliot says. 'I've never been rescued so ... insanely.'

Roxanne smiles. 'It beats go-karting,' she agrees.

In an instant their celebrations are turned upside down as the car flips onto its side, Roxanne's head smacking hard against the door frame, knocking her out cold. The car is sinking fast. Through the windscreen the horizon has changed. The stream has ended and they have tumbled into a river.

He cannot remember having fastened his safety belt. Now, with the freezing waters pouring into the car through the smashed back window he struggles to find the catch to release himself. He doesn't notice Roxanne's inert form slumped in the rising water.

twenty seven

A few more seconds and all the air in the car will have gone. Eliot tugs at the door handle, but the pressure of the water is too great, the door will not budge.

'Can you open the door your side?' he shouts over his shoulder.

Stupidly he tries smashing the window with his fist.

'A crow bar or ...' he says turning towards Roxanne.

She is already submerged, her eyes closed. The rear of the car bumps against the bottom of the river and starts to level out, the remaining pocket of air leaving the front of the car moving backwards towards the space where the rear window has been. Eliot gulps a lungful of the remaining air as the precious bubbles rush away from him and out of the car.

Suddenly Eliot understands. He tears at Roxanne's seat belt catch, freeing her, then turns towards the back window. No escape that way because of the headrests. Even if he could squeeze through he won't be able to pull Roxanne after him.

Though the engine has cut out, the headlights are still on. Maybe just maybe ... The window switches are still working. Unbearably slowly the windows open. With every second more precious than the last, Eliot propels himself out, lungs bursting, towards the light. His head explodes the surface of the river like a football hitting the back of the net. Another huge lungful of air and he dives back down towards the car. Grabbing the roof he pulled himself round to the driver's side, braces himself against the door and manoeuvres Roxanne round to pull her out.

He breaks the surface a second time, gasping for air. Freezing water has got into his lungs and he coughs and vomits the dirty brown water. Holding Roxanne's head above water, Eliot swims the few short metres to the riverbank. He lays her down on the riverside path and is beside her on his hands and knees coughing as he hears foot-steps rushing towards him.

'On her side, you have to roll her on her side to let her cough up.'

A bearded man in a homburg hat towers over Eliot. Beside him an elderly labrador drops onto its haunches.

Eliot shakes his head. 'She's not breathing. She's dead.'

'No, son, get the water out of her lungs and get her heart beating.'
The man throws himself onto his knees and sets to, clearing Roxanne's airway, checking for a pulse.
'You'll have to do it. Dicky heart,' he explains, patting his chest.
Too numb to protest, Eliot does as the man instructs, pumping Roxanne's chest to get her heart beating. Water pours then dribbles from her mouth as the river is pushed out of her lungs.
'And again. One, two, three, rest. That's it. Now breathe some air into her lungs. Hold her nose. The chest again. One, two, three, rest.'
Eliot is on automatic, his body numb from the cold, his head in overload. But sufficiently alert as to wonder how it is that his first contact with the mouth he has waited to kiss should not be an intimate sensual act, but a public act of salvation. There he is on a river bank, an old codger for company, blowing up the object of his desire as if she were a party balloon or paddling pool.
A cough.
'That's it! Again,' the man prompts. 'One, two, three.'
The cough becomes a splutter then, suddenly, Roxanne is thrashing about, coughing up water, gasping for air.
'You stay there with her, young man, and I'll rush off and call an ambulance.'
With that the bearded man is off, almost running, his dog in pursuit.
Roxanne's eyes open, her lips slightly parted, her hair wet across her face.
'What are you smiling at?'
'You saved me, I saved you, I guess we're quits.'
'Where's the car?'
Eliot points down into the river.
'You owe me a car.'
'And a wig, I imagine.'
Roxanne's hand goes to her head.
'I shouldn't worry about it, I prefer brunettes.' Eliot helps her onto her feet. 'There's a man calling an ambulance.'
Roxanne shakes her head. She can barely stand but she is adamant. 'We need to disappear.'
He carries her along the riverside in the opposite direction to that taken by the old man. After some eight hundred metres he is exhausted.
'Don't kill yourself, Eliot. There's a road over there.' She points

BENEATH THE BITTERCREST

towards a copse some fifteen metres from the riverside path. A flash of orange between the tree trunks as a car rushes past. 'Leave me there propped up against a tree and find us a car. I'll be OK. I'm feeling better.'

He doesn't argue and he carries her towards the copse. Having made sure she is hidden from anyone on the path, he removes his jacket and wraps it round her. She is shaking and pale.

'It's wet but ...'

She smiles weakly and coughs. 'And something hot to drink would be good.'

The road flanks the eastern edge of the copse and Eliot has only been on the road for a minute when, by good fortune, a bus appears. In ten minutes he is back in town. He works quickly and methodically. First the banks. He draws a total of twelve hundred pounds from three accounts, if they are to disappear they will need money. Then a supermarket where he buys biscuits, cakes and a bottle of rum. Finally, he crosses the road and enters the station, passing through the car park where, just over an hour earlier, he saw the red post van lurch forward to give chase.

A bored receptionist at the car hire franchise shows no interest in Eliot's bedraggled appearance. Barely having glanced at him, she hands him a form to fill out and takes his money while conducting a phone conversation with a friend who is clearly besotted with news about minor royalty and the possibility that Prince William may have found true love.

'There's your keys, Love. Just hand them in at your destination. Where did you say ...?'

'Leicester,' he lies, not wanting to leave a trail anyone can follow.

The car is parked on the station forecourt, a large Citroën. In minutes he has left town and reached the copse.

The copse is empty. Bare tree trunks, dead brambles that twist and curl like barbed wire, and rotting leaf litter. But he is sure he is at the right spot. He shouts out her name. To his left the leaf litter rustles. Roxanne emerges from under a pile of leaves she has used to hide herself from view.

'Don't argue,' he says. 'I'll carry you to the car. I think there is a hospital ...'

'No hospital. Use your head. I just need hot coffee. I'll be OK.'

He puts the heater on full blast and helps her down a shot of rum. For the coffee they will need a service station.

As they head away, they see through the hedge the flashing lights of an emergency vehicle arriving on the river bank close to where Roxanne's car disappeared.

Ninety minutes later they are south of Birmingham on the M42.

They haven't spoken much, both are too numb from the near drowning. Roxanne sits shivering in the passenger seat while Eliot drives. Jazz and blues on the radio warm the mood, removing the need for conversation. There is nothing to say, there is too much to say.

'How long was I unconscious?'

'You weren't unconscious,' he corrects her. 'I'm coming off this junction.' Eliot takes the exit off the motorway. 'No heartbeat, no breathing. You were dead. We have to go back,' he explains as they reach the roundabout.

'Thanks, that makes me feel a lot better. Go back where?'

'Everything's in the rucksack. In your car. Without it we have nothing. The evidence, photos, receipts, phone numbers. Your hair.'

'So it's my fault?'

'I didn't say that.'

'It's too late, Eliot. Ten foot under water. The place is crawling with police. You saw for yourself. We have to go on.'

She is right. They will have found the post van and the bodies. Shit. Eliot smashes the steering wheel with his fist and slams his foot down. The car screeches round the roundabout until Eliot reaches the exit that takes them back onto the motorway, still heading south.

The cloud cover is threateningly low. Spots of rain streak the windscreen.

'I need someone I can trust.' Roxanne turns the radio off.

'Don't we all?'

'You've no idea.'

'Try me.'

Roxanne smiles fleetingly but says nothing. She grabs a biscuit from the bag Eliot has put at her feet.

'OK, I'll start. I killed a man.' Eliot takes a deep breath, suddenly overwhelmed by the memory of his futile attempt to save Han's life, the bloated corpse in the trunk, and the sound of the guard falling down the stairwell.

'I heard. It was self-defence. It'll pass.'

BENEATH THE BITTERCREST 199

'No. It won't pass.' Eliot wonders how it is that she is so sure feelings of horror and self-disgust ever fade.

'Illegal immigrants,' he says, changing the subject. That's what this is all about, isn't it? There's a smuggling ring in Swindon. Peter Han told me a great deal about your friend Mr Brown. In the newspapers they say people pay five grand each, or more, to get in. From Iraq, Africa, China, wherever. Fifty people in a lorry would make a quarter of a million per trip. No tax. No visas. If there's any trouble, dump them. By the roadside. In the sea... How am I doing?'

She doesn't answer. Eliot continues.

'Of course, not all of them survive the journey. Exposure, hunger, illness, and so on. Like the body I found by the Gas Tower. Of course, since they don't officially exist, they don't officially disappear. For the police it's just another dead tramp. Blind eyes turning in all directions. No doubt helped by a little cash, tax free.'

'What do you imagine happens to them when they arrive?' Roxanne asks quietly. 'The ones who survive the journey.'

'What I don't understand is this. You're in business with them. You set me up. So you tell me what you do with them. While you're at it you can tell me why you followed me onto the train in Doncaster. Where are we going by the way?'

'What if I told you dozens of people have gone missing?'

'When you think how many smugglers there are and how many people ...'

'I'm talking about this one operation.'

Eliot's eyes leave the road for an instant to return her gaze.

'I think you stumbled onto something with that friend of yours,' she continues. 'The private investigator...'

'Han,' he supplies the name.

'I want you to take me to the crematorium you visited.'

Eliot looks confused, he does not recall mentioning the crematorium to her.

'Your interrogation,' she offers by way of explanation. 'Brown seemed put out when you mentioned the crematorium. What kind of a man agrees to burn bodies in the middle of the night? And why?'

Eliot absorbs the information. The interrogation in the house by the river already seems like a dream. But it was not a dream. Roxanne was there. And Brown. 'OK, but what's your angle? If I'm going to risk my neck then ...'

'You don't need to know.'

'Don't patronise me. No information, no crematorium.' He puts his foot on the brakes, pulls over onto the hard shoulder and folds his arms. 'I've earned it.'

Roxanne thinks for an eternity about what she might tell him, what he needs to know, what he doesn't need to know, what he will believe, what he could be pursuaded to believe.

When it finally comes, it's a two word answer.

'My brother.'

By the time they reach Swindon, warm and finally dry, it will be late afternoon and dark. Eliot has convinced Roxanne that barging into the crematorium during office hours would be a big mistake. Instead he has proposed buying a few supplies then stopping off to grab a proper meal.

'Tell me about your brother,' Eliot says while they wait for their pizzas to arrive.

Roxanne shakes her head, 'the less you know the better.'

'Are you ... Yes, maybe you're right,' he concedes, remembering the 'interview' he has endured.

He stares at the couple across the room, the only other people in the restaurant. Their faces glow in the light of the candle that flickers on the table between them, their voices whispering intimacies, their eyes smiling. He feels Roxanne's eyes on him.

'This isn't a great idea. Maybe we should ask them for takeaway boxes,' she says uncomfortably 'If someone recognises us ...'

He shrugs and smiles. 'They're interested in each other. We're OK.'

Roxanne gazes at the couple for a moment then turns towards Eliot. 'He's a business man. My brother. Same thing as BitterCrest, import export. The family firm, we trade with various companies around the Mediterranean.'

Eliot waits for her to continue.

'Six months ago a friend of the family, in the same business, was introduced to a company trading in the UK. The more my brother saw the more suspicious he became. Large lorries were coming down to the Loire and driving back to the UK half empty. It didn't add up. He told the friend to be careful but there was too much money involved and the friend thought my brother simply wanted a cut of the action. Maybe he was right.'

'Nice family,' Eliot comments. 'You didn't grow up in Sicily, did you?'

'Didier, my brother, decided to follow one of the lorries,' Roxanne ignores the jibe. 'He knew that whatever was being smuggled would have to be loaded onto the lorries before they left France. That was four months ago.'

The pizzas arrive.

'And you set out by yourself to find him?'

'I can look after myself.'

Eliot raises his hands in surrender to show he isn't arguing.

They drive past the crematorium entrance a couple of times, checking it out. The gates are open and there are lights on in the main building but, from the road, it is impossible to see the car park. Maybe the lights are just for security.

They are approaching a third time, some fifty metres away from the entrance, when a long dark saloon emerges and disappears up the road at speed.

Eliot parks out on the main road. Keeping to the shadows of the trees that flank the footpath, they approach the crematorium. Except for the lamp posts, the lights are now off and the building seems deserted. Eliot leads Roxanne round to the side of the building. The car park is empty. A breeze shakes the laurel bushes and whistles the empty branches of the trees. The thick cloud cover that has lasted all day has gone but there is no moon.

The doorbell goes unanswered but a slither of light escapes under the double doors. The doors are not locked.

Bright fluorescent strip lighting run the length of the corridor. The floor is a mess of scuff marks, where trolleys have been pushed up and down, thousands of final journeys, year in year out. Aside from a gentle hum, the building is silent.

They take opposite sides of the corridor, trying each door.

Eliot gets lucky. He recognises the room immediately. The oak table laden with floral tributes, the tall cupboards, the mops, buckets and brooms.

'Here we go.' Eliot points at the row of pegs where a dark mackintosh is hanging. 'Look, our man is still here.'

'This is the room you saw before?'

'Yeah. That's the oven over there, where he sent the body.'

Her eyes have a distant look, as if she were seeing another room where people were stacked into ovens in their thousands, or a lorry packed with frightened people dreaming stupidly of a better life. All the stupid dreams. People longing for homelands they will never be given, work they will never find, food they will never eat, freedom they will never enjoy.

'Let's nail the bastard,' she says.

At the end of the corridor is another open door. The light is on. Through the doorway they see a mug tree bearing four chipped mugs sitting on a cheap red veneered desk. Beside it a cartoon of milk and a small pile of teabags. The staff rest room, Eliot decides. The carpet, an ugly green colour, has countless cigarette burns and various dark stains. The back of an upturned chair is visible. Music plays gently, a swing band tucking into Moonlight Serenade.

As they draw closer more of the room comes into view. A desk. A plastic kettle beside the pile of teabags. A thin waft of steam kisses the kettle's spout. A teaspoon sits beside a jam jar which bears a label secured with a vast swathe of Sellotape. The label reads 'Timothy Wesley's Sugar' in bold capitals underlined several times in thick red marker pen. Eliot steps forwards, clearing his voice, so as not to scare the man out of his wits.

He needn't have bothered. He turns away, putting his arm up to prevent Roxanne from stepping into the room.

'We're too late.'

'No,' she shouts, pushing past him.

Eliot feels his stomach yield. Helplessly he leans forwards and retches, his vomit leaving a trail down the wall and the door frame.

When he lifts his head, he finds Roxanne still standing there, staring into the room. Beyond her, tied to a chair, are the mortal remains of Timothy Wesley, his face a bloody pulp and three of the fingers of his left hand snapped right back to show the gleaming white of his knuckle bones. His Brylcremed hair hangs over his face in a lank yellow-white curtain specked with blood. Flecks of blood are sprayed across the wall beside the body, each trail of flecks a silent witness to the savagery of the attack.

The card on the front porch warns of a large dog. Eliot asks himself how many of the properties displaying such signs actually have a dog, of any description. They are parked outside a very ordinary looking end of terrace house in Stratton, in north east Swindon. Lights are on, upstairs and down. Roxannes passes Eliot binoculars. Eliot notices she is coughing again.

The front room is painted in a creamy magnolia. Not a hint of

BENEATH THE BITTERCREST   203

peach or apple, but the real thing, magnolia in all its mind-numbing glory. Brass light fittings. In a state of wonderment Eliot notices the armchairs have antimacassars, how many of those are there left in the country? A through lounge cum dining room. The television is on, there seems to be one facing the street in every house, like square Christmas trees, twinkling and flickering away the winter hours.

The dining room table is set for two, table cloth and place mats, brown sauce and porcelain cruet. A painting of geese flying over a frozen pond hangs over the dresser. Eliot flinches as someone steps into the room, entirely filling his field of view. A woman in her late fifties places a tray on the dining room table. She wears her hair in a silver bun. A pink apron protects her skirt and blouse. He watches as she loads the cruet and brown sauce onto the tray, crosses into the lounge, skirting a coffee table and disappears through the doorway into the hall. Her face is tired and drawn and Eliot reflects that in a few hours her life will be harder still. He shudders at the memory of what they have seen at the crematorium.

After a few moments, Gwen Wesley's silhouette, still bearing the tray, appears behind the lace curtains in one of the first floor windows.

Havering is about to leave for home at the end of yet another long day when the phone finally rings. He grabs an envelope and scribbles down the address.

'Thanks for that, Winston. I owe you one. '

It has taken all day to find out where Peter Han lives. The day has been busy with other business, two urgent cases requiring progress, and a meeting with local councillors that he could have done without. Han, it appears, lives so far west he is practically in Wales. It will keep till morning.

'We should have spoken with her.'

'That would have been an interesting conversation,' Eliot answers. They are heading into a storm. Both are tense and unhappy.

Eliot has become a fugitive in his own country. His life is falling apart because of a bunch of illegal refugees and smugglers and, to cap it all, the one witness he has found has been murdered, seemingly only minutes before they arrived.

For Roxanne the situation is no less threatening. It has been hours since the rescue. Alarm bells will be ringing because they will know someone tipped Eliot off. Nor will it have passed unnoticed that she failed to turn up to a lunch time meeting in London.

It is her idea to drive north. She knows somewhere safe and Eliot, for want of a better plan, has readily agreed to leave everything in her hands.

Eliot rubs at his eyes with one hand while steering with the other. Around them the fog slowly gathers, first licking the verges then pouring onto the motorway itself. Roxanne turns the heater up.

Eliot drives as far as Penrith at which point his eyes are completely shot. After shovelling a plateful of processed sludge that passes itself off as lasagne in a roadside café, Roxanne insists she is fully recovered and takes the wheel. Eliot cannot sleep, the headlights of approaching vehicles have burnt holes in his retinas and the drone of the engine buzzes in his ears like a circular saw. They leave the motorway at Carlisle and waste an eternity driving about looking for aspirin.

The cold light before dawn. The fog has cleared sufficiently to reveal a sullen charcoal sky studded with concrete monoliths. Roxanne nudges Eliot to wake him.

'Where are we?'

'Fullhill.'

Eliot lifts his head to look out of the window. They are on a flyover above a bleak urban housing estate. The orange street lighting staining the pavements remind him of the urine-soaked stairwells he played on as a child growing up in south London. Brutal tower blocks squat in a despondent landscape like cardboard boxes abandoned in an alley.

Down at street level the area looks even less inviting. Every shop is either boarded up or protected by heavy metal blinds. Chip wrappers, discarded drink cans, polystyrene burger boxes, empty fag packets, and a used condom rolled down the pavements in the harsh wind. A Wild West complete with urban tumbleweed.

'Where's Fullhill?'

'Glasgow.'

From below the housing blocks are menacing, each identical window a dull narcotic eye staring down into no-man's-land. Above the housing estate is a large cemetery, its grey tombstones scattered in the overgrown grass, looking for all the world like a scale model of the housing estate itself.

'OK, what the hell is Fullhill?'

BENEATH THE BITTERCREST   205

'No-one will look for us here.'

'I'm not surprised. The only people who would call this shit-hole home have broken noses, wear slippers to the shops, have ugly dogs, and cigarette stains on their hands. They have nothing to do and all day to do it in, eat chips or Mars Bars with everything, and are full of hate and completely without hope.'

'What would you know about that?' she says.

In a doorway a tramp huddles in a sleeping bag, flattened cardboard boxes gathered round him, a clutch of empty beer cans tumbled at his feet. The graffiti of racial hatred in angry red across a shop front reads 'Wogs fuck off home'. A mangled bike frame hangs padlocked to a lamp post in front of the dentist's, which has heavy iron bars across every window.

'I grew up on an estate just like this in south London,' he answers quietly, 'and I've spent the past fifteen years trying to forget it ever happened.

Roxanne knows where she is going, turning left and right without hesitation. She pulls up in front of one of the blocks. The city council has decided to beautify the block by painting fat stripes of different colours to break up the huge facade. It is like painting a Tellytubby on the side of an armoured car, Eliot reflects. Roxanne cuts the engine and steps out of the car.

'This is a joke, yeah?' Eliot joins her on the pavement.

Her look suggests otherwise.

'I guarantee it will be propped up on bricks, no doors, no seats, by lunchtime. Probably torched too for good measure.'

'What?'

'You can't leave the car here.'

'I did last time.'

'What? A car like this?'

They park four miles away, in a quiet street of elegant terraced houses, and hire a cab to take them back to Fullhill.

Fullhill is, if nothing else, honest. It does not pretend to be anything other than it is. Anyone who has money, family or opportunity has long since escaped the soul-sapping prisons of its tower blocks, leaving only the desperate poor.

The early mornings are calm enough, no-one has jobs to go to and few of the children go to school, sleep and hangovers keep the streets empty. Commuters into Glasgow won't even drive through the area, such is its reputation.

Lunchtime, when the solitary, and much barricaded, off-licence and the three pubs open their doors, the first residents come out in search of a liquid breakfast.

By late afternoon a few dealers hang out on street corners, five quid wraps of various drugs secreted about their persons, if they are stupid. The smarter operators do everything by mobile phone, in a few minutes one of an army of twelve year olds will have cycled round to pick up downers, uppers, crack, dope, ecstasy, heroin.

Early evening is the busy time. Pale junkies fan out from their dingy flats high up in the blocks, emerging like a cloud of bats at twilight, striding out with one thing on their minds, the need to steal something to feed their habit. Like vampires they disappear into the night, seeking out an open window, an unlocked door, a pensioner out and about after dusk, a motorist imprudent enough to stop at one of the district's traffic lights.

In the junkies' wake come their girlfriends, kids in their teens or early twenties, dolled up for a night of whoring, their short lives already tottering on the high-heeled edge of the abyss, their eyes furtive, sad, and defeated. Fat men from smarter parts of the city, where they jolly well look after their children and know right from wrong, slink into the dark Fullhill streets in their family saloons for a quick blow job with a fifteen year old on their way home for supper.

As the evening wears on and the residents get tanked up, the air becomes almost euphoric, banter, shouting, kids larking about, stolen cars racing up and down in front of the off-licence then, by half-eleven, the stragglers are screaming abuse at the landlord as he finally throws them out. The usual fistfights. Police sirens. After dark the police only venture onto the estate in groups. Every few weeks, gunshots ring out as the fifteen year olds fight over ownership of this or that drug fiefdom.

The fish and chip shop is the last door to close. The counter has heavy iron bars across it to protect the staff. The windows have been smashed so many times that the owner has given up replacing them and has settled instead for thick boarding hammered into place with six inch nails.

By about two am everyone returns from their labours and the anger moves indoors. Occasional screams pierce the night for a while as spouses and partners and girlfriends and pimps and drunks indulge in a bit of slap and tickle.

Finally, when all is quiet, the rats and foxes emerge for a few brief

BENEATH THE BITTERCREST 207

hours' foraging before the whole cycle starts up again.

Roxanne crunches the numbers into the intercom by the door.

'Maxwell Tower,' Eliot reads the grubby name plate. 'Do you think they named it after Robert?'

Roxanne looks none the wiser.

'Doesn't matter,' he says.

'Yes?' says the intercom. 'Who is this?'

'Roxanne.'

'Roxanne!'

The door clicks open.

A video is playing somewhere down the corridor as the heavily reinforced front door swings shut. The window over the door has been boarded up. It is dark and warm. They emerge into the lounge. Three kids of primary school age, two boys and a girl, are bouncing on a bed in front of the television, watching a Wesley Snipes movie full of vampires. The children cheer and laugh as Snipes blows the vampires away.

'Roxanne!'

A large African woman clutches her face in her hands, shaking with joy. She runs across the room and takes Roxanne's hands in her own.

'Welcome, you are welcome, come in. Oh my God, what has happened to you?'

Roxanne grabs the woman and hugs her. 'Oh, Alima, it's a long story. This is Eliot.'

'Eliot, you are welcome. Come in, come in.'

A second woman appears, who Alima introduces as Fatima, a neighbour. The introductions made, Alima and Fatima withdraw. Without being asked, the children get off the bed and indicate to Eliot that he should sit down.

Moments later a breakfast of eggs, bread and coffee have been prepared and, while Roxanne and Alima chat animatedly about various friends of Alima's, Eliot fills his plate and eats.

The room is sparsely furnished. Aside from the bed, there are a couple of tatty chairs, a television, a video machine, and a table. In a corner are cardboard boxes that contain children's books, two jembe drums, and a few old toys.

'So, Eliot, you like Fullhill? I am Dudu Bondembe.'

The two men shake hands and Eliot makes space on the bed for Dudu to sit down. He is a tall well built man with a high forehead and very dark skin; ten shades darker than Laurie, the new guy at the office. Dudu wears a large Fair Isle jumper in spite of the hothouse heat in the flat.

Eliot struggles to think of a diplomatic reply. Seeing his discomfort, Dudu bursts out laughing.

'It is our prison. Alima has been out just twice.'

'It's a jungle out ...' Eliot stops in mid-flow, tired and suddenly embarassed about his choice of vocabulary.

'No, it is worse than a jungle,' Dudu corrects him. 'I will not go out after five o'clock. At home we say one arrow is not safe. Too many bad things. Some bad people and many poor people. Everyone has given up. When they see us they are angry. They spit at us, say we are rich.' He sweeps his hand about the room to indicate his wealth. 'As you can see.' Dudu roars with laughter. 'Still, my children have English lessons and learn to swim so ...' his voice trails off.

When Dudu smiles, his eyes are somehow out of sync with his mouth. There is a guardedness, a holding back, like someone hovering warily at the edge of the circle at a party where he doesn't know the other guests. Eliot has a memory of rare days playing in the park as a child when a sun bright sky was simultaneously pouring rain.

The Snipes video finishes and clicks off. The news is on.

'How do you know Roxanne?' Eliot asks.

'She has lost her brother. My brother too is lost. He was coming to stay with me and has not arrived.'

'How do you know he isn't still at home in ...?'

'In Kinshasa. He rang me from France. In November. He has been in France for one year. There was a lorry to bring him over to England. Five thousand pounds. All his savings.'

'Did you know ...'

'Eliot, stop. Look.' Roxanne interrupts, having re-entered the room.

Eliot turns towards the television. A newreader is talking but Eliot doesn't hear the words, he sees the photos over her shoulder. Two shots side by side, him and Roxanne, tinted blue to match the virtual studio the newsreader is supposed to be sitting in. The picture changes to a wide shot of the crematorium in Swindon.

'... have said that the murdered man, Timothy Wesley, was attacked in the early hours of yesterday evening.' The newsreader's voice continues over shots of the crematorium car park and side entrance.

BENEATH THE BITTERCREST

'Police are keen to interview Eliot Balkan and Roxanne Lepage who were seen approaching the crematorium early yesterday evening. Balkan is also being sought with regard to another investigation in the Swindon area. The police have warned the public not to approach the couple as they are both believed to be armed and dangerous. '

'Bullshit,' shouts Roxanne, as the newsreader moves on to a story about a conceptual artist, desperate for attention, who is claiming that the destruction of the twin towers in New York was a work of art.

Eliot walks over to the window and stares out over the estate. How long will they be safe, even here?

Alima changes channels and seeks to reassure Roxanne. Dudu looks nervous. Eliot gazes out at the Glasgow skyline.

'You are a dangerous man, Eliot.' Dudu joins him at the window.

'I'm a danger to someone. Tell me, Dudu, you still haven't explained how you met Roxanne. How did you find her?'

'He didn't find me, I found him,' Roxanne says behind him. 'Shortly after my brother disappeared a letter arrived. He had sent me a photocopied list of names. Foreign names, African, Middle Eastern, East European. I came over to England and contacted various refugee centres and agencies, telling them I worked for the French Government and that the people on the list had been receiving assistance in France. I simply needed to confirm they were in the UK so that we could take them off our files in France, where they were listed as missing persons.'

'And they bought it?' Eliot sits down on the thin carpet and leans back against the wall. He instantly regrets asking the question, he is too tired to listen to the answer. What is he doing in Scotland in the company of strangers, miles from home? What can it possibly benefit anyone for Eliot to understand the hurt lurking behind Dudu's eyes? What can Eliot offer the other man other than sympathy?

Eliot concentrates on slowing his breathing. He has to relax.

'No, not all of them,' Roxanne is saying. 'But eventually someone did recognise a couple of names.

'We were happy to speak with her.' Dudu interjects. 'There is no other way to find out what happened to my brother. We are refugees. No-one is interested.'

'They thought Dudu might be the person I was looking for because the family name, Bondembe, was the same. It was his brother,' Roxanne adds. 'Eliot? Eliot?'

Eliot's head has slumped down, his chin on his chest, eyes shut.

twenty eight

The aroma of cooking fills the air. Spice, chicken, rice. He stays there on the carpet, eyes closed, breathing in the smells. Peppers, sweet plantains, lemon, onion.

He listens to the voices. Another video is playing. Children's voices whooping with delight as punches are landed and baddies hit the deck. The mother is calling. The kids jump up and run out. Moments later they come back into the room. Enveloped in the sounds of family, Eliot keeps his eyes tight shut, imagines himself at home, safe, warm, happy.

When finally he opens them he finds himself staring straight into the cheeky eyes of six year old Mili, a chicken leg in her hand, casually tugging meat from the bone while studying the contours of his face.

'You've got a funny nose,' she observes solemnly.

'So have you,' Eliot laughs.

Mili sticks her tongue out and races off. 'Mama, Mama ...'

The rest Eliot doesn't understand but the gist is clear, the strange man has woken up.

Getting to his feet he crosses the room, picks up a jembe drum standing in the corner and starts doodling a few riffs and rhythms. The skin whispers roughly, booming low notes falling out of the bottom end of the drum whenever he smacks the skin bang in the middle. He is perched on the edge of a chair, eyes closed, the drum resting on his insteps, hands enslaved to the dry lilting beat when Mili returns carrying a plate piled high with food. She places the plate in front of him on the carpet then, with the sweetest of smiles, rejoins her brothers on the bed in front of the video.

'I do not understand why do they want to kill you,' Dudu says softly, inspecting the oranges.

They are in a church community hall, one end of which has been transformed into a shop. Fruit and vegetables, principally, but also dried fish, rice, lentils and flours of various types. The vicar and two bright faced students stand behind trestle tables wearing aprons, serving customers.

'Join the club.' Eliot says. 'I wish I knew.'

BENEATH THE BITTERCREST

'The lizard stirs the water then is surprised that it cannot see,' Dudu suggests then, turning to the vicar, 'Ten oranges please, Sir.'

'No, you've lost me there,' Eliot confesses.

'Your confusion is created by yourself. At home we say it is the lizard who ...'

'Are you sure proverbs are going to help?'

'Proverbs are the oil with which thoughts are eaten.'

'Yeah. I see,' Eliot says, none the wiser.

The noise in the church is impressive, maybe forty shoppers, all talking. Dudu has to repeat his request several times before the vicar hears him.

'Is it my imagination or is everyone here a foreigner? ... I mean a ...'

'Eliot, you can call us what you want. It does not change anything. Foreigner, refugee, wog, paki, bogus asylum seeker ...'

'What I meant was where are the locals?'

The shoppers are plainly not fifth generation Glaswegians. Their clothes, skin tones and voices mark them as coming from various parts of Africa and the middle east. Dudu pays the vicar and takes his oranges.

'The local diet does not include fresh fruit and vegetables,' Dudu says. 'This market is for everyone. The church does not make a profit so prices are cheap, but the ah ... local people, they prefer chips and fried chocolate bars.'

Eliot smiles, his childhood diet wasn't much better.

'We have to prove Brown is organising the illegal importation of immigrants.'

Eliot turns towards Roxanne. Since they left the flat, forty minutes ago, she hasn't said a word, following Dudu and Eliot like a sullen shadow. He has forgotten she is there.

'Prove to who?' Eliot says. 'I mean, until we find someone we can trust ...'

'Yes, OK, OK,' Roxanne cuts him off.

'We've lost any evidence we've found as quickly as we've found it,' Eliot remarks as they step out of the church into the cold Glasgow air. 'No doubt the low building was cleared out almost as soon as I escaped. Aside from my testimony there's nothing to ...'

'I know he is involved,' Roxanne says.

'So he says he had no idea what the drivers were up to. He prepares accounts for an import export business. How should he know what other employees are doing? His presence in the low building no more incriminates him than it does me.'

'You don't believe that.'

'It's not about what we believe. He is so far ahead of us he's managed to steer the media into labelling us the killers. Now we can't even show our faces, let alone establish what is happening.'

'Maybe I can help?'

Roxanne and Eliot both stare at Dudu who is standing between them, a carrier bag in each hand, smiling.

'I am a refugee. Dispensible like my brother. Invisible. I can get close to them.'

Eliot and Roxanne look at each other, then back at Dudu, who senses their lack of enthusiasm and shrugs his shoulders.

As they leave they fail to notice the squat figure of a woman who has been standing at the back of the church for several minutes studying Eliot and Roxanne's faces.

They return to the flat laden with food. While Alima cooks, Dudu finds an envelope containing a handful of photos and bits of paper, all that remains of the family's life before they became refugees.

'This one is of me and my brothers and sisters in Kinshasa, three years ago.'

Smiling politely, Eliot passes the photo to Roxanne. He is feeling frustrated. Somehow, he and Roxanne have to get away and talk together, alone. Dudu's offer of help, whilst well intentioned, simply clouds the issue.

'And this,' Dudu is saying, 'is the last letter I had from him. A few days before he travelled.'

Dudu passes Eliot a flimsy sheet torn from a notepad.

'I think this will make more sense to you.' Eliot passes the note to Roxanne.

Roxanne reads the note, which is written in French, several times.

'I don't understand, Dudu, what was this medical he writes about?'

'Medical?' Eliot interjects.

'Yes, here.' Roxanne makes a show of passing the note over to Eliot for his expert analysis but he shakes his head.

Dudu rereads the letter. 'I remember. He had a medical before he left.'

'Yes. It says that here,' Roxanne says flatly.

'Sorry.' Dudu says, looking at Eliot.

Eliot, none the wiser, shrugs.

BENEATH THE BITTERCREST   213

'Before they agreed to carry him to UK he had to have a medical.'

'They made him sit a medical?' Eliot says.

'Yes. They wanted to be sure he was healthy,' Dudu explains. 'Alphonse rang me the day before he left. The smugglers told him someone had become ill and died on the journey and they didn't want the risk of it happening twice.'

'Did he tell you what the tests were?' Roxanne asks.

'No.'

'You didn't find this strange?' Eliot asks.

'Why?'

'Did you sit a medical before travelling?'

'There are many different trees in the forest. I came by plane with my family and claimed asylum at the airport. I was not smuggled in.'

The three sit in silence for a few moments.

'Are you thinking what I'm thinking?' Eliot asks Roxanne.

'Possibly,' Roxanne says non-commitally.

'Dudu, do you mind if Roxanne and I speak in private?'

'You are welcome.' Sweeping the kids out ahead of him, Dudu withdraws, closing the door behind him.

'Who would organise a medical, and for what purpose?' Eliot says. 'I can't believe a man like Brown cares about the health of the people he smuggles in. Assuming Brown's involved, that is. And if it's just the drivers ...'

'Assuming Brown's involved?' Roxanne explodes. 'You were the one ...' She pauses. 'Look, if there was a medical then there's a doctor. If there's a doctor then maybe he could be persuaded to talk ....'

'OK, let's assume for one minute that Dudu has got his story straight. Big assumption. Anyway, what kind of doctor would get involved?'

'Tell me, Eliot, is this because Dudu's an immigrant or because he's black?'

'Get lost.'

'No, I really want to know. Because...'

'Oh, grow up.' Eliot paces the room, trying to keep his head clear. 'OK. How do we get into France?'

'We?'

'Yeah, how do we get into France? I'll need you there to translate.'

DS Store puts the phone back in its cradle. It has taken some pursuading to convince the Glasgow police to let him send his own men up to apprehend Balkan and the French woman, after a member of the public rung in claiming to have spotted the pair in Fulhill. Store is increasingly nervous that they are losing control of the situation and that, if that happens, he will be the one hung out to dry. He picks the handset up to make a second call.

'Are you sure about this?'
'No,'
They are sitting in the car in the dark, forty miles from Glasgow.
'Is he reliable?'
'He'll come,' Roxanne says.
'Yes, but when?'
'I don't know,' she shouts.
Eliot looks at his watch. Midnight. A couple of hours sleep before setting off has barely scratched the surface of his weariness. They are both on edge. There is no way they could approach any port or airport, the news bulletins identifying them as the killers of Timothy Wesley have put paid to that. Their photos will be everywhere. So instead they wait on the edge of a tiny airfield, awaiting the arrival of a light aircraft. Huddled in the car, woolly hats on, wrapped against the cold, scanning the horizon for the telltale silhouette in the sky.
'How long have you known Jacques?'
'Four or five years.'
'Through business?'
'Yes.'
'And he still carries a torch for you?'
She turns towards him but it is too dark for either of them to see the other's face. Eliot hears her sigh.
'Your text message finished that. I screamed at him for two minutes before he was able to tell me he was responding to my text message. Which I hadn't sent.'
'He's a good pilot though?'
'I have no idea. He and my brother took their pilot's licence at the same time. Six years ago, maybe seven.'
More silence.
'Do you have any cigarettes?' Eliot says presently.
Roxanne coughs. 'I stopped last year.'
'So did I. I keep a few in the glovebox, just in case.'
'This is a rental car. We left mine in a river, remember?'
'Right.' Eliot's hand drifts to his ear, as if hoping to find a fag

tucked behind it. 'By the way does Jacques know that we're an item?'

'What?'

'You know, lovers.'

There is a sudden movement, a rustling of clothing. The car's interior lights come on. Roxanne looks ready to kill.

'Joke,' he says, hands up defensively. 'It's a joke.'

She continues staring at him.

'OK, it's not a joke. I have the hots for you. There, I've said it.' He nods dumly to confirm he is telling the truth.

'The hots?' mouthing the word as if it is the most ridiculous expression she has ever heard. She switches the light off, then adds softly. 'You pick your moment.'

'Love's like that.'

'It is?'

'I feel like I'm about to freeze,' he says after a moment.

'So freeze,' she answers, gently running her hand through his hair. 'You should relax more.'

'Tell me something I don't know.'

More silence.

Roxanne leans forward and switches on the radio. A bossa nova track, Desefinado. Cool, sophisticated, sexy.

'You know why I love this song?'

'Amaze me,' he says, reaching out and pulling her towards him.

'It's the only song I know with the word Rolliflex in the lyrics.'

'Amazing.'

His mouth closes over hers and they kiss. The bossa nova melody meanders an effortless but improbable arc as their breaths intermingle. He feels the tip of her nose brush his cheek.

'Eliot,' she says, pulling away.

'What?' He opens his eyes.

'I think that's him.'

'Is his timing always this good?'

A couple of flashing lights are visible less than fifty metres away, barely above the treeline, hurtling straight at them.

twenty nine

If Jacques understands who Eliot is, he keeps it to himself. Having all but scraped the paint off the car roof, the plane lingers on the ground just long enough for Roxanne and Eliot to clamber on board. They bounce about on the grass as the aircraft picks up speed and takes off. The Cessna climbs steeply over the airfield carpark. Eliot hopes the car will still be there when they return.

Jacques is a little older than Eliot expected, mid forties maybe, with short greying hair, dark eyes and a Roman nose. Eliot, stuck in the back of the four seater, listening to Roxanne and Jacques chatting away in French, soon tires. He allows the constant hum of the engine to lull him into a dreamless sleep.

Touchdown wakes him up. As seems an increasing occurence, he has no idea where he is. He shouts as he sits up and bangs his head.

'Ah Eliot, ça va?'

'What? Oh, Jacques. Yeah, ça va. Where are we?'

'Near Saumur,' Roxanne says, turning round. 'Hungry?'

Breakfast comes from a small boulangerie, the best croissants Eliot has ever tasted. It being only six in the morning the shop isn't open but Jacques leads the way through a side door straight into the bakery. As Jacques and Roxanne chat with the owner, Eliot breathes in the fantastic yeasty aromas of baguettes and pains au chocolat. The croissants are still cooling on a rack beside the oven.

Jacques drops them back at the small airfield where he has also organised a car, a large Mercedes.

'Happy hunting,' he calls over his shoulder, heading back towards the plane.

Roxanne drives. For a while the road flanks the Loire. It being winter the river is broad and full, sparkling in the moonlight. Eliot munches croissants and lets the tension drop from his shoulders. For the first time in a week he feels safe and relaxed. A bath, a shave, and a change of clothes are all he needs. He glances over at Roxanne and smiles to himself, well maybe not quite all. They head north, leaving the river behind them. A row of troglodytic houses clings to the cliff

BENEATH THE BITTERCREST

face. A few brief glimpses of the Loire beneath them before the road enters a forest.

'Not much further,' she says.

When the road emerges from the forest, Eliot sees row upon row of heavily pruned vines disappearing into the mist. They speed through a village, after which Roxanne turns onto an avenue lined with tall poplar trees, their empty cages rocking in the wind.

'You live in a chateau?'

'This is my parents' house. It is not really a chateau.'

'Really? So what is it then, a worker's cottage with fifty extra rooms, two towers and a stone staircase?'

As they climb out of the car, two huge hounds appear around one corner of the house, pounding across the gravel, their sleek short hair emphasising their powerful musculature. Eliot takes a step back, he has never liked dogs and recent events in Swindon have done little to help.

Roxanne steps in front of him and catches the dogs in her arms. There is a flurry of dribbling tongues, huge canine teeth, tender words spoken in French.

'Offer them your hand.'

'Oh right. Give them a snack then the rest of me gets the freedom of the chateau? Blood dripping from the stump ...'

'Let them smell your hand, stupid,' she laughs.

Eliot is suddenly aware of the warm smell of Roxanne's neck, millimetres from his nose. Intoxicated, he does as he is told and gingerly extends his hands around the sides of her body. He flinches as animal fur brushes his skin and two wet noses press against the backs of his hands. Roxanne speaks to the dogs. All at once they stop sniffing, back away, bark once in unison and race away in the direction from which they have come.

Eliot, watching the departing hounds over one of Roxanne's shoulders, becomes aware that his arms are still extended to either side of her body, his chest pressed up against her back. Roxanne steps forwards, turns and gives him what might be read as a smile. He lopes after her across the gravel.

They enter the house by a side door which opens onto a huge kitchen with dusty pale blue walls and dark hardwood furniture, the windows shuttered against the night. Roxanne, having set the coffee machine going, hurries off. He hears her greeting someone, it is clear from the sounds of delight that she has been sorely missed.

'Maman, je vous présente Eliot.'

In the doorway beside Roxanne stands an elegant woman in a floor length green dressing gown, covered with delicately stitched dragons in a Chinese style. Her red hair is swept into a bun, her eyes blue and full of warmth.

'Bonjour, monsieur, c'est un plaisir.'

'She says it's a pleasure ...'

'It's OK, my school French can deal with this,' Eliot reassures Roxanne. 'Bonjour, madame. Votre petite maison est très jolie.'

Roxanne gives him a look.

'Vous allez rester quelques jours chez nous?'

Eliot looks to Roxanne uncertainly.

'It's OK, have your coffee. I'll take Maman outside and explain things to her.'

Roxanne returns some five minutes later, grabbing a coffee before she speaks. 'Are you ready?'

Eliot gulps his coffee and follows her out. The hounds appear briefly then withdraw. Out of the corner of his eye Eliot notices an old blue car with huge round headlights parked in a barn at the side of the house.

'Something I said?'

'No, your French was ...' Roxanne struggles to find the word she wants.

'I meant is everything OK?'

'Why?'

'Your mum seemed kind of ...'

'Is there a croissant left in that bag or did you pig the lot?'

The car rips down the drive, spraying gravel in all directions.

The moon has sagged towards the horizon where a bank of dark clouds are gathering. The night sky is being diluted by the feeble light of a winter dawn. Roxanne, jaw set, throws the car round the bends, heading north. Three small villages come and go in a flurry of grey stone, lights in downstairs rooms indicating the early risers. Eliot wonders what day of the week it is.

'Why do people always make assumptions?'

Eliot decides she is speaking rhetorically.

'That's what really annoys me.' Roxanne glances briefly in Eliot's direction before launching into a bout of coughing.

'We woke her up in the middle of the night. How long is it since she saw you?'

BENEATH THE BITTERCREST

Eliot's head is thrown back as Roxanne drops down a gear to speed up the hill. The dark branches of a pine forest shake in the wind.

'By the way, I think you should see a doctor about that cough.'

'I'm fine. We're going to see one of my ... my brother's friends.'

'OK.' Eliot puts his head back against the headrest and closes his eyes.

His head rolls from side to side as the car rides the bends. The passing villages are as easy to hear as to see. The car only slows a fraction but the change in the sound of the engine's roar bouncing back off the walls of the houses is obvious even with eyes closed. Sight renders the ears lazy. The escalating morning light imprints itself on his eyelids. He wants music but can't be bothered to go through the rigmarole of sorting it out. The car stops suddenly and he opens his eyes to find Roxanne scowling at him.

'Hi, Eliot, are you feeling better?' he says. 'Yes, thank you, Roxanne, it's really good to know that however bad things get we still have each other.' He arches his eyebrows.

Her scowl softens. She sighs and coughs. 'Look, all I ...,' she starts.

'It's OK. Take it easy.'

They are in a village square, flanked by an army of maple trees which, in summer, no doubt provide welcome shade. In the cold light of a January morning, however, their empty branches reveal a butchery of stumps reminding Eliot of octupuses with their legs tied in knots.

Lights are on in the café. Gusts of wind toss long dead leaves about.

The chairs are up on the tables except one. At the far end of the room sits a large man in a black leather blouson jacket, hair sleeked back from his face, nose bulbous, wrists heavy with gold chains. The triangular Ricard ashtray in front of him already contains the remains of four Gauloises cigarettes and the air is acrid with their smoke. A single light is on over the bar. The shutters are shut.

'Salut, Pierrot.'

Roxanne and Pierrot exchange kisses, three times on each cheek.

'Café?' Pierrot indicates the machine behind the bar with his eyes.

'Oui, allez.'

Roxanne pours two coffees, for herself and Eliot. Pierrot studies Eliot, his clothes, his face, his hair.

'L'Anglais, qu'est-ce qu'il fait là?'

'How does he know I am English?' Eliot says.

'Your shoes,' Pierrot says disdainfully in English.

'He is a friend,' Roxanne replies in French.

Pierrot shrugs.

While Pierrot and Roxanne speak, Eliot inspects the jukebox. It is intriguing. At home the machines, when you can find one, usually play only the top forty and a handful of golden oldies, a bit of Elvis, some Beatles, Stones, George Michael, Simply Red. Here, in the middle of bloody nowhere in rural France, it is altogether different. French, English and American pop music; but also Zairean soukous, Brazilian sounds, jazz, blues, flamenco, North African stuff, Italian opera. He chooses Desefinado and sips his coffee. The mechanical arm grabs the CD and bossa nova trickles from six speakers recessed into the ceiling.

He has barely dipped a toe in the sophisticated minimalist asymmetry of the bossa nova beat, when he feels a hand on his arm.

'Come on.' She steers Eliot towards the door. 'Merci, Pierrot,' she calls out.

'De rien. Bonne chance.'

As they head out of the village, Roxanne looks worried, glancing in her rear view mirror several times.

'Did we find anything out?'

'My brother's friend has left the country.' She answers. 'He sold everything and moved out two weeks ago. Pierrot said there was talk of a great deal of money changing hands. The staff were told on the Friday afternoon that they should not turn up for work on the Monday. Just like that.'

'What do the police say?'

'He's gone on holiday. There's no law against closing a company down. He had told someone he was thinking of leaving the country so that's what he's done. They think he's in the Caribbean, drinking cocktails and partying.'

'I thought employees had rights in France,' Eliot says.

'Until Marc comes back there is nothing they can do.'

Eliot pinches his nose, they are too late again, another door has closed.

'So, two businessmen go missing and nobody bats an eyelid.'

'The police listed my brother as missing but they believe he simply had an argument with his lover and walked away to cool off. No body, no crime.'

'Great.'

'Same with Marc. He did give me something though.'

'Who?'

'Pierrot. A phone number for one of the women who worked in Marc's office.'

'What are we waiting for?'

'We're not waiting. She lives here.'

They are entering a village, a one street affair with the houses flanking the road on either side for half a kilometre. It is properly light now, almost half past seven. They pull up outside a row of terraced houses. Another bout of coughing.

'This time you stay in the car, OK?'

Eliot nods. 'Remember, we want the name of the doctor,' he calls after her as she steps out of the car.

She waves to show that she has heard.

The door is answered almost immediately. A huge whale of a man in blue pyjamas shuffles off to be replaced by a short woman in thick fluffy slippers and a beige woollen dress. She stands arms akimbo in the doorway while behind her a group of children are fighting. Roxanne exchanges a few words with the woman who steps aside and lets her in.

Eliot turns on the radio, finds something classical and waits.

'So, do we have a name?' he asks, when Roxanne returns.

'Better than that. Office keys. We are going to Saumur.'

Havering climbs out of his car and approaches what remains of Han's cottage. The morning has been a disaster. He had just reached the M6 when the call came through. Peter Han's body has been found in a ditch some fifteen miles east of Swindon by a woman walking her dog. The body appears to have been dumped the previous night. An autopsy is scheduled for later in the day.

It is a little after eight am. A phonecall has established that the fire took place yesterday morning and that by the time the fire services arrived on the scene the building had already collapsed. Having satisfied themselves that no-one was trapped inside, the fire chief and local police cordoned the area off and left. Insurance inspectors are expected during the course of the morning.

Walking round the smouldering remains, stepping over shards of glass and distorted debris that have fused together in the heat of the fire, Havering reflects on the developing situation.

However many noses Peter Han put out of joint, he has not deserved this. Furthermore, it is years since the Fraud Squad investigations, hard to believe that feelings would still be running high after all that time. Of course it is possible that someone has just come out of jail with a score to settle, but it seems unlikely. Apart from anything else Han has found himself a very quiet backwater. Even his own office haven't known his address.

Arson is suspected, but it will be a few days before anyone will offer an official opinion as to how the fire started. Empty cottages aren't a top priority.

Trees flank the garden on three sides. From the ground floor of the cottage, the lie of the land is such that it is impossible to see down into the valley below. Someone approaching from that direction would not be seen until they were almost at the front door. On the other hand, the cottage is so tucked away that Han will have been invisible to anyone who has not known where to find him.

The wind is whispering the trees beneath a pewter sky. Although the garden is dormant, Havering can see enough to know that it has been tended by a loving hand. Flowerbeds cleared and tidied, shrubs lining the path up the garden all neatly pruned. No doubt snowdrops and daffodils will soon spike the cold soil.

Havering walks up the path towards the top of the garden, partly to look at the plants and partly to gain a vantage point from which to view the site. Seeing the gate and the path beyond, leading up between the trees, he experiences a pang of envy imagining Han going for a morning walk.

Solitude and tranquillity. A far cry from city streets.

Muffled birdsong hung between the trees. Has Eliot Balkan been here? Havering asks himself. His intuition tells him yes.

As he turns back towards the cottage, his jaw drops in surprise.

Saumur was once the centre of Protestant resistance during the wars of religion, four hundred years ago, its narrow streets witness to the barbarity of intolerance as the Huguenots were driven out of France and Catholic Europe, to seek refuge in England and Scotland. Now the town is on the tourist trail, renowned for its imposing castle overlooking the Loire, and its fine wines. On the pedestrianised streets away from the river, people hurry on their way, collars turned up, as if the past were a different country. Which indeed it is.

The offices of TransEuro Exports are in a side street close to the town centre, tucked between a designer optician's on the one side and a charcuterie on the other. Every building is hewn from blocks of warm sand-coloured local stone. Above every shop front is spread a balcony with elegant black railings. Roxanne finds the right key and pushes the door open against a thick flotsam of unopened mail. A church clock strikes nine o'clock.

They climb the stairs to the first floor only to find a second locked door. The key requires considerable wiggling about before the lock tumbles. Eliot guesses the key is a copy of a copy, made without permission, possibly by the secretary.

The office has clearly been vacated in a hurry; papers strewn over desktops, half drunk cups of coffee hairy-festering near the window, an umbrella hanging by a radiator. Someone has scribbled on the wall 'le boulot c'est con', work is shit.

Through the window you can see into the office on the other side of the street; they will have to work quickly.

'Anything about doctors or medicals,' he says, crossing over to a filing cabinet.

Havering stumbles as he runs across the wet grass towards the shed.

Invisible from below, no-one would know of the shed's existence unless he or she had climbed the path to the top of the garden. Even then a casual observer might miss it, partially hidden as it is by vegetation and an outcrop of rock.

With mounting excitement, Havering pulls at the unvarnished wooden door.

It is locked.

There is nothing of interest in the first room. Company brochures, packing materials, toner cartridges, headed notepaper and other stationery.

The second room, which overlooks a small courtyard at the back of the building, has a slightly smarter desk and chair. The manager's office.

'I'll go upstairs,' Eliot says. 'It's docteur or médecin, right?'

'Chirurgien is a surgeon and infirmière is a nurse.'

Eliot mouthes the words back at her to memorise them.

The second floor is organised pretty much like the first floor, two main rooms, but where there is a toilet on the first floor there is a small kitchen on the second. There are three desks and a locked filing cabinet in the front room, and two desks in the back. Eliot pulls open drawers, inspects the piles of paper stacked up on each desk.

In the front room, and partially obscured by foliage, a large day-planner above the fireplace catches his eye. To get a better view, he moves the pot plants from mantle piece to nearby filing cabinet. The day planner, which runs to the end of January, provides him with exactly what he is looking for.

Three days, two in December and one in January, the last entry just days before everyone was laid off and the offices were closed.

'Et voilà!' Roxanne is in the doorway clutching a sheet of paper. 'Three names, and phone numbers. I recognise one of them, my father visited him a few years ago. He lives just outside Saumur.'

'Brilliant. And look at this,' he shows her the wall chart. 'Swindon. Here, here and here. Three separate entries.'

What's through here?' Roxanne asks, walking out onto the landing.

'Nothing worth looking at.' He follows her into the back room.

Roxanne throws open the window and stares down at the courtyard below. 'I want to check something downstairs.'

Back on the first floor, they enter the manager's office. Eliot watches Roxanne as she rummages in the desk drawers for a few seconds.

'No, there's nothing,' she says. 'We've got the list, let's go.'

They both hear the click of the door.

The man pushes the pile of junkmail and letters aside with his foot. Producing a long hunting knife from inside the folds of his black blouson jacket he steps forwards. The stairs groan as they take his weight.

A sound upstairs.

Is there someone else in the building with him?

He stops on the fifth step, listening carefully.

A loud crash reverberates in the stairwell. Launching himself up the stairs, the man rushes past the first floor offices and on up to the top of the building.

On the second floor landing he pauses. A noise from the back room. He launches himself forwards, blade in front of him ready for action.

Shards of pottery lie among soil and broken plants and various pieces of paper on the floor in front of a filing cabinet. Fresh sheets of paper fly off the cabinet as gusts of wind billows into the room through an open window that looks out across the rooftops. They can't have escaped from two floors up.

BENEATH THE BITTERCREST

Suddenly he realises he is not alone.

'No wait!' someone shouts.

The man spuns round and glimpses Roxanne standing in the doorway at the very instant something heavy connects with the side of his head. He slumps to his knees then tips forwards, his head smacking the floor. As the world fades he recognises the Englishman's awful shoes in front of his nose.

'How was I to know who he was?' Eliot protests.

They walk briskly through the narrow streets. Roxanne is coughing again. Eliot grabs her arm and drags her into a side alley.

'It's OK. Catch your breath. No-one's following us.'

Roxanne leans against the wall, fighting to bring her lungs under control.

'He was coming to warn us,' she insists.

'So why was he carrying a knife?'

'I've known him for years.'

'And you call me naive.'

Reluctantly, she acknowledges that Eliot is right. Her lungs succumb to another bout of coughing as she considers who Pierrot may have spoken to in the past hour.

'We have to get you to a doctor.'

'It's nothing. You're sure he can't escape?'

They have left Pierrot bound and gagged where he fell.

'I'm more concerned that he'll starve to death if no-one finds him. Anyway, let's worry about you. You breathed in several litres of river water yesterday.'

'Leave it, Eliot.'

Havering doesn't call a locksmith, he has long ago learnt how to force doors.

A musty smell of dried grass, dormant bulbs, garden tools, and creosote hangs in the air. Propped up in one corner are a couple of tatty deckchairs. In front of them an old watering can and a hover mower. Balls of twine hang on the back of the door along with secateurs, an assortment of trowels, and a tired toothless saw. The wooden floor is dusty, flakes of caked mud fallen from drying tools or from between the tread of wellington boots mingle with dried leaves and papery fragments of loose skin from the bulbs.

But what really catches Havering's eye is the twelve inch telescope partially hidden beneath a dust cover. It is a beautiful piece of kit and must have cost Han an arm and most of a leg. Havering pictures Han on a summer's night beneath the stars, drink in hand, hunting supernovae. Whisky or beer? Whisky probably. And a thermos of coffee.

The shed has no window so Havering moves further in to allow more light in through the door. Everything is just as one would expect in a garden shed.

And yet somehow too perfect.

Acting on instinct, Havering starts carrying stuff out of the shed to clear the floor. It doesn't take him long to find what he was looking for.

thirty

The waiting room is all but empty. Eliot chooses a chair by the window and gazes down at the bright waters of the Loire. Roxanne collects a magazine from the low table and joins him.

A fifty year old man in a brown suit fiddles with one of the cuffs of his shirt, head downcast, hair untidy. His left leg twitches to a rhythm playing in his head.

Across the room a couple are whispering, he hesitantly, she passionately. She holds his hand and looks into his eyes. She appears fifteen years younger than him, her elegant jacket and skirt perfectly offsetting the various items of gold that adorn her neck, ears and wrists. He too is well dressed but, like a snake about to slough its skin, his clothes seem detached, as if he will soon be rid of them. He smiles nervously, his eyes looking sadly into hers.

Reflected in a mirror hanging beside the couple, and sitting by a window across the room, are a second couple who Eliot fails to recognise momentarily.

Eliot turns to look at Roxanne. She is completely transformed. A voluminous shoulder length auburn wig. The nose stud is gone, the makeup now classically elegant, the clothes and jewellery identical in intention to that of the woman opposite. I am wealthy, the look says, I have property, taste, and refinement. Similar to the woman Eliot met on the train at Doncaster but more French.

It hasn't prevented her from stepping into the clinic through the 'out' door, of course, and it isn't stopping her from tearing pages from the magazine she is reading when she finds something interesting. Some things you just can't change.

While the disguise is principally intended to avoid any possibility of the doctor recognising her, Roxanne has insisted that Eliot also be metamorphosed, if they are going to talk business they have to look the part. Designer stubble and the slept-in look are not 'private clinic' apparently.

'You know dressing up is not really my ...'

'We're all pretending, Eliot, pretending to be things we're not. Putting on a show. That's life.'

The black leather moccasins are snug but not too uncomfortable.

Not yet anyway. The dark blue suit cost more than he has spent on clothes in his entire life. Roxanne has paid for everything on a French credit card. Since it is clear any cash withdrawls or other transactions from his accounts will run them grave risks of being traced, he has not complained, though he refuses the yellow shirt she selects. They compromise on a white shirt and the darkest thinnest tie in the shop. His makeover is rounded off with a haircut and shave at a swanky hairdresser's. Finally, he looks the part, to her satisfaction anyway. He isn't himself convinced that having his head practically shaved by a camp giant smelling of roses will do anything other than lay him out with flu the minute they arrive back in Scotland. And the sideburns will take weeks to grow back.

Purchases concluded, and with the earliest doctor's appointment being for mid-afternoon, Roxanne takes Eliot to a restaurant to celebrate.

'You look good,' she says, kissing him on the cheek before sitting down. 'So young that what we're doing may not be legal.'

'And what are we doing exactly?' he smiles, pushing a saucer of olives across the table towards her.

A waiter glides forward silently.

'You choose,' Eliot says after glancing at the menu.

She does. The waiter withdraws.

'I don't think I ever met this doctor before but he may have visited the house when my father was ill. My mother might have showed him my photo. I'm sorry but I had to change the way I look.'

'No need to apologise for sitting across a table from me dressed like that,' he replies, his eyes hungrier looking at her than they were studying the menu.

She looks disappointed, picks an olive from the saucer and licks it slowly before popping it in her mouth.

'It's not that you don't usually look fantastic anyway, it's ... oh shit, I'm just digging a hole, aren't I?'

She smiles and coughs. Behind the makeup she looks unwell.

'You know I chased round half the hospitals in Yorkshire looking for you, after the crash?' he says as the waiter arrives and hovers, wine bottle in hand.

'Maxine Foulcaut'

Eliot snaps back to the present and looks up.

In the doorway is a nurse, immaculate white dress, a watch pinned to her breast pocket. Eliot waits for the whispering couple to stand

BENEATH THE BITTERCREST

and follow her out of the waiting room. Instead it is Roxanne who stands and tugs at his sleeve.

Havering studies his haul: two large sealed bags in thick plastic, containing hundreds of sheets of paper, some hand written, some printed; two audio cassettes; and a laptop computer.

A large packing crate, also hidden beneath the shed floor, is crammed with a professional sleuth's tools of the trade. Night vision goggles, lock picking equipment, glass cutters, various bugging kits, false ID, knives, cameras, a pistol ... Han's arsenal is impressive.

Everything Havering isn't taking with him goes back as he found it, if anyone else spots the shed at the top of Han's garden then Havering is determined not to make it easy for them. He sets about replacing the loose floorboards, kicking dirt and dry leaves about to cover his traces, before hauling the lawn mower, the telescope and all the other junk back inside the shed. Finally, satisfied with his work, he pushes the door shut, dragging a large rock into place to prevent the door from flapping open.

The sky is charcoal grey. Rain is only minutes away.

'Entrez, entrez.'

Monsieur Boutet is in his very well-heeled fifties with a deep tan that tells of many hours of leisure pursuits on a yacht or tropical beach, closely cropped white hair, a perfect set of teeth, and a booming voice that speaks of decades of success. The furnishings in his office are all period pieces, magnificent leather-backed chairs, glass fronted bookcases, a real fire and, on the walls, various paintings of chateaux of the Loire, prints of hunting scenes, and a set of Sherlock Holmes first editions.

Boutet indicates the two chairs in front of his desk with a wave of his hand while he quickly looks down at his list of appointments.

'Alors, Madame Foulcaut et ...?'

'Peter Eavesham,' Eliot says.

'Ah, an Englishman.' Boutet smiles.

'Oui.'

'Ah, vous parlez le français.'

'Non, not really.'

Boutet looks disappointed.

'Vous preférez que je parle en français ou en anglais, Madame?' Boutet says, addressing the beautiful and obviously wealthy woman sitting opposite him.

'En anglais,' Roxanne replies, without looking at Eliot.

Boutet waits for Roxanne to finish coughing. 'Daccord.'

'I am keen to explore the services you might be able to offer my organisation,' Roxanne starts.

'Certainly,' Boutet smiles again, his open hand gesturing encouragingly.

'We are considering entering into a trading arrangement with a British company.

While Roxanne speaks Eliot studies Boutet's face closely.

'This company has set preconditions that include the need for services I am hopeful someone such as yourself might offer.'

If Boutet knows what is coming, he hides it well. The smile sits on his tanned face as comfortably as a cat sprawled across a sofa.

'Does Monsieur Eavesham represent the British client?'

'No,' Eliot answers for himself. 'Madame Foulcaut has retained my services ... in an advisory capacity.'

'I understand.' Boutet's attention returns to Roxanne. 'And someone has recommended our services?'

'Exactly.' Roxanne coughs again.

Eliot notices that the colour is draining from her cheeks.

'As you will know, our services are founded on discretion and client confidentiality ... ah ...'

' ... but can I divulge who has given me your name?' Roxanne says, pulling herself together and finishing the sentence for him.

'You are very perceptive.'

Roxanne makes a show of considering the question. She looks towards Eliot who nods as if giving her permission to reveal a previously agreed detail. Eliot feels Boutet's eyes on him briefly.

'I will say only that our recommendation came from Swindon,' Roxanne says.

The mask slips momentarily. The smile remains in place but the eyes shift. It is subtle, and all too brief, but it is enough, they have their man.

'I am told your fees are appropriate and your service excellent,' Roxanne says.

'Such praise is an honour for the clinic. We will be happy to assist you. When shall we start?'

Roxanne looks again towards Eliot. His eyes seek confirmation from her that his opinion is sought. She nods.

BENEATH THE BITTERCREST   231

'Prior to deciding to whom this contract should be awarded,' Eliot says, 'a comparison of the services being offered would be prudent.'

Roxanne nods again and turns towards Boutet, her eyebrows raised.

'We will offer, of course, the same service we have offered previous clients, and at the same price,' he says smoothly.

'And what service is that exactly?' Roxanne says, producing a hankerchief and mopping her brow.

Boutet's fingertips build a cage in the air in front of him as he considers his reply.

Eliot does his best to look disinterested, while at the same time praying that the dictaphone in his pocket is actually working and that the microphone is getting enough level to make a viable recording. He makes a show of checking his watch.

'Maybe we should return when we have heard what the other ...' Eliot suggests blandly.

Finally Boutet commits himself.

'There will be the routine physical examination, a general health check: pulse, blood pressure, pulmonary tests, to confirm the absence of tuberculosis or other infection, urine, saliva, etc. and, of course, the blood tests.'

Eliot wonders why the surgeon seems so reluctant to divulge any information, and why a man of his standing interests himself in matters as basic as health checks.

'The cost we have been advised to expect seems extraordinarily high for a routine health check, Mr Boutet,' Roxanne says. 'As I explained we are not yet committed to this arrangement. The projections so far discussed, coupled with what I have learnt this afternoon, suggest that this opportunity might not be as interesting to us as we had hoped.'

Boutet's smile slips, he appears torn between his desire for the contract and caution. Greed wins out. 'May I speak frankly, Madame Foulcaut?'

Roxanne indicates that he may.

'The costs are as they are for two reasons. Firstly, there is the nature of the job. It will be obvious to you that work like this has to be carried out with the utmost discretion. This is as true for us at the clinic as for yourselves. The staff are picked very carefully and the work is carried out in such a way as to leave no trail.'

Boutet pauses to allow time for his words to sink in, then

continues. 'Secondly, the blood tests are far more complex than those required for an ordinary medical examination. There are many different major histocompatiblity (HLA) proteins. Human leukocyte antigens are not unique to the individual but since each of the antigens exists, in different individuals, in as many as 20 varieties, the number of possible HLA types is about 10,000, each white blood cell having a double set of six major antigens, HLA-A, B, and C, and three types of HLA-D. You will understand that such work is necessarily highly specialised and requires very specialist equipment and skilled personnel. I supervise the work myself and I can assure you that we are, without question, the finest facility in the region.'

Boutet sits back in his chair. The smile returns, reassuring, warm and confident.

'Mr Boutet, I thank you for your candour.' Roxanne says. 'You will, I am sure, appreciate that, given the sums involved, we needed to reassure ourselves of the professionalism of all involved.'

Boutet is nodding vigourously.

Roxanne looks towards Eliot, who simply raises his hands to indicate that he is satisfied. She stands up and the two men do likewise.

'Thank you for your time. You will, I am sure, be hearing from either myself or one of my colleagues shortly.'

'Madame, it will be a pleasure, and may I be permitted to say that I am very much in support of this ... ah ... this project. There is a great need out there.'

'Thank you, that is most kind.'

'And may I suggest, Madame, that you see a nurse before you leave? You have a nasty cough and I am sure we can provide you with a few antibiotics.'

Roxanne glances in Eliot's direction.

'Thank you, most kind,' she repeats, clutching her hankerchief.

Boutet holds the door open for them. 'Madame, monsieur.' The smile is broader than ever.

As the door closes and Roxanne and Eliot make their way back down the corridor, Eliot fancies the surgeon's smile lingers and shimmers in the air behind them like a dew sparkled cobweb trembling over a tombstone at sunrise.

Before they are even out of the clinic car park, Roxanne is on the phone to Jacques. After a brief conversation she passes the phone to

BENEATH THE BITTERCREST   233

Eliot so that he can scribble down directions to an airfield in Normandy where Jacques will pick them up, the Frenchman having been adamant that he will not return to the airfield where he dropped them off earlier in the day.

Eliot reads out the directions to Roxanne.

'We've just got time if we don't stop for anything but petrol. We have to use the N roads, the motorways are too dangerous, we might get traced and stopped at a toll booth.'

'What about the other doctors on that list?'

'What's the point?' Roxanne swallows a couple of antibiotics.

'Fair enough,' he concedes. 'Did you understand any of that stuff Doctor Smiley told you, by the way?'

'Did the dictaphone work?'

Eliot fishes the tiny recorder out of his pocket, rewinds the tape and presses play. The sound quality is worse than from a call box in Patagonia but the voices are intelligible. He holds the machine to her ear so that she can hear for herself.

'We simply need to find someone who does understand it.'

They stop for petrol just outside Rouen. In the next bay a Rover with UK plates is receiving a large measure of unleaded. While Roxanne goes to pay for the fuel, Eliot watches two kids bouncing about on the rear seats of the Rover.

'Keep the bloody noise down, Tiffany,' the mother yells while fiddling with her lip gloss in the vanity mirror.

It is a vortex that sucks Eliot straight in and spits him out somewhere in North Wales six months ago. A holiday in Anglesey, the usual torment of rain swept beaches, damp sandwiches, and bawling kids.

'Keep the bloody noise down, Alexandra,' Sue says as she struggles with the lid of the thermos flask.

Overwhelmed by the need to hear his kid's voices, Eliot grabs Roxanne's mobile, which she has left on the dashboard.

'Yes?'

'Sue, it's me?'

'What do you want, Eliot?'

'I just want it all to stop. The running, the fighting, the nastiness.'

'I'm busy. The children are in the bath.'

'Sue, it's all got out of hand.'

'You should have thought of that when you were ...'

'Please, listen to me. I haven't much time. People are being killed and no-one gives a toss.'

'You've been on television,' her voice unimpressed.

'It wasn't me. You have to believe that. Look,' he struggles to find the right words, to ignore the ice in her voice. 'I want you to get a message to Stephen for me. About BitterCrest. The accountant there, a man called ...'

'You can tell him yourself.'

'Eliot, hi,' says a new voice.

'Stephen. What's going on?' Eliot's head is swimming. He hears Sue in the background, shouting at the kids.

'I came round to see if Sue needed anything,' Stephen says, answering the unasked question. 'What are you playing at, Eliot? Why haven't you ...'

'You have to help me. There's no-one else. Gustave Brown at BitterCrest, he's the one behind the smuggling. He has to be. People are dying, Stephen. They're smuggling people. I saw Brown in the low building where ...'

Roxanne emerges from the shop.

'I have to go. Tell Sue I'll call again. And kiss the kids for me.'

Eliot cuts the call.

'Who were you calling?' Roxanne asks as she sat down. 'You know how long it takes them to trace a call from a mobile phone?'

'What?'

'Don't bullshit me.'

'Checking to see if there's a decent signal. I'm about to send an email.' He shows her the screen which is indeed partially filled with text, then continues crunching keys. 'Didn't realise you had a WAP phone.' Eliot really doesn't want a conversation with Roxanne about a wife and kids. 'I need to let someone know I'll be a little late supplying the papers he requested.'

Roxanne picks up the card balancing on Eliot's right leg.

'Detective Inspector Havering?'

'One of the good guys. I hope.'

thirty one

The 'good guy' has decided to work from home. Just as well, since Havering's trawl through the papers taken from Han's shed reveal that the ex-policeman seems to have spent much of his spare time investigating the police. Havering knows there won't be much sympathy at the station for a man who turned on his own.

To save time while he waits for the kettle to boil, Havering puts one of the tapes into the cassette player in the kitchen. On the cassette label are scribbled the words 'G.Brown - 20.11.01'

The sound quality is poor but audible. A bugged telephone conversation between two men.

'What do you want?'

'I'm concerned,'

'Go on.' The tone bored, disinterested.

'It's Wesley. We need to keep an eye on him.'

'Well keep an eye on him.'

A pause.

'Was there anything else?'

'I'm not happy about the girl. If she finds any ...'

The dialing tone cuts in. The other party has hung up.

Presumably one of the voices belongs to G. Brown. Who is he and what is the link between him and the letter in Arabic that Eliot Balkan has been carrying? And who is the girl?

The front door slams.

'How was your trip?' Niveen calls out from the hall.

Havering retrieves the tape from the cassette player, it will have to wait.

They touch down in Scotland just after eleven. Roxanne has been arguing with Jacques for almost half an hour and Eliot understands enough to know that she has been pleading with him to rest before heading back. All she has managed to extract is a promise to put the plane down at the first airfield over the Channel.

'Look after her,' Jacques says quietly to Eliot as he prepares to follow Roxanne out onto the wing and down onto the ground.

'She's not the looked after type, is she?'

Eliot watches Roxanne heading off towards the car park. Though they have exchanged barely fifty words, meeting Jacques in person has left Eliot feeling bad about using him to reach Roxanne, the more so given the help Jacques has provided.

'You get some rest,' Eliot advises.

Jacques nods. 'By the way. Your change of image. Nice suit, very French.'

Eliot smiles and watches as the Frenchman revs the engine and taxies away to the pumps to fill up. Clutching the sports bag containing his normal clothes, Eliot runs off across the grass to catch up with Roxanne.

The moon, which has been following them on their journey northwards from France, is now prowling behind a cloudbank gathering in the south, its cold light flaring the edges of the uppermost clouds. Eliot wonders if their rented Citroën has heated seats.

The airfield buildings are a squat collection of ugly single-storey structures housing various offices, store rooms, and, most importantly, the members' bar. It being not long after eleven, the bar is in full swing, muffled music drifting in the air, a thin tungsten glow sneaking past the edges of the closed curtains.

'Drink?'

Roxanne shakes her head. 'We have to get back to Fulhill.'

There are twenty, maybe twenty five, cars in the car park which forms an L-shaped plot around two sides of the airfield buildings. The Citroën is in the furthest corner. Eliot wonders how many of those in the club house bar have been flying during the course of the day and how many have simply turned up for the booze. As they pass the main entrance to the buildings he notices three men wrapped in coats, hats and scarves standing in the doorway. Red spots of light in the shadows indicate the presence of cigarettes; even in this weather smokers are treated like lepers Eliot thinks miserably before remembering that he is an ex-smoker.

'Hold this a minute, I'm going to the ladies.' Roxanne thrusts her bag into his arms.

He watches her stride towards the entrance. At the last moment the men step aside to let her pass into the building. As the door slowly springs back in Roxanne's wake, direct light falls on two of the men. They are muttering as they glance towards the closing door, Eliot guesses the remarks concern Roxanne. He can't blame them, she looks stunning and how are they to know she is wearing a wig?

BENEATH THE BITTERCREST 237

Suddenly he realises that one of the men is familiar to him. Frantic cerebral overdrive, as he struggles to recall where has he seen him before. One of the men casts a look in his direction. Eliot quickly turns away. In the distance Jacques is standing by his plane, lit by the arc light that illuminates the area by the hangar and around the fuel pumps. A towtruck squats in front of the hangar. An airfield mechanic pumps fuel into the tanks in either wing, while Jacques rubs his hands together against the cold.

A surge of music as a door opens then slams shut. Eliot turns to find a couple staggering out of the building, a blonde on high heels clinging tightly to a fat man in a sheepskin coat. Her drunken giggles echo across the carpark as the man starts to dance.

The door opens again and Roxanne emerges. She steps briskly past the three men still smoking in the entrance, their faces turning to follow the progress of her hips, lust smeared across their faces. As the faces turn, bathed in light from the closing door, Eliot finally makes the connection. One of the men was in the lorry that went from the low building to the crematorium.

Roxanne is walking towards him. She is smiling. Behind her, the three men have gone back to their conversation.

A car starts up, something large and throaty, one of the 4 x 4 vehicles perhaps. More hysterical giggling. Roxanne is maybe five metres away now, her hand reaching up towards her head.

'Thank God, I don't have to wear this any longer,' she says, grabbing her hair.

'No,' he shouts but it is too late.

She lifts the auburn wig and brandishes it like a scalp. Behind her the conversation stops. Three heads turn in unison.

'Run.' Eliot struggles not to shout.

'What?'

'Run!'

Behind her the three men are beginning to move away from the entrance. Eliot turns and races to the car, praying Roxanne is following as she has the keys. As he reaches the car the doors click open. He throws open a back door and tosses the bags onto the back seat.

'The keys,' he shouts as he flings open the driver's door.

She throws the key. He catches them, drops into the driver's seat, and stuffs the key in the ignition. At that moment, his fingers gripping the key as Roxanne flings open the passenger's door, Eliot notices something strange in the wing mirror. The three men have suddenly stopped. Two are running backward and the third throws himself to the ground, causing the 4 x 4 to swerve violently to avoid hitting him.

'Get out of the car!' Eliot yells, throwing the door open and falling out onto the tarmac. He picks himself up and sprints towards the car park exit, hoping to intercept the 4 x 4, waving his arms wildly. At the last second, Eliot dives out of the way and the vehicle speeds past.

Roxanne has caught up with him and together they race across the grass towards the hangars. Too late to change course, they realise that Jacques has finished refuelling and is at the end of the runway preparing for takeoff. They keep running. Ahead of them the hangar door is open. There is nowhere else to go.

Behind them they hear the shouts of their pursuers. The escalating whine of an engine away to their left as Jacques' plane starts picking up speed.

'The hangar,' Eliot shouts above the noise.

They are less than forty metres from the fuel pumps when Roxanne loses her footing and slips on the grass, falling heavily. In an instant Eliot is there, grabbing her arm, hauling her onto her feet.

Their pursuers are maybe thirty metres behind and gaining.

'Twisted my ankle,' Roxanne says, kicking off her shoes and stuffing them into the bag she has over her shoulder.

'Keep going.'

He drags her forward. Behind them Jacques' plane roars as it leaves the ground. They are only fifteen seconds away from the hangar now. Their pursuers are closing fast. A shot rings out.

'Holy shit.'

'Just keep running.'

Roxanne is slowing with every step, her bare feet sliding on the cold wet grass. As they pass the pumps Eliot glances over his shoulder, she looks like she might pass out any minute.

Off the grass and back on tarmac now. Another shot, closer this time, Eliot feels the bullet whistle past by his ear.

'Weave from side to side,' Eliot says, dragging Roxanne in his wake. 'Like this. I saw it in a film.'

'In a film?' she says incredulously.

The roar of the plane is so loud he thinks his ear drums will burst. They are halfway across the tarmac, level with a small towtruck. All at once there is a massive crunching and grinding of metal and blood curdling screams. A fraction of a second later Jacques' plane flies

BENEATH THE BITTERCREST

directly over their heads. It banks steeply, avoiding the hangar by no more than a couple of metres.

Looking over his shoulder ,Eliot sees that two of the men are down, by what remains of the fuel pump. A fountain of aviation fuel rains down on them. The third man is on his knees struggling to get up, soaked in petrol. In the background the sound of Jacques' plane is getting louder again. The third man raises his arm.

'He's going to shoot. Get down,' Roxanne screams.

They dive behind the tow truck as the shot is fired.

Just as well, firing a gun while ankle deep in aviation fuel is the last mistake a man can expect to make.

The explosion blows him fifteen metres into the air. A fireball sweeps over the top of the tow truck behind which Roxanne and Eliot are hiding. They see the mechanic reach the hangar door at the very instant the blast passes over them, blowing him off his feet and back into the darkness of the hangar.

Seconds later they are on their feet. The blast has blown away the arc light and plunged the area into darkness. Roxanne takes Eliot's arm to help her bear the weight on her ankle.

Jacques' plane flies overhead. They wave frantically, more in hope than expectation, it was unlikely that Jacques can see anything on the ground other than the fire around the fuel pump. They watch the plane climb steeply, heading south.

'He's lost a wheel,' Eliot comments.

'Another favour I owe him,' Roxanne says. 'No more fake emails, promise?'

Eliot nods. 'Wait here.' He runs towards the hangar and disappears inside.

He emerges a minute later, shaking his head, the mechanic is dead.

'Why, Eliot? Why do all these people have to die?'

Eliot has no answer. 'Is it broken?' he says, looking down at her ankle.

She shakes her head, crams her feet back into her shoes and, with Eliot supporting her, they head back towards the car park, keeping to the shadows as best they can.

The club house party is over, everyone has spilled out into the cold night to gawp at the fire.

'How long do you think it will take the fire engines to get here?'

'It's not the fire brigade we have to worry about but they'll probably have to come from Glasgow like us.'

'Why did I have to take my wig off?'

'It probably saved our lives that you did. If those bastards hadn't reacted, we would have got into the car, turned the ignition and been blown into a thousand pieces.'

'How can you possibly know that?'

'They saw us get into the car and they backed off. They knew something.'

'Maybe they thought we were armed.'

'Whatever.'

'So, how do we get away from here?'

They reach the club house, walk round the back of the building and emerge behind the car park. Confusion reigns. Two dozen people wander about on the edge of the grass in a state of shock, staring at the flames and smoke billowing up into the night sky. There is confusion as to whether the explosion was a freak accident or something more serious.

'Does anyone know what happened?' Eliot asks two women in their fifties who are trying to light cigarettes.

'George said he thought a plane had crashed, didn't he, Moira?' one of the women asks the other.

'That's what he said, yes,' her friend answers. 'But what the silly bugger knows about planes you could scribble on the back of my thong.'

The two women collapse in a fit of drunken laughter.

'The people we came with seem to have left without us,' Eliot says when the laughter has died down. 'Are there any local cab hire companies?'

'Round here?' one woman manages to say before erupting into another bout of helpless laughter.

Roxanne meanwhile has approached a couple standing at the edge of the group who are staring at the fire.

'Did anyone see what happened?' she asks.

'It's awful, absolutely awful,' the woman said, her hand pressed to her lips.

'It'll close the airfield down.'

'No, surely not, Duncan.'

'Well, if the insurance pays up, which I doubt, next year's premium will be so high we'll none of us afford the membership fee.'

The woman turns to face Roxanne. 'I'm Rhona, sweetheart. Are you all right? Have you hurt yourself? You look a wee bit frazzled.'

BENEATH THE BITTERCREST 241

Roxanne smiles. 'I've twisted my ankle. It's just ... oh, no, I shouldn't bother you with ...'

'It's no bother at all, sweetheart.'

Roxanne looks embarrassed. 'it's just ... well, I came here with friends, my boyfriend and I, and they seem to have panicked and left without us. We're stuck here in the middle of nowhere. I don't know what we'll do if we don't find a taxi ...'

Rhona takes Roxanne's hand and pats it maternally. 'There's no question of it. Duncan and I will take you home.'

'That's very kind, Rhona, but we came from Glasgow. It's a long drive and we wouldn't want you to ...'

'Don't be ridiculous, pet. There's plenty of room in the Land Rover. Duncan and I are happy to help, aren't we, Love?'

Duncan grunts noncommitally, still staring at the fire. Eliot arrives.

'This is Eli ... Elison, and I'm Catherine,' Roxanne says. She turns to Eliot. 'Elison, I was just telling Rhona and Duncan about our friends driving off and forgetting us.'

'Did you have an argument?' Duncan probes. 'Didn't notice you at the bar.'

'No, not all,' Roxanne insists. 'In fact we had been having a lovely evening. We've been thinking of signing up for flying lessons.'

'Oh, you won't regret it,' Rhona says enthusiastically. 'It's been wonderful, hasn't it, Love?'

Another grunt.

'And you too, Elison?' Rhona asks.

'Well, yes, we have been discussing the possibility.'

Eliot's attention is distracted by the sight of two youths running towards the rented Citroën. He looks towards Roxanne, who gives him an almost imperceptible shake of the head.

There are almost twenty metres and two parked cars between the Citroën and the spot are they were standing. Eliot watches in horror as one of the youths reaches the open door and climbs in. The key is still in the ignition, he has left the bloody key in the ignition. He raises his hand to his head; oh Jesus, what can he do? What if he is wrong? What if the car is fine? What if it isn't?

The last grains of sand have almost escaped the hourglass. Eliot makes a decision, hurls himself forwards as if he has slipped, grabbing Roxanne as he falls, sweeping her in his arms, dragging her towards him. As they hit the ground, the Citroën explodes.

The blast isn't more powerful than that of the fuel pump, but it is more deadly. Fragments of shrapnel, metal and glass, rip through the air like a scythe, peppering the parked vehicles, smashing windows and slicing into bodies.

When it is over and inanimate objects have stopped moving, only the sounds of the injured remain. With blind animal instinct Eliot and Roxanne cling to each other. They sit up, finally, to find themselves surrounded by carnage. Rhona and Duncan lie a few metres away, neither is moving. Over by the edge of the airfield, other people are sitting up, clutching bleeding limbs, tending the dying and those too badly hurt to move.

Eliot wonders if the Swindon operation is itself no more than a fragment of a much larger game? How on earth have their pursuers closed in so quickly?

'Can you walk?' he asks Roxanne. 'The police will already be on their way.'

'Look at this.' Her voice is thick with fury. 'Look at all these people. And all the others, the ones who are missing. How many missing people?'

'We have to get away now.'

'Now we've got proof we can ...'

'We've got nothing,' he says. 'Look at the bloody car, what's left of it. Everything was in the fucking car. Twice in two fucking days.'

Roxanne swings the sports bag off her shoulder. Pulling the bag open, she fishes out the dictaphone and waves it in front of his face. 'I took the bag out of the car before I followed you across the grass, you idiot.'

Eliot grabs her and kisses her.

Breaking away from his embrace, Roxanne crosses over to the dead Duncan and starts rummaging in his pockets. She quickly finds what she is looking for and tosses the car keys at Eliot.

'Don't look at me like that. The dead don't need cars. You have a better idea?'

He doesn't.

'It's somewhere in the car park. A Land Rover. Let's hope it still works.'

It does, being about as far away from the remains of the Citroën as it could have been. Eliot revs the engine, and releases the clutch, steering carefully round the debris scattered across the tarmac. A couple of people shout at him to stop but to stop now would be fatal.

The twisted metal remains of the Citroën lie close to the exit, seats, tyres and plastic trim billowing foul black smoke thick enough to bang your head against.

He turns west towards Glasgow and puts his foot down.

The moon has broken free of the clouds, bathing the fields with a cold light. The needle moves up painfully slowly, old Land Rovers aren't exactly built for speed, but as long as it carries them to the city they will be safe.

They have travelled maybe half a mile when Roxanne grabs Eliot's arm and points. Further along the road and visible across the fields, a convoy of emergency vehicles has appeared, heading directly towards the airfield.

Eliot slams the brakes and swings the Land Rover round in an arc that takes the vehicle up off the road. They need to head back the way they have come, but the verge is seriously rutted and the car's wheels start to spin. With the engine screaming, Eliot wrestles with the steering wheel but the tyres sink further and further into the mud.

Havering has had enough. For four hours he has been in his study, grappling with the laptop he retrieved from Han's shed. Keychain access password required, user name and log in password, no unauthorised access. Round and round in bloody circles. Defeat isn't just staring him in the face, it has headbutted him and broken his nose in the process.

Of the hundreds of sheets of paper he has found, none has really moved him any further on. True, he has a better idea of Han the man, his meticulous notes, his careful research, his evident hatred of corruption. But it is all cold potatoes.

Havering thinks of the telescope in the shed. How many people know of Han's interest in the stars? So many elements of a person's private life remain hidden from view.

The phone rings. Havering answers it immediately so as not to disturb his wife who is already in bed.

'Thought you might like to know Eastfield has guests. A BMW and a Subaru, arrived five minutes ago. We're running a check on the cars' plates.

'Excellent. Well done, Mullen. Keep me in the loop.' Havering checks his watch, almost midnight, an usual time to be starting a party.

thirty two

The sirens are clearly audible and the flashing lights of the emergency vehicles strobe the empty branches of the trees overhead. Are there police cars or only ambulances and fire engines? Eliot doesn't want to wait around to find out.

Revving furiously the Land Rover lurches from side to side, mud spraying in every direction. The road is tantalisingly close but time is all but spent.

A chance glance towards Roxanne suddenly provides Eliot with his solution.

The lead police car turns the corner, tyres screeching, closely followed by a second and a third. Behind them come the ambulances and, bringing up the rear, a fleet of fire engines. The doppler of their sirens shakes the air in a cacophony of falling pitches.

As the third police car accelerates along the straight one of its rear tyres slips on a film of mud that has been sprayed across the road. The driver loses control and spins away across the road and on over the verge before slamming its rear end against a low stone wall.

Hazards flashing, one of the ambulances leaves the convoy and pulls up at the scene of the accident, while the other vehicles thunder on towards the airfield.

Eliot and Roxanne hear the accident, but see nothing.

At the last instant, Eliot has spotted that the land on his side of the road falls away towards a track some three metres below them. If the car won't go back up onto the road maybe it will go down.

A short bone-shaking journey down over grass and loose stones and they reach the track, just as the first police car draws level with them on the road above. Eliot kills the headlights and lets the Land Rover coast gently down towards an open gate below them.

From there the track leads up and away towards the hills.

Thankfully the siren of the crashed police car, and that of the ambulance that has stopped to lend assistance, are still blaring, masking out any noise from the Land Rover. With his head stuck out through the side window to see where he is going, Eliot drives slowly away.

At the top of the hill the track joins a minor road leading north.

BENEATH THE BITTERCREST

They pause briefly to look at the activities on the airfield far below. Eliot wonders how long it will be before a police car is dispatched to track down a missing Land Rover.

The landscape is bleak and, except for the occasional dry stone wall, there is no obvious sign of human presence. They drive on, praying the road actually leads somewhere, praying it doesn't just become a dirt track.

The moon disappears behind the huge curtains of rock that towers above them and Eliot, safely away from the airfield, turns the head-lights back on and puts his foot down. Rocks and pine trees in all directions. For a city boy like Eliot the environment is so alien he might as well be on the moon. He finds the heater, turns it up full, and winds his window up.

Roxanne turns on the radio. It is tuned to a local station, some radio host is abusing all comers, three callers cut off in mid-sentence in under a minute.

'This confrontational English thing is so stupid. Insulting people isn't clever.'

'Scottish.'

'What?'

'It isn't English, the man's Scottish.'

'You're as bad as he is.'

'I was just ...' he starts.

'Joke, I was joking.'

She pats his trouser leg soothingly.

'Yeah, right,' he says, she is throwing his own lines back at him now. 'You do realise we can't drive this car into Glasgow?'

'Why not? If we leave it in Fulhill, it'll be stripped to the chasis by tomorrow morning, remember? No-one will be able to trace it.'

'Possibly. But if it isn't ...'

'What do you want to do?'

'Dump it. Where it won't be found.'

They continue along the winding road, the foul mouthed shock jock insulting his listeners, the pine trees jostling for position on the steep hillsides. The road runs along the edge of a small loch, freezing waters black as night, barely a ripple breaking the oily surface. Then on from the loch and away into a narrow gorge. Minutes later they enter a tunnel. When they emerge, they find the landscape has opened out to a wide valley and below them are the lights of a small town.

The town is nothing special, corrugated iron roofs of an industrial estate, terraced streets where squat houses huddle together for warmth between pubs and kirks. A small river meanders through, passing a football pitch with its tatty noticeboard showing the month's fixtures, before leading on to the high street where a boarded up cinema that has served as a bingo hall, until that too ceased to draw in the punters, nestles between a tobaconist's and a laundromat.

But the town does have one asset - a railway station.

They drive back the way they have come. On the other side of the tunnel, Eliot spotted a track that led off up the gorge. It runs for a couple of hundred metres, ending in front of a rundown house. A door hangs off its hinges on a small barn flanking the house. Eliot climbs out of the car and hauls the door open. There is just room.

With the car safely in the barn, he pulls the door closed.

'What do you want to do?' he asks.

'How far are we from that town?'

'Two and half miles, maybe three.'

Eliot observes Roxanne, realising that she hasn't coughed in a while, the antibiotics must be having an effect. She looks tired.

'You look how I feel,' he says.

'Thanks.'

'How's the foot?'

Roxanne shrugs.

'It's down hill all the way.'

'Where would we stay?'

'We can hammer on the door of a pub till they let us in, or break into a church.'

They stay in the car. The first train is just after seven o'clock according to the board outside the station. An hour to walk down ... he will carry her if he has to. He sets his watch to go off at quarter to six.

Eliot walks round the other side of the house to piss. The air is alive with the sound of the wind. It must have rained earlier, the ground is still damp and the clicking of water droplets falling from the trees onto the leaf litter remind him of a work of installation art he saw in a London gallery.

London seems an infinity away, a different lifetime. He wonders what his children are doing, pictures them asleep in their beds, Toby snoring under his Thomas the Tank Engine quilt, Alexandra curled up in a sea of soft toys. The orange glow of the urban night sky, the

BENEATH THE BITTERCREST

hum of traffic, the all night shops, the cats that leap from fence to fence through the night, fighting and mating on the table cloth-sized plots of grass that pass for gardens. His body aches for life to return to normal, for the nightmare to pass.

'Get in, get in,' Roxanne urges as he approaches the car.

The radio is on.

'... from eyewitness accounts that an aircraft may have been involved. The incidents at the airfield, the worst in living memory, have left at least ten people dead and many more injured. The police just issued a statement to say that they have reason to believe that Eliot Balkan, who they are already pursuing on other charges including the murder of a crematorium operative in Swindon, may have been involved. He is thought to be in the company of a French national, Roxanne Lepage. The couple is armed and dangerous. The public are advised not to approach them. We will bring you more news as we ...'

Roxanne switches the radio off.

'You and me against the world,' she says.

Eliot reaches up for the light switch. They stare into each other's eyes.

'We'll most likely freeze to death before morning,' he says with a rueful smile. 'And the world will be safe again.'

Roxanne stretches over the back of the seat and produces a bottle of whisky and a box of oatcakes. 'I found blankets. Rhona and Duncan prepared for all eventualities.'

Except getting caught up in a car bomb attack on an airfield Eliot thinks to himself. 'Do the seats go back?' he asks.

'They do better than that.'

The back of the Land Rover converts into a double bed. They drink some whisky then lose themselves in each other's arms. As the whisky does its work they pull at each others' clothing. Eliot senses each and every hair on his body standing on end against the chill air. He pulls the blankets over them, but the urgency of their passion pushes the blankets off again in seconds. The windows steam up. The long plastic bench covers stick to her arching back. In the pitch dark they become two animals, become one animal, become the primal urge to survive the night. He plunges forwards as if he had never made love before, as if the movements are completely fresh to him, as if he were discovering his own body as well as hers. She whispers softly in French, her words caressing him in the darkness, guiding him like a lighthouse. Her fingers dig into the small of his back, urging him on, urging him on.

He arches his back, banging his head against the roof of the Land Rover but nothing can distract him, the humdrum repetitiveness of his love making with Sue, the years of routine, of bodies too familiar, of almost mechanical relief, falls away in this moment of defiance. If they are to be hunted like dogs then they will live as dogs. He finds her nipples with his lips, finds her mouth.

She pushes him back, turns him over and, tossing her wig away, straddles him and impales herself. He grabs her breasts as her body rocks back and forth. She crashes her head against the roof as he has done and they laugh outloud while their bodies continue the quest that neither of them can now do anything to stop.

'Slap me,' she says.

'What?'

'Slap me, smack me, hard. No. Harder. Like I've done something bad.'

He tries to oblige but his heart isn't in it and soon she tells him to stop and climbs off him. They lie there in each other's arms, gasping for breath, their bodies radiating so much heat that, now his eyes his acclimatised to the dark, Eliot can see the steam rising from her shoulders. He pulls the blanket higher and reaches out to kiss her but she pulls away.

'Pass me the whisky.'

Reaching out for the whisky, Eliot's hand finds her wig and snaps back as if he has suddenly found a third person in the car. Roxanne guesses what he has done. She props herself up and grabs the wig which she puts on his head.

'You look like a Viking,' she laughs.

'Is that some cheap way of inviting further pillaging?' he banters, trying to sound casual.

'Maybe. Maybe sometime.'

Eliot gets the message, sits up and retrieves the oatcakes while Roxanne puts her clothes back on.

'Eliot?'

'Why is everything so complicated with you?'

'Hold me. Just hold me.'

They pile the blankets over themselves and, lost in each other's arms, huddled together against the cold, sleep like babies.

BENEATH THE BITTERCREST   249

Brian Eastfield has lost much of his composure and a couple of teeth. He has been blindfolded and handcuffed to a dining room chair in his own living room.

'Let's start again shall we?' the voice is dry, calm and pursuasive.

Eastfield flinches, expecting another blow. He feels the blood congealing on his upper lip.

' What ... what ... I've told you. Gustave and my brother go back a long way. All he said was that he needed my gaff for a couple of hours. And I said yes. I go out. I come back. Leave him to it.'

'Go on.'

'Next thing I know the police are all over me.'

'He's lying,' says another voice.

Something solid smashes against Eastfield's shoulder. Pain floods his senses.

'I was at the dogs with the wife. You can check. I used a credit card. I'll give you the details. Please, just check.'

'Nobody steals from me.'

'Please, I've ...'

'Shut up.'

The sound of footsteps walking round the chair. Eastfield is trembling. He feels a warm puddling in his trousers, the shame of pissing himself.

'You've made a big mistake.' The voice is suddenly whispering in his ear. 'And so has Gustave.'

The chair is kicked away from underneath him and Eastfield falls heavily to the floor. He lies there with his throbbing head, weeping silently.

The footsteps walk away, a door slams and he is alone. At the end of the garden the River Thames laps gently at the jetty.

thirty three

By the time the alarm goes off, condensation has frozen on the windows in an intricate latticework of crystals. Roxanne is already up, stuffing things into the sports bag. Eliot reaches across and kisses her. She smiles, but he senses she is distracted, her mind elsewhere.

They climb out of the car, push the barn door closed and set off down the track, wolfing down the last remaining oatcakes as they walk.

Eliot feels more alive than he has for days, months even, and suddenly he realises why. He is consumed with thoughts about Roxanne. Instead of thinking about himself, he is thinking about her.

What is it like to lose a brother? As an only child he will never know. What makes her tick? Why does she blow hot and cold? How is she feeling? What does she want from him? From life?

The track is badly rutted and treacherous underfoot. Eliot carries the sports bag. Roxanne follows in a pair of walking shoes she found in the back of the car. Rhona had clearly had bigger feet than Roxanne but with two thick pairs of socks, also found in the car, the shoes support her bruised ankle far better than the court shoes she has been wearing.

They are quickly back on the road. Overnight the wind has died down and the trees are white with frost. Their shoes ring out in the still air. Eliot hums a blues song in time with his footsteps. He wants to talk about the previous night, tell her he won't pressurise her, that he doesn't expect anything. It is a question of picking the right moment.

'It's bloody cold,' he says.

'Yes.'

'Nothing but trees and rocks.'

'No.'

'No chance of finding a decent expresso.'

'No.' A moment later she adds, 'While you were asleep, I listened to the recording we made with the doctor and copied it down.'

'Make any more sense?'

She shakes her head.

Ahead of them looms the tunnel entrance. In the car they went through the tunnel in ten seconds, on foot it will be a different matter. Inside the cavernous belly of the rock the air smells damp. The tunnel is awash with sound, water dripping from overhead, water trickling down the walls, their footsteps reverberating back and forth. Roxanne gives a high pitched yelp to hear the echo. She likes what she hears and does it again at the top of her voice.

The tunnel curves to the left and pretty soon they walking in the gloom, unable to see out, either behind them or in front. Their eyes have adjusted to the low light when, suddenly, the walls of the tunnel ahead are awash with the light of an approaching vehicle.

'Quick, up against the wall,' he shouts. 'No, this side.'

Roxanne joins Eliot on the left hand side of the tunnel.

What if the approaching vehicle isn't a hill farmer going about his business? What if it is someone out looking for them? Stuck in the tunnel they are as easy to pick off as flies in a web.

'We have to run,' he shouts. 'We have to get out.'

He charged ahead, following the leftward curve of the tunnel. With every step the reflected light from the tunnel wall, and the noise, grows exponentially. He can no longer hear if Roxanne is following him. A rush of colder air sweeps his cheeks, immediately followed by the full beam of four powerful headlights. Deafening and disorientating. He loses his footing and staggers forwards, throws his right foot out then pushes back against it, away from the lights. The sound of screaming brakes is followed by an ear-splitting grinding of metal against stone as the car scrapes against the tunnel wall. Temporarily blinded, Eliot panics and falls. Moments later Roxanne crashes down on top of him.

Get up, get up, Eliot tells himself, his vision a mess of stars and fluorescent streaks of colour. As Roxanne picks herself up, Eliot draws himself up onto his hands and knees. The air in the tunnel is thick with exhaust fumes. Behind the dancing colours on his retinas is a red glow. Behind the noise of his coughing, the engine of the crashed car revs wildly.

'Where's the car?' Back on his feet now.

Roxanne points back down the tunnel. 'The driver may be hurt.'

Eliot nods. His eyesight is returning. He turns to leave.

Roxanne grabs his sleeve. 'What about the ...'

'Leave it.'

The red glow from the crashed car's brake lights cuts out suddenly.

Total darkness, as terrifying as his first day at school. Eliot staggers blindly forwards, his hand feeling the wall. The crashed car's engine revs and thumps and whines like a blender mincing fingers.

The tunnel seems to go on for ever then, all at once, the darkness has charcoal clouds above and the air is fresh. They are back outside. The road veers to the right. Far below in the valley are street lights. In ten minutes they reach the edge of town.

An all night service station. While Eliot buys a handful of chocolate bars, Roxanne pursuades the attendant to let her use the staff toilet. When she re-emerge a couple of minutes later, Eliot notices she has put on weight, but says nothing. By the time the morning shift arrives, the overnight attendant will find that his outdoor clothes have all disappeared.

'Clean up and put these on, we can't get on a train looking like this.' Roxanne produces various items of clothing from under her bulging jacket.

She passes Eliot an anorak and bobble hat. It is true that his expensive suit looks much the worse for wear. He wipes his shoes clean with paper towels, also taken from the service station. Roxanne pulls a shapeless blue fleece on over her jacket and ties a scarf around her neck. They hurry towards the station, wolfing down the chocolate bars as they go. Both are so jittery they'd see spies in a kindergarden.

In the fug of the waiting room fourteen people wait stoically, as they do every morning. Three women stand further up the platform smoking. An old man occupies one of the benches, clutching a canvas shopping basket to his chest, his nose dripping onto the handles. From behind a pillar, curling plumes of steam reveal the presence of someone hidden from view. Eliot leans back casually, trying to see round the back of the pillar. Roxanne keeps an eye on the exits, making sure they have an avenue of escape. Her foot taps out a nervous rhythm.

The train arrives. They sit with the smokers, a defensive bunch used to protecting their own against the fascism of the non-smoking lobby.

Every few minutes the train stops to pick up more commuters. Everyone knows each other, chatting across the aisle, swopping anecdotes, discussing the previous night's football. Roxanne and Eliot keep their mouths shut, their foreign accents zipped up.

Pressing his face against the window, Eliot, who is in a backward-facing seat, looks eastwards to where the first traces of pre-dawn light

BENEATH THE BITTERCREST

splinter the night sky. Should they have rung the police? Is the driver still stuck in the tunnel?

Eliot ponders what he is becoming. A fugitive in stolen clothes, tossed into a world where survival of the fittest is the only rule, where nothing and no-one else matters, where everyone is guilty until proven innocent. The young man sitting across the aisle, what is in his bag? The woman with her face hidden behind a newspaper, is she really interested in the sports pages or is it a pretence? The bald headed man chatting to the pipe smoker with the moustache has glanced three times in Eliot's direction, while prattling on about Rangers' chances the following weekend. There is something shifty about the lot of them.

Absent-mindedly Eliot rummages about in his anorak pockets, forgetting that they are not his own. He finds a pack of chewing gum, passes Roxanne a stick across the table and takes one himself. From another pocket he retrieves a wallet. It contains neither money or cards, only a handful of photos.

'She's a wee looker.'

Eliot spins round. A large middle aged man in a duffle coat has stopped on his way back from the toilet and is peering over Eliot's shoulder. The photo shows a young girl on a swing.

'What's her name?' the man asks.

'Er ... Catherine,' Eliot answers, hastily putting all the photos back in the wallet.

'Bright as a button too, eh?'

'Pardon? Ah, yes. Yes she is.'

'Aye, you can see that. She'll be what, eight years old?'

'Just nine.'

'You must both be very proud.' The man catches Roxanne's eye. 'Are you staying in the town or just visiting?'

The situation is slipping out of hand. Roxanne hasn't followed the conversation and seems totally non-plussed.

'She's in St Mary's.' Eliot says. 'We're hoping she'll pull through, though the doctors have said ...'

'Oh dear.' The man prepares the ground for a hasty retreat. 'Well, good luck to you both.' He moves away down the train.

Roxanne's eyebrows seek an explanation. Eliot shakes his head and returns the photo wallet to the pocket of the anorak. The duffle coated man sits down next to an old lady and talks to her in a low voice, glancing occasionally in Eliot's direction. The woman's eyebrows pucker with concern.

The train reaches Glasgow at twelve minutes to eight. Instinctively, Eliot takes one side of the train and Roxanne the other as the train eases into the station, He scours the platforms for signs of danger; a familiar face, a police presence, a person behaving suspiciously. Behind him people queue to get off the train. The doors open with a pneumatic hiss and they pour out onto platform nine.

The platforms are arranged in pairs. Passengers leaving platform nine mingle with those boarding the train on platform ten, a heaving mass of people heading in both directions. Eliot and Roxanne join the queue heading towards the exit. It is fortuitous that Eliot glances towards the exit at the exact moment when the couple in front of him bend down to deposit their bags. A group of uniformed police are waiting at the exit barrier.

Eliot grabs Roxanne's arm and pulls her back, away from the exit. 'Brilliant, here we go again, down a coal mine under a frog's arse.'

There are no other ways off the platform, no connecting stairs, no lifts. Only when they reach the far end of the train do they see what they have to do. The passengers are heaving en masse towards the exit. It is now or never. Roxanne and Eliot jump down, cross the tracks and climb up onto platform eight, run across platforms eight and seven and repeat the whole process, climbing down and negotiating a path over the rails and sleepers. In less than a minute they are standing on platform six, well away from their reception committee.

A wall between platforms six and five supports the huge iron arches that span the roof. Having crossed over to the other side of the wall they are no longer visible from platform nine. It is a gamble, but Eliot feels sure that resources will be concentrated on those platforms used by local trains arriving from near the airfield.

An intercity train stands on platform five and the catering staff are loading drinks and sandwiches from a trolley onto the buffet car. A huge loaf of a man with a face and ears resembling the victor ludorum cups handed out at school sports days, has removed his jacket and hat and placed them on the trolley. Sweating profusely, he grabs two multipacks of lager cans and heaves himself up onto the train.

The paper stuck on the train door reveals it is destined to leave for London in just a few minutes, at eight a.m. Eliot turns to Roxanne.

'I've been thinking.'

Roxanne arches an eyebrow in mock surprise.

BENEATH THE BITTERCREST

'Ha Ha. Listen, let's separate and meet up back at Fulhill. A better chance of getting away. It may not only be uniformed police down there.'

'Agreed,' Roxanne turns to scan the end of the platform. 'So who goes first and who takes the dictaphone?'

As she speaks a trolley hits the back of her legs. She leaps out of the way as it sweeps past her towards the exit barrier.

'Arsehole,' she shouts at the back of the departing porter. 'Eliot. Eliot?'

He has disappeared, leaving only the sports bag sitting on the platform.

Eliot pushes the trolley down the platform towards the exit. Why do train companies oblige their staff to dress like backing singers in a seventies soul band? Purple with yellow trim, for pity's sake. Fortunately, the jacket is so large that Eliot has been able to slip it easily over his own clothes.

About thirty metres from the exit he tugs the hat down over his eyes. This is insane, he thinks, reality is being replaced by a cartoon spy fantasy. It will never work, the uniform is way too big, he must look like a sheep in an elephant skin.

Two men loiter at the exit, smoking. He hates them for that more than anything. Five metres and closing. If they spot him he will push the trolley at them and topple them like skittles.

The taller of the two is talking into a mobile phone while the other looks to his right. Checking with a colleague on another platform? One side of the gates is closed, there will be just enough room to squeeze past. Three metres. Eliot keeps his head down, steering the trolley to pass by the left of the two men. Too late he realises he hasn't done the jacket up. He isn't wearing a proper uniform, only the jacket. He has blown it but he has to press on. Shouting behind him, back along the platform.

All at once his path ahead is blocked as two sets of legs fill the gap between the two men and the closed gate.

'Mind yer backs. Mind yer backs.' He ploughs forwards.

They leap aside to let him through. A posh Scottish accent curses him as he passes. Fortunately he cannot understand a single word of it. He allows himself a brief recce. Across the concourse another trolley is emerging through a set of doors, pushed by someone in a uniform similar to his own.

'Mind yer backs. Mind yer legs,' he shouts again, wrestling with the trolley.

'Who's been a stupid boy?'

A hand grips his shoulder. His blood runs cold.

Eliot takes a deep breath, staring at the people waiting to catch trains, the people queuing to buy the morning papers, the steam rising from the cappucino machine. He hears the crinkle of cellophane being removed from a baguette sandwich, hears a child laughing loudly. The concourse clock says seven forty nine, another ninety seconds before the trolley will be missed.

'Got the wrong fekking platform, have we?'

Two men laughing behind him.

'Good job they don't let you drive the fekking train, eh?'

The grip on his shoulder relaxes. Eliot doesn't wait. He pushes away, steering the trolley towards the double doors at the far end of the station. Over his shoulder the jibes continue.

'Yellow and purple? For a uniform? And you'd win better fitting clothes in a bloody raffle.'

Eliot dumps the caterer's trolley outside the double doors. Tossing hat and jacket onto the trolley, he heads briskly towards the station exit.

Gustave Brown steps out of the shower and grabs a towel hanging from the door hook. He stares through the doorway at the woman sprawled across his bed. Plump, common and happy to indulge whatever fantasy comes to mind. Just how he likes it.

'You'd best be on your way,' he calls out.

'What's for breakfast?'

'Just get dressed and get out.' He ogles her fat arse as she hauls herself off his purple sheets. There isn't time to do what he wants to do.

'Same time next week, Pet?' she says, squeezing into lycra running shorts. She takes a small bag of cocaine from the bedside table and crams it into her purse.

He crosses the bedroom and holds the door open, slapping her bum as she passes.

'Wednesday or Thursday,' he says.

'OK, Pet.'

Brown returns the bathroom to shave.

He doesn't see the two men who push their way in as the tart opens

BENEATH THE BITTERCREST 257

the front door to leave. Nor does he hear them walk quietly down his hall, enter the master bedroom, and cross the deep pile of his blue carpet towards the partially open door of the en-suite bathroom.

The cold tap is blasting away. Brown, stark naked, has his head down in the basin, rinsing away the remains of his shaving foam and allowing the cool water to rush through his ginger hair. He lifts his head, eyes closed, right hand reaching blindly towards the towel rail. Beads of water leap from his chin, splash against the porcelain. Finding the towel, Brown buries his head in it, rubbing vigorously.

The steamed up mirror reflects only the vaguest of shapes but the movement is clear enough. Brown spins round, his temper boiling, how dare the slut return?

But the whore is long gone.

'He told us to make sure you were up,' says one of the men.

'Well you can bloody well wait outside.' Brown barks, quickly regaining his composure. 'Unless he sent you here to wipe my arse?'

Tonto and Goatee exchange glances. Brown stands his ground, water dripping down from his hair onto his bare chest.

'He said you need a plan,' Goatee says.

'You think I don't know we need a plan?' Brown sneers. 'Get out.'

Eliot reaches Fulhill a little over an hour later, having stopped to purchase a map of the city and a sandwich. He takes care not to take a bus directly to Fulhill but to an area some two miles east.

Fulhill is at its safest in the early morning, the junkies, pimps, drunks and whores all safely tucked up in bed. The housing blocks are still drab. The wind is still icy, throwing spikes of freezing rain into Eliot's eyes. He pulls up his hood but might as well not have bothered, the weather is more than a match for a cheap anorak. The gathering storm clouds are so dark that the street lighting has come on. Twilight at the end of the world.

Eliot remembers which block Dudu lived in, Maxwell Tower, but has no idea of the flat number. As he walks along the path that flanks the cemetery, looking down on the estate, he pictures standing at the entrance to Maxwell Tower with Roxanne, her fingers poised over the buttons of the intercom. Which ones did she press? Forty four? Fifty four? Sixty one?

He cannot remember. Should he just try every flat above the ground floor and hope he gets lucky? That would be both stupid and dangerous, there is no point in drawing attention to himself.

The path leads steeply down towards the car park. The only vehicles are a tatty pale blue Austin Allegro with padlocks fitted on each door, and a burnt out Mercedes that is still smouldering. Its owner, in a nicer part of town, might only now be discovering that it has been stolen.

While he considers his next move, Eliot buys a bottle of milk and a limp ham sandwich from one of the boarded up shops. Next, he seeks out a doorway overlooking Maxwell Tower and finds just what he needs round the side of the shops. Nestling down and pulling bits of cardboard box around him, he is thankful the cold air deadens the aromas of urine and vomit that cling to the cardboard.

With time to think, Eliot considers the possibility that paranoia has overwhelmed him. He did not even question his assumption that the police at the station were waiting for him. Everyone is guilty until proven innocent. Is there a way back from that state of mind?

At ten o'clock, when Roxanne still hasn't appeared, Eliot decides he might as well buy a paper. The choice in the shop isn't exactly inspiring; The Sun, The Mirror or some Scottish paper he's never heard of. He buys all three, along with a box of 'jam' tarts as fluorescent as traffic lights, a small bag of assorted boiled sweets, a can of Iron Bru and, in an act of defiance against the run of bad luck destiny is hurling at him, a lottery scratch card.

By eleven o'clock he is an expert on: celebrity underwear; the alleged bedroom antics of three footballers; how Europe is on a mission to stop us eating sausages; and how the Scottish parliament is, depending on your viewpoint, the best thing to happen north of the border for a thousand years or the most disgraceful confidence trick in the history of politics. The lottery scratch card is a loser.

There is still no sign of Roxanne. Has she arrived while he was in the shop? He doesn't think so, he looked up and down the road before running in to make his purchases and was back outside in less than a minute. From the shop door he can see almost three hundred metres up the road in one direction and over two hundred in the other. Nothing to do other than wait.

By eleven thirty he is seriously worried and cold. It is over two hours since he arrived back in Fulhill. Has she managed to leave the station? If they have caught her, where have they taken her? Who are 'they'? The police? Brown's thugs?

Chain-sucking boiled sweets, he curses himself for not paying more attention when they first arrived in Fulhill. All he needed to do was to memorise a two digit number. Failing that, he could have asked Roxanne for the number before he left the station. How much longer should he sit there? Half an hour? All day? Quite apart from the risk of dying of hypothermia he knows he must continue to be invisible. As things stand, the conversation with docteur Boutet recorded on the dictaphone is possibly the best chance of finding out what is happening in Swindon, and Eliot knows he has a duty to get the tape to someone who will understand it and can make use of it.

To add to his other woes, it starts to rain steadily.

Up ahead a figure carrying a broken umbrella is shuffling along the pavement in his direction. The tramp's face is obscured by the umbrella; come to reclaim his piss-soaked cardboard boxes before the rain finishes them off, no doubt.

Sure enough, upon reaching the shops the vagrant turns towards Eliot.

'Don't even start,' Eliot says as the figure stops in front of him. 'No, you can't have the boxes and no, you can't pinch the doorway. So sod off.'

'It didn't take you long to resort to type.'

'Bloody hell, what happened to you?' Eliot says, completely stunned.

'What happened to me?'

The umbrella tips back to reveal Roxanne.

'Things became a little difficult after your stunt at the station.' Her tone of voice is ugly.

'Pear drop?' Eliot uses the same soothing tone his grandad used to employ when tackling domestic arguments. He offers Roxanne the bag of sweets. 'There's toffee as well.'

'It'll take more than boiled sweets, Eliot. Within minutes the station was in total chaos, police everywhere. You could have told me what you were planning.'

'I should have called a press conference,' he retorts sarcastically.

'Don't be stupid.' She kicks Eliot's boxes. 'You could have warned me, given me a moment to sort out how I would get away.'

He finally snaps. Boxes tumbling around him, Eliot leaps to his feet and grabs her by the arms.

'Right. This is such bullshit. Spoilt brat with your family chateau and your dodgy business deals. I never asked to be part of this. I don't need you. I don't need to find your brother, or anyone else. I'll just go home and forget the bloody lot of you. Get off my case and ...'

She silences him with a finger pressed to his lips, gazes up at him with her green eyes. Eliot tries to read her face but finds he cannot. Is she happy to have provoked him to anger, to a raw outburst of emotion? He remembers her demands in the Land Rover the previous night. Or is she sad that he has buckled under pressure, lost control? Is she measuring him up against other men, other lovers? He takes a deep breath. Women. He releases her arms.

'You're right,' he concedes. 'I was a shit. So what did you ...?'

'Don't say anything. Let's find Dudu.'

Roxanne hands him the sports bag.

'It is your fault,' someone shrieks behind them. 'Your fault. They will die and their children.'

An African woman Eliot recognises from his arrival at Dudu's flat is standing a few metres away, on the pavement, incandescent with rage.

'They trust you and you have kill them all.'

'Fatima, please, what has happened?' Roxanne takes a step towards Fatima but the other woman clenches her fists, shaking with fury.

'You send people to take them away.'

'Take who away?' Eliot says.

'Alima, Dudu, all of them.'

Eliot and Roxanne exchange glances.

'It is not enough we are dirt. We must die as dogs. We live this shit, this stinky life. No money, no work. And now we die.'

Eliot looks about. Two boys have stopped on their bikes to watch. He wonders what they are making of what they see, hopes they see only a refugee screaming at a couple of tramps.

'Fatima, when? When did they take them away'

'At night, yesterday. I hear banging on door, then shouting. They take all of them. Your fault. Children crying and Alima. They beat Dudu and take all away.'

In the background the two boys snigger and make wanking gestures behind Fatima's back.

'Who took them?' Roxanne says quietly. 'Do you know who took them?'

Fatima shakes her head and suddenly the anger ebbs away, leaving only sorrow and pain. She clutches her head in her hands and bends over.

The two boys start laughing.

'Stupid fecking wog,' one says to the other's amusement.

Eliot has had enough and races towards them, his face thick with anger. At the last moment the boys run off down the street, chanting something unintelligible.

Eliot returns to find Roxanne with her arms round Fatima. They are talking in French.

'She stood behind her front door when they took them out of the flat,' Roxanne says presently. 'She heard them say something about Dudu's brother, they were taking him to be with his brother.'

'God,' Eliot mutters. 'They're going to kill them.'

Fatima looks up briefly at Eliot then starts to sob.

'That was helpful.' Roxanne says sarcastically.

Eliot raised a hand in apology.

'She says they spoke like you, not like the people here.'

'English accents?'

'Yes, I think so. We have to get back to Swindon.'

'We still don't know about the medical tests.'

'Forget them,' Roxanne says angrily. 'Dudu and his family are more important right now.'

'OK, but listen. We need access to the Internet. It won't take more than a few minutes.'

They leave Fatima outside the shop, her life a downward spiral of broken dreams.

Double Tragedy hits police station.

Police have confirmed the identity of a woman found dead in her car in a lay-by off the London Dover road. PC Alison Walsh, 32, was found yesterday morning in her car.

A spokesman confirmed that she had worked at the same police station as PC Thomas Hampton, the policeman who died two days ago along the same stretch of road when his vehicle overturned at the notorious Shooter's Hill corner in the early hours of Tuesday morning.

Detective Inspector Machin, said the incident was a double tragedy for the force. 'It is a tragedy to lose two fine officers in this way. The two had been lovers for some time and it would appear that PC Walsh felt unable to carry on following the death earlier in the week of PC Hampton.'

The couple are said to have had a stormy relationship.

Police sources confirmed that they are not looking for any other persons with regard to either incident.

thirty four

They decide on chancing the bus south. Their first port of call, however, is a thrift shop on the edge of Fulhill.

With the help of several banknotes, Roxanne pursuaded a drugout sleeping under the arches close to the station to swop clothes, but the fetid rags that sneaked her past the police will almost certainly prevent her from boarding a bus.

She refuses to even enter the shop and stays hunched up in a doorway opposite, while Eliot goes inside with instructions on what is acceptable. He emerges a few minutes later with black slacks, two t-shirts, baggy jumpers, an ex-army greatcoat for him and, in reasonably good nick, a leather blouson jacket for her. As he is leaving the shop he remembers the state of his trousers and returns inside to buy a pair of jeans.

An alley serves as a changing room.

'You look like your clothes were thrown on with a pitchfork.'

'From a man who makes scarecrows look elegant,' she counters, shivering.

He takes her in his arms and hugs her, rubbing her back vigorously to warm her up.

'Have you taken those antibiotics?'

She nods. 'Wait there.'

She breaks away and disappears into the thrift shop. She returns wearing a large Russian style hat of thick fake fur. Her eyes have changed from brown to green.

'Do they sell secondhand eyeballs in there?'

'I threw away my contact lenses.'

First her hair, now her eyes. On the train before the crash, her eyes had been green he now remembers. Eliot wonders idly how many other parts of her body can be discarded or transformed at will.

By good fortune they pass an Internet café on a side street close to the bus station. Roxanne gives Eliot the piece of paper on which she has scribbled her transcription of the conversation with Boutet. She goes to the counter to buy two coffees while Eliot joins the line of internauts crunching away on brightly coloured iMacs.

Out of habit, Eliot keys in his email address, name, password and he is staring at his in-folder before he has even thought about what he is doing.

The usual spam, offering him personalised website design, cheaper holidays, bigger breasts, smaller breasts, a clean breast, share trading tips ... and an email from DI Havering.

```
Eliot hi,
Having trouble accessing Han's laptop.
Everything's password protected. A little bird
has told me computer security is one of your
specialities. Any ideas?
David Havering
PS: did you know Han was dead?
PPS: in his shed.
```

In a state of total confusion Eliot reads the message a second time.

How does Havering know about Han? Han didn't have a laptop, Eliot searched the entire house and found nothing. How does Havering know what Eliot does for a living? How does he know Han is dead? What the bloody hell does 'in his shed' mean? Han didn't die in his shed. And most of all, how has Havering got hold of Eliot's email address?

The last question is actually the easiest to answer. Scrolling the text, Eliot finds his own email, the one he had sent from Roxanne's WAP phone from the service station in France, beneath Havering's reply.

So how has Havering found about Han, and does it matter?

No. What matters is that, in Havering, Eliot has found someone who is listening, a fellow traveller, an ally. God knows he needs all the allies he can find.

In his shed.

Eliot suddenly sees Han's shed in his mind's eye. At the top of the garden overlooking the cottage, not far from the gate to the woods. Why hadn't he thought of looking in there? What is on the laptop? What did Han know?

Eliot hits the reply button and starts typing.

```
you must know all this. the key to cracking
passwords is information. a password almost
always relates to its owner in one way or
another, sometimes its as simple as an object
```

```
close to hand. people struggle for inspiration.
second, because we are asked to supply so many
passwords, to banks or email accounts, to
access computers at work, on the internet, etc.
etc. most people end up using the same one or
two passwords for practically everything. so
find the password for han's email account, or
his bank log in on the internet, or his user
log in at work, and chances are you'll have his
password on those discs. attempt to access one
of his accounts then choose the password hint
option if there is one. work backwards from the
hints han gave himself.
good luck
eliot
```

He clicks send. For a few seconds he stares into space, lost in thought, then he remembers what they have come in for. He chooses a search engine and types. It takes 3.43 seconds to complete the search.

'Well?' Roxanne says moments later, pulling a chair up and sitting down beside him.

Eliot's face is expressionless. He turns the screen towards her and clicks the mouse to print a copy of the web page.

HLA (human leukocyte antigen)

HLA (human leukocyte antigens) are proteins present in the cell membranes of nearly every nucleated cell in the body. These antigens are in especially high concentrations on the surface of leukocytes (white blood cells).

HLA antigens are the major determinants used for by the body's immune system for recognition and differentiation of self from non-self. There are many different major histocompatiblity (HLA) proteins and each individual possesses only a small, relatively unique set that is inherited from their parents. It is unlikely that 2 unrelated people will have the same HLA make-up. Children, on average, will have one-half of their HLA antigens that match one-half of their mothers antigens; the other one-half of the child's antigens will match one-half of their father's antigens.

Many HLA molecules exist, but some are of special interest because they are more common in certain autoimmune diseases. HLA-B27 antigen is found in 80 to 90% of people with ankylosing spondylitis and Reiter's syndrome, for example, and can aid in the diagnosis of these diseases. However, HLA-B27 is also present in 5 to 7% of people without autoimmune disease. Thus, the presence of this HLA molecule is not indicative of disease by itself.

HLA antigens are particularly important in identifying good "matches" for tissue grafts and organ transplants, such as a kidney transplant or bone marrow transplant.

'My God,' she whispers.

'I was thinking about the crematorium employee.'

'Timothy Wesley?'

He nods. 'Do you remember at his house, something had struck me as odd. The table was set for two and the wife took a tray upstairs.'

'She was fed up of waiting for him to arrive and decided to eat in bed.'

'Maybe. I'll pay the bill and we can get out.'

Ahead of him in the queue at the till is a large brunette with the top buttons of her blouse undone. Gazing absent-mindedly at the cleavage in front of him, Eliot thinks of Roxanne's breasts hovering over his face the previous night in the car. She is getting to him. He turns away, thinks of something else.

On the wall beside him is a board covered in small ads: shiatzu massages, kittens looking for a vegetarian home, a half price introductory colonic irrigation, and so on.

Eliot wonders if vegetarians really love animals or if they just hate plants. 'Yoga and yoghurt - an introduction to real culture' reads a hastily scribbled note promising an evening of tantric growth at the Tabernacle Hall. Next to this is half a sheet of A4. Under the heading 'Save the planet - share your car' is a text urging people to offer any spare places they might have in their cars with other patrons of the café. Attached is a list detailing a wide variety of journeys: Glasgow

BENEATH THE BITTERCREST

to Edinburgh, Glasgow to Carlisle ... and, somewhere in the middle, Glasgow to Bristol. Eliot checks the date and time. Using the pen that is swinging from a piece of string, he scribbles the number down before barging to the front of the queue and slapping ten pounds on the table.

'Number four, by the window, keep the change.' He turns towards the queue. 'Sorry folks, must dash.'

He grabs Roxanne's arm.

'We need a phone.'

'What wrong with my mobile?'

'What was that you said about being pinpointed to the nearest foot?'

'Wait,' she calls as he opens the door. 'What's wrong with that?'

There is a payphone hanging on the wall by the toilets.

Eliot has fed Freddy a story about needing to hitch south to attend a drumming workshop. It isn't really in keeping with the spirit of the exercise but, for an extra thirty quid, the hippy is happy to take a diversion and drop them off in Swindon.

'Besides, it would be good for the old girl to see the world,' Freddy says, laughing out of the corner of his mouth that doesn't grip the skinny rollup.

The 'old girl' is a dilapidated Bedford van, room for Eliot up front by the driver and Roxanne tucked in the back between sacks of muesli and rice. To Eliot's relief Freddy prefers music to conversation; Van Morrison, The Doors and a world music CD, featuring some 'I know you're gonna dig this, man. Mega heavy talking drums' from Nigeria.

The drumming is solid, but Eliot soon drifts to dreamless sleep. Roxanne dreams of muesli. Shortly after seven, the van pulls up in a Swindon side street.

'Listen, man, you need a lift back, ding me tomorrow before three.' Freddy holds open the back door. 'Got the number?'

Roxanne clambers out and stretches her cramped legs.

'It's all in here,' Eliot pats his pocket. 'Cheers, Freddy.'

'Keep the faith,' Freddy shouts as he pulled away.

They trudge northwards along the dark streets that lead to Stratton.

'Home sweet home,' Eliot says.

'It's colder here than in Scotland.'

'What do we do if there's no-one in?'

'She'll be there,' she says, taking his arm.

He takes a deep breath.

The estate is a monument to the Seventies housing boom. Mile upon mile of terraced houses. Houses set back behind identical patches of grass. Eliot is amazed at the startling conspiracy of conformity. Each garden with its small flower bed in exactly the same place and, in the orange glow of the street lights, he can see that each flower bed has daffodil spikes thrusting upward. Probably the exact same number of bulbs in each garden. A shrub under the window. Empty milk bottles by the door, they still have milk delivered.

He pictures summer Sundays, a lawnmower humming away in every garden for precisely twelve minutes, then ten minutes off for a cup of tea and a biscuit, followed by a ritual car washing, followed by lunch at one, followed by walking the dog ... or does walking the dog come before mowing the lawn? It is mind mashing.

He has a fleeting image of himself and Roxanne settled in such a house then remembers that he already has a family, of sorts.

'Is everything all right?'

'Yes. Why?'

'You flinched.'

'I was thinking ... Ah, there's the house.' He stops and looks at her. Under the street lights he can't tell that she has changed her eye colour. 'Did I tell you I want to have your babies?'

Roxanne rolls her eyes .

'Yeah, maybe you're right,' he frowns. 'Oh well, here goes.'

Eliot steps onto the lawn and peers through the net curtains into the front room to ensure it is the right house. Everything looks just as it did on their previous visit except that in the dining room the table is set for one and not two.

The two tone tubular bell chimes probably come with the house. A brief twitching of the curtain in the front window. The security lens in the door darkens, someone is peering at them from behind the door.

'Who is it? Is it you?'

'Hello. Mrs Wesley?'

'Yes?'

'We were hoping,' Eliot continues, 'we might have a word ...'

A light comes on in the porch, they are floodlit like a football pitch.

' ... about your husband's work at ...'

'He's dead.' The voice angry now. 'Now go away or I'm calling the police.'

BENEATH THE BITTERCREST

'If you do that, Mrs Wesley, you will only be helping your husband's killers.'

'How dare you?' The voice has risen another notch.

Roxanne steps forwards.

'Mrs Wesley, I am going to push a sheet of paper through your letter box. Please read it, people's lives depend on it.'

She pushes the folded piece of paper through and, taking Eliot's sleeve, hauls him back down the drive. They wait by a telegraph post.

'We can't stay here long,' Eliot says. 'Not like this, out in the street.'

They don't have long to wait. The front door slowly opens. Gwen Wesley stands in the doorway, clutching the piece of paper.

They take their shoes off, as requested, and pad through to the lounge. Seeing the violent and swirling reds, oranges, purples, and browns of the Axminster carpet Eliot, for the first time in his life, offers a silent prayer of thanks for dull magnolia walls. She leads them through to the dining room, where she removes the table setting and deposits it through the service hatch doors that lead, presumably, to the kitchen. A deep barking and frantic scrabbling of hard nails on lino is heard through the hatch. She closes the doors.

'Doesn't take to strangers,' she explains. 'It's the breed, all brawn and no brains, Timothy says.'

Haunted by a present tense that no longer serves, she turns away, her eyes brimming with heartbreak and desperation.

'Sit yourselves down,' she says eventually.

She joins them at the table.

'How much do you know, Mrs Wesley?' Eliot says gently.

Gwen's hands appear to have a life of their own, the fingers running over and over each other like a wheel within a wheel. Her fingernails are chewed right back, leaving the ends of her fingers looking raw. She doesn't look directly at Roxanne, hasn't even glanced at Eliot as yet, instead she keeps her gaze fixed on the geese in the painting across the room.

'I knew about the overtime,' she admits at last.

'Overtime?' Roxanne prompts.

'Till two or three in the morning sometimes. At first, I thought he'd found himself some floozy uptown. I walloped him for it, told him to move himself into the shed until he could mend his dirty ways. But then he showed me the money, said it would go towards Andrew's operation.'

'Andrew's your son?' Eliot asks.

She nods, then lifts her apron and rubs her eyes. As if on cue they hear the front door open and close followed by footsteps going up the stairs.

'That's him now.' A pause. 'Of course, I had no proof of where he were getting the money. He could have been lap dancing, for all I know. I were a fool. So long as money were coming in ... Can you imagine a life on dialysis?' Her voice rose a notch, anger glimmered in her bloodshot eyes. 'Week in, week out, strapped to that bloody machine hour after hour. And I'm the mug who does all the work. He just lies there. Thirty two and he'd rather be dead. Without operation ...'

'I'm sorry.' Eliot says simply.

'Aye, and so am I.' Gwen's hands stop moving for a moment as she glances at Eliot, then her gaze returns to the geese and her hands set off once more. 'Anyroad, there won't be any more money.'

They sit in silence for a moment.

'Can we tell you what we know?'

'That's why I asked you in.'

'Do you know who we are?'

'I may be a fool but I'm not blind, your photo's been in every bloody newspaper this side of Timbuktoo. Even if you have had a shave.'

'We didn't kill your husband.'

'Would I have opened the door if I thought you had?' Gwen slides the piece of paper across the table towards Roxanne. 'Tell me about this.'

'Some friends of mine have been abducted. They're refugees, husband, wife and three children. We believe they've been brought here, to Swindon, and that they are in great danger. We also believe your husband was involved in the smuggling ring. I'm sorry, I don't know how to say this without ...'

'Don't look for pretty words, Love, just be out with it.'

Roxanne considers where to start.

'An organisation has been smuggling immigrants into this country. For money. A number of people have disappeared. It's hard to know how many because there are no records. Or none we can find. Maybe some died on the journey and the company needed to dispose of the bodies. Maybe they approached your husband and ...'

'No, he would never have done that,' Gwen says. 'He were many things, my Timothy, but I won't have it said ...' her voiced trails off.

BENEATH THE BITTERCREST

Eliot starts to pace the room. 'What if, from the word go, he set everything up deliberately?' He stops to stare at Roxanne, who stares back. 'As a way of getting access to cheap organs? That would explain the blood tests and the tissue typing. Christ, they could be bringing people in to order.'

'Who is he talking about? What's tissue typing?' Gwen stands up and pulls open a drawer in the dresser to retrieve a pack of twiglets, which she opens and places on the table in front of her. She sits back down, a little heavily.

'It's a test done to match organs for transplants, kidneys, bone marrow and ...'

'That's not possible,' Gwen says, ashen-faced, suddenly alert. She pushes the twiglets across the table, a little too hard. They tumble over the edge and clatter to the carpet.

'Why not? That's where your husband fits in. Maybe he made a deal in return for ...'

'Did you say your son has had an operation?' Roxanne asks.

'No, Love,' Gwen says then adds, almost inaudibly, 'He's booked in for one. Next month. Fingers crossed.'

'In a private hospital?'

Gwen looks over at Roxanne. Her eyes register the implication of what Roxanne has said.

'I need a drink,' she declares. 'In the dresser, at the right.'

Eliot finds a bottle of whisky and an assortment of tumblers. He pours Gwen Wesley a glass and places it on the table in front of her.

There is a shuffling noise upstairs as if furniture is being moved about, followed by a loud rhythmic banging on the floor.

Gwen drops her hands from her face and wipes her eyes on her apron. 'Andrew,' she explains, pulling herself together. 'I'd better check the machine.'

She gulps down her whisky. As she crosses the lounge she draws the curtains.

'Now what?' Eliot says after she has left the room.

He sees how exhausted Roxanne looks. He turns and studies the painting with the geese, the almost green tinge to the twilight sky, the dark maze of bullrushes, the half open gate across the field. The flying geese forever caught in a frozen 'v' that points south but never arrives, silhouetted against the green sky above an ice bound pond and skeletal winter trees. Roxanne busies herself picking up the fallen twiglets.

'This has to be huge,' she says at last. 'Not just Brown but ...'

'Police, medical people, harbour officials. Exactly. After all there's no point in going to the trouble of tissue typing if they aren't sure of getting the donors in.'

'The donors?' Roxanne bristles. 'Doesn't that imply consent on the part of the person whose organs are being taken?'

'But that's the point, isn't it?' Eliot answers, suddenly understanding. 'In order to be smuggled in the immigrants have to agree to sell a kidney, or have bone marrow removed, or something. That's how they pay. How much is a kidney worth? Ten thousand? More?'

An outside door slams. The dog scratches and growls behind the kitchen door. Gwen reappears holding a black book.

'I want you to know I loved my husband. He weren't much, certainly not a looker, even as a young man. Not much nous, or fire in his belly. No ambition, me mam said and she were right. And God knows he were no Cassanova, but he did right by me and Andrew. A good provider. He earned the money and I put food on the table. We were a team, of sorts. For forty year. There are many as can't say that down this street.'

She puts the book on the table.

'He kept this in his shed. Oh, I knew it were there,' she says, noticing the looks on their faces. 'He told me, said that if anything were to happen I were to take it and do as I saw fit. I've been a loyal wife, as God is my witness, never once looked in the book. Maybe I'm a fool but it's how I were brought up. I could see he were in trouble this past two year.'

She steps back from the table.

'If I'd moved sooner he might still ... Well, that won't get us anywhere, will it? Anyroad, I'm going to ask one thing of you both. It's time secrets were out, but I want you to promise me you won't disgrace this family's name. And you'll keep my son out of this.'

Gwen's eyes betray her understanding that such a commitment isn't possible. She stands there, a tired Yorkshire woman in her late fifties, facing the aftermath of her marriage. Forty years of trying to make something of a union that has never heard the sound of fireworks and now never will. And yet, mixed in with the fear of what will be found in the diaries is a small, palpable sense of relief that the silence is over, that the charade will be laid to rest.

'Right,' she says, visibly making an effort to pull herself together, patting her silver hair into place and adjusting her apron. 'I'll be in the kitchen cooking. If you don't eat, the pair of you will be as much use as a chocolate fireguard.'

As the door to the kitchen closes, Eliot and Roxanne throw themselves on the book.

It is a five year office diary, a black hardback slightly spotted from damp. Secured to the inside of the backboard with a rubber band is an envelope with so much crammed into it that the book won't shut properly. Roxanne removes the envelope and tips the contents out. Several dozen clippings flutter down onto the dining room table. All neatly trimmed, most are identifiably from local newspapers or from the national press. Where the date isn't printed on the page it has been added in a margin in black pen. Articles about immigrants, items about dead vagrants.

Eliot feels the hairs on the back of his neck bristling.

'Look at this.'

Roxanne pushes a clipping towards him. It is a photograph cut out from the Swindon Gazette showing the front of a building under scaffolding. The caption reads 'New hospital to be completed ahead of schedule'. The clipping is dated nineteen ninety nine. Further down the page is a second, smaller, photograph showing a group of men in hard hats. The men are all pointing inanely towards the entrance of what was, presumably, the same building.

'Why do they always make people pose like that in local papers? They look like total twats.'

'Three from the right. It's him, isn't it?' Roxanne points at one of the figures.

Eliot peers closely at the photo. The faces are deep in shadow beneath the hats and the image is grainy.

'Bloody hell. Mr Pompous himself, Neville Draper.'

The caption beneath the photo reads "Thrilled by progress at the site".

Other clippings show a government minister cutting a ribbon in front of a large building. The same building? Gustave Brown in the photograph this time, smiling proudly.

Eliot leaves Roxanne to arrange the clippings in some sort of order on the table while he opens the diary.

The diary begins in 1998 but there is nothing in it for the early months beyond entries detailing the dates of summer holidays, meetings with relatives, and sporadic references to the weather, along with caustic comments about global warming.

In early 2000 everything changes. The tenth of March contains a frantically scribbled entry in black ink.

> *Andrew diagnosed with acute kidney failure. By what right does God visit this on us? I've done everything for the boy, given him everything he bloody wanted, treated him as my own son. Five year wait for a kidney! They asked me if I wanted to donate one of mine! Not that mine will help him.*

So Timothy Wesley isn't Andrew's natural father. Eliot continues flicking the pages and, on the fifth of May, he finds what he is looking for.

> *Sold my soul. Is he worth it? He is my son, even if he isn't flesh and blood. Six weeks I've seen him plugged into that machine for hours at a time. I can't bear it. What happens after Gwen and I are gone? So the traitor's shilling. Stay later at work for a spot of overtime, head down, mouth shut. They're promising a transplant in six months.*

So that's it. It was all to help save her son.

Eliot remembers another conversation from weeks ago. Jesus, it can't be true. Can it? His head is spinning. How's Chloe? he asked Stephen in the wine bar. They have to find a donor Stephen answered. Serina's daughter needs a transplant. Could the whole thing have been a set up from the start? With Eliot as patsy, unwittingly helping to protect the smuggling operation as payment for Serina's daughter's kidney? They knew all along. What had Brown said about deleting entries without leaving traces? Eliot keeps turning the pages, his mind rushing, barely reading the entries.

Roxanne, who has finished arranging the clippings, joins him, peers over his shoulder.

'Stop.' She holds his hand to prevent him turning the page. 'Look. Look at this,' She taps the entry at the top of the page.

> *2 am. Two incinerations*

They turn the next few pages in silence.

Gwen enters the room with coffee and biscuits.

Three weeks later another incineration.

On the 26th of June Wesley notes his anxieties about the quantity of fuel that is being consumed for these nocturnal activities. He is worried about his colleagues becoming suspicious.

Then, on the 10th of August, there it is, in black on white.

Eliot stabs the page with his finger. 'Bingo.'

Havering sits at the back of his office watching his two officers trying to access Han's laptop. Discarded plastic coffee cups lay strewn across the desk, pizza boxes cram his wastepaper basket. The lights are low. PC Mullen's fingers hover over the keyboard as he struggles to think. The glow from the computer screen illuminates the broad dome of his balding head. Beside him PC Faulkner scribbles onto a notepad. They have been working at it for hours, without success. First Faulkner at the keyboard, then Mullen.

Havering scratches his ear and considers whether to call it a night, Faulkner has a young family, she will be missed at home. Absent-mindedly Havering wonders if Faulkner's children have her dark skin and fine Ethiopian features or their father's fair skin and hair.

Eliot was right, obtaining Han's password hints proved relatively straight forward. A little arm twisting at P. S. Partners delivered the name of Han's bank and his office email address. A colleague even provided Han's office email password, apparently Han revealed it in order to get an email read one day when he was away from his computer and in urgent need of information.

eclipse

They tried, of course, using the password to access the laptop but without success. So, on a neighbouring computer, they attempted to access his bank account on line. In moments a password request popped up on screen. Mullen entered eclipse. Password refused. A box appeared on screen asking if a hint was required. Mullen clicked yes. The text changed .

Your hint has been sent to your email address.

'Pray to God that it's been sent to his office email or we are totally totally stuffed,' Faulkner said, clicking away furiously at the keys.

To everyone's relief they found an email from the bank in Han's in-folder.

how far from jim the blessed soil?

'Oh great. That helps.' Mullen said in frustration.

'Coffee break?' Faulkner suggested.

That was an hour ago, since when they have tried anagrams and letter substitutions. They have rung P. S. Partners, again. Did Han know a Jim? Did he have a relative called Jim? They have trawled through the Fraud Squad days, did Han help to prosecute a Jim. Why blessed soil? Hallowed soil? A burial perhaps? A dead ex con called Jim? Someone Han helped to put away?

'It's life, Jim, but not as we remember, or something,' Mullen offers. 'Star Voyager, or whatever they called it,' he explains when he sees Havering's confused expression.

Havering goes over in his mind what Eliot wrote. A password always relates to its owner in one way or another. There's no such thing as random.

'You can thank your lucky stars you've got the day off tomorrow,' Faulkner is telling Mullen.

'That's it. Lucky Jim!' Mullen shouts with mock enthusiasm.

Havering feels the germ of an idea forming in the back of his mind. 'Say that again. Repeat what you just said.'

'That's it. Lucky Jim!'

'Not that. What you said,' Havering looks at Faulkner.

'You've got the day off ...'

Havering shakes his head, that's not it.

'Oh ... You can thank your lucky stars you've got the day off.'

Stars. Something to do with stars. Not Star Voyager. Something about Han. A password relates to its owner ... people struggle for inspiration ...

'Telescopes,' he blurts out.

Mullen and Faulkner are nonplussed.

'Han had a telescope. Let's think astronomy.'

'I tried Star Voyager, Star Trip. It didn't work.' Mullen says.

'Jim, Lucky Jim, lucky stars ...'

'Sunny Jim!' Havering loses them again. 'Before your time. It was a cereal promotion. Before my time.' Havering looks down at the password hint he must have scribbled a hundred times in his notebook. 'If Jim is sunny...' think astronomy '... if Jim is ... the Sun ... then the blessed soil is ... is what?'

'How about blessed soil is the Earth and Jim is the Sun?' Faulkner volunteers.

'The distance between the Earth and the Sun,' Havering shouts excitedly, suddenly understanding. 'That's it! It has to be. Type it in Mullen.'

'So what is the distance?' Mullen says, stating the obvious.

BENEATH THE BITTERCREST

'I don't know. There has to be an encyclopedia somewhere,' Havering says.

'Internet,' Faulkner directs.

There are various options. Miles? Kilometres? Accuracy? They choose the measurement that goes down to the nearest metre: 149,597,970.691 kilometres.

The password is refused.

'Try it again,' Faulkner urges Mullen, 'but separate the numbers into pairs.'

'Why?'

'Just do it.'

14 95 97 97 06 91

It is perfect, Havering thinks to himself, a seemingly random set of twelve numbers that can be found in an any decent encyclopedia.

The password box dissolves. They are in.

thirty five

The bright staccato of slamming dominoes filters out into the corridor. A cleaner wanders past, pushing a huge cloth covered brush in front of him. As it is less than six hours since his previous visit and as the corridor looked immaculate before he started, it will probably take one of the electron microscopes housed on the floor above to spot the difference. Passing the closed door of Room 9, he shouts a greeting in Kurdish, which language he shares with the room's occupants, then returns to the song he has been humming.

Inside Room 9, three men are whiling away the hours as they do every evening. The dominoes are divided out and another game begins, as loudly as before. There are no windows, the room is deep underground. On the one occasion they have been taken upstairs they saw the frost on the trees, and a mantle of snow puddling the huge lawn behind the building. While the weather outside remains cold, down in the entrails of the earth they are warm and well fed. If the men are frustrated at their continued incarceration, they do not show it.

They have, of course, noticed that all large items of furniture, table, bookcases, beds, are screwed to the floor but they have concluded that in the land of opportunities all furniture is secured in this fashion.

The trauma of the journey has faded over the six weeks since they arrived. Although they have no access to television or radio there is a library with books in a dozen languages, a good collection of music CDs, and various games. They are allowed to write to their families in Iraq though it has been explained to them that they can expect no replies until they have left the centre to start their new lives, incoming mail would attract the attention of the authorities and compromise the centre's work.

The previous week the other three men in their group were finally given their papers, national insurance numbers, passport, bank account details, social security and housing benefit, and a provisional address in West Ealing. They left the same evening. With luck, the domino players tell themselves, it is now their turn to make their way to London to start their new lives.

They play for money, not money they have but money they will earn when they reach the city. A penny a game. Not a fortune but enough to make the nightly games worth playing. Already Naseem is way ahead of the other two, who owe him £23 between them. Having found a gift catalogue in a bookcase, he has planned how to spend his winnings, though in truth he will send it all to his parents at home.

Double six finishes the game. Naseem pulls out his notebook and adds to his tally while the other two shake their heads sadly.

The door opens and Big John, one of the security staff, pokes his head round.

'Big John' Grey, so called because he is the older of two Johns on the staff, is in fact of below average height. A man struggling to maintain appearances. Beneath the well pressed trousers and ironed shirts lies an itchy skin condition he has yet to show his doctor and, over the past few months, his hair has thinned dramatically. He no longer attends the gym and seldom cooks for himself, preferring to stop off on his way home and buy takeaways that he munches in front of late night television shows. Grey lives alone and hasn't seen any of his family for months but, if he had, they would have noticed that his once relaxed smile has lost its shine.

Still, he makes sure that while people are in his care they are treated well.

'Big John!' Naseem calls out. 'Pull on a chair. How is the bicycle?'

'Pull up a chair,' Grey corrects him gently. He finds a chair, sits down and scratches his shoulder. 'That'll have to be the last game, Gentlemen. I've just been informed that tonight's the big night.'

The three men leap up from the table and cheer. Linking arms, they begin to dance a dance from home, three steps to the right, four steps to the left, round and round the table. Naseem drags Grey up off his chair into the centre of the room to join the dance.

'You'll be first, Naseem,' Grey says. 'All your papers are ready and in order. Once everything is checked and signed you'll be on your way. I'm told they are getting everything ready.'

The three men burst into song, dancing round Grey who stands there with an embarassed grin for a few moments before taking his leave.

'I'll be back in five minutes. Gather together any belongings you want to take.'

The door closes. The three men hug each other then wander off to assemble their few possessions. Naseem runs a hand over his face, is there time for a shave? Not his moustache, of course, but a smooth chin would be nice.

When Grey returns, Naseem, Hasan and Domar are back at the table, hair combed and ready. They have been provided with a set of warm clothing and this they now wear, along with a palpable sense of relief. Naseem fiddles with the steel bracelet on his right wrist, pulling the chain round and round nervously.

Grey nods. Naseem stands, bows mock-formally to his friends and follows Grey out.

A quick pass of the swipe card and the main door opens. It is two floors up to ground level and Naseem is practically bouncing up the steps, keen to feel fresh air on his cheeks. Who cares how cold it is?

They do not go up to the ground floor, however. Grey uses his card to open the door to basement level one and hurries Naseem through. If Naseem is disappointed he doesn't let it show, he has been patient to this point and a few minutes more will do no harm.

'All my papers are here?'

'That's right. Everything is just down here on the left.'

'Pardon me?'

'It's OK, follow me.'

Naseem does as he is told. The last door on the left is ajar. Room 2B. They enter.

'2B or not 2B,' Naseem says smiling, proudly vaunting his knowledge of English literature.

Grey stares uncomprehendingly at the small Kurdish man with his thick moustache and his watermelon grin.

'The room. 2B. Like Shakespeare. Yes?'

'Sit down here, Naseem,' Grey says. 'I'll be back in a moment.'

There is not much in the room, a chair, a table. The lighting is recessed into the ceiling, as it is on the floor below. A long, floor to ceiling mirror runs half the length of one wall. Next to the mirror is a second door. On the opposite wall is a large clock. Aside from the mirrored wall the room is tiled from floor to ceiling, and spotlessly clean. In one corner a number of pieces of electronic and mechanical equipment are stacked and shrouded in plastic sheeting.

Naseem sits down and waits. There are twenty three power points in the room, he counts them all, and numerous faint skid marks across the floor.

'At last we meet.'

BENEATH THE BITTERCREST

A statement of fact. The voice is professional, polite but lacking in warmth. Naseem looks towards the door.

'Neville Draper,' the man introduces himself. 'You must forgive me, we are very busy tonight.' An order rather than an entreaty.

A tall, hard-looking man in his fifties stands in the doorway. Immaculately dressed in a double-breasted dark blue suit, white shirt, black shoes, maroon tie, and crocodile skin belt. An emerald green hankerchief pokes out over the breast pocket of his jacket. He holds a black leather briefcase. On one of the fingers of his right hand is a curious ring embossed with symbols Naseem does not recognise. Naseem smiles and starts to stand up, extending a hand as he does so.

'Stay seated.'

Draper crosses the room towards Naseem.

'You appear to be in good health.'

'Thank you, yes, very much.' Naseem looks up. 'Everyone has been most ...'

'Before you go, there are a couple of formalities. Certain papers to sign. A covenant between the parties, if you will.'

The briefcase is placed on the table, turned away from Naseem, and opened.

'Remove your jacket for me.'

Naseem obeys, laying the jacket on the table in front of him. The man is busy with something inside the briefcase.

'My papers. Do I sign my name on all of them? And my family, I am wondering ...'

'Roll up your sleeve for me. A last innoculation and you can be on your way.'

'My papers,' Naseem says again as the syringe comes close to his arm.

'Yes, yes, your papers. As soon as this is done we can attend to them.'

Naseem relaxes and rests his hand on his hip.

'There. It shouldn't take long. A couple of minutes or so.'

'Thank you. Everyone has been most kind.'

Given how apprehensive he felt six weeks earlier, Naseem is now feeling a little foolish. Far from treating him badly, as some of his more cynical friends had suggested would be the case, he has found the English both polite and helpful. Over formal and cautious perhaps but those aren't necessarily bad qualities, at least everything works, unlike in Iraq. He smiles and looks up.

The eyes looking back into his own are not smiling. In fact they are as cold as science. The mouth is offering a smile of sorts. The face stares casually, as if observing a moderately interesting phenomenon.

Naseem feels the hairs all over his body spring up. He starts to blink rapidly. His heart gives the impression of having suddenly doubled in weight and a thumping headache rips across his temples.

'Don't worry, you'll soon be on your way.'

The eyes as lifeless as a shark's.

The room beginning to spin. Naseem grabs the table's edge with both hands.

'It's all quite normal. I'll be back to have a look at you in a couple of minutes.'

'My pa...ers,' Naseem speaks with difficulty.

Draper closes his briefcase and leaves the room.

Naseem tries to shout but finds he cannot. He tries to stand, but finds he cannot do that either. Very confused he decides to rest his head on the table and wait for the moment to pass.

In the confusion that follows he is aware of acute embarassment when his bowels leak into his pants. The room is suddenly full of people and noise. As he attempts to mumble his apologies, he is lifted up and laid on a bed. He seems to no longer have any muscle control, he cannot move his limbs or even blink.

His ears are, however, functioning with awful normality.

'Can we get a move on?'

'I want that plugged in now.'

'How is his respiration?'

A machine clicks on somewhere to his left. His eyes are staring at the ceiling. Figures move in and out of view on the periphery of his vision. White uniforms, green face masks. A woman bends over his face and peers into his eyes. A torch looms into view, the bright light burning a hole in his retina.

'When you're ready,' a voice calls out

A dull pressure on his arm. A cable passes his face.

'Roll him onto his side.'

A number of hands (how many hands?) turn him onto his side. He stares at their white coats, right up against his face. A pocket full of pens. A watch pinned to a breast pocket. Noise, rushing about.

'Do we have a time yet?'

'Ten minutes.'

'Good. Strip him off and clean him up.'

BENEATH THE BITTERCREST 283

Naseem catches sight of a large pair of scissors. There is the sound of clothing being cut. They are cutting his clothes? What has happened? Has he fallen ill? No, he is not ill. He was fine just a few minutes ago. He was playing dominoes with Hasan and Domar. They have been told they are going to London. He is meant to be collecting his papers. A mistake then? But Big John has told him he will have his papers.

Naseem sees his clothes, cut into strips, passing in front of his eyes. He has the vaguest sensation of his limbs being moved here and there but these sensations are so remote as to evoke no more interest than watching a herd of goats walking across a landscape. An alarm rings in the depths of his consciousness, as distant as the glow of a fire beacon on a cliff top. A signal. Urging him to respond, to stand and flee. But the possibility of flight is as remote as the cliff top and even swallowing is beyond him.

All at once the figures clustered around him withdraw and he no longer imagines himself down in a valley looking up but on the cliff top itself, high in the mountains of Amadiyah in his beloved but brutalised homeland, Turks to the north, Sunnis to the south, the roar of the fire crackling in his ears.

A variety of machines gather around him like tourists round a tour guide, their faces a mass of electronic displays and readouts.

But the machines are as nothing compared to what lies beyond.

The room is suddenly much larger than he remembers. Figures dressed in white gowns are clustered together, bending over something he cannot see. A bank of machines line the walls behind them. Overhead a bright light on a stalk looks down, like the shining face of a praying mantis. Naseem experiences a vague flashback of seeing a similar scene before. He grapples with this elusive memory, reaching out towards it like a tendril, cajoling it, begging it. What is happening? Why does it feel familiar? People gathered in a group like ants around their queen, like footballers celebrating a goal, like ... an operating theatre.

Several figures step back. If Naseem could feel any worse he will surely feel worse now for he is looking at a human being laid out on a table. For a brief second he almost believed he was looking into a mirror image of himself but he is wrong. The person on the table is partially covered in a gown and appears to be unconscious. Red tubes run up the side of the table, disappearing beneath the gown. A line is attached to a hand with a piece of tape. A clear mask with a tube projecting from the bottom nestles over the sleeping person's mouth and nose.

As Naseem watches, a masked man handles a scalpel which glints momentarily in the bright light. The masked man leans over the person on the table. The knife descends and when it is raised Naseem can plainly see the trace of blood collecting along the bottom edge of the blade. They are cutting the man open! It is an operating theatre. What is he doing watching an operation? Why are they putting him through this? He becomes aware of the noises around him, voices talking behind his back in low voices. What are they saying? Why is he naked? A door openes and closes.

'Not long now.'

The voice is familiar, curteous but cold.

'Soon be on your way.'

It is the man with the silver hair. Surely he will help, he must see that something very wrong has happened.

'Quite a sight, isn't it? Must be gratifying to know that your life won't have been totally worthless.'

Naseem wants to see the man, to be sure he isn't dreaming. That is it, it is a dream. He simply has to wake himself up, as he learnt to do when he was a small child. When he would run to his mother and tell her about the pictures in his pillow and she would tell him about dreams and that when dreams turn into nightmares all you have to do is wake yourself up. Or fly out of the room. He has had this kind of dream before, where he cannot speak or he cannot run. He must have fallen asleep after the dominoes.

A figure walks into his line of vision, at the foot of the bed. The embossed ring, the silver haired man.

'Now you see why it has been so important to ensure you are healthy. Did you know that a procedure, such as this, can take upward of four hours sometimes? Such stamina these surgeons have. And dedication. And yet the whole process depends not on their expertise but on the availability of donor organs. It is criminal, all those wasted lives. Productive lives blighted by misfortune.'

Naseem watches the scene beyond the glass. A gruesome metal clamp has been produced and is in the process of being positioned over the sleeping man's chest. Now would be a good time to wake up, before the nightmare gets out of hand. There is the sound of the door again, opening and closing.

Another voice. 'They are almost ready, Sir.'

BENEATH THE BITTERCREST 285

'Yes, of course,' replies the silver haired man's voice. 'Well, Naseem, it is Naseem, isn't it? This is where we part company. I must go and attend to your colleagues. Looking at it from a philosphical viewpoint, we will all take the journey you are about to embark on. I have never attended an execution, as such, but I imagine there is much the same mixture of relief and regret. Just think, if this country had not banned executions, we might have been in a similar position to China, with its murderers and rapists repaying their debt to society by serving as a ready supply of donor organs. All our lives might have turned out differently.'

'Sir?' the second voice cuts in.

'Yes, yes,' the voice suddenly sounds irritated.

Naseem realises that as well as seeing through to the operating theatre he is seeing a shadowy reflection of himself. Behind his head, metallic arms like cranes catch the light. The only time he has ever seen anything like them was in a car assembly plant. They are robots, he is sure of it.

He has to speak, to protest, to beg for assistance. He focuses all the power of his soul, if he cannot wake up then he will speak. Where is his mouth? His head? His head lies behind his eyes, so his mouth must be close by. If he knew the word proprioceptor he would also know where his problem lies, for he has lost the spatial awareness of his own body. He is disembodied, his body has become lost and does not know whether it faces up or down. Are his legs bent or stretched out? Are his hands open or clenched? Is his mouth gaping or closed?

From somewhere beyond comprehension he finds his voice. No words just a stuttering gargle, no more meaningful than a fart. It is enough. The silver haired man turns. He sees him! He looks into his eyes and smiles. It is a smile, isn't it? Please, please, I'm trapped Naseem's eyes say. Or that is what he hopes they say.

'This one needs attention,' the silver haired man says to someone Naseem cannot see. 'I'll be preparing the next one. Theatre Three.'

With a further glance down at Naseem, he is gone.

'Three minutes,' a voice says as the door closes.

Naseem is rolled onto his back. The masked and gowned people gather round him again. He has an idea that he is being washed from far far away, like being hugged through a mattress.

'We're taking eyes and skin as well on this one?'

'You programmed the ARU?'

Naseem manages a gurgle, surely someone will notice.

'Can someone deal with this?'

The green mask moves in and out as the woman speaks. Naseem looks into her eyes. Brown with beautiful long lashes. Can she not see?

She can see! He sees her jaw clench, sees sadness in her eyes. She nods to someone on her left.

It comes upon him like a wave, a roller breaking way out to sea. First the faintest hint of white foam that gathers and bubbles on the viscous black surface then a rising surge rushing towards the shore, unstoppable, irresistible. A chemistry of finality surges through his veins towards his heart, his head, his soul. He remembers his mother at the school gate, his father eating bread, his brother, his sisters, the dates gathered in the dust behind the house, the sun rising behind the sugar cane. It isn't a dream anymore and he understands, finally, that he will not be waking up.

Draper steps out of Theatre Three, removes his gown and mask, hands them to an assistant who is already burdened with charts and files, and sets off purposefully down the corridor, the assistant in pursuit.

'Any news?' Draper asks.

'Yes. The new arrivals,' the assistant replies. 'It is too early to be a hundred percent but the preliminary glycoprotein result shows that one of the children might be an almost perfect match for someone who has been waiting for two years.'

'Excellent. Have parents and children been separated?'

'It was thought that might cause problems.'

'Chart.'

The assistant prises a folder out from under her arm and hands it over. Draper pulls out a file and flicks through it.

'Curious name for a grown man. Dudu.'

thirty six

The files on Han's laptop relate primarily to police enquiries from the eighties and early nineties. Mullen, on the edge of a migraine, rubs at his temples. Faulkner, who has taken over at the keyboard, scrolls up and down the folders, wondering what they are looking for.

'So ...' Mullen says, as if nudging a pawn forward to start a game of chess.

'So what?' Faulkner snaps back, knowing Mullen is needling her to take his mind off his headache. She glances at her watch, she has to ring home.

'There you go. G.Brown,' Havering points at the screen.

Faulkner opens the folder. There are ten files within it.

'Brown chronology,' Havering prompts.

Scrolling through the text, they discover Han first became interested in Gustave Brown during his investigations of the fraud squad. A pornography racket smuggling dirty magazines in from Scandinavia. What distinguishes Brown from the other invertebrates in his pond are his qualifications. A chartered accountant, he ran a bona fide string of newsagents before succumbing to temptation. His intelligence and business nous gave him the edge over the shysters, pimps and fraudsters he worked with and, adept at playing the nonentity as a way of deflecting attention away from himself, he has consistently been underestimated. Although unable to collar Brown, Han has kept detailed files going back years. When Brown became involved in a prostitute smuggling operation based in Yugoslavia, Han was onto him. When Brown met senior establishment figures linked to the arms industry, Han was there keeping notes. Even after leaving the force, Han's interest in Gustave Brown's activites continued.

In a file, entitled Office Solutions, they find details of Han's telephone conversations with Eliot Balkan. The 'date modified' column shows the file to be the last item Han accessed on the laptop, just five days ago. The final sentences in the file concern a call from Eliot regarding a body found on wasteland in Swindon. Han notes he has given Balkan directions to the cottage.

Havering leans over Mullen's shoulder and clicks the mouse to open the file entitled Swindon. Now they are getting somewhere

'Do you think it's true?' Faulkner asks quietly.

Mullen shakes his head. 'Someone would have spotted it.'

Havering is not so sure. He admires the faith of his junior officers, envies it even, but he knows it is still so easy for villains to slip from one county to another without the paperwork ever catching up. No criminal record, no obligation to pass anything on to neighbouring police forces. A suspected serial rapist in Somerset can upsticks to Yorkshire and find work in a primary school without anyone being any the wiser.

'So Store gets suspended in the eighties on suspicion of involvement in a human trafficking racket ...' Mullen starts.

'Ferrying prostitutes into east London,' Faulkner corrects him.

'Whatever,' Mullen says. 'According to Peter Han, Store was taking bribes.'

'Accused of taking bribes,' Havering corrects him.

Mullen rolls his eyes and continues. 'And instead of being sacked, he gets moved out to the sticks and ends up in Swindon, in charge of immigration crime.'

'It's worse than that,' Havering says. 'Our Detective Inspector Store is policing the activites of local businesses, including BitterCrest Imports and a certain Gustave Brown, the self same man he was accused of taking money from in Han's original investigation.'

Back in Swindon, Gwen has seen enough. Without saying a word she withdraws to the kitchen. Roxanne leans over Eliot's shoulder, following his finger.

> *... and if it might be possible for Brown or someone else at BitterCrest to authorise payment and delivery of extra fuel outside hours.*

Finally, a link between Brown and the deaths. Energised by this discovery they continue working their way through Wesley's diary.

As month followed month, and Andrew's transplant failed to take place, Timothy Wesley realised that he had been duped. In his desire to save his wife's son he sold his soul and became party to a crime of enormous magnitude. Unfortunately, he had no bargaining power. He was like the man buying a bottle of whisky in Saudi Arabia who

BENEATH THE BITTERCREST

arrives home to find he has bought coloured water. Who could he complain to?

The diary is his private confession, a meticulous record of the amount of fuel delivered to the crematorium, the names of the people who brought the bodies, the vehicles they employed. A finger pointing from beyond the grave. His daily entries are also testimony to his shifting emotional landscape, from initial frustration, to despair, to anger. If he revealed the acts he was a party to he would bring disgrace on his family. If he said nothing, the horror would continue.

Eliot and Roxanne begin to see that Eliot was quite wrong to suggest that the smuggled immigrants were donating or selling a kidney or a cornea to pay for their passage. Turning the pages, they realise with mounting dispair and disbelief that there are far too many deaths for that. It simply cannot be the case that a few people have died in transit from exhaustion or hunger or cold.

Wesley has been involved in the systematic disposal of nearly eighty bodies. And they haven't finished reading.

Wesley himself was astute enough to realise that if he made the wrong move it might not simply be disgrace that would be visited on Gwen, and Andrew. Those who kill with such impunity would surely have little compunction about killing a crematorium operative and his family. He appears to have concluded that he must carry on, in the hope that sooner or later Andrew would get his transplant. Once that happened, he would find a way to escape.

Gwen has told Eliot and Roxanne to stay. Having read a few pages of the diary for herself, she now understands the torment of her husband's last months and is determined he should not have died in vain. News that a family with three small children has been abducted brings with it the possibility of rescue. Of redemption.

While Eliot and Roxanne eat, Gwen goes upstairs to pursuade her son, whose dialysis has just finished for the day, to get up and carry down the computer he keeps in his room.

A lumbering pallid loaf of a man, Andrew does as his mother asks, appearing in the dining room in his pyjamas with an armful of kit. He helps Eliot set the computer up on the dining room table, connects the modem to the telephone socket on the wall, then returns upstairs without uttering a single word. Through the ceiling they hear the television. Kung Fu videos by the sound of it.

Roxanne leafs through the diary, calling out figures and dates to Eliot who enters them into the computer.

'Do you have a mobile phone charger?' Roxanne asks Gwen as she comes in from the kitchen

'Andrew does. Where's he gone?'

Eliot points up at the ceiling.

'Right, that's it.' Gwen rushes out.

They hear her feet heavy on the stairs, and shouting in the room above. The music is turned down one decibel.

'Useless bloody lummox,' Gwen says, re-entering the lounge. 'Timothy were right, we should have swopped him for sommat better when he were still a nipper. Anyroad, you wanted one of these.'

Roxanne takes the phone charger and plugs everything together. The battery charging icon appears on phone's screen.

They continue leafing through the diary.

By midnight the list of the dead has reached over a hundred and sixty. One entry, listing the cremation of three bodies, reads:

> ... *the bodies as stripped down as it is possible to imagine. They taken absolutely everything, internal organs, eyes, skin, bone marrow, everything.*

'It beggars belief,' Gwen whispers. 'How could so many people go missing and no-one complain?'

'Nothing much was said when that midlands doctor murdered all those patients.'

'No,' Gwen concedes, 'But they were all old folk, expected to die.'

'Not all of them,' Roxanne protests.

'These were all refugees,' Eliot explains. 'With no right to be here. No-one knew they were here, except those who had arranged their travel and were planning to kill them. They were people without names or family or friends.'

'Who knows whether they had right of asylum or not?,' Roxanne corrects him. 'Their cases were never heard. They did what they had to do to escape from .. '

'France,' Eliot offers, somewhat unsympathetically.

'Not France. From their countries of origin. Do you think people abandon their home, friends and families without a reason? Can you imagine what it must be like to arrive in a foreign place with nothing, no money, no suitcase, nowhere to stay, unable to speak to people or even to understand what they are saying to you.'

The volume of the video upstairs increases to drown out the noise

BENEATH THE BITTERCREST

downstairs. Gwen looks up towards the ceiling and then towards Roxanne and Eliot. She shrugs.

'All I'm saying,' Eliot says in a stage whisper, 'is that no-one complained because no-one knew they were here.'

Roxanne glares him out angrily. Eliot throws up his hands in despair and turns his attention back to the computer.

Underlying their rising tempers is the lack of a clear sense of how to deal with the situation. For days now every hour has brought further revelations that defy understanding. The barefooted man chased and beaten became the tramp found frozen on wasteland, became the unfortunate deaths of a few refugees no-one cared about, became the pre-meditated deaths of possibly hundreds of people.

Eliot saves the file on the computer then emails it as an attachment to himself and Laurie at the office, along with instructions to keep it hidden and secure. As an afterthought he asks Laurie if he can find out who owns the Sopford Industrial Estate.

Will Laurie still trust him? It is strange how you can go from being the wrong person at the wrong place at the wrong time to being a serial murder at large. The world is on its head, as if a fox were being accused of chasing and hunting defenseless men and women in red coats and their equally defenseless hounds and horses. Such is the power and influence at work that, to the media and the public at large, Eliot will be whoever his opponent wants him to be. The hare becomes the hound, the model the paparazzi, the victim the rapist.

'Let me ask you a question, Eliot.'

Eliot stops typing.

At the same moment Roxanne's mobile rings. She grabs it.

'Why are you doing this?' Gwen asks Eliot.

'Hello? Hello? Sorry?' Roxanne presses the phone hard against her ear.

'Only you don't seem the crusader type, Love.'

'And you are?' Eliot retorts.

Roxanne waves her hand angrily to shut them both up. 'What do you want?' she says into the phone, then mouthes something at Eliot he doesn't understand.

Roxanne crosses the room to get a better signal, the charger cable first stretching then falling away onto the carpet. She stands by the window talking urgently in a low voice.

'She's on a mission,' Gwen comments in a whisper, 'but you ...'

Eliot ignores the old woman. Who is Roxanne talking with?

'Why would I do that?' Roxanne shouts into the phone then glances at Eliot.

'Do you know who ...' Gwen starts.

'Just shut up for a minute,' Eliot hisses.

Roxanne has a hand pressed against her free ear. 'What? You're breaking up. Shit.'

She turns back towards Gwen. 'Have you got a car?'

Gwen nods.

The heat in the car is overbearing. Eliot feels a bead of sweat trickle down the small of his back.

'What makes you think he'll be there?' He pulls at his collar.

'I've just spoken with him.' Roxanne, sprawled out across the back seat, bites the words off one at a time. 'Are you actually awake?'

'Ha ha. So he told you he was at home?'

She shakes her head pityingly then turns away to stare out at the deserted streets. Tension is stratospheric, they all feel it.

Gwen has not spoken since insisting that she would drive. They followed her round the back of the house to the garage block that served the terrace and watched as she backed the spotless beige Nissan out a little too quickly, scraping the rear bumper against the wall. Though she has said nothing her agitation is palable.

Eliot's thoughts turn to BitterCrest's accountant.

Flashback. He is at the computer, Gustave Brown beside him, leaning into his face, the odour of garlic and sweat so strong it is like acid eating at his cheek.

'We need a plan of attack,' Eliot says.

'Agreed,' Roxanne answers. 'You stay in the car. I go in to cut a deal.'

'Hello? A man who has organised the deaths of hundreds of people and you're going to cut a deal with him? By yourself?'

'Use your head. If we both wander in off the street why does he need to negotiate at all? It's the two of us he's after.'

Eliot has no answer to that.

'He frees Alima, Dudu and the children and we agree to keep quiet.

'That's it? That's the deal?' Eliot is dumbstruck. 'What guarantees can you offer? And what about your brother? What about all the other ...'

'They don't matter.'

'They don't matter?'

'I gave Dudu my word. There are three children, for God's sake. They're innocent.'

'They're all innocent. All the people they've murdered. Don't they matter?'

Roxanne's eyes are as dead as stone.

'We've missed something,' Eliot continues, trying to steer her towards a more constructive approach. 'Why would he ring you? We must know more than we think we do. Something that makes him vulnerable. Maybe he needs us as much ...'

'Drop it.'

They pull up outside a large house in the centre of town.

'Park further up the street,' Roxanne says, having checked the house number.

'It's too dangerous. I'm coming with you. '

'Think about your wife and kids, Eliot.'

Out of a clear blue sky. How does she know? He has no riposte.

Gwen advances another twenty metres then cuts the engine.

He hears the car pull up, twitches the curtain, watches the two women in the car, Roxanne at the back, the old woman behind the wheel. Doesn't spot Eliot, hidden from view by the car's roof. As Roxanne opens her door and steps out into the orange halo beneath the lamp post, Gustave Brown lets the curtain fall back into place. There will be no more cock-ups.

He still curses himself for not having acted at the start, when others were being taken in by her kiss-me-quick eyes, the Front National membership card she conveniently used as ID, and the Free Trade mantras she peddled at her interview. He held back, not sure whether she was asset or liability.

Well, they have certainly found the answer to that question.

He kicks the sofa, then smooths his hair, calms himself.

He will welcome her, sit her down, put her at ease. Everything forgiven, no recriminations. When he has won her over, he will explain that she has picked the wrong man. He can help her. He will help her flush out the real villain.

Deflect the heat away from himself.

But first he must finesse the two clowns that have been assigned to him. They are slouched across his sofa, their eyes glued to a house makeover programme on the television, their boots scuffing his coffee table.

'She's here,' Brown announces.

Tonto and Goatee look up, eager grins smeared across their faces.

'I want the both of you out of here while she and I have a little chat.'

'We were told to ...' Tonto starts.

'I don't give two shits what you were told.'

Days wasted trying to locate her, without success, and then suddenly she answers her mobile and all bets are on again. No-one is going to tell him how to deal with her. If she hadn't been protected, if others hadn't been thinking with their pricks instead of their brains, everything would have been different and Eliot Balkan would be on his own right now. Easy to pick off.

That is the difference between professionals and amateurs. A professional never lets pleasure cloud judgement.

And now?

Now there is just a chance the genie can be pushed back into the bottle.

'Are you deaf?' he shouts at the two monkeys sprawled across his sofa. 'In the bedroom, out of sight.'

The two monkeys have other plans.

Roxanne climbs the front steps. There are eight flats in the block, two to a floor. Her finger is hovering over the bell for flat 4 when she notices the front door is not quite closed. She pushes it gently open.

The door clicks shut behind her.

The block has retained its period features. The glow from the streetlights filter through etched and frosted glass around the door, dimly illuminating the geometric tiled mosaic that spans the floor.

A lift occupies a cage in the middle of the stairwell. Roxanne takes the stairs.

As she reaches the first floor landing, a muffled groan cuts the air. She freezes, listening intensely. Has she misheard? Is it simply the sound of settling joists? A dreaming dog turning in its sleep?

The seconds pass in silence. Finally, Roxanne relaxes and crosses over to Brown's door. Finding no bell, she knocks. The odour of a fry up hangs in the air, and the smell of damp.

She knocks again. Harder this time. Brown has to be in, it is only minutes since they have spoken. They saw lights on as they arrived.

The key is to pursuade him that if the African family are released that will be an end to it. To offer him reassurances that she will leave the country. Maybe she can convince Brown that she will take Eliot with her. Eliot is easier to read than a colouring book, the tiny hesitations in his advances telling of his family at home, a couple of kids no doubt, a wife no longer wanting sex. A man drooling for an affair, a bit of fun, no commitments. They are all the same. But will Brown buy it? Or will she have to come up with something better?

Still no answer. In every bone she knows something is wrong. A warning voice screaming in her head, but she has no choice. She reaches for the door handle.

'It's different for her,' Eliot protests. 'She's trying to find her brother. And you ... you have a husband to avenge, and a son. Well, I've only got me. If that's not glorious enough ... Anyway, you heard her.'

Gwen's breath is visible briefly in the cooling air. The forefinger and thumb of her right hand slowly rotate the wedding ring on her left hand that lies on its back in her lap like a dead spider. It won't be long before frost laces the car windows.

'I were only asking, Lad,' Gwen says gently.

The reproach hangs in the air.

Suddenly Eliot has had enough. He steps out of the car, slams the car door, and heads towards the appartment block.

The fresh air brings instant clarity. He has no obligation to Roxanne. Eliot realises he has never even properly asked her what she knows about Gustave Brown and BitterCrest.

Why has she colluded with Brown? Why has she allowed Eliot to be knocked out and interrogated? If she swopped sides before, how can he be sure she might not do so again, if it suits her purpose?

As he climbs the steps to the front door Eliot considers the possibility that Roxanne might at that moment be trading him over to Brown in exchange for the release of the African family. Is that why she wants him in the car?

There is only darkness. Roxanne flicks a couple of switches in the hall. Nothing. Someone has cut the power. Her heart thumps so loudly the noise is echoing off the walls of the corridor but, if Brown hopes to mess with her head, he has underestimated her.

'Hello?' she calls out softly.

By choosing the stairs instead of the lift, and by refraining from switching lights on outside the flat, Roxanne has given her eyes a moment or two to adjust to low light levels. Just as well, since inside the flat the only illumination comes from round the edges of a pair of closed curtains at one end of the hall. It is a world drained of colour, of light barely reflecting off flat surfaces, a graveyard seen in moonless midnight mist. Ahead of her the darkness is almost absolute. She inches forwards, her hands out in front of her as a second pair of eyes, her feet silent on thick carpet.

The chemicals pulsing through her body are determined to steer her back towards the door and out of the building but adrenalin can be refused. Roxanne learnt that as a child and now exerts her will, her absolute desire not to abandon the African family to their fate.

Her fingers touch a wall, find a dado rail.

Another sound, away to her right. A moan? A creaking door?

She takes a step. The sharp tap of her heel on a hard surface causes her to flinch, the carpet has ended. Has she crossed into a room?

Suddenly she sees him. Upright in an armchair, the side of his face outlined in the faintest whisper of light coming from away to his right. He is looking straight at her, his gaze cool and steady.

'How about you put the lights back on? I'm not into this Count Dracula shit.'

Gustave Brown says nothing, stares at her with insect-like disinterest.

'You rang me,' Roxanne reminds him, her fear rapidly turning to anger. 'So cut the shit and let's get on with it.'

In five steps she has crossed the room and stands before him.

Brown continues to stare ahead, contemptuously ignoring her.

She is a lone swimmer in a tank full of sharks.

'Enough, you bastard,' she shouts, poking him in the chest.

Her finger comes away sticky and Brown begins to move, his head tipping forwards, slowly at first and then with quickening momentum. Roxanne leaps backwards as the body slumps forwards and falls from the chair.

In the fraction of a moment she races to the source of light, tears open the heavy curtains. But in doing so she has her back to the room.

Rapid footsteps tell her she is not alone.

Eliot looks down. He is maybe three metres above the ground, no great height but far enough for the ground to smack him a great

BENEATH THE BITTERCREST

thump if he falls. All that prevents him from obeying the laws of gravity are the toe- and fingerholds he has on a pattern of ornamental bricks that run up the end of the building. Although the bricks stand less than two centimetres proud of the rest of the brickwork it is enough; months on the climbing wall are finally proving to be of purpose.

In moments he reaches the height of the first floor windows.

The flat number beside the name plate at the front door has led Eliot to conclude that Brown lives on the first floor, he hopes he has chosen the right end of the building.

To his left is a large sash window. The lights are off. The question is how to reach it.

From below, access to the window is blocked by an old vine that spans the wall to first floor level. Eliot, who is no gardener, knows of only one plant that grows like that. His grandfather's pride and joy was a massive wisteria that thrust and curled along the entire south wall of their tiny terraced house in Lewisham. But in Eliot's memory the wisteria was an evergreen. In any event Eliot is loath to rely on the plant's branches for support. When, from ground level, he put his weight on the thickest branch the vine snapped in half.

The ornamental bricks stop a metre or so short of the window. A drainpipe will get him a further twenty centimetres, after that he is on his own.

He wants to see Brown and Roxanne together, he needs to be sure.

The drainpipe feels very cold but solid and strong. He clings to it, his insteps resting on a joint in the pipe and one hand wrapped around the pipe itself as he swings his body out towards the window reveal. If he grabs a firm hold of the ledge, he will be all right.

His left foot suddenly slips away from under him.

The pain is excruciating as his whole body lurches to the left, threatening to wrench his shoulder from its socket. Desperately he clenches the fingers of his right hand to haul his body back from the void and towards the drainpipe.

It is a losing battle. The girth of the pipe is too broad. With only one hand round it his fingers begin incrementally to slip. Eliot peers to his left, towards the window. The ledge is now above his head, almost within reach, but to commit himself in that direction will be to precipitate his separation from the drainpipe.

The seconds are ticking away and the knuckles on his right hand threaten to explode from the pressure. What if the window ledge is brittle? What if the whole thing crumbles away from the wall?

The hourglass is empty, he has no choice. As he throws his left hand up, and finds the ledge, his right foot falls away from the pipe. For a moment he hangs there, one hand on the ledge, the other round the drainpipe, his face squashed against the bricks, like a man crucified. His feet tangled in the upper branches of the vine. The fingertips of his right hand continue their inevitable arc until finally they snap away from the pipe.

Eliot attempts to bring his right hand across to join his left, but gravity is not on his side.

His body crashes downwards.

The night air is thick with the noises of straining branches, snapping twigs, supporting wires stretched taut as guitar strings and nails being prised out of the brickwork one by one.

Eliot keeps his body as still as he is able. It is like trying to lie down on a busy trampoline, with forces juddering and shaking him in every direction, tossing his body this way and that. He is dropping slowly as nails pop out and part of the plant peels away from the wall.

He braces himself for impact.

And then, like a coiled spring coming to rest, the shaking subsides and the noise is over. Eliot hangs there, a fly in a spider's web, with no idea as to how he might extricate himself. Gingerly he lifts his head, torn between the desire to get safely down to the ground and the urge to complete the mission he has set himself.

Reaching up with both hands, he finds the window ledge and hauls himself up. The vine groans, its branches scraping over each other beneath Eliot's shifting weight.

The stone is solid and Eliot pulls himself up to the point where he is able to swing his elbows up onto the ledge. It occurs to him that he has made so much noise that the occupants of the room, if there are any, will be waiting for him.

The curtains are open and the orange glow of the street lamps lights the upper half of the room. Paintings on the walls. The top of an armchair. A mantlepiece. A glass topped coffee table.

The sound of a wire snapping.

Beneath Eliot's feet the branches are shaking again.

A light goes on elsewhere in the flat, spreading through an open door, illuminating the carpet.

More pings as nails fly out of the brickwork beneath him and supporting wires slacken and fall away.

BENEATH THE BITTERCREST

On the floor, surrounded by a dark patch that catches the light, is the body of Gustave Brown. Eliot hears raised male voices.

The vine finally tumbles away from the wall and Eliot, who had been resting most of his weight on it, goes with it.

They have tied her to a chair in the kitchen. Over and beyond the call of duty, since they have only been asked to catch her and bring her in, but with a litany of recent failures behind them, Goatee is of the opinion that a little initiative and extra spadework might stand him in good stead with his employer. Besides, he enjoys his work.

Roxanne for her part has said nothing since her capture. She tastes blood in the corner of her mouth. Something is trickling down her cheek, itching like a procession of ants on her skin.

Who killed Gustave Brown? Who are the two thugs who have caught her? If Brown is no longer a player, and plainly he is not, who is the key to securing Dudu and his family's release? Who is pulling the strings?

'It would be a source of considerable appreciation if you would divest yourself of the whereabouts of Romeo,' Goatee says.

Roxanne looks over at the other man who is cleaning his nails with a bloody kitchen knife.

'Where is Eliot Balkan?' Tonto's face is suddenly right up against her own, his breath thick on her cheek.

Might screaming be productive? She has already had the knife pressed against her throat and has been warned but, in the circumstances, with Brown's body in the next room, what does she have to lose?

'I came here to make a deal,' she says finally. 'With Brown.'

'He isn't making deals any more.' Tonto walks away towards the sink.

'Then we have nothing to discuss,' she says simply.

Goatee puts a hand on her thigh. 'You may find this hard to believe, but what we can do to you is nothing compared to what he might do.'

'Who's he?'

Goatee smiles and runs a finger up the inside of her leg.

Roxanne's subconscious already knows who he is talking about but her conscious mind has to catch up. She plays for time. Eventually Eliot and Gwen will worry about the time she is taking. How long since she left the car? Ten minutes? Five?

'Why don't you two tell me what's going on? Then I tell you where he is.'

Goatee's hand stops moving.

'I'm not going anywhere.' she adds, stating the obvious.

A mobile phone rings. The dance of the Sugar Plum Fairies. Goatee straightens up and fishes his mobile out of his trouser pocket. He grunts his name into the phone and listens.

Roxanne's eyes dart from one man to the other. A couple of times the shorter man appears to be about to speak into his mobile, then stops and listens some more.

Suddenly an alarm sounds, loud and pulsating. Calculated to wake people up.

'A fire alarm?' Goatee shouts into the phone. '... Yes. OK.' He looks down at Roxanne. A thin smile crosses his lips. 'Yes, if that's what you want.'

Footsteps rushing about on the floor above. Tonto rushes out of the room. The front door opens briefly then slams shut. In seconds smoke billows into the kitchen.

Goatee trousers his phone as Tonto reappears.

'The whole place is going up,' Tonto explains, rushing to the window.

Goatee checks the ropes tying Roxanne are secure.

'There's smoke out the back as well,' Tonto shouts. 'What are we doing?'

'Somebody's done our job for us,' Goatee says happily. 'Joan of Arc stays here. She can fry with Brown.'

Tonto throws open the kitchen window. Immediately below is a garage roof. The smoke is coming from a window on the floor below, to the right, possibly the stairwell. The orange glow of flames licks the windows. He climbs out and drops down onto the roof.

Goatee kicks the chair out from under Roxanne. She falls heavily against the kitchen units, knocking her out.

'Burn in hell, bitch,' Goatee snarls, tossing the kitchen knife across the room and following Tonto out through the window into the night.

Moments later there is the sound of splintering wood as Brown's front door is torn from its hinges. With the door open, the racket from the fire alarm is deafening. Black smoke pours into the flat. Distant shouts of slippered residents running about on the landings.

Through the window the sound of a car roaring away at high speed.

BENEATH THE BITTERCREST

Eliot appears in the kitchen, a hankerchief pressed to his face against the smoke. He grabs the knife at his feet and cuts Roxanne's cords. Coughing, he drags her over to the window, grabs the nearest liquid to hand, an open bottle of white wine, and poured the contents over her face. She splutters and comes round.

'We're climbing through a window. Can you do that?'

She nods. He hauls her to her feet and helps her out.

They reach the car as the fire engines sirens become audible.

'What the bloody hell ...' Gwen says, startled by the sudden reappearance of Eliot and Roxanne.

'Go, go, go,' Eliot yells.

'I dragged a couple of dustbins in from outside and set fire to them in the stairwell. It was just a load of smoke. Trust me.'

'Famous last words,' Gwen observes. She checks the rear view mirror for the tenth time, convinced they are being followed.

'I told you to stay in the car,' Roxanne says, between coughs. She is sprawled out across the back seat, with Eliot up front beside Gwen.

'Thanks, Eliot, you saved my life,' Eliot suggests.

'Didn't you just say the fire wasn't a fire?'

'Oh, right. And you tied yourself to that chair?'

'I'll see you get a medal.'

'Do that.'

Eliot clenches his eyes shut, he has a headache the size of Spaghetti junction.

Nearly twenty four hours have passed since Dudu and family were abducted. In that time anything may have happened. In that time he has read a diary detailing the cremation of almost two hundred people, killed possibly for their organs. With Brown dead how will they find Dudu and his family? If they are still alive.

They don't even know that.

The game is up. They have lost their prime suspect. Unless the attack was a random act. Two burglars chancing upon that particular flat on that particular night. Yeah right.

'Can we not involve the police?' Gwen asks out of nowhere.

Eliot opens his eyes. Gwen looks tired and worn, looks her age. Through the window he recognises the street, they are almost back at the Wesley house.

'We could ring them and ...' Gwen continues.

'Too many rotten apples.' Eliot hates the cliché even as he utters it.

Gwen sighs heavily, flicks the indicator on to turn right.

'What about that policeman in Guildford?' Roxanne asks.

'Oh yes, the village bobby, my close friend Detective Inspector Havering,' Eliot says sarcastically. 'What will we tell him? We don't even have a bloody suspect anymore.'

The car pulls up outside the house.

With the engine off, their breaths quickly become visible. The despairing silence is total.

'How about the industrial estate?' Eliot says eventually. 'Maybe we should go back to the low building and ...'

'It's too late for that,' Roxanne answers wearily.

All at once Gwen sits bolt upright in her chair and turns the ignition key.

'Why the bloody hell didn't I think of it before? I know where to go.'

She sets off so fast the wheels skid and she all but loses control of the vehicle. They head north west.

It begins to snow, a few dandruff flakes at first then, within minutes, a steady flow like breakfast cereals tumbling into a bowl. Once out of town the hills become steeper and the wind picks up. The wipers are working at double speed, smearing fat snowflakes across the windscreen like cream cheese over crackers.

Lacking ideas of their own, neither Eliot nor Roxanne feels inclined to challenge the older woman.

Eliot puts his head back against the headrest and tries to relax.

He is surprised to feel Roxanne's hands on his shoulders. Reaching over from the back seat, she massages the knots in his neck and shoulders. The sensation is overwhelming, he hasn't realised how tense his body is. Waves of pain and release sweep through his upper body, bringing tears to his eyes. He submits to her probing fingers, focusing his mind on the rising and falling sounds of the engine and the G forces passing through his body as Gwen throws the car into first one curve then another along the narrow country road.

At one point the wheels lose the grip. His heart flies to his mouth as the vehicle lurched sideways. He shuts his eyes.

'Nearly there.'

'Nearly where, Gwen?' Roxanne asks.

'Up here on the left.'

Eliot opens his eyes. They are in the middle of nowhere. A high brick wall runs along the side of the road, partially obscured by

BENEATH THE BITTERCREST

bushes, the overhanging branches of mature trees and dead brambles. The snow deep and crisp and even. Eliot starts humming the carol.

'There, those gates, do you see?'

Beyond the gates as they speed past, a modern building is briefly visible, all glass and stainless steel.

'The hospital. That's where Andrew were to have his operation. That's where they'll be.'

They pull up on the verge a hundred metres beyond the gates.

'Well, what do you think?' Gwen cuts the engine.

Eliot finds Roxanne's hand, still on his shoulder in the darkness.

Roxanne sighs. 'I don't know, Gwen. Maybe ... I don't know.'

'A hospital?' Eliot mutters disappointedly.

'You saw press cuttings Timothy kept,' Gwen insists. 'This is where the photos were taken. That man you were after, and the other one, they were stood there, in front of the hospital.'

Draper? Patron saint of pomposity. What had Peter Han called him? Small potatoes. Draper as master criminal? Eliot struggles to believe it. It is like being told Snow White was actually abusing all those helpless dwarves.

And yet, with Brown out of the picture ...

Could they have been wrong all along?

'We're talking hundreds of people killed over two and a bit years,' Eliot says. 'They couldn't do that in a hospital. It couldn't be done.'

'Maybe there's a special wing,' Gwen offers.

'People would know. It would leak out.'

'Something hidden away.'

'It's a modern hospital. There would be people who knew, builders, architects, town planners, surveyors. Never mind the nursing staff. The whole thing would have been plainly visible during construction.' Eliot turns to Roxanne. 'I'm all for conspiracies but it just isn't possible.'

'I'm sorry, Gwen.' Roxanne agrees with Eliot. 'Maybe later ... if we can get anyone to listen, this place should be investigated. They might be carrying out transplants here, but I can't see Dudu and family locked up in a hospital.'

They sit in the dark, snow slowly gathering on the windows.

'Oh well,' Gwen says eventually, 'no point catching our bloody deaths.' She starts the car up and drives back onto the road. A few hundred metres on she finds a spot to turn the car and they head back the way they came.

Drawing level with the entrance Gwen slows the car to a crawl.

Eliot notices that on top of the pillars that stand on either side of the gates there is a large irregular-shaped lump hidden beneath the blanket of snow. A memory stirs deep in his subconscious. Something on a pillar? He tries to empty his mind and force a coherent image to the surface, but it remains tantalisingly beyond his reach.

He is lost in thought as Gwen put her foot down and sets off, driving as fast as conditions will allow. The sooner they get back to studying her Timothy's diaries the better, the answers must be there somewhere. But the feeling that he has been close to a significant discovery refuses to go away.

They reach the outskirts of Swindon. Street lighting bathes the snow orange. Gwen wonders what time it is, the clock in the car stopped several weeks ago. Timothy not fixing the clock should have been a sign, she realises, he was always so fastidious.

A flashback to a memory of childhood. Gwen is in her father's car, perched on the back seat. The smell of leather upholstery. No seat-belts. Nineteen forty six or forty seven. It is raining so hard the windscreen wipers have given up. She is wrapped in a large tartan blanket and they are all singing a song. How did it go? Something about a big house.

She slams on the brakes.

'I've just remembered,' she shouts. 'The hospital, it weren't always a hospital.'

'What?'

'It weren't always a hospital.'

'It's only just been built.'

'No, that's just it. There were a building there before. An older building.'

Eliot and Roxanne don't seem impressed.

'After the war, when the National Health Service were being set up, the place were converted into a hospital for ex servicemen. It had been used in the war, you see, for training spies or something. Like those places where they tried breaking enemy codes. Then, after the war, they turned it into a nursing home.'

Roxanne and Eliot continue to stare back uncomprehendingly.

Gwen continues slowly as if talking to two simpletons.

'It were a country house, I think. What if they converted it during the war? The old building, like. Built bunkers underground or some such? And there's caves all about round here. No-one would know.'

BENEATH THE BITTERCREST   305

'But you're saying they knocked down the old building to make the new hospital?' Eliot is struggling to follow Gwen's story.

'You've cloth ears, the pair of you,' Gwen's voice is rising in frustration. 'The old building's still there. We went there, Timothy and I, to discuss Andrew's transplant. It's an administrative centre now.'

'So where's the new hospital?'

'Oh, heaven help us. The new buildings are in the grounds.'

'OK,' Eliot says cagily. 'So you're saying there might be underground levels hidden beneath what is now the administration block?'

Gwen lifts her hands to the Lord in grateful thanks.

Roxanne looks at Eliot who stares back.

'But why would they keep illegal refugees in a hospital?' Roxanne is thinking aloud. 'We know Brown wasn't interested in their health or ...'

'If it was Brown,' Eliot cuts in, 'Before you give Gwen a heart attack the point is this. If these bastards have been ripping the organs out of refugees for money, what better place than a hospital? They kill the refugees, rip the organs out, carry them down the corridor and sew them into someone else.'

Roxanne turns towards Gwen. 'Do you have friends who might remember what the building was like in the war, anyone who might have visited the place back then?'

'How bloody old do you think I am?' Gwen's voice is thick with mock indignation.

Out of nowhere Eliot remembers a fragment of time during his initial interview at BitterCrest. The intercom had buzzed and the receptionist had announced a call from a hospital. 'I have the hospital for you.' What had Draper said? 'I'll deal with it ... Tell them to wait, I'll deal with it later.'

Then all at once another memory surfaces.

'Dudu and his wife and children come first,' Roxanne is saying to Gwen. 'We can always visit the hospital later.'

A car door opens, then slams shut. Gwen and Roxanne look at each other.

'What are you doing?' Roxanne says, catching up with Eliot who is striding off down the road.

'What do you think I'm doing? We've been wrong. Right from the start. It was Draper not Brown. It was Draper.'

'How can you know? You said you didn't believe that ...'

'Forget what I said.'

Eliot keeps walking.

'It's five miles, Eliot.'

'That African tramp on the platform at Doncaster. You knew him.'

She doesn't answer him, but he has her attention.

'At the time I thought he was just a drunk but he wasn't, was he? You knew him and he was trying to tell you something. I think I understand what he was trying to tell you.'

thirty seven

The floor is awash with splattered blood. On the metal trolley in the centre of the room are the remains of a human being. The body has been stripped as if by demons. The skin has been flayed, the abdominal cavity cut open and the internal organs removed. Liver, heart, kidneys, lungs, pancreas, the lot. The intestines and stomach are to be found to the left of the cadaver in a large metal bucket. Moving up to the face, the eyes have been removed, leaving empty staring sockets. Moving back down, several bones appeared to have been sliced opened, most notably the femur of each leg.

The overall effect is of an empty and bloody ribcage to which were attached four flayed limbs and a grotesquely disfigured head. The only immediately recognisable components are the hands and feet, which remain intact, and the hair above the vacant eye sockets. A steel bracelet hangs round the corpse's right wrist.

If someone chancing upon the room were able to shift his or her gaze from the corpse they might notice the long mirror that runs almost the length of one wall. There is something strange about the mirror, its reflection imperfect, as if it were reflecting two rooms, one brightly the other vaguely. Beyond the reflection of the trolley and its dismembered corpse there seems to be another trolley, around which figures appear to be working.

Beside the corpse stands a man. He is staring at himself in the mirror, studying the scene, him in his white coat beside the body, as if committing it to memory. His nostrils are slightly flared and he looks as if he might throw his head back and howl at the night. His shoes are encased in protective outer shoes, his hands wear protective transparent gloves. His breathing is even and calm. If any part of the scene before him causes him disquiet, he does not show it. His eyes take in the corpse, running from scalp to toe, lingering briefly when he reaches the genitals. He reaches out and takes the dead man's balls in his hand, as if weighing them, his eyes darting up to the mutilated face as he does so.

There is a slight metallic squeal as a handle turns and a door opens. A middle-aged woman, very smartly dressed, stands in the doorway. Still gripping the cadaver's testicles, the man turns towards her.

308   christian vassie

'Mrs Bryant, what a pleasure. A senior consultant still on the premises at this time, how diligent. Your reputation is undeserved.'

Bryant's face is composed, but Draper can see her knee is twitching uncontrollably. Avoiding the carnage in the room, she keeps her gaze fixed on him, while holding the door open.

'What a waste that we should bury these with him,' Draper says, rolling the scrotum about in his hand, enjoying Bryant's discomfort. 'Of course, we wouldn't want to clone him, God knows there are already more than enough of them cluttering up the planet, but think of the genetic material, the potential for research. Stem cells perhaps?'

'While we all agree that the work we do here is unfortunately necessary in order to save lives,' Bryant says coolly, 'we do not all take such barbarous pleasure from the procedure.'

'Well said that woman. Good for you.' Draper lets the testicles fall from his grasp and smiles kindly. Her twitching knee is getting worse. 'How are they doing?' he says, indicating with his eyes the room beyond the mirror.

'Another two hours.' Bryant avoids eye contact.

Draper pulls an object, resembling a tv remote control, from his pocket. Locating the button he wants, he presses. The long mirror becomes transparent and the room beyond the glass becomes visible.

The operation is in full swing. A team of uniformed surgeons, anaesthetists, and other theatre staff busy themselves around their patient. Metal tools glint briefly beneath the bright lights. Around the room, light emitting diodes and liquid crystal displays blink and pulse like tiny hearts.

'Marvellous,' Draper whispers quietly. 'Pass me some of that,' he says casually, indicating what he wants with a slight wave of the hand.

Bryant hesitates.

'Come on, come on.' Draper insists.

The woman steps carefully into the room, grabs a fistful of paper towels and carries them over to Draper who is still by the corpse, gazing through into the next room.

Draper takes the towels without looking at the consultant who stands beside him, the colour draining from her cheeks, her jaw clenching and unclenching. Draper dabs slowly at his brow and around his neck. When he is done, he drops the ball of damp towels into Naseem's empty abdominal cavity.

'Excellent,' he says. 'Excellent. All right, I am all yours, lead on.'

Bryant grabs more paper towels as she leaves the room. She crouches in the corridor wiping away at her shoes like Lady Macbeth trying to clean her hands after the murder of her king. Behind her, Draper removes his gloves, gown, over-trousers and outer-shoes, tossing each item back into room 2B.

'You should have thought of that before stepping into the room,' he reproaches her.

Bryant does her best to ignore the taunt, though she cannot help regretting that she has allowed herself to be so compromised. By the time she found her conscience, it was too late and she is now an accessory to every crime committed in the name of medicine by a hospital that has forfeited its right to exist.

'Throw it all in there,' he orders impatiently, seeing her hesitating with the bloodied towels.

She does as she is told.

'Carry your shoes. You can, I am sure, find something else to wear till the end of your shift.'

Draper closes the door on the remains of Naseem's corpse.

'Right, let's go.'

He follows Bryant down the corridor.

'I understand your sister is coming in soon,' Draper says as they passed through a set of swing doors, twisting the knife.

Bryant doesn't need reminding of how her silence has been bought.

It has taken Laurie less than ten minutes to find the answer to Eliot's question. He sits in his flat watching the late night football roundup with his laptop on his knees and a can of Red Stripe in arm's reach.

Companies House to start with, then a couple of other sites a hacker friend introduced him to. Sopford Industrial Estate, when you get past all the foreign holding companies and other bollocks, is owned by Neville Draper, Gustave Brown and a San Marino based outfit called The Institute.

He emails back, hoping Eliot checks his inbox regularly.

They descend two flights of stairs. Neither having anything they wish to say to the other, they walk in silence. Draper fiddles with his suit, which has been rather constrained beneath the gown and other items of protective wear. He fishes the hankerchief out of his breast pocket and refolds it before replacing it, making sure that an exactly equilateral triangle of emerald green protrudes to offset and heighten the dark blue of his suit.

Unlike the floors above, basement level three is carpetted. Many years ago it was the accommodation level, the level to which staff retreated during the periods when German air raids were at their peak. The carpets are beginning to show their age but the doors and fittings are of real quality, lending the corridor the air of a very respectable, if slightly old-fashioned, seafront hotel.

Halfway down, Bryant stops and hands Draper a set of keys.

'If you don't mind, I do not wish to be a party to this.'

'Run along then.'

It is so quiet three floors underground that Draper can hear the levers in the lock tumbling as he pushes the key home. He pauses, composes himself, then pushes the door open.

There are ten appartments on sub-level three, each with its own bedrooms, bathroom, kitchen and living area. A child's voice fills the air, shouting excitedly in a language that sounds to Draper as if it must come from west Africa. A second child answers, protesting noisily. Then an explosion of helpless laughter. It is after one o'clock in the morning but, in the windowless basement, the occupants have no idea of the time, their watches taken from them and there being no natural light. Draper walks towards the noise.

In the lounge Alima looks over at the boys. She and Dudu are seated at the table. Dudu has his head in his hands and Alima, her arm around him, is seeking to console him. He blames himself, as he always does. If only he hadn't taken Eliot and Roxanne to the church market, if only he had told them to leave, if only he had put his family first ... She has been trying for hours to reassure him.

'Excuse me.'

Alima jumps and spins round towards the voice.

'I hope I didn't startle you. The door was open. I did call.'

'Who are you?' Alima asks.

Beside her, Dudu lifts his head and opens his eyes. The three children sit quietly on the sofa, heads downcast.

'Of course, forgive me. My name is Draper, I am ... in charge of catering. The door was open. You have wonderful children.' Draper's eyes linger slowly, all three children have such long eyelashes. 'I was ...' he turns to the woman, '... concerned to ensure that we were meeting your dietary requirements.'

'I do not understand,' Alima says nervously. She glances at Dudu

BENEATH THE BITTERCREST

for support, but he shakes his head, since the abduction he has been too frightened to speak.

'I'm sorry, Mrs Bondembe. I am talking about food.'

Draper smiles and steps into the room.

'I am concerned about the food. I know we cannot produce what you are used to, cassava, yam, plantain stew, bush meat.'

As he speaks Draper walks past the table and on towards the sofa.

'But I want to be sure that you are all happy ...'

He reaches out and takes the girl's chin in his hand, pulling her head up to oblige her to look at him.

'...that the children are well fed.'

He can feel the girl's jaw trembling as her dark eyes plead with his own. He feels the father's eyes burning the back of his neck, the mother's hands bunching into frightened fists.

'You see, my staff are not always as concerned as they might be to cook food that is appropriate or appreciated,' he continues, warming to his theme.

He lets go of the girl's jaw and rubs the top of the head of one of the boys.

'We do want your stay with us to be pleasant.'

He turns to face the parents.

'So please let me know if there is anything you need, or anything you would rather not eat. Maybe I could show the children round the kitchens?'

They stare at him. He feels their questions, dozens of them, caught in their throats. There are leaders and followers in the world: those who get things done and those who are done to, those who provide the raw material, so to speak. What was Brown thinking, abducting the whole family? Even if they have learned something from Eliot Balkan or Roxanne Lepage, who will believe a bunch of African refugees? And for the sake of a handful of kidneys ... it would have been more prudent to simply set fire to their home, with them inside.

'Oh, I almost forgot. I was asked to tell you that some tests have to be carried out, general health, educational assessments, and so on. Not really my field, of course, the caring professions are always understaffed. It's all to decide on where you're going next.' Draper's eyes glance from mother to father as he speaks. 'They usually do the children first. So ...'

He pats the top of each child's head in turn as if playing a tune on a musical instrument,

three blind mice,
three blind mice ...

He smiles reassuringly.
'... which one shall it be?'
He looks down at the children.
'Shall we let Mummy choose? Or Daddy?'
Oh, he has their full attention now, master of all he surveys. The father is weak, barely able to look him in the eye. It is the woman who will give them trouble and lash out when she finally understands there is to be no escape. Draper continues playing the children's heads,

... see how they run,
see how they run ...

One of the children is whimpering.
'Let's pick Mum. So, mum, which one do you choose?'
Alima's eyes are dark with hatred. She answers Draper in a steady voice.
'If anyone tries to take my family apart ...'

... who cut off their heads with a carving knife ...

'Stop touching them,' she shouts suddenly.
Dudu flinches, his eyes glancing momentarily at Draper, who also seems taken aback at the woman's show of resistance.
'Well, mustn't keep you,' Draper says blandly, his hand dropping to his side. 'Promise me you will speak to someone if there is anything you need. Someone will be round in a little while to start the tests so I will leave it to you to decide who will go first.'
He crosses towards the door.
'Why are we here?' Alima blurts out as he is about to leave the room.
Draper stops on the threshold. He pauses, soaking up the seconds, before turning back to face her.
'I only deal with the catering,' he apologises. 'Well ... I'd better be going. Good evening.'

thirty eight

'Don't be daft,' Gwen answers.

'But we might be gone for hours,' Roxanne insists.

The two women stare out at Eliot who is in front of the hospital gates leaping repeatedly while swinging a branch about, to sweep away at the snow on the top of one of the pillars. A grey, animal form is slowly emerging.

Eliot tosses the branch aside and races back to the car.

'I knew it! Look. It's a bloody lion!'

'And?' Roxanne says.

'That's what the drawing meant. I thought it was a cat on a box but it was a lion. Two lions on pillars.' He cannot believe she doesn't see it. 'The picture the African guy drew you at Doncaster station. He was trying to tell you about this place. About this hospital.'

Suddenly Roxanne remembers the train pulling out of Doncaster, the picture pressed to the window. It's a long shot but it's better than nothing.

'Please, Gwen, go,' she says, stepping out of the car. 'We'll call you later.'

'And if you run out again in five minutes, desperate for a lift?'

'Talk to her, Eliot.'

'You're right, she's wrong,' Eliot says to Gwen.

'I'll be all right, Love.' Gwen gives Roxanne a motherly smile. 'I may look like an old fool, but I've no desire to freeze to death in this car.'

Roxanne cannot be bothered to argue. She joins Eliot at the gates to the Fairley Manor Hospital. It is one fifty a.m.

'Good evening, Sir.'

The guard at the reception desk quickly slides the book he is reading under an emergency procedure dossier.

Draper, like a predator that has eaten his fill, glances disinterestedly at the guard, then at the falling snow visible through the large and elegant windows across the hall. A soft click indicates that the security door behind him has swung shut. A quick discussion with the head of the transplant team in the main hospital block and he will go home.

'Excuse me, Sir.'

Draper's eyes drift back towards the guard, whose badge identifies him as Colin Spall. Spall, barely out of his teens, is clearly an oaf for whom "work" consists of nothing more taxing than parking his backside on a stool and feigning servility to those who pass by.

A casual visitor to the hospital will see the barely sentient louts in chocolate brown uniforms as a token force, a sign that security isn't really an issue. Which was exactly what is intended.

Draper's heels click against the marble floor as he strides towards the exit.

'Are you going home, Sir?' Spall calls out after him.

Draper spins round, a small involuntary tic twitches beneath his right eye.

'In case someone calls for you.'

Draper shows the man his mobile phone, smiling ironically.

'Sorry, Sir ... but if someone calls round in person ... shall I tell them you have left for the night or ...'

Draper walks away, anyone who matters will know where he is.

The administration block is a large country house, Fairley Manor, built in a mock gothic style at the top of the hill. Imposing if not pretty, it would make a great location for a Hammer horror film if, instead of modern hospital buildings and car parks, the manor were surrounded by woodcutters' huts and family vaults.

There is no indication of subterranean levels, no large vents sitting in the middle of the lawns, no signposts. If Gwen is right then great care will have been taken to make the underground development invisible. Eliot and Roxanne keep beneath the shelter of the trees that skirts the perimeter of the grounds. Apart from anything else, the snow has been falling for some time and their every footprint will point an accusing finger in the direction they have travelled.

'You never told me who the African was. The man at the station.'

'He was someone Dudu and Alima put me in touch with. Claimed to know someone who had escaped a smuggling gang.' She stops while they negotiate a fallen tree. 'I met him early that morning, before attending your conference, and paid him to keep a lookout for you. His story didn't make sense, he was wierd. Creepy. I assumed he was a crack addict who would say anything to get money for a fix.'

BENEATH THE BITTERCREST   315

But could the man have been right all along? Eliot is certain they won't have to wait long for the answer.

The back of the house gives onto formal gardens and a wide lawn almost the size of a football pitch. The boundary wall is of fairly recent construction, no earlier than the second world war Eliot guesses. Prior to that, the view would have extended to the open countryside to afford views of grazing livestock and rustic yokels toiling in the fields.

A few lights are on in upstairs windows but not on the ground floor. Working their way round, Roxanne and Eliot find their path blocked by a dense wall of dead brambles and are obliged to step out from under the trees onto the path that skirts the edge of the lawn. In full view of the house, they walk briskly through the snow. They have covered maybe twenty metres, with no sign of an end to the thicket of brambles beneath the trees, when an arc light mounted high on the house bursts into life, turning the snow-carpetted ground a dazzling white. They stand transfixed, like third division footballers experiencing a floodlit premiership ground for the first time.

A red light starts flashing above one of the cluster of television monitors facing Spall but, as the security guard is only six lines away from finishing a magazine article about the best shags on tv, he ignores the light and carries on reading. The arc lights at the back of the building go off fairly frequently, usually as the result of deer, or even hedgehogs, crossing the lawns.

Every unusual event has to be logged in the incident book, but a few minutes either way won't change anything. Whatever is out there can stay there and bloody well freeze to death for all he cares.

The distraction makes him lose his place and he starts again at the top of the page. Above his head, the television monitor shows two figures starting to run, silhouetted against the white lawn.

An alarm bleeps, quietly at first but Spall knows that every ten seconds it will increase a notch, until eardrums start to bleed.

'Yeah, OK,' Spall says aloud, his eyes glued to the page. 'Shut the fuck up, will you?'

Apparently if you want to shag a tv star the best night to try is when there is a film premiere in town. It seems that the combination of adoring fans outside the cinema, an action movie, and the piss up afterwards is almost guaranteed to get every z-list celebrity moist between the hams and gagging for it. Spall licks his lips as he reads.

The alarm rises a notch. On the monitor, still unnoticed, the figures continue running. Spall presses his finger to the page to ensure he doesn't lose his place a second time and, with his free hand, reaches out for the button that will cut the alarm.

'That's right, get on my tits.'

One woman, famous for nothing more than volunteering to be locked in a flat with a handful of other equally vacuous nonentities, has apparently got so excited while attending the premiere of a thriller in Leicester Square that she whipped off her knickers and ...

His fingers finally find the button and the bleeping stops. He glances at the display. Twenty five seconds. Shit, he will have to explain why it has taken him so long to respond. Shit, shit, shit.

He raises his head. He catches sight of a movement on the monitor, something disappearing into the trees at the bottom of the screen.

A leg? A foot?

It will just be another deer, dumping a load when the lights came on and racing for cover.

He scribbles the time of the incident into the logbook. Unfortunately it doesn't end there. His contract specifies that every incident has to be investigated immediately. He picks up the phone to raise his boss. No answer. No answer. No answer. The phone is almost back in its cradle when he heard a voice.

'Speak.'

'Philip, yeah. Where the hell were you, man?'

'Piss off, Colin.'

'Suck my dick.'

'Is there a point to this or do you just want to talk dirty to someone while you jerk off?'

The two men laugh.

'A code 45,' Spall says. 'I need someone to check the back of the house.'

'Short staffed, you'll have to do it.'

'Yeah right, dump me in it.'

'Oh, for fuck's sake. Look ... all right, when Grigston gets back I'll send him over.'

'You're a litte tart and I want to have your babies. How long?'

'Twenty minutes, half an hour?'

'Fuck off, you know a code 45's got to be checked within eight minutes.'

'I'll see what I can do but ...'

BENEATH THE BITTERCREST

Spall slams the phone down, checks his watch, two minutes gone already. Drumming his fingers on the desk, he waits for the phone to ring. If he has to go out he will need his coat and hat. He finds a torch in a drawer at the end of the desk, along with a can of Mace and the remote control for the main alarm.

'Come on, come on,' he mutters, staring at the phone.

They are such bloody cheapskates at the hospital, never enough staff. Three minutes gone. His shift is due to end in twenty minutes and he has been hoping to pop into The Pull Stop, a late night bar and Swindon's newest club. With luck, he might get in half an hour's drinking, and maybe even get lucky.

With the snow falling steadily there is a good chance that a trip outside will leave him soaked through, his hair plastered to his head like vomit on a pavement. Spall climbs off his stool and opens all the doors and drawers under the reception desk, on the off-chance of finding an umbrella. No such luck.

Four minutes gone. He picks up the phone and slams it back down on the counter.

'Fuck!'

A quick glance round all the monitors. There are six cameras, two at the front of the building, two at the back and one on each side. Five of the cameras are working on infrared, showing a reddish white snow tumbling like static over the duller and darker reds and blacks of the background. Where the arc light was tripped by the remote sensor, the colours are all different but the content is essentially the same, grass, brick walls, darkness, snow.

Spall grabs the torch and the can of Mace and runs to the cloak-room to fetch his jacket and hat. Suitably attired, he heads towards the exit.

The tall glass doors swing open noiselessly.

As he crosses into the lobby, the can of Mace falls, unnoticed, from his pocket. Spall pulls open one of the exterior panelled hardwood doors and steps outside.

The path leading down towards the hospital complex is devoid of life. The directional orange light of the nearest lamp post frames the swirling snow as if trapping it in an inverted funnel.

Spall sets off round the building in a clockwise direction, cursing the snow and the sodden ground, knowing he'll look a right state by the time he gets all the way round.

Eliot and Roxanne have seen the guard emerge from the building and, for a moment, they fear he has spotted them and will intercept them. When the guard heads off in the opposite direction, Eliot grabs Roxanne's arm.

'Wait. Like this.'

He walks backwards towards the front entrance. Roxanne shakes her head but does as he suggests.

'Don't tell me,' she says, joining him by the doors. 'You saw it in a film.'

'You have a problem with that?'

The can of Mace Spall dropped has fallen onto the mat and wedged itself between the doors, preventing the mechanism from locking. As Eliot pushes open the large, hardwood outer doors and steps into the lobby, the inner glass doors opposite swing open automatically ahead of them. Eliot picks up the can of Mace. Behind them the glass doors swing shut and lock.

The hall is impressive. Dark oak panelling lines the walls. A wide staircase winds round two walls towards the upper floor, from which a balustraded landing affords a view of the reception area below. Several large stag heads peer down, testament to the huntin' and shootin' days of the Fairley family, original owners of the house. Elsewhere hang large glaring portraits, several braces of old pistols, and a pair of crossed swords. A large aspidistra completes the period feel. Offset against this rather heavy Victorian aroma are the hard black lines of the reception desk and three very curvaceous and modern sofas, in grey and shocking pink, that sit on the white marble floor like yawning hippos on an ice rink.

An alarm bleeps steadily.

Spall reaches the floodlit section of lawn. As expected there is no sign of life. On top of everything else, he catches his heel on the ceramic bordering around a flower bed that is hidden beneath the snow. Limping, he makes his way round the house, cursing the snow, cursing the alarm system, and the floodlights, and the fact that he'll probably be too late for a drink at the Pull Stop.

He is on the home stretch, round the back where various ugly extensions were added during the war years to provide a kitchen annex, when he spots footsteps in the snow.

It occurs to him that the whole thing has been cooked up by the other security guards for a laugh. Well, ha ha. If he is going to have his evening buggered, they can bloody well go down with him. Once the general alarm is sounded they will have to join him. He reaches into his pocket, finds his keys, some loose change. Another pocket, more money, a pack of chewing gum. He has a bad feeling. The inner pockets of his coat, a small lump of dope, some Rizlas, his wallet.

In his mind's eye Spall sees the remote control, sitting on the reception desk, where he left it. Shit. Not only is he unable to set off the main alarm, he will now also have to run back inside to cancel the code 45 at the main terminal, and he has less than two minutes to do it. He races off, stupidly destroying all the evidence the intruders have left.

Halfway across the final stretch of lawn, he notices two sets of footprints to his right, leading away from the main door. He stops, about turns. The footsteps lead off in the direction he has just come from. Someone has entered the building, probably while he has been outside checking out the back lawns.

Unless they broke in earlier in the evening.

Or maybe Draper took that route when he left the building. But there are two sets of prints. Head buzzing from the unaccustomed physical exertion, Spall rushes to the doors.

Once in the lobby, out of the snow, he uses his swipe card to open the glass doors.

Everything seems in order. At the reception desk he cancels the code 45, as protocol requires. Only then does he realise that, since he has seen evidence of intruders, he shouldn't have cancelled the code 45 at all. With every passing second he is digging himself deeper and deeper. He can kiss the drink goodbye and, worse still, he has a hunch he may soon be kissing his job goodbye. His hand hovers over the main alarm button: trigger the alarm and have your incompetence revealed straight away or do nothing and have your incompetence revealed in the morning.

Great bloody choice.

Except ... that there is as yet no sign of a break in or a compromising of security, other than some footprints in the snow ... and ... if the weather goes his way, warms up a bit, it is just possible the snow will be gone by morning. No snow, no evidence.

Satisfied with his reasoning, Spall removes his jacket and disappears into the cloakroom to hang it up.

Three minutes later Eliot and Roxanne emerge through the same cloakroom door into the quiet splendour of the hall. Eliot wonders how long it takes for the effect of Mace to wear off and hopes he hasn't given the guard a fatal dose.

The alarm has stopped bleeping.

If reception desks provide an opportunity to control access to a building, they also signpost a building's heart. While Roxanne checks behind the desk, Eliot inspects the solid oak door behind the desk.

In the absence of either door handle or swipe card slot or coded button entry device, Eliot concludes the door must open either by remote control or by some device secreted in or around the reception desk. It might have been prudent not to have knocked the guard out.

The cctv monitors over the desk each show a different view of the grounds around the house cocooned in a thick white shroud. Eliot flinches as the arc light that lights up the lawn at the back of the house switches off and the monitor switches back to infra red mode. He pulls open drawers without really knowing what he is looking for.

'Yes,' Roxanne says excitedly. 'A pedal on the floor, here under the desk.'

She presses it and behind them they hear a gentle click followed by a pneumatic hiss as the door opens. A phone on the reception desk immediately starts to ring. Have they triggered an alarm?

'Useless tosser,' Philip Lawson, head of hospital security, says as the new boy returns from the canteen with two coffees and a couple of cakes.

The new boy, Mr Grigston, a large timid looking man in his early fifties, stares unhappily at his boss.

'Not you, Colin, the wanker up the hill,' Lawson elaborates. 'He's only gone and left his post unattended. Made us all look like bloody amateurs.'

'Might there be a problem?' Grigston asks, eyes glued to the floor.

Lawson looks out of the window across the grounds, towards the house, its dark Victorian bulk dimly silhouetted against the night sky at the top of the hill.

'Should we go over there perhaps?'

'No.' Lawson shivers at the prospect, 'you should go over there.'

Grigston, a loaf of a man better suited to waddling than walking, blows his cheeks. 'I should go now, should I?'

Lawson stares into the half-baked eager-to-please eyes, it is like having a puppy. He moves away from the window and settles back in

BENEATH THE BITTERCREST   321

the armchair he has taken from the senior staff room, puts his coffee on the table beside him and takes a bite from the larger of the cakes.

'No, there's something else I want you to do before that.'

The air beyond the security door is as still as a tomb. Steps lead down into the guts of the earth. Gwen is right, there is something beneath the old house.

While Roxanne heads straight down, Eliot lingers at the top of the stairs. A tv camera mounted on the ceiling stares impassively down into the stairwell. Directly opposite Eliot is a door, which is curious because there is no floor between Eliot and the door. Immediately in front of him the steps lead down and, by the time a person has travelled far enough towards the door to have reached it, they will find themselves almost three metres below it.

Roxanne turns back. 'Come on!'

'There's a camera,' Eliot whispers angrily, pointing up at the ceiling. 'What's your problem?'

'Time's running out, Eliot. If you're not up to this ...'

'What?' Eliot descends the stairs towards her.

'It's not your fight, I see that. Gwen will still be waiting.'

'And you're the Lone Ranger. Is that it?'

'This isn't a game anymore.'

'It never was.'

Eliot studies Roxanne with mounting unease. It isn't simply that there is no proof the African family are down there. And it isn't that he minds her being feisty. He likes feisty. But there is feisty and there is reckless, he isn't sure Roxanne knows the difference.

While understanding her determination to rescue Dudu, Alima and their children, the fact is that the age of chivalric heroes has gone with the advent of infra-red cameras, motion sensors, poison gas, pass cards ... Shit, the list is bloody endless. Breaking into the heart of a multi million pound operation is unlikely to be as easy as cutting a slice of cheese. Peter Han underestimated the situation and where is he now?

Gwen has promised to hand her husband's diary over to a trustworthy authority if they don't come out alive. With Roxanne acting as she is, Eliot hopes Gwen has the envelope written and stamps ready. She also promised Eliot she would make a phonecall to the number he gave her, if they aren't back at the car within the hour.

At the foot of the stairs they are presented with three options: two sets of double doors, and a lift. Small windows set into the doors reveal stairs descending further into the ground behind one set and, straight ahead, a dimly lit corridor behind the other set.

Eliot pushes the doors leading to the stairs. A flashback to the stairs beneath the low building on the estate. The doors are locked.

'Swipe card.' Roxanne points to the box mounted on the wall.

'Yeah, I know, I can see that.'

'Same with the lift.'

Eliot turns and pushes the second set of doors. They swing open soundlessly.

'The corridor it is then.'

Roxanne shrugs her assent.

As they cross from stairwell to corridor, the lights suddenly brighten. They stop, scarcely breathing, the seconds swinging to and fro like a huge pendulum.

'It's an energy saving thing,' Eliot whispers eventually. 'The lights go on and off to save energy. We're OK.'

Gwen was wrong. The sub-level appears to be of modern construction, concrete walls and ceiling with cleverly recessed lighting. A faint trace of hospital disinfectant hangs in the air. The doors are numbered like houses on a street, even numbers on one side, odd numbers on the other. Fourteen, thirteen, twelve … all locked. They get as far as six when the numbering system suddenly changes. 6A and 6 on one side, 6C and 6B on the other. Then the fives, fours, threes.

The door to Room 3C is open. They enter.

Overhead fluorescent lighting comes on automatically to reveal a smallish office, magnolia walls, heavy filing cabinets, two desks, a book case containing a dizzying array of technical manuals and medical books, and a cluster of computers.

The computers have all drifted into a gentle digital sleep. While they are rousing from their slumbers, Eliot considers his options. Time is short, an hour trawling through files for evidence or explanations is not possible. But if he could somehow bring some chaos …

'There's nothing here, let's go.' Roxanne says from the doorway.

'Two minutes.' Eliot has an idea.

He finds his house keys and pulls the flash drive Laurie gave him for Christmas from the key fob and inserts it into the USB socket on the keyboard of the nearest computer.

Eliot recognises some of the file names: BadTrans.b, W32/Goner, Parite, Nimda, I-worm.Lee.o, Magistr, and twenty others that are unfamiliar. He imagines the police's reaction if they had noticed Laurie's Christmas present on his key ring, and checked what was on it. Given his profession, it is like wandering about with the plague virus in a test tube.

'Come on, will you?'

With increasing impatience Roxanne watches Eliot's fingers dance across the keyboard, opening files, installation wizards, and set up windows, one after the other with the easy fluidity of a seasoned programmer. It's like re-introducing wolves to Richmond Park. In under three minutes it is done.

'Right, we can go.'

They step back into the corridor.

'What have you done?'

'The mother of all headaches.'

'What's that?' Roxanne points at the flash drive dangling from Eliot's key fob.

'Silicon plague. Viruses, worms and trojans. Infectious polymorphic algo-rithms that will spread through computerland, wiping out sectors of the hard drives, infecting files, corrupting databases and generally reducing Digital World to mush. With luck, every computer in the building will be connected to that one and ...'

'Can you hear talking?' Roxanne whispers anxiously.

'Quick, in here.' Eliot says, discovering another open door.

At the same moment they hear voices further down the corridor. Roxanne throws herself towards Eliot and together they tumble through the open door and out of sight. The door has barely swung shut when conversation and feet drift past in the corridor. An animated discussion is taking place, much to Eliot and Roxanne's good fortune. They sit in the darkness waiting for the voices to fade.

A cloying odour clings to the walls. Subtle but ugly. The floor is damp, viscous to the touch. Silence creeps into the room and envelops them. It is the kind of moment where, if he heard a pin drop, Eliot would worry about where the grenade must be. The barely audible sound of Roxanne's breath in the darkness brings him no comfort, only the realisation of how frail human life is.

He rummages in his jacket pockets and finds his torch.

They both leap back as the dazzling light from a torch shines directly at them from across the room, Roxanne gasping audibly as she falls. Then, as his eyes acclimatise to the light, Eliot understands.

'It's a mirror, it's a bloody mirror! Look.'

He shines the light on himself and his reflection appears in the mirror. They pick themselves up. Eliot raises a hand to his nose and smells it. Disinfectant, and something else, the floor has just been cleaned.

Back against the walls are a number of large appliances, dust covers over them obscuring their function. Crossing to the far end of the room the dark smell is stronger, slightly sweet but sulphurous.

The room isn't silent after all, there is a faint mechanical humming from air vents recessed into the ceiling.

'Look at this,' Roxanne whispers.

Eliot turns.

Roxanne has pulled the dust covers off several of the appliances.

'What do you think they are?'

Most are the kind of devices expected in a hospital, what looks like an ultrasound scanner, Eliot saw one used when Sue was pregnant with Alexandra. He remembers the strange v-shaped image with a vaguely humanoid form drifting in and out of shot like those ugly fish seen in nature documentaries swimming lazily around a diving bell in the murky waters of the Atlantic.

'Not that, I know what that is.' Roxanne prompts him, 'This one.'

The machine she is pointing at is altogether different. A metal box on wheels would be an adequate description of the base but the upper portion of the machine defies such easy analysis. Eliot finds himself thinking of the machines he has seen in a car plant, the robots that build and paint vehicles on the assembly line. A collection of arms are clustered around a pair of cameras, that must presumably serve as eyes. The metal arms are folded in on themselves like the front legs of a preying mantis. At the end of these limbs are a variety of different appendages, soft rubber claws, blades, saws, tweezers, pincers, suction tubes, lights, and what Eliot takes to be tiny fibreoptic cameras.

'Are you thinking what I'm thinking?' he asks.

'I have no idea.'

Eliot catches sight of something glinting on the floor partially hidden under one of the machines. He bends down and picks up a bracelet slick with blood.

'Looks like they missed this when they were tidiying. Did Dudu ... or Alima ...'

'How should I know?' she cuts him off angrily before turning away.

BENEATH THE BITTERCREST 325

He waits silently. Slowly he reaches out and touches her, draws her to him, wraps his arms about her. Her body is rigid. He wants to say something but finds no words, words are too slight, too impoverished and gauche, too direct, too vague, too distant. He holds her until the muffled sobs shrink and the shaking subsides, until his own cheeks are wet with tears. Tears for what? Self pity? Rage? He doesn't know. It hardly matters, his own feelings are only a minor scuffle in the fairground of her emotions.

Roxanne looks up, wipes her cheeks gently with her thumb.

'If they are here, we'll find them. I promise you. Whatever it ...'

She presses a finger to his lips to shut him up. Her lapse of focus is over.

'Let's go,' she says.

Her mouth smiles but her gaze is hard and cold, Eliot notes as he crosses the room, pulls open the door and steps out into the corridor.

It is unfortunate that he chooses to go left rather than right but, in truth, either way spells trouble.

thirty nine

Grigston speaks anxiously into his radio. 'Well, it might be helpful if you were able to come over and see for yourself.'

Lawson finishes his cup of coffee and brushes cake crumbs from his jacket.

'If Spalley Boy's talked you into taking the piss, I am going to get Neolithic with the pair of you. Understood?'

'Spall's not here, I'm afraid, and I can't see him on the monitors. In fact ...'

'Where are you?'

'At the reception desk. He's not here.'

'You've told me that already.'

Lawson peers through the window out into the night. The snow is still falling, the house on the hill is still standing. Lawson kicks the wall.

Eliot stands still, as requested, his hands high above his head.

'Keep the other hand up there where I can see it.'

The owner of the voice is right behind him. From the sound of it the man is a little shorter than Eliot. Eliot's right forearm is pulled sharply downwards and behind his back. Something hard snaps shut about his wrist.

'Now the other arm. That's it, nice and relaxed. Then you can tell me who you are and what you're doing down here.'

Had he turned right instead of left Eliot would have held a brief advantage as the man had passed the door to Room 2B and was walking away ... it hadn't happened that way. Eliot imagines running the back of his boot down the other man's shin but there might be a weapon pointing at the back of his head. He feels the handcuffs snap round his left wrist.

'Okey dokey, you can turn round now.'

Eliot, wrists cuffed behind his back, finds himself face to face with 'Big John' Grey. As he thought, the man is almost a head shorter than him but he is armed. From his thick black belt hangs what appears to be some sort of truncheon, and a gun.

'To my office. Do you have ID? Why do I think I recognise you?'

BENEATH THE BITTERCREST

Eliot shrugs. Out of the corner of his eye he sees a movement within the room he has just left, a movement the guard can't possibly have seen because the door blocks his view. Eliot steps backwards and, sure enough, Grey moves forward to close the gap.

She is so fast that Eliot has trouble following what happens next, but it ends with Roxanne standing very closely behind Grey, one arm pulling against his chest and the other arm, holding a vicious hunting knife to his throat.

'This is not the time to make any sudden moves,' she hisses into Grey's ear.

To prove the point she presses the blade against his neck. Grey flinches as she draws blood. 'I understand,' he says quietly.

'Which pocket are the keys in?'

'What?'

'For the handcuffs.'

'Left,' Grey answers.

'Very slowly,' she orders. 'Good. Now, undo his cuffs.'

The cuffs fall open and Eliot feels the blood return to his hands.

'Your turn.' Roxanne's voice is as cold and hard as the blade she presses against the guard's throat.

Eliot handcuffs the guard's hands tightly behind his back then, looking Grey in the eye, pulls a swipe card from the guard's shirt pocket.

'I think we've just found our passport to the lower levels.'

'How long ago did this happen?' Draper demands.

On the floor in front of him is Spall, eyes watering, trussed up turkey, gagged and bound and served up warm against the radiator to which he is attached with cords removed from the windows in both the gentleman's and the ladies' toilets. Lawson and Grigston stand by the door.

'It can't have been more than twenty minutes ago,' Lawson answers. 'I spoke with him at ...'

Without warning, Draper kicks Spall hard in the thigh.

Spall groans and recoils. Lawson steps forwards and begins untying the cord that secure Spall to the radiator.

'I said LEAVE HIM TIED UP,' Draper shouts.

Lawson's hands drop to his sides. Draper leans forwards and rips the tape from Spall's face.

'Now,' Draper speaks barely audibly, 'suppose you tell me what went on here?'

Spall looks to his colleagues then at Draper.

'A code forty five,' he whispers.

Draper crosses the room to pick up the discarded can of Mace he has spotted in a corner. 'What did you say?'

'A code forty five, Sir,' Spall repeats, clearing his throat. 'I went out to investigate and, when I returned, they were waiting for me in here.'

'How many of them?' Draper turns the can of Mace over in his hand.

'The last thing I remember is opening the door and stepping into the room.'

'If I can explain,' Lawson starts.

Draper suddenly lashes out, smashing the trussed up guard across the face with the can, causing Spall's nose to spurt blood. 'Follow me,' he says to the other two guards, tossing the can away across the room.

At the reception desk Draper, orders the two guards, who are both in shock, to show him what the cameras have seen. The video playback is, as ever, of poor quality, the exterior cameras showing only blurred shadows, two figures, one taller than the other, walking briskly across the snow.

The camera in reception, above their heads and pointing down into the hall, is of much more use. He freezes the picture as two figures step from outside into the hall. Eliot Balkan and the French snake in the grass.

'Right, raise the alarm. Ring that pinnacle of human intelligence, Detective Superintendent Store. That's what we pay the police for, isn't it, to help in times of crisis?'

Draper pushes Lawson roughly against the wall and leans into his face.

'If so much as a fart squeezes past you and through that door,' he indicates the security door behind him, 'I'll kill the pair of you.'

Lawson flinches as a speck of spittle hits his cheek. Grigston turns away as Draper grabs Lawson's chin and twists the guard's face until he is obliged to look him in the eye. Draper sees the terror he is hoping for.

'Understood?'

Lawson nods as best he can. Draper smiles and pats the man's face playfully.

BENEATH THE BITTERCREST   329

As the lift descends, Eliot observes Grey. The khaki uniform, the obligatory epaulettes, key chains and polished boots; security guard's clothing is always designed with an eye towards military nostalgia. From car park attendant to the surly guardians of shopping centres, the message is always the same, we mean business. Eliot is usually in the habit of totally ignoring such people but the gun suggests this man has actually been trained to do his job.

The lift stops and the doors open.

'Looks like a bloody museum,' Eliot mutters, taking in the period fittings. Gwen was right after all, the place can't have changed since the Second World War. Churchill himself probably walked on this carpet. And Turing.

'What floor is this?' Roxanne asks.

'Sub-level three,' Grey answers. 'Do you mind moving that knife away from my eyes?'

'Is this the lowest level?' Eliot is suddenly suspicious..

'You said you wanted to find the Africans.'

'And now I'm asking if this is the lowest level.'

Grey stares back at Eliot, his eyes dark with anger, but he says nothing.

The three of them walk down the corridor.

'How many exits are there?' Roxanne asks. 'Apart from the lift and the stairs we passed.'

Grey hesitates a moment too long.

'None. The stairs and the lift, that's all,' he replies. He stops about halfway down the corridor. 'In there. Unfortunately, I don't have the keys for this level, my work is all on level two.'

'That is a shame,' Roxanne agrees, pressing the point of the knife against his temples.

A trickle of blood drips down into the guard's eye. Eliot stares at Roxanne. The knife itself has been a surprise, he had no idea she was carrying it, but her state of mind is giving him greater cause for concern.

'Just open the door,' Eliot says.

Grey turns slowly towards Roxanne. Her eyes are impassive, distant.

'In my right pocket.'

Eliot shoves his hand in the man's pocket and finds a set of keys.

'The dull key. No, next to that one ... it's a skeleton key.' Grey keeps his eye on the knife.

Eliot slips the key in the lock. 'I think your employers might be disappointed with you.'

'Ha ha,' Grey replies, mirthlessly. His shoulder is itching like hell.

The appartment is brightly lit. From down the hall a curious sound hangs in the air, a collective sigh that rises and falls like the sound of the sea.

The living room is empty. Dirty crockery lies on the table, in the corner of the room a video is playing silently on the television. A couple of chairs have been tipped over. The voices are more distinct now, not a sigh but the muffled sound of weeping.

'Where does that door lead?' Eliot asks.

'The kitchen,' Grey replies.

'Eliot, take the knife.'

Eliot takes the knife.

'If he twitches or makes a sound, slit his throat.'

She disappears into the kitchen. The sound of weeping grows louder.

'Makes you feel proud, eh?' Eliot says sarcastically.

The guard grunts something under his breath.

'What was that?' Eliot asks.

No answer.

'I suppose killing people requires some skill,' Eliot continues, taunting him. 'Precision, an eye for ...'

'I don't kill anyone,' Grey blurts out, 'I look after them. I make sure they are well fed and fairly treated.'

'Oh? Like a turkey farmer?'

Eliot, standing behind the guard, sees Grey's neck muscles twitch with tension and notices the red rash around his collar.

Grey doesn't answer immediately. 'I do my job, that's all,' he says finally.

'Well, they all sound very happy, don't they?'

Grey says nothing.

'So, what's your excuse? Mum needs a kidney?' Eliot persists. 'Or is it your brother? Or do you just enjoy watching people suffer?'

Grey's skin is crawling beneath his uniform. His fists pull at the handcuffs.

Roxanne emerges from the kitchen, her arms wrapped around Alima who is sobbing into her shoulder, her body shaking with grief. Having settled Alima on the sofa, Roxanne returns to the kitchen.

BENEATH THE BITTERCREST

Eliot and Grey stand clumsily, Eliot with the knife at the guard's throat while the guard stares vacantly across the room, his eyes fixed on a bland print of a bowl of fruit hanging on the far wall beside the empty bookcase. Alima weeps softly.

Roxanne reappears with the two boys, their faces blank, their eyes furtive and frightened. Roxanne steers them towards their mother. Alima takes them and holds them to her like a drowning woman clinging to flotsam. The eldest boy, Cissé, is sniffing loudly. The younger, Femi, buries his face under his mother's arm.

'They've taken Mili,' Roxanne says. She walks up to Grey and stares him in the face. 'You bastards. Look at me, you shit.'

With the knife at his throat, Grey is not about to move his head. He glances briefly at her then continues his study of the painting across the room.

'Found a more deserving six year old?' She spits the words in his face. 'Some rich kid with important parents? Someone who has more right to a little African girl's heart than she has? Is that it?'

Grey is a rock, looking at no-one, wishing he could close his ears.

'Sit down on the floor,' Roxanne orders him. 'Dudu is in the kitchen,' she explains to Eliot. 'He won't come out from under the table. Alima says he's reliving the torture he suffered in the Cameroons.'

'What a touching scene,' a new voice says.

They all turn towards the voice.

Draper is in the doorway. At his side, a guard with small dark eyes beneath a luxurious thatch of blond hair, and a large gun. He points the gun at Eliot, and the dark sneering eyes at his colleague, Grey.

Draper lets out a sigh. 'Quite a merry dance we've had.' He indicates Grey with a nod of his head. 'Has he taken you on the grand tour?'

'He hasn't taken us anywhere,' Roxanne says.

'Saving the world again?' Draper sneers, stepping forward into the room.

'Stay where you are,' Roxanne shouts. 'Any further and we slit his throat.'

Draper studies the scene; mother and cowering children on the sofa, Roxanne, Eliot and the hapless John Grey.

'I'm sorry.' Draper stiffles a laugh. He takes a deep breath and composes himself. 'Here you are, thirty feet underground, no possibility of escape, and you're laying down the law?'

'Cut him,' Roxanne tells Eliot.

Eliot presses the knife against Grey's jugular. Grey looks anxiously towards Draper. Eliot's eyed lock onto Roxanne's who nods and mouths 'go on'.

Draper sighs. 'The trouble is I hold all the cards. You want to waste a guard? Be my guest.'

Grey flinches as the blade snicks his neck. A thin trail of blood trickles stickily down towards his shirt.

Roxanne's eyes drift towards Grey's gun, still in its holster and hanging from his belt. A soft click as Hewitt, the guard with the golden bouffant, flicks back the safety on his handgun.

Roxanne's gaze flies to Draper who, with the blandest of smiles, shakes his head, Grey's gun is out of bounds. Draper returns Roxanne's gaze for a moment longer, then shifts his attention to Alima and the children on the sofa.

'While lover boy finishes with the knife,' Draper says to Roxanne, 'maybe you can help me decide which of these two boys to take next. Their mother is impossibly indecisive. And the father ... well, he's out with the fairies, isn't he? I tell you what, you might like to help prepare them, so to speak.'

Draper takes a step towards the sofa. Hewitt's gun continues to point at Eliot. Big John Grey feels the rash burning around his neck. Alima looks up, first at Draper then at Roxanne and finally at Eliot. She shakes her head.

Eliot lets the knife drop, violently pushing Grey away from him. Draper chooses not to catch Grey as he staggers forwards. His wrists still cuffed behind his back, the guard falls heavily.

Draper turns towards Eliot. 'Pick the knife up.' He holds out his hand.

Eliot is lost. How has he so profoundly misjudged Draper?

'Shall we ask one of the boys?' Draper suggests maliciously.

With a speed that takes the others by surprise, Roxanne grabs up the knife. The power balance in the room shifts once again. There is a feral look in her eyes, she is close to the edge. Eliot has sensed it, ever since he told her it was Draper behind everything and not Brown. Something has snapped. She has become colder and more distant. And more dangerous.

Draper senses it, the smirk leaving his face, his body posture suddenly less casual. The blond guard senses it, targetting the gun on Roxanne instead of Eliot.

BENEATH THE BITTERCREST 333

Roxanne faces Draper across the room, three metres between them, his hand still outstretched, her knuckles white from the grip she has on the knife. If she lunges at Draper and the guard fires she will lose, but will the guard fire? Draper certainly would, but he isn't holding the weapon. Roxanne considers her options slowly. With Draper dead might Alima, Dudu and the children be saved? How many other people are involved? Can the horrifying acts being committed in the name of medicine be stopped or is Draper no more than another cog on the wheel? No need to rush now, nothing gained by rushing.

For her own life she feels nothing, it is this the others sense, it is this that makes her dangerous. She gazes into Draper's eyes and feels his disquiet, he does fear death.

The older boy starts to cry. Roxanne glances at Alima and, in that moment, she feels her legs fly away from under her as Grey, who has been lying at her feet all the while, takes advantage of her lapse of concentration and sweeps his leg round the back of her ankles, bringing her crashing down beside him, the knife falling away from her across the floor.

Draper doesn't make the same mistake twice. He leaps forwards and snatches the knife then steps back.

'It's better this way,' Draper says softly, watching Roxanne rubbing her elbow. 'Let's be honest, coming to rescue a bunch of black Africans in a snow storm isn't the most intelligent plan in the book, is it? Even if they could face the temperature out there, they are hardly going to blend in with the decor. And that's assuming you could prise 'daddy' out from under the kitchen table.'

'Fuck off, Draper,' Roxanne growls. 'You racist shit.'

At that Draper seems to tire of them all, the sooner they are only memories and separated organs being whisked away towards deserving recipients, the better. A fleeting recollection of canopic jars sitting stoically beside a pharaoh's embalmed corpse fluttered through his mind like a lazy butterfly.

The Africans are left where they are, under lock and key.

Eliot and Roxanne are moved across the hall.

All that remains of the original wartime furnishings and fittings, Eliot notes as they are pushed unceremoniously into the new appartment, is a set of very ordinary watercolours of rural scenes, and some tatty lampshades in scarlet and yellow, lipped with gold tassels. No other furniture aside from three steel trolleys.

Draper, taking the gun, orders the blond guard Hewitt to tie the intruders to the trolleys. Eliot initially refuses to co-operate but when Draper responds by casually firing a round into the wall, Eliot changes his mind.

The heavy leather belts dig into his wrists and ankles, the chest strap compresses his ribs to the point where he struggles to draw breath and, by the time the job is done, Eliot finds he can only move his head. He watches as Roxanne receives the same treatment. Also watching, from a corner of the room, is the disgraced 'Big John' Grey, his wrists still cuffed behind his back.

Draper steps forwards to check the knots and buckles are secure. He hovers over Roxanne, licking his lips, a spider studying a fly.

'Were you born a bastard or is there a special school?' Eliot says, hoping to distract Draper. 'I don't think I'd sleep well, playing God slaying the innocent.'

'Slaying the innocent,' Draper repeats the words dramatically. He turns towards Eliot, a carrion crow on a battlefield distracted by the superabundance of food.

'Yes, I play God,' he continues, 'but to give life, not to take it away. We give people the organs they need to save them: people with worthwhile lives, people who will be missed, beloved sons and daughters stricken by disease, parents who want to see their children grow up, leaders of industry with thousands of employees, diplomats, ambassadors, ministers … you would be quite impressed by the list.'

'And the people you kill?'

'Who misses them?' Draper replies simply, running a lazy hand over one of Roxanne's breasts.

'Their families.' Roxanne speaks coldly and quietly, if she feels Draper's hand she gives no indication of doing so. 'Their children. The villages and towns they come from. The people who count on the extra money they send home.'

'You mustn't believe everything you read.' Draper looks disappointed with her. 'These people are the world's worthless and unwanted. Their lives are boring and empty even to themselves. They come to get away, to forget. And the people they leave behind forget them. They disappear and no-one is ever any the wiser. It's the perfect solution.'

Eliot realises how easily he himself has been seduced in the past by arguments similar to Draper's, it only requires the dehumanisation of the victim, a recitation of the mantra about consumer choice, and anything becomes acceptable. Jackboots linger in the shadows and doorways of almost every mind.

'They even pay to transport themselves over here. Can you imagine? It's like a box of cornflakes taking itself to the supermarket. And after all that, their generosity is still not at an end. Litres of compatible blood available to the operating theatre.' Draper smiles to himself in congratulatory wonderment at his own acheivements. 'Still,' he says, abruptly changing tack and stroking Roxanne's hair. 'Did I forget to tell you? I checked up on a certain Didier Lepage.'

'Let me guess, you were suddenly overwhelmed with guilt at having murdered her brother?' Eliot says.

'Is that what she told you?' Draper is amused. He looks at Roxanne. 'I didn't think Eliot was your type. But then I didn't think the other one was either. I must be a poor judge of character.'

Eliot is looking quizzically at Roxanne whose face is unreadable.

'Shall I tell him? Oh, may I?' Draper claps his hands together happily. He assumes a crestfallen look for Eliot. 'It would appear Mrs Lepage has been keeping secrets. She did the same to me. Caught me off-guard. Simply didn't occur to me that a dull business man like Didier Lepage would have been interested in marrying a hippy whore with a taste for Indian food.'

Eliot is struggling to keep with the flow of Draper's story.

'I saw the fast-lane callgirl with an appetite and assumed all she wanted was a night at the Cinnamon Club, some easy money and an occasional ride in a flash car. We had some nice rides, didn't we, Dear?' Draper licks his lips suggestively. 'Does lover boy here know about the little terraced house in Calais, the waitress mum who turned tricks and absent English sailor dad?'

Eliot thinks he sees a brief flash of regret in Roxanne's eyes.

'That's sweet,' Draper smiles sympathetically at Eliot. 'Now I imagine you're going to have to tell her about the wife and kids. Oh, I'm sorry, have I spoken out of turn?' He looks back at Roxanne. 'By the way, I may have soured things a little between you and your in-laws.'

'What happened to Didier?' Roxanne's voice is flat, emotionless.

Draper considers his answer.

'I think you're going to find this amusing ...' he says, his eyes full of smiles, ' in a way. It's true, he did meet a sticky end. Nose a little too close to the fire. Another of your countrymen found him snooping about, panicked, slapped him about a bit and threw him in the back of his lorry along with the other passengers. Didier didn't last long, I'm afraid, not really the right stuff for arduous journeys. Very helpful though, gave us his name, his business and so on. With a little prompting. Then, sadly, he died of his injuries.'

'Bastard,' Roxanne says.

Draper holds up his hands.

'Guilty as charged. But here's the interesting bit. I was suffering at the time, had been for a couple of years, with cataracts. As you know, the trouble is finding a tissue match. Without a corneal transplant one's sight becomes progressively worse until, eventually, one can't see anything at all. For a visionary like myself ... Anyway, it was the strangest thing but your husband was a perfect match. Can you imagine? A chance in fifty thousand.'

Draper walks round the room, giving his words time to sink in.

'So, in a curious way, he is still with us.'

Draper leans over Roxanne, his gaze drifting lazily over her crotch, breasts and finally her face.

'The look of love,' he explains softly. 'I see you through his eyes, so to speak.'

She spits in his face. Draper calmly wipes the spittle away with his handkerchief.

'We keep everything in storage. His skin is still somewhere in the building, I'm sure. His kidneys went to a deserving, and very wealthy, woman in Chelsea. Oh, I've had an idea. Maybe I could arrange for his skin and yours to be stored side by side. Who knows, we might even have a his and hers operation. Sometimes happens, a fire at an underground station, or some such, a young couple in love both needing skin grafts.'

Draper's mobile phone rings.

'That will be the technical staff. The procedure is fascinating. We take the lift upstairs to the theatres. Practically the whole process is automated. Not pain free exactly ... we usually administer drugs to take the edge off, but in this instance I don't know, perhaps you should atone for all the irritation you have caused. '

He answers the phone.

'I think you had better come upstairs, Sir.'

'Is there a problem?' Draper's voice is calm.

'There's a ... situation developing, Sir.'

Draper recognises the voice of one of the guards he had left in reception.

BENEATH THE BITTERCREST
337

'Then deal with it,' Draper says, sweetness laced with barbed wire.

There is a pause on the line, as the guard hesitates between fear and duty.

'It's the police ...'

Draper takes a deep breath.

'We sent for them,' Draper speaks slowly, as if explaining the concept of corruption to a four year old. 'You made the call. So, let Detective Superintendent Store in, and tell him to wait for me in reception.'

'There's rather more of them than that.' Grigston says nervously. 'A helicopter and ...'

Draper pinches the bridge of his nose, you ask for backup and they send the charge of the bloody light brigade.

'Tell Lawson to deal with it.'

'He isn't here, Sir.'

Draper cuts the call.

'Right, Hewitt, you come with me. And you ... you over there, by the wall.'

Grey is preoccupied with the chafing of his wrists, convinced that the sharp metal edges have cut through the skin and are now grinding directly against bone. He jumps as the hand touches his shoulder.

'You, my friend,' Draper says, 'you are going to have the opportunity to redeem yourself. Where is the key?' He looks down at the cuffs to show Grey what he is talking about.

'She has it,' Grey looks over at Roxanne.

Draper turns predatorially. Roxanne says nothing. He rummages in her trouser pockets, lingering a little longer than is strictly necessary, and finds the key. Key in hand, he slaps Roxanne hard across the face, drawing blood as the metal cuts across her cheek. He crosses over to Grey and unlocks the cuffs.

'You are going to guard these two while I go upstairs.'

Grey inspects the damage to his wrists, raw but unbloodied.

'You should be safe,' Draper tells Grey, with just a trace of sarcasm. 'Unless you get too close and they try to bite.'

The humiliated Grey doesn't reply. Hewitt smirks.

'Returning to the subject of keys,' Draper continues, 'Later on you'll tell me how it is you had access to individual appartments on this level. For the time being, you'll hand over all the keys in your possession.'

As he speaks, Draper unfastens Grey's holster and removes his gun.

'He has them,' Grey says, indicating Eliot.

Draper tucks Grey's handgun into his waistband then retrieves, and trousers, the thick bunch of keys Eliot has in his pocket.

'Theatre staff will be here soon,' Draper tells Grey. 'Maybe that might be the moment to put some lotion on that nasty rash you've got.'

In the doorway Draper stops and turns. 'Oh, did I forget to mention we found an old lady in a car outside the gates. I think she will have died of hypothermia. So close to a hospital. Very sad but then ... the recent tragic death of her husband may have left her feeling very confused. Probably for the best.'

Draper and his blond sidekick leave the room. A key rotates in the lock.

forty

The footsteps receding down the corridor are still audible when Grey rushes across the room to Roxanne. He stands over her, his face flushed, a nervous tic pulling at his left cheek.

Roxanne and Eliot exchange glances. Where is Roxanne's knife? Who has the knife?

'Enough!' Grey suddenly screams at the top of his voice. 'Enough!'

Eliot and Roxanne strain against their straps, desperately trying to loosen their bonds to free their hands. Grey is muttering under his breath, his jaw flinching as he spits out vicious oaths, lost in a world of his own devising. He lunges at the strap securing Roxanne's ankles and pulls at it.

'Get off,' Roxanne shouts. 'Get him off me.'

Eliot watches helplessly as Grey yanks Roxanne's trolley back and forth. Two of the trolley wheels leave the ground, threatening to tip it over with Roxanne bound to it. Somehow in the chaos an ankle strap comes free.

'Over here you bastard,' Eliot calls, to draw Grey away from Roxanne.

But Grey is not to be distracted. He hasn't yet looked either of them in the eye. Having undone the belt that bound Roxanne's ankles to the trolley, he moves up and starts on the thigh strap then, all at once, he pushes the trolley away from him and grabs his temples, rocking backwards and forwards.

'Fuck you!' he screams at the ceiling.

Roxanne is frantic, wriggling, attempting to push up with her knees to loosen the thigh strap, as Grey lurches forwards blindly, grabbing the spare trolley and hurling it across the room. It crashes against the far wall with a grinding and splintering of metal. Grey turns towards Eliot, the muscles in his neck bulging, his eyes wild and unfocused.

'Hey, it's OK,' Eliot says gently, sensing that the guard's rage is not directed at his captives. 'You'll give yourself a heart attack.'

Time crawls as ugly rage burns and smoulders in Grey's unseeing eyes. He is gasping for each and every breath.

Finally he slumps forward onto his knees and closes his eyes.

Months of self deceit are collapsing about him and the truth is finally bursting through his carefully constructed defences. Dozens of hopeful faces, people who counted him as a friend, people who have given him letters to send to relatives in far off places, letters that he has handed over, as requested, letters that have no doubt never been sent, people who turned to him for comfort, people like Naseem, like Alphonse, like Fatima, like Cisse ... and maybe a hundred others.

While he hasn't been directly involved in the killing, he has understood. He has understood.

As an ex-service man who served in the Gulf War, he struggled to find a job he was suited to after he left the army. So when the friend of an acquaintance approached him with an 'interesting job that requires discretion' he was happy to take any opportunity to reduce his burgeoning debts.

Grey knows when to shut up and turn the other way, he is familiar with the chain of command. For a while it has been OK, he has done his shifts and pocketted the cheques, but over the six months little things have begun to eat away at him.

He scratches violently at his itching shoulder and at the rash around his neck.

The young men he has kept locked up haven't mattered much to Grey. By and large they have been a surly bunch, often arrogant, convinced of their right to enter the country whatever the laws to prevent their entry. Many of them have been sexist and racist, not in the least interested in the value system of the country they have entered. He knows their type from his time in Turkey, Kuwait and Iraq. Economic migrants playing the system don't exactly get what they deserve but to Grey they are cheats. Their pretence simply devalues the claims of those who really need help. But the others, and the women and children ... the real victims of torture and persecution. It is in their eyes, a sadness and pain that nothing can ever remove. But then again what does he know?

To find that his boss doesn't give a toss whether he lives or dies, however, that is different. That has brought him to his senses. The boot is on the wrong foot.

Eliot flinches as Grey approaches him.

'I'm OK,' Grey reassures him as he begins untying him.

Grey hasn't seen the man cowering in the kitchen across the corridor, but he has seen several like him. Men who have suffered electric shock to their genitals, men who have seen their families

BENEATH THE BITTERCREST 341

raped before their eyes. The oppressed, the humiliated, the broken. He has seen the look in the African woman's eyes, her trembling children. How many people's lives can he trade against his pay cheques?

'Fucking shits,' Grey shouts again from the depths of his being.

Eliot stares up at the broken man before him. The guard hasn't suffered like the lost souls he had been paid to incarcerate but he is a victim nevertheless, a casualty of brutalisation.

Rage and torment continue to skate across the surface of Grey's irises like storm clouds.

'If you had slit my throat, that shit Draper ...' Grey blurts out.

'Join the club.' Roxanne says.

'Hey,' Eliot reproaches Roxanne. 'Give the man a break.'

'No, she's right,' Grey says, undoing the last of Eliot's straps.

Eliot sits up and swings his legs over the side of the trolley, flexing his muscles to get the blood flowing. He watches Grey undoing the last of Roxanne's straps.

'Now what?' she asks.

Eliot puts his arm around Grey's shoulders, seizing the initiative. 'With this man's help anything is possible.'

Eyes fixed on the floor, Grey nods. He looks up at Eliot and Roxanne. A grim smile ventures across his face. He nods again, more convincingly this time. Yes, maybe anything is possible.

'Otherwise we'll have to tunnel out,' Eliot says, trying to lighten the mood. 'Remember Colditz?'

Roxanne rolls her eyes. 'Ha ha, I think I'm going to die laughing.'

Three floors above, Draper, mobile phone pressed to his ear, steps out into the reception area.

'I don't give a toss what the bloody time is,' he shouts into the phone. 'Shut up and listen. We've had a code 45 .'

Christopher Goodlife hates interruptions. Especially at his club. Especially when he is playing bridge. South has just bid three spades following his partner's two no trumps. Looking again at his own hand he is reminded of the case of the doubleton queens. A strong lead from west again and they will be seriously squeezed. He grimaces an apology to the others around the table and sips his whisky.

'Look, Neville. This code 45 ... is it really ...'

'We've caught Eliot Balkan and the French girl.'

'So what is the problem?' Goodlife asks wearily.

Across the table Goodlife's bridge partner and sister, Serina Falcon, leans back and beckons the waiter over for a fresh cup of coffee.

'Security has been breeched. We found another one in a parked car. There could be more.'

Draper notices the dull chopping sound of helicopter blades, dropping in pitch as the rotors come to a stop. He crosses over to a window.

'What was that?' he says, realising he has been asked a question.

'I said what about the local police? That ugly chap with the fat nose. Stone? Store? What's his name?'

'He just arrived,' Draper answers, staring at the helicopter in the carpark.

'Well, let him deal with it.'

'I need firepower, not village bobbies.'

'This isn't Texas, old boy. Listen to yourself for a ...'

Draper snaps. 'No, you fucking listen to me. If I go down, I'm bringing everything crashing down with me - you, the minister, the police, Customs & Excise, the hospital, everything.'

'There's no need to hector me, Neville. No-one has suggested for one moment that we wouldn't ...'

Draper takes his ear from the receiver, parliamentary private secretaries have turned obfuscation and evasion to an artform. He turns towards the reception desk.

'Who are they?' he asks Grigston, silently mouthing the words while pointing out of the window at the helicopter.

'I'm afraid I don't know,' Grigston answers. 'I rang you as soon as I saw them arrive. There were two squad cars as well but they left shortly after the helicopter landed. Should I have ...?'

'Just give me the number for whoever can immediately authorise increasing security,' Draper says into his mobile.

'I'm sorry, what number is ...?' Grigston says in some confusion.

Draper raises a hand to shut Grigston up.

'Sorry, Christopher, missed that last bit,' Draper says into the phone.

'I said that the cost implications of contracting extra security will have to properly evaluated. You already have at your disposal a large ...'

'All we have at our disposal above ground is a collection of poorly trained misfits in fancy dress.'

BENEATH THE BITTERCREST   343

'If I hand out phone numbers willy-nilly I shudder to think what ...'

Draper cuts the call, he has heard enough. His erstwhile backers are wiping him off the hard drive. He is on his own.

He steps outside. A group of three men and two women have climbed out of the helicopter and are crossing the tarmac. A large man in his fifties with a walrus moustache breaks away and hurries forwards.

'Is Store with you?' Draper asks, shaking the man's hand and wondering who he is.

'Detective Superintendent Store?' the man answers. 'I believe he may have left a few minutes ago. We had been hoping to speak with him but, apparently, he had other matters to attend to. DI Havering, by the way, Guilford police.'

'What can I do for you, Detective Inspector? Are you lost? If it was Superintendent Store you were hoping to talk to, then you will have to go to Swindon police station, we are a hospital.'

'You were expecting him?' Havering says.

'Swindon police help us with security,' Draper answers carefully. 'Today was scheduled for the monthly visit.'

'At half past three in the morning?'

'Most burglaries happen at night,' Draper's delivery is smooth, controlled.

'Yes, quite so,' Havering concedes.

'Anyway, I'm sure you are too busy to stand idly about in a snow-storm. And hospitals don't run themselves so, if you don't ...'

'My, my, they keep you working late.'

'The caring profession never sleeps, Inspector. Anyway, I'm due at a meeting ...' Draper indicates the hospital buildings with a sweep of the hand.

'Actually we're here to visit this very building, Mr ...?'

Havering points behind Draper to the house on the hill.

'Draper.'

'Ah, it's Draper, I thought you might be Mr Brown.'

'I'm afraid the administration block is closed.'

'And the lights?'

'To deter thieves. I had been hoping to show DS Store the measures we had introduced since his last visit but, unfortunately ...'

'You can show me.' Havering's voice is friendly but firm.

If Draper is inconvenienced, he hides it well. He leads the party back towards the administration block. As they step inside, out of the snow, Draper puts his hand briefly in his trouser pocket, a gesture Havering notes but doesn't comment on.

'Hippopotami on an ice rink,' Havering remarks.

Draper seems confused.

'Those sofas, on the marble floor. Don't you think?'

Draper smiles politely.

'Right, let's get down to business, shall we?' Havering says. 'Is Mr Brown about? Gustave Brown?'

Draper makes no comment.

Behind Havering, the four officers who arrived with him in the helicopter are shaking the snow from their coats and boots.

In their wake Lawson slinks across the hall towards the reception desk hoping Draper hasn't noticed him.

Havering indicates with his eyes what he wants doing. PC Thorne and PC Day break away from the group and head up the stairs.

'When you've finished upstairs, take a look outside.' Havering turns back to Draper. 'We have reason to believe that within this building criminal activity may be taking place. I intend to search the premises as I have reason to believe lives may be in jeopardy. We can discuss Brown's whereabouts as we go.'

'I trust you have a warrant.' Draper stalls.

'You can trust what you like,' Havering replies pleasantly. He has just noticed the security guards. 'I've seen scarier newspaper delivery boys.'

He saunters over to the reception desk and leans across.

'Boo,' he says into the face of the shorter one.

The two guards flinch, their eyes darting from Havering to Draper and back again.

'Open this door for me, sonny,' Havering orders.

Having first glanced at Draper, who nods disinterestedly, Grigston presses the pedal . The door to the lower levels clicks open.

'Nice uniforms, by the way,' Havering says to Grigston and Lawson. 'Chocolate. Suits you both. Hides the stains.' He breezes past the reception desk and pulls the door open before turning to his officers. 'Faulkner, you're with me. Mullen, you stay here and look after our two Brownies.'

Havering leads the way. Beyond the door, they cross a small lobby. Havering pulls open a second door and they enter the administration block. Draper permits himself the shadow of a smile.

'I should never have brought you along,' Roxanne says.

'Brought me along?' Eliot splutters.

'No commitment, no action.'

'This your theory or Che Guevara's? If I'd listened to you, our friend here would be dead and we'd still be strapped to those trolleys.'

'Can I say something?' Grey interjects.

Eliot and Roxanne stop shouting at each other and turn towards Grey.

'Always carry a spare.' He is holding up a key. He has their full attention. 'There are five ways out of here: in a coffin; up the stairs, in the lift, or through one of two tunnels. Disregarding the first three, and the first tunnel, since it hasn't been used since the second world war and might well have collapsed by now, there's one alternative, the tunnel that connects this building with the main hospital.'

'Assuming for a minute that I trust you,' Roxanne answers, 'what are the chances of getting through as far as the main hospital buildings and then escaping to the outside?'

'If we move quickly, fetch the African family and head off straight for the tunnel, we stand a chance. I can get us through the first few doors. There are security cameras when we reach the other end. We'll have to convince hospital security to let us through and ...'

'What was that you said?' Eliot interrupts.

'We have to convince hospital ...'

'No, no, before that.'

'The connecting tunnel?' Grey is confused.

'No, something about world war two.'

'There isn't time, Eliot,' Roxanne says, already at the door.

'Oh that.' Grey finally understands what Eliot is talking about. 'The trouble with that ...'

'No, you're both wrong. If it was good enough for Churchill, it's good enough for us. It's the last thing anyone will expect.'

Grey shrugs ambivalently then, with the skeleton key, pushes past Roxanne into the corridor.

'I don't trust him,' Roxanne says.

'Who said anything about trusting anyone?' Eliot retorts.

Alima and the boys haven't moved from the sofa. Alima is quickly persuaded to fetch Dudu. Within a couple of minutes, she re-emerges from the kitchen with her husband. Dudu looks terrible, his gaze fixed on the carpet, his shoulders sagging, a broken man. The boys get up and hug their father but he seems unaware of their presence.

Grey, visibly moved by events, fidgets nervously. He has switched sides and there can be no turning back. Every wasted minute is dangerous.

'We must go now.'

'What about Mili?' Alima asks.

Grey shakes his head sadly.

For a moment, Eliot thinks Roxanne will refuse but she says nothing. Her face is hard as granite.

'I will not leave her,' Dudu protests.

'Are we all to die then?' Alima asks.

'How can you ...' Dudu explodes with rage then sees his wife's face, registers the immensity of her pain, feels his sons' arms around him. Have they escaped one hell to all die in another?

Alima throws her arms around him, turning to Grey as she does so. 'You are right, we must go.'

Grey nods, but is unable to look her in the eye.

As they step out into the corridor, Alima notices a light flash on; the down arrow has lit up above the lift doors at the far end of the corridor.

'Hurry,' Grey shouts, running away down the corridor in the opposite direction.

They reach a T-junction and turn left. Grey has already reached the end of the corridor and is opening a door with the skeleton key. As Eliot, who is bringing up the rear, tumbles through the open door and pushes it shut behind him, he hears the lift doors opening at the other end of the corridor.

'It's OK, I have a torch,' Roxanne whispers in the darkness.

The space they are in is cold and smells musty. The torch reveals why.

In the darkness he can hear the constant dripping of water. His lower back is burning, his face and legs throb.

Spall jerks his head back and smacks his cranium against the radiator to which he is still tied. How long has he been unconscious? Where have Lawson and Grigston gone?

Spall shuffles on his buttocks away from the radiator, a couple of centimetres. Is his back blistered? He licks his swollen lips, tastes

BENEATH THE BITTERCREST

blood, remembers Draper swiping the tear gas canister across his face.

The urinals flush automatically away to his left. Muffled through the door he hears voices. Pulling at the ropes that bind him, he opens his mouth to shout for help. Then thinks better of it.

What if Draper is still out there? The sick bastard. No, the best thing to do is to see if he can wriggle free and run away. He'll get his mates to come back in the small hours and torch the place, kick shit out of a few cars in the car park.

He starts to rock his body backwards and forwards to loosen his bonds, cursing under his breath. Fuck Draper, fuck the job, fuck everyone.

Fifty years of dust shroud the room. Stacked up against one wall are a pile of green metal helmets and thirty or more cardboard boxes. Bully beef, chocolate powder, dried egg, tea, and sugar the boxes announce in typefaces Eliot has only seen in films or museums. Between two doors at the far end of the room hangs a map of the United Kingdom. In the middle of the room is a large desk upon which sit a cluster of bakelite phones, an inkwell, a blotter with an elegant hardwood handle, and a collection of in-trays and out-trays; all hairy with the dust of nearly six decades.

In a corner, on a green felted bridge table, is an old gramophone player complete with horn over the stylus. Shouldn't there be a dog sitting in front of the speaker, head cocked to one side, listening to his master's voice? Eliot picks up one of the records propped up against the gramophone player.

'Jesus,' he says. 'Moonlight Serenade. It's like the Imperial bloody War Museum.'

'Where do we go now?' Roxanne asks.

'I'm not sure,' Grey answers.

'What?'

Grey shrugs.

'You mean you don't even know that there is a tunnel?'

A second torch beam brings more light to the room, Eliot has remembered that he too is carrying a torch.

'These hills are riddled with tunnels, caves and potholes. Cheddar Gorge is just down the road. I haven't seen this tunnel myself but a while back I met an old man at the village pub, down the road. He worked here in the war. Told me about this place, asked me to check if it was still here. He wanted me to collect a few things for him, old 78s, pencils, and so on. For a car boot sale. I've never been further than this room.'

The boys play excitedly with the ancient telephones, turning the dials and watching them spin slowly back.

'He told you where the tunnel was?' Eliot says, urging Grey along.

'It's that way, I think.' Grey points towards the door to the left of the map of Blighty.

'Lead on, Lothario,' Eliot declaims exhuberantly.

'Shhh,' Roxanne hisses, her finger to her lips.

At that moment Alima pulls the boys away from the telephones. Femi howls outloud. In the silence that follows, broken only by occasional whimpering from Femi, all eyes turn towards the door. Have they been overheard?

The seconds pass lazily, all eyes glued to the whisker of light visible under the door, all ears alert for the sound of running footsteps. Whoever came down in the lifts will have found the appartments empty and will soon be on their trail.

Finally the tension subsides a fraction. Grey turns and leads them to the door at the far end of the room. Beyond the door is another corridor. An odour of musty leather, cold damp, and acrid animal droppings hangs in the air like smoke. Distracted by a scratching sound, Eliot flashes the beam of his torch down at his feet. A fury of grey rushes between the legs of first Dudu then Alima before disappearing into a large hole where the skirting board has either rotted or been eaten away.

'Mama?'

'Shh,' Alima soothes. 'It was a mouse, a tiny mouse.'

'What? That size?' Eliot says in a stage whisper.

Alima glares at Eliot.

The doors are all painted green. Numbers are pinned to the doors along with wilting and yellowing pieces of paper, curling at the edges, upon which any writing has long since faded and run in the damp air.

Ope .. tions Room Eliot manages to read on one door where the writer has used pencil instead of ink. The hinges groan as he pushes the door open and swings the torch about. Thirty or forty typewriters, or what look like typewriters, are arranged side by side along the length of a long bench against one wall. On a simple set of shelves sit a large collection of teacups, tin mugs, a huge brown teapot and several large mess tins. Multicoloured mould pockmarks the walls and the leather backed chairs.

'Eliot,' Roxanne hisses from further down the corridor.

Eliot steps back into the corridor and hurries to catch up with the others.

'You have to be joking,' he says.

Roxanne is four doors down from the operations room Eliot has been surveying. In her hands are several large egg-shaped devices. Grenades.

'Have you any idea how unstable that shit will be?'

'They might be useful,' she answers simply.

Behind her Dudu appears, holding a heavy iron bar and a fistful of flares.

'There are in this sealed cupboard. Like it was put there yesterday,' Roxanne explains. 'I also liberated this bottle of rum, for later.'

'The key word being 'like',' Eliot retorts.

'We found food and ...' Dudu starts.

'Don't even go there,' Eliot holds up his hand. 'I'm glad you're back in the land of the living, Dudu, but a fifty year old porkpie is little more than a suicide pill.'

Femi and Cissé squeeze out between Dudu and Roxanne. The boys have found gas masks and are trying unsuccessfully to strap them on. Eliot pushes his way past everyone into the room.

'There are two cupboards,' Roxanne explains over his shoulder. 'On the first one the seals must have broken and everything is rotting but in the other there are things we need.'

As if to prove the point Alima, who has been rummaging on the shelves with Grey, turns round. In her hands are a large monkey wrench and another tool that looks like a chain cutter.

'I think that's everything,' Grey announces, his head still in the cupboard. He backs away and faces the others. In his arms he holds a large length of stout rope, a hammer, two hunting knives, a paraffin lamp and Roxanne's torch. 'Here, you'd better take one of these.'

Eliot takes one of the knives.

Further on, they find a room in which hang a number of heavy greatcoats, not in great nick but, given the weather outside, they will be better than nothing. Alima and Dudu each take a coat at Roxanne's insistence.

Things are going well and everyone's spirits are up.

Some thirty metres on, at the far end of the corridor, set in a solid iron frame and secured with six heavy bolts, is an iron door. At the centre of the door is a large wheel and Eliot guesses it must function like the doors on submarines, sealing one section off from all the others.

The euphoria that has enveloped the group evaporates.

Grey places the items he is carrying on the ground. The others watch him heave away at the metal wheel for twenty seconds or more. To no effect.

'Shine the torch over here,' Grey says, panting from the exertion.

The black paint that once covered the metal of door, frame and wheel has perished and blistered. There is rust everywhere, the wheel is jammed solid. Dudu joins Grey and together they push and pull while the sweat pours down their faces.

'Are you sure this is the right way?' Eliot says. 'I mean before we all break our backs trying to open it.'

'The old man said there was a heavy sealed door between the bunker and the passages that led outside, to stop anyone breaking in,' Grey said between breaths.

'Kind of you to tell us. What if there's another ...'

'Shut the fuck up, Eliot,' Roxanne lashes out. 'If you're not going to help, just shut up.'

Eliot resists the urge to shout back. Grey has started hitting the bolts with the hammer he has found. Dudu joins him, using the monkey wrench to pound away at the wheel. Flakes of rust float to the floor. Dudu and Grey are both powerfully built men, Eliot knows nothing will be gained by adding more brawn to the mix.

Suddenly it hits him. He races away back down the corridor.

'Here, come back with the torch, we need more light.'

He ignores everyone and reaches the room with the cupboards.

By the time he returns, some three minutes later, nothing has changed. The door is still locked, the wheel still jammed.

He crouches on the floor, propping his torch up against the wall to give maximum light, and pulls the hunting knife from his pocket.

'This I must see,' Roxanne says sarcastically. 'What are you going to do, eat your way out of here?'

On the floor in front of him is a very large tin of tunafish. Eliot stabbed at it with the knife, pierces the lid, then twists the blade through the hole and works it round until he has torn open a three inch gash in the top of the tin.

'Here we go.'

BENEATH THE BITTERCREST

He stands and approaches the door.

'Excuse me, gentlemen.'

Dudu and Grey stop heaving and hammering.

'This might help.'

Eliot pours the contents of the tin over the screw of the wheel and each of the bolts around the door.

'Tinned tuna,' he explains. 'The rich man's WD40. A minute or so and I think everything will be in order.'

Aware of the total silence behind him, Eliot slowly turns to face his critics. He glances from one to the other. They gawp back.

'Well?' he ventures.

The faces continue staring impassively. Eliot shrugs. Roxanne's face betrays the ghost of a smile, which she duly tries to suppress.

'What?' Eliot asks.

Roxanne shakes her head.

'What?' Eliot insists then, seeing he wasn't getting an answer, 'it's a case of brine over brawn.'

Or, more accurately, vegetable oil over brawn. A further two tins are required but eventually the oil penetrates the rust sufficiently for the wheel to turn and the bolts to draw back. Grabbing the massive handle, Dudu heaves the door back on its hinges.

'Holy shit, what's that smell?' Grey blurts out as the door swings open.

'The river is dry except during the flood,' Dudu says, wrinkling his nose.

'What?' Grey says.

'I was being ironic,' Dudu explains.

'Oh, right. Yes. It's a proverb,' Eliot explains to Grey, having by now become familiar with Dudu's speech patterns, whilst not having the faintest idea what Dudu means.

Dudu continues, 'Times of adversity are always followed by times of plenty.'

Eliot has the facial expression of someone who has just woken up to find himself floating in an elephant's stomach.

'I believe we have found the sewers,' Dudu says.

'Right.' Eliot shakes his head rapidly as if trying to clear his ears. He notices the two boys have taken to wearing their gas masks on the top of their heads.

Far away behind them a crash echoes in the darkness.

'What's that?' Alima asks.

'Just something falling over,' Grey reassures her.

'Excuse me,' Draper fishes his mobile phone out of his jacket pocket.

They are in a large open plan office on the first floor. Along one wall a dozen filing cabinets stand shoulder to shoulder. Clustered about in the huge space are groups of desks, each with its own computer. Ornate plasterwork covers the ceiling from which hang long lines of fluorescent tubes.

Draper puts some distance between him and the others before speaking.

'Yes?'

'They've escaped.'

It is Hewitt.

'How? When?'

'Grey's with them. The Africans have gone too. About ten minutes ago.'

'Find them.'

'Dead or alive?'

'Just get on with it,' Draper says, cutting the call.

He turns to find Havering staring at him.

'My wife,' Draper explains. 'Spiders in the bath. She wanted advice on how to deal with them.'

Havering smiles amiably and makes a theatrical show of consulting his watch. 'Shall we continue the tour?'

The walls of the tunnel are carved out of the solid rock and glisten beneath an oily film of water that meanders slowly down towards the wooden floor, rough hewn planks, the outermost of which have been sculpted to follow the contours of the rock. A muted gurgling of running water is in the air. Is it just water? Eliot hopes so, but wouldn't place a bet on it.

The children's excited shouts echo in tunnel, their voices further distorted by the gas masks they wear.

Every few metres are alcoves or passages leading off in other directions, hidden behind crudely made doors made of vertical wooden slats secured by heavy padlocks and rusting chains.

For Eliot the temptation to make music is irresistible.

Maybe it is the faint but growing hope that they might actually escape.

He fishes his house keys out from his trousers and runs them along the slats, savouring the dry xylophone sounds and the tight echoes of the tunnel every bit as much as he did when he was a six year old running sticks along the school railings. For a moment, he is no longer trapped, hunted, fighting. Like a Tibetan pilgrim spinning prayer wheels, for a moment peace and order return to Eliot's existence in the form of rhythm and pitch and touch.

Fifty metres on, the roof of the tunnel starts to rise and the sound of their footsteps becomes more and more disorientating as the echoes grow longer and more complex. Roxanne stops and shines her torch upwards. The roof of the tunnel is now some eight metres above their heads, maybe more. Clusters of stalactites hang in millennial silence. Beneath their feet infant stalagmites, resembling gobbits of discarded chewing gum, lump the wooden boards.

Their noses have acclimatised to the smell of the place, the sulphurous odour is no longer so painful. The adults walk in silence while the two boys play a war game, firing imaginary guns and clutching their bellies to stem the flow from imaginary wounds.

Roxanne, who is leading, notices that the beam of her torch is beginning to lose power. 'How much further?' she asks.

'I don't know,' Grey answers truthfully. 'The old boy simply said there was a long tunnel that eventually leads out onto the hillside to the west of the house.

'He had never actually been along it himself? Oh shut up, Eliot.'

Eliot, who is running his keys along a line of stalactites, shrugs and puts his keys away.

'It was an escape route,' Grey answers, 'not a general thoroughfare.'

A thud as something drops to the floor, followed by a scratching as whatever it is that has fallen picks itself up and rushes off into the darkness behind them. With the torch beam Eliot locates the rat just as it disappears into a crack between the floor and the tunnel wall. On his knees Eliot shines the torch down between the planks. The sound of running water is noticably louder now, the river must lie beneath their feet.

'What can you see?' Grey asks, startling Eliot who has assumed the others have all gone on ahead.

'Sod all.'

Grey looks back down the tunnel, the way they have come. Thirty or so metres behind them the faint but unmistakeable glow of an approaching torch beam casts a shadow on the tunnel wall. Grey taps Eliot's shoulder. 'Come on, we've been left behind.'

The two men hurry to catch up with the others.

'Left or right?' Roxanne says.

'Left,' Dudu insists.

'I was asking them.' Roxanne points towards Grey and Eliot.

They have a problem. The path bifurcates, one path leading gently upwards and the other downwards.

Grey hesitates, the old man's story didn't mention multiple paths.

'There are steps,' shouts one of the boys.

A rush of clattering footsteps and the boys appear around the corner up ahead on the left hand path. Without further discussion, the adults follow the boys who are already racing away and out of sight.

'Wait,' Alima calls out after them.

The path descends steadily, snaking this way and that, following an ancient watercourse that has, over millennia, eroded and gouged away the softer rock to leave the harder stone. The boy's voices echo up ahead. With every step the sound of water grows louder, the source is surely beneath the wooden boards at their feet.

Up ahead and out of sight, a sudden sound of splintering wood, followed by a child's scream. Dudu is charging ahead as they hear the splash.

'My God,' Alima shrieks.

Roxanne, Eliot, Alima and Grey, racing to catch up, turn a corner to find Dudu sitting on the edge of a large hole, where two steps have disintegrated.

'Careful, all the steps may be rotten,' Roxanne shouts. 'Keep to the side of the tunnel, Dudu.'

The gurgling water sounds very close. Beyond the broken planks sits a terrified Femi. They can just make out Cissé's voice calling out from below.

'Dudu,' Roxanne says a second time.

The haunted look has returned to Dudu's eyes. He peers up at his wife for a second then pushes himself forward into the void.

'No,' Alima shouts but it is too late.

A second splash, followed by a second shout, an adult shout this time.

'Grey,' Eliot calls out. 'Grey!'

Grey, who has been looking back down the corridor, turns to face the others. 'I can't swim,' he says, answering the question that had not

BENEATH THE BITTERCREST

yet been asked.

'Just pass me the rope,' Eliot says.

Grey does as he is asked. Eliot quickly unravels the rope, ties one end around his waist and hands the other end back to Grey. Grey, distracted for some reason, makes no attempt to move or to secure the rope and Eliot is obliged to pass the rope round Grey's waist himself. Roxanne, seeing what Eliot is doing, takes charge of tying a knot. She then takes grip of a section of rope and beckons Alima to do the same.

'Lower me down slowly,' Eliot tells them. 'I'll shout when I reach the bottom.'

'I don't know how much longer the torches will hold out,' Roxanne says. She takes Eliot's hand and gazes briefly into his eyes and, for a moment, Eliot dares to believe in happy endings.

With Grey and Roxanne taking the strain on the rope, and with his torch tucked into his waist band, Eliot lowers himself gingerly into the void.

Descending into the gloom, Eliot gazes up towards the receding pool of light and understands how astronauts must have felt heading away from the earth on the long journey to the moon. As his eyes gradually acclimatise to his new environment Eliot, spinning slowly on the rope, sees the water two metres or so beneath his swinging feet. A jumble of eddying currents agitate the black oily surface. To one side of the river is a short stretch of shingle beneath an overhang in the rock face. No sign of Dudu or the boy but it is too dark to see very far with his fading torch. If he can somehow land on the shingle instead of in the water ...

With the tips of his toes he reaches the rock face that arises straight up out of the water. Eliot pushes himself away from the rock, swinging back towards the shingle. Coming back in an arc towards the rockface he pushes away again, harder this time, gaining momentum.

A howl of protest drifts down from above but the noise of the river drowns out the words. Eliot keeps at it, hoping Grey, Roxanne and Alima will bear his weight. With every push he is swinging further back, towards the shingle, but the rope is juddering against the splintered wood of the walkway above his head.

He starts to spin so that his feet are no longer facing directly towards the rock. Lashing out desperately at the rock with his right foot on his next approach, Eliot manages to stop the spinning but at the cost of dislodging the torch from his waist band, sending it tumbling into the water.

More shouts from above.

Over the sound of the water he thinks he hears a voice, down and to his left. Dudu and Cissé must be on the shingle.

Eliot becomes aware of light shining down from above, lighting up the rock and the oily waters.

Another shout. From below this time. It is the boy, he is sure of it.

'It's OK,' he calls out, 'we're going to pull you out of here. Just keep calm.'

Eliot is now no more than a metre and a half above the water. The rope is digging painfully into his ribs and the rockface is beyond the reach of his feet. He realises he is going to have to get wet.

'More rope,' he shouts repeatedly up towards the light.

Eventually they hear him and feed out the rope, lowering him into the icy waters. The water is deep but the current not too strong. Eliot swims to the bank and hauls himself up onto the shingle. He lies there for a moment catching his breath then stands up and unties the rope.

'My papa, you must help my papa.'

A wet hand reaches out and finds Eliot's. Cissé has made it to the shore. A beam of torch light sweeps over them both and Eliot hears excited voices high above their heads. The boy is soaked and shivering but otherwise all right. Eliot starts tying the rope around the boy.

'Where is your dad? Your papa?' he asks.

'He fell in the water but he did not get out,' the boy says in tears.

'It's OK, we'll find him,' Eliot says, unconvincingly. 'Where were you?'

'There is a hole over there,' Cissé points towards a crevice set into the rock a short distance away.

Eliot secures the rope around Cissé's small frame.

'They're going to pull you up out of here then ...'

'What about my papa?'

'I'll find him while you're on your way,' Eliot ruffles the boy's hair. 'Don't worry.' He looks up towards the torch light. 'You can pull him,' he shouts.

The rope tautens as the slack is taken up.

'You'll be up there in just a few seconds,' Eliot reassures him.

He holds the boy steady as his feet leave the ground. Then suddenly the boy isn't going upwards anymore but falling back down into Eliot's arms with the rest of the rope tumbling after him. Eliot stares up at the hole.

'What going on?' he screams.

A gunshot reverberates against the rock. Roxanne shouts out. The light level diminishes dramatically. Maybe they have dropped a torch. Yes, that's it, not a gunshot after all, Eliot tries to rationalise the situation and de-escalate his fear.

The sound of footsteps running on the wooden walkway over their heads.

'Get down and ... your ears,' Roxanne shouts.

A brief silence follows during which Eliot hears the sound of something small and metallic dropping onto the rock a few metres away.

When you hear a pin drop, worry about the grenade.

Eliot grabs Cissé and throws himself backwards toward the crevice the boy has described. As they hit the ground, he wraps himself around the boy, burying the boy's head against his chest and covering his own ears as best he can.

The blast lifts them from the ground, the sound so loud he wonders if he indeed has his hands over his ears. A terrible twisting and tearing of wood and splintering of rock fill the air. It begins to rain masonry. First planks of wood, then fragments of stalactites plunging down like arrows at Agincourt, then massive chunks of rock that have become detached high above their heads. In a split second, they are drenched to the skin as a lump of rock the size of a car crashes into the water no more than three metres from where he and the boy lie. Then the noise subsides and Eliot takes his hands from his ears. An alarm is ringing somewhere.

The ringing is in his ears. It is pitch black, total and absolute. He feels the boy wriggling against his chest, he has clung to him so tightly that the kid is probably suffocating. Eliot loosens his grip. The boy pulls himself away.

'Where is the light? I want ...'

'Stop,' Eliot cuts him off in mid-sentence. 'Stay close to me.'

Up on hands and knees, Eliot feels his way forwards, almost immediately touching water. The water level is rising.

'I think we can drop the pretence now, don't you?' Havering smiles at Draper.

The explosion, whilst barely audible above ground, has packed enough of a punch to shake the chandeliers and bring plaster down from the ceiling in the reception area. An alarm is sounding behind the reception desk and Grigston is looking anxiously in Draper's direction.

'Your source was plainly mistaken,' Draper retorts, turning away from the reception desk to face Havering. 'I have taken you round the entire building, encouraged you to open every door. There is no basement to this building. And now, you will forgive me, it is very late and I intend to go home.'

'I think we should investigate the source of that alarm.' Havering walks towards the reception desk but Draper blocks his path.

'I have already afforded you every courtesy, in spite of the hour.' Draper's voice remains icily calm but his eyes betray his agitation. 'Unless you are intending to arrest someone or produce a search warrant I must ask you to leave. My security staff are quite capable of handling the situation and I will not have them hectored by you or anyone else.'

Havering looks from Grigston to Draper then back to Grigston.

'You still deny knowing Eliot Balkan and Roxanne Lepage?' Havering asks.

'I have never denied knowing either of them,' Draper corrects him. 'They have both caused innumerable problems for my business. You should be aware that everything has been reported to the police.'

'What exactly is your business here at the hospital, Mr Draper?'

'I am a trustee and non-executive director.'

'And how did ...'

'You can address all your other questions to my solicitor.'

The conversation is brought to an end by the sudden arrival of a uniformed officer who runs in from outside.

'There's something you should see, Sir,' Day says into Havering's ear.

Without a word to Draper, Havering follows his officer out into the snow and round to the back of the house.

'Over here, Sir.'

'Lead on, lead on.'

Havering pulls his coat collar up around his ears. They trudge through the snow, the motion sensors triggering the arc lights and turning night to day.

'I wondered why he didn't follow us out,' Havering mutters to himself. 'The bugger's watching us in comfort on television.'

Some forty metres from the house, a section of the lawn has

BENEATH THE BITTERCREST   359

disappeared to leave a crater five or six metres deep and four metres across. The lack of snow along the sides of the crater suggests it has only very recently appeared.

'I suppose he'll be telling us they have trouble with moles next.'

Day grins.

'No point standing about out here, this hole's not going anywhere.' Havering calls out to Thorne who is standing on the other side of the crater. 'I want you both inside with me, and I've a feeling we'll need reinforcements.'

Scrambling along the rock ledge with the boy in his wake, Eliot calculates he has travelled maybe four metres. He should be directly under the hole he descended through. God only knows how big the hole is now.

'Hello,' he calls into the darkness. 'What happened?'

Stupid question, he knows what happened, Roxanne or Grey used one of the grenades they found. But why? Are they being pursued? Or has one of the grenades simply gone off and killed them all.

'Hello?'

Eliot inches forwards hand over hand, the icy water rising all the time, above his wrists now.

He feels fabric. A sleeve, an arm, a body. His fingers fumble and find the face.

'What is it?' Cissé asks.

'A man with a goatee.'

'What's a goatee?'

'it's ... look it doesn't matter. A kind of beard,' Eliot answers. 'So it's not your dad, and it's not the man who was with us, the guard.'

'Who is it?'

'I don't know. In case you hadn't noticed, kid, it's pitch dark.'

'I can't see.'

'Join the club. Here look, have one of these.'

From one of his trouser pockets Eliot produces the packet of boiled sweets he had bought in Glasgow. He finds the boy's hand.

'It's wet. And sticky. What is it?'

'Just put it in your mouth. It's a sweet.'

The sweet seems to do the trick, shuts the kid up.

Eliot feels the body for a pulse. Nothing, either at the wrist or at the neck. A corpse then. Fighting his fear, Eliot explores the body. There are papers in the jacket pocket. He searches the other pockets and finds a knife and some loose change. Around the man's waist is an empty holster. Maybe the man fired the shot Eliot heard before the grenade went off.

Eliot works his way round the corpse, groping with his hands as the water rises inexorably around them. How long do they have? It doesn't matter, if it isn't possible to answer a question, jettison the question.

'What is this sweet called?' The boy's voice close by.

'Henry. David. I don't know, whatever you want.'

'That's silly,' Cissé laughs.

Eliot's fingers close on what might be a gun. He curses, giving a blind man a gun is like giving a goldfish a pair of skis. But it isn't a gun. Barrel-shaped, yes, but ... he scarcely dares hope. Then he finds the switch.

'And then there was light!' he shouts ecstatically.

How could the torch have survived the fall? It doesn't matter. Cissé is smiling so broadly it might split his face. Damply, they hug each other.

When Eliot manages to prise himself away from the boy he shines the torch about. Beyond the dead guard lies a second body, Grey's. Fragments of broken stalactites and lengths of wooden planking lay all about in the dust and debris that has fallen from the ceiling. The river is almost twice as wide as it was. Rocks that have fallen into the river have blocked off the water's natural course and the river is rising to circumvent the obstacles in its path.

If Eliot has hoped to climb up and regain the walkway he is disappointed. The distance is too great. Without someone to pull them up there is no possibility of escape that way. He finds one end of the rope and, with Cissé's help manages to pull it clear of fallen debris. Next, he rifles through Grey's pockets, taking keys, pass cards, and a pack of chewing gum.

'Can you swim?' he asks the boy.

Cissé nods cautiously. 'A little. Are there any more sweets?'

'Later. Follow me. That's the only way out of here.' He points downstream to where the river vanishes into the darkness of the tunnel ahead. The rock comes down to within thirty centimetres of the surface of the river.

'What about Femi and my mother? And Roxanne? And my papa?'

'We'll see them when we get out. They're ahead of us. Come on, help me with this.'

The boy seems satisfied with Eliot's explanation. Eliot wishes he could have anything like the same degree of confidence himself.

Together they haul the largest pieces of wood they find around the huge rock that blocks the river's flow. Eliot ties the rope around the wood, lashing the planks together as best he can, and leaving a number of loops he and the boy can hang on to.

'Are you ready?'

'How far is it?'

'Not far at all.'

'Is the water cold?'

'- ish.' Eliot admits.

'There are fish in the river?'

'No, of course not.'

'Is my papa ...?'

'He'll be waiting for us on the other side.'

'Are you lying to me?'

'What's with all the questions, kid? I tell you what, tomorrow I'll buy you all the encyclopedias you can eat, OK?'

'OK.'

'Let's go.'

They throw the raft into the water and jump in after it.

'No, you listen to me, Goodlife. You have precisely three minutes to get Havering off my back. I don't give a flying fuck who you have to speak with.'

Goodlife whinces, Draper can be so uncouth.

Serina pokes her head round the door. They have lost over two thousand pounds between them. She has her coat on. An attendant hovers with her bags.

Goodlife puts his hand over the receiver. 'We'll win it all back next week, darling. I'll deal with Draper, don't worry. Mustn't miss your cab. Lots of love.' He waves his sister goodbye, then takes his hand off the receiver. 'All right, Neville, calm down. I'll ask the minister ...'

'Wrong, you won't ask the minister, you'll fucking tell him. Three minutes.'

Draper cuts the call and turns to the trembling Grigston.

'Have you contacted everyone on the list?'

'I spoke with four of them and left messages for the others. Should I have ...?'

Draper composes himself. Through a window he sees Havering

trudging through the snow towards the entrance, talking into his mobile phone. The other officers are gathered beneath a streetlight, awaiting instructions. For the first time in months, Draper notices the slow ticking of the grandfather clock that stands at the top of the stairs overlooking the reception area.

Outside, the snow swirls about like television static. Havering is a caged tiger, pacing up and down, talking, listening, cajoling, protesting. Suddenly he erupts in rage, shouting abuse at the mobile phone, which he holds at arm's length. In the next instant, he hurls the phone away over the trees and turns towards the house. Their eyes meet for a moment, Havering's furious and outraged, Draper's calm and controlled. A thin smile flickers briefly on Draper's lips.

Havering spins round to face his officers, arms gesticulating wildly. One of the female officers approaches, appearing to reason with him, and is pushed away so powerfully she staggers and falls back in the snow. Havering turns back towards the window, waves his fist at Draper and shouts. The words are lost but the sentiment is clear, for Havering it is far from over.

Draper stares impassively as the police return to the waiting helicopter. The blades start rotating, slowly at first as the engines power up, then the helicopter heaves itself off the ground and moves away towards the south.

Draper has bought himself time.

forty one

A powerful current propels them forwards towards the end of the chamber. Swept along in the freezing viscous waters, Eliot barely has time to heave Cissé up onto the raft before they disappear beneath the overhanging rock and on into the claustrophobic confines of the tunnel. As the heat drains away from his legs, Eliot understands that if they are still in the water in fifteen minutes it will be as bodies floating face down.

'Hold on to the torch and keep your head down,' he shouts at the boy.

The air is full of the sounds of water, a bright rippling against the irregular stone walls that have been eroded by the river's action through the centuries, and a deep sub-aquatic rumbling that shakes the raft. The water buffets them from side to side, smashing Eliot's shoulder repeatedly against the wall, disregarding his frantic attempts to push the raft into the centre of the river. The current claws at Eliot's legs, trying to pull him under. He clings to the rope, using all his strength to keep his head above water.

The river is less than four metres in width. The roof of the tunnel varies in height between a metre above the water and a mere thirty centimetres. Cissé is shaking uncontrollably. Eliot reaches up and squeezes the boy's shoulder.

'Fun, isn't it?' Eliot shouts, hoping he sounds convincing.

Gripping the torch with all his strength, Cissé shakes his head. Eliot wraps a further loop of the rope around his arm, it is unimaginable that Dudu could have survived such a journey with nothing to keep his head above water.

All at once the acoustic changes as the sound of the water, no longer constrained, flies away into the space around them. The tunnel has opened up. They have entered another large chamber.

'The torch, shine the torch!'

The beam is still focused on the water. Cissé is lying flat out, the torch grasped in both hands, his head down and his eyes tightly shut. Eliot reaches up and prises the torch away.

They are in a large cave the size of a church, with stalactites and stalagmites fused together in columns eight metres high. A massive stalagmitic structure, seemingly composed of flacid tripes stacked one above the other and glistening beneath a film of creeping water, dominates the centre of the cave. Eliot cranes his neck to see if there is a path or an exit, but he is too low in the water to see much beyond the river banks. He shines the torch downstream, they have maybe thirty metres before the cave comes to an end.

'You have to open your eyes,' he shouts, shaking the boy. 'Need you to stand up and see if there is a way out.'

Cissé does as he is told, climbing gingerly to his feet, taking the torch and directing the beam at the walls while Eliot attempts to steer the raft towards the shore.

'What do you see?'

'Are there monsters?'

'Is there a way out?'

'I don't want to stay here.'

'We aren't staying here. Can you see a path? A hole? Quickly.'

They are almost at the river's edge when a submerged rock smashes into Eliot's thigh. At the same time he feels his foot catch in a hole or fissure beneath the waterline. He howls with pain as the raft is spun round in the current, twisting his leg until he fears his foot must snap off. With his free leg he pushes frantically against the rock attempting to free himself.

'Get down,' he orders the boy. 'And hang on to the torch.'

The rock holds him with the predatory passion of a moray eel. The raft has rotated well over ninety degrees, grinding against the river bank and threatening to break into its constituent parts. Worse still the weight of the raft is bearing down on Eliot, pushing him under the water. He pushes his head above the surface, grabbing a huge gasping lungful of air. The cacophony underwater is overpowering, a gurgling and churning of sound that threatens to burst his eardrums. Why isn't the boy shining the torch down into the water?

Another lungful of air.

Maybe if he turns himself over. He tries rolling his body over, but realises he cannot complete the movement without letting go of the raft. The rope is so tightly wrapped round that he is losing sensation in his arm. He feels so tired he should maybe stop fighting and let nature take its course.

He comes up for air.

'Please, Mr Eliot, don't leave me,' a voice says close to his ear.

He disappears beneath the surface again. There is only one thing he hasn't tried. With all his remaining strength he twists his body round, pulling himself down against the water's flow towards his trapped foot. His fingers reach out, following his trouser leg and finding his sock. The water throws itself at him with the brutal force of a tug-of-war. Eliot grips his sock in his frozen fingers, refusing to let go.

The current relents for a second. Eliot grabs his bootlace and pulls. His fingers slip away. Suddenly there is light, Cissé is shining the torch down into the water. Eliot tries again and again to reach his bootlace. Finally, his fingers grip the lace and pulls and the knot begins to slip apart. His lungs are burning, desperate to expand, even if only to be filled with several litres of freezing water. Ignoring the cravings of his lungs, he pulls at the lace, loosening it by degrees and, when he can take no more, he pushes violently with his free foot against the rock that holds him.

It works.

His foot comes out of the boot and immediately the raft is on its way again with Eliot travelling backwards as the current sweeps them on through the cave.

'Yes, yes,' shouts the boy.

Eliot smiles up at him. 'Are you trying to blind me with that thing?'

He knows they should try to reach the river bank and climb out of the water but Eliot is too tired. He lets the raft pull him along, staring up at the cave roof, catching his breath. His body feels so cold, so cold. A warning voice in his head reminds him that it is better to face in the direction of travel, so he carefully unwraps the rope from around his left arm and turns to wrap the rope around his right arm.

It is by chance that he looks up ahead when he does. No time to think. He acts on impulse, pulling the boy off the raft and into the water. As the boy hits the water, the roof hits the raft. The cave has ended and so, apparently has the tunnel. The torch falls away into the water. Looking back underwater, Eliot sees the torch tumbling slowly before hitting the bottom, its faint light flickering for a moment, then going out. Above their heads the raft is scraping along the roof, dragging and pulling at the rough surface in a cacophony of splintering wood. If they continue holding onto the raft they must surely die, but what option do they have?

Grabbing a last lungful of air, Eliot prises Cissé's fingers from the rope and holds him close as, together, they tumble away in the dark embrace of the icy current. The sound of the juddering raft is submerged in the rushing gurgling of the torrent that engulfs them.

forty two

Draper watches as the last member of the medical team gathers his belongings and heads for the tunnel that connects the house's sub-levels with the rest of the hospital. With luck the whole situation will be under control within twenty four hours.

Draper isn't in the habit of counting on luck.

He runs various imaginary scenarios through in his head. In the first, the police, that is Haversham, or whatever the man said his name was, gives up. Either his Achilles heel is found, a penchant for photos of little girls perhaps, and he will be pursuaded to forget all about a midnight flight to Swindon, or maybe he can simply be leaned on. He is a big man and doesn't seem the type to be easily intimidated but Draper's sponsors are not without allies in the police force.

What about the officers who accompanied him? In a sense Havering, yes, that's the name, Havering is easier to control as senior officers have more to lose. His subordinates, on the other hand, are on the way up. It only takes one eager beaver. Draper crunches a number into his mobile phone.

'Christopher.'

'Yes, Neville.' Christopher sounds tetchy and tired. 'I take it they've gone?'

'The minister must have been very persuasive.'

'I'm delighted to hear it. Now, if you don't mind, I ...'

'Are my reinforcements on their way?'

'If this turns out to have been a false alarm you will be footing the bill.'

'Answer my question,' Draper demands with what little patience he retains. 'You did organise the firepower I requested?'

'Against my better judgement. The minister says you're on your own from here on in. Loose cannons, etc.'

The bastard is enjoying this, Draper thinks to himself. 'You have to arrange an accident. Two helicopters. Shouldn't be too difficult, bad weather, snowstorm, fuel line fault ... internal enquiry and so on.' As he speaks, Draper turns towards the sound of approaching footsteps. The woman, a tall willowy black woman in her thirties, who assists in theatre. She nods. Reinforcements have arrived.

'You've been reading too many adventure stories,' Christopher Goodlife's voice is saying in Draper's ear. 'They got their marching orders, you should be grateful for that. Someone will follow it all up in the morning. Goodnight.'

The line dies.

Draper isn't sure the Minister is in a position to organise the downing of two police helicopters but if you don't ask, you don't get.

As he follows the woman back up the corridor, his eyes lazily perusing the contours of her behind, Draper imagines himself far away, on a tropical island. What a life: go for a swim or lie on the beach, eat a mango or sip warm coconut milk, peel a banana or go for another swim. Decisions, decisions. And if he has his girl Friday with him, well ... Maybe it is time to retire, to quit while he is ahead. Fortunes have been made, lives saved, and lost. There is no certain way of knowing how much Eliot and Roxanne have said, and to whom. Out of nowhere Draper remembers the remaining two Kurds and the African girl.

'I have something to attend to,' he calls out.

The woman turns. She doesn't challenge him but her eyes speak volumes.

'No, you're right,' Draper says, 'first things first. We'll meet the cavalry and give them their orders, then deal with our guests.'

The world is soft as cotton wool. The noise has retreated to a whisper. The darkness envelops him in a mother's arms and he is at peace. Almost eagerly he floats, away from the tumult and towards an inner light, a light without colour, radiant and warm. His inner ear tells him he is tumbling, over and over, but he feels no fear. There is nothing to fear.

The bone jarring contact smacks him back to reality. A sudden mad rush of water pounding in his ears. His head rising above the surface, an insane cacophony of noise.

He is wet. Freezing water spraying against his face, his head banging repeatedly against something hard and angular. He hears himself take a breath, a rasping gasp, then coughing in spasm, as if his lungs will fly up out of his mouth. An object banging hard against his stomach. His tired fingers reach out with a trembling grip.

He opens his eyes. Why has the world returned to haunt him? He longs for the gentle peace that clung to him beneath the water.

It takes a while to make sense of what he holds in his hand; the light is poor and his head is fuzzy with cold. An arm, its skin flayed away. The finger bone connected to the wrist bone, the wrist bone connected to the arm bone, the arm bone connected to ... The eyeless sockets of a flayed face bob up in front of him.

The jetsam around him answers the question of how bodies are to be disposed of now the crematorium is unavailable.

Eliot jerks his head back, away from the carnage. His cheek crunches against a grid of metal bars. Behind him he hears a howl, a child's voice, the boy has survived the tunnel.

'Over here,' Eliot shouts above the noise of the water. 'swim over to me.'

He catches sight of the boy's jacket as the boy sinks from view. Eliot pushes the corpse aside and dives towards the boy. His fingers find what his eyes cannot see and, with what remains of his strength he holds the boy and swims back towards the surface. Beneath his kicking feet he feels other limbs hanging in the dark freezing water.

It is so cold. He wraps the boy's fingers around the metal bars that block their path. A large sodden expanse of fabric rises to the surface, Eliot guesses it must be the great coat Dudu was wearing.

'You have to hold on,'

'I'm tired,' Cissé cries.

Eliot looks up. Through the bars is the outside world, they have reached the end of the tunnel. Snow has gathered on the bars higher up. He sees the gnarled silhouette of an oak tree, black against the cloudy sky. From somewhere beyond his line of sight, the moon is casting its weak light onto the snow.

There appears to be a gap overhead.

'Can you climb?'

'I'm tired.'

'I know, you said so just now. Can you climb?'

Cissé looks up into Eliot's eyes. Eliot sees his own son's eyes in the boy's gaze and fights back the tears that immediately well up inside him.

'Please,' Eliot smiles, 'We're not meant to die down here.'

'They did,' Cissé answers flatly, looking at the flayed corpses bobbing around in the water beside them, diving for the boy must have dislodged other bodies.

'We're not joining them. Go on, climb,' Eliot insists.

'Hey,' a voice shouts above their heads.

Cissé's face lights up. 'Papa!' he shouts back.

'Cissé. Climb, there is a gap. My son, oh God.'

The boy seems reborn. Hauling himself up, hand over hand, he scrambles up the laticework of iron bars towards his father's voice, with Eliot following in his wake.

Sure enough, three metres up they find the gap at the top of the gate. Dudu hauls his son over and guides his feet to help him down the other side before returning to assist Eliot.

Having embraced his son, Dudu embraces Eliot.

'Eliot, thank you, you have saved my son. You must think of me as a spoon.'

Eliot pulls back from the embrace in some confusion. Dudu smiles.

'Another of your proverbs.'

'Yes. It means think of me as your friend.' To prove his point Dudu spins Eliot round and rubs his back and shoulders energetically to increase Eliot's circulation.

'Maybe they lose something in translation,' Eliot says, his teeth chattering with cold.

As Dudu turns his attention to his son, massaging his arms and legs and speaking gently to him in a language Eliot doesn't understand, Eliot looks at the surroundings. To their right, the ground slopes steeply down towards the river. To their left is the gate that blocks the entrance to the cave system beneath the hill. Without the gate they would have been swept away to certain death in the black icy waters. The river is in full flood.

'My wife?' Dudu avoids Eliot's eye as he asks the question. He rubs Cissé's back so vigorously that the boy's breath stutters like a machine gun.

'They're safe. I came down to save you and the boy,' Eliot explains, rubbing his left elbow, which is throbbing painfully. 'The others were safe.' He says nothing of the explosion.

Dudu clings to his son, relief at the news of his wife eliciting an involuntary gasp that shakes his shoulders. Blood drips from a large gash in his forehead.

'Now we must find warmth or we will die.'

Eliot nods.

They clamber up the bank, heading away from the river towards the safety of the trees. The journey through the tunnel has disorientated them and they have no idea in which direction the hospital lies. Their wet clothes cling to them, growing steadily colder in the winter air. The boy is coughing and shivering so violently he can hardly walk and Dudu, Eliot notices, is walking with a limp. It is a race against time. Eliot, with only one boot, the other being wedged under a rock back in the tunnel, reasons that the faster they move the more quickly their bodies will heat up so he drives them on, shouting at Cissé to lift his feet and run.

Eliot is unclear in his mind whether they should try heading towards the hospital or away from it. He has no idea of how the land lies, or what other buildings there might be scattered about. He remembers seeing a couple of farms in the distance when he and Roxanne circumnavigated the house earlier on but he cannot recall seeing woodland.

They reach the crest of the hill. Eliot sinks to the ground clutching his unshod foot. In spite of the cold, his toes feel as though they are on fire. With only a sock between his foot and the frozen ground he has repeatedly stubbed his toes against the rocks and roots that lay in their path. He is sure he feels blood on the surface of his sock. Removing his jacket, Eliot tears strips from his shirt, binding them round his foot to protect it while Dudu and Cissé stand beside him, resting with their hands on their knees, gasping for air.

Eliot is tying the third strip of material around his foot when the first shot flies over their heads. He might well have mistaken the whistling of the bullet for a gust of wind but the thud, as the bullet buries itself in a tree to his left, is less open to misinterpretation. Stupidly, he spins in the darkness, trying to see where the shot has come from. All he sees are trees, the dark cages of their empty branches devoid of foliage, and falling snow.

'Great, I knew something was missing. Brilliant, fire away,' Eliot shakes his fist at the night. 'Sitting ducks all present and correct.'

Dudu pulls at his sleeve. 'Cissé says it came from over there,' He speaks in a stage whisper, pointing up the hill. 'He has good ears.'

Eliot peers up the hill into the gloom.

'We cannot fight them,' Dudu says, sensing what Eliot is thinking.

Eliot whips his head round towards Dudu, emotions in turmoil. Why listen to a coward, a man who hides under tables?

'Come,' Dudu says quietly. 'It doesn't matter. Come.'

Dudu is right. They run back down towards the river. As they run Eliot hears the hum of an engine. The wood ends just ahead, the wind is whistling through the trees and he wonders if his ears are playing tricks on him. He is dizzy with cold, maybe the noise is only tinnitus resulting from the explosion.

Below them the snow swirls over the black waters of the river. There has be a option that doesn't involve descending to the riverbank; out in the open they will be sitting ducks. Another bullet smacks a tree trunk overhead.

'Stay in the trees to the right,' Eliot hisses out to Dudu who is a few metres ahead of him, dragging Cissé along as best he can.

Suddenly Eliot hears barking. Guns, snow, a traumatised torture victim and his young son for company, all three of them soaked to the skin and close to hyperthermia, and now a pack of bloody dogs ... all the aces.

Ahead of Eliot, the boy slips, almost bringing his father down on top of him. Another flurry of shots. Eliot helps Dudu drag the boy to his feet.

'Do you hear dogs?' Dudu asks.

'Keep running,' Eliot answers.

They set off again, following what appears to be a path leading round the hill. The ground on either side of them becomes progressively steeper. Conifers replace deciduous trees. Finally the path disappears altogether and they find themselves stranded. Ahead of them a vertical rock face maybe ten metres high. To their right, the hill climbs at an impossible angle. To their left, the land falls away vertiginously.

'We have to go down,' Eliot says.

'It is too steep.'

'We can't go back.'

The dogs are getting closer, their yelps clearly audible. Dudu stares down between the trees. The valley floor is faintly visible fifteen metres or more below, a pool of snow beyond the dark silhouettes of the tree trunks. Dudu closes his eyes, looking down is making his head spin.

'It's easy,' Eliot says encouragingly. 'We slide down on our bums.' He adds, 'Many a mickle makes a muckle.'

Dudu is confused.

'It's a proverb,' Eliot explains.

'What does it mean?' Dudu asks.

'I haven't the faintest idea. You're the expert, I thought you'd know.'

Both men laugh.

'Papa,' Cissé tugs at his father's sleeve.

The snarling of the dogs is audible. Eliot looks over Dudu's shoulder and sees movement along the path. Time is all but out.

'Watch me,' Eliot instructs. 'Keep your legs closed. You don't want your feet taking separate routes round one of those tree trunks.'

'Take Cissé,' Dudu says, peering nervously down into the gloom.

'No,' the boy yells, clinging to his father.

'It's our only chance,' Eliot insists then squats down and launches himself down through the trees. 'Come on,' he shouts at the top of his voice.

Behind him the boy screams as the dogs cover the remaining few metres.

'Go, Papa. Go.'

Eliot does his best to steer himself round the trees in his path, digging his heels into the leaf litter to slow himself down. The rushing sound behind him suggests the boy has persuaded his father to slide down the bank. The boy is shrieking with excitement, above the baying of the dogs.

Some five metres or so before the edge of the wood, Eliot digs his heels in too hard. His whole body jack-knives up and catapults forwards, slamming into a tree trunk before bouncing back and continuing downwards, out of control, tumbling head over heels. As he falls, Eliot fancies he again hears the humming of an engine.

He flies out from under the cover of the trees into a thick bank of snow. All at once the sky is a furnace of blinding light. The noise is now unmistakable, a helicopter's rotor blades slicing the thick frozen air directly above him, sending the falling snow into a whirling frenzy.

Dudu and Cissé come crashing out of the trees, slamming into Eliot and completely winding him. They lie there in a heap, gasping like landed fish, too tired to move. Somewhere above them, the dogs continue to bark.

The helicopter descends slowly, the downdraft from its blades chilling Eliot, in his wet clothes, to the bone. He sits up, looks around for somewhere to hide, but it is way past hiding time. Falling back in the snow, he resigns himself to his fate. They have lost. It is down to Roxanne, Alima and her second son. If they have escaped and managed to raise the alarm in time then ...

It is a big if.

The swirling whiteness that pours out of the black night, the rhythmic white noise of the chopper blades, the tingling tiredness of his body, all conspire to take Eliot far away from the snow drift on the bank of a river whose name he doesn't know. He thinks of his children, of what he might have done to change the way things have turned out. He thinks of his wife, Sue, and of how promises unravel, you don't have to try, it just happens. One day you are staring so deeply into each other's eyes, the whole world might vanish and you'd never notice, and the next you find that brushing the kids' shoes has become more important than making love.

He thinks of Dudu's children, and the children and families of those many others who have been murdered to provide transplant organs for those who can afford them. The memory of a pile of discarded clothes in a basement room in the low building rises up from his subconscious and mingles with other memories, photographs of genocides in Rwanda, East Timor, Nazi Germany, Yugoslavia ...

The baying of the dogs is drowned out in the noise from the helicopter as it touches down.

Eliot has never been motivated by political fervour, he has always considered he had enough worries of his own, but now, staring failure and death in the face, he is angry not for himself, but for those who will die after him. With him and Roxanne and Gwen dead, Draper's project will continue. The poor will keep coming, they always keep coming, from Africa, the Middle East, the Far East, from where there is war, or hunger or persecution or tyranny or intolerance.

He hears shouting as people leap out of the helicopter. Gunshots from up the hill. Further shots from close at hand. Eliot flinches, imagining each shot is for him. He wants to run, but is too tired to even lift his head. He closes his eyes. Please let Roxanne get away. He feels the world receding at great speed, feels he has already left it.

Suddenly, he is being shaken roughly.

'I think this one's almost gone,' a voice calls out.

'They're all soaked to the skin. Hypothermia. We have to get them out.'

'There isn't room on the chopper.'

A gunshot is followed by a metallic ping.

'If we hang around much longer there won't be a chopper.'

Eliot feels himself lifted up and carried. His senses are so weak he no longer knows which way up he is. Tumbling onto a hard surface he takes to be a seat ... the noise is deafening ... he must be in the helicopter. Another ferocious exchange of gunfire.

'Who the hell is up there?' a voice shouts.

A voice Eliot recognises, but cannot place.

'They're not amateurs, Sir, I can tell you that. Three or four of them I'd say.'

'Have we got everyone on board?'

'Balkan and the boy. We may have to come back for the other one.'

There is a yelp as someone close by is hit.

'Take us out of here.'

'You can't leave him,' Eliot mutters with what strength he can muster.

A hand on his forehead. Eliot forces himself to open his eyes.

'You OK?' A woman in uniform looking down at him.

'Who ...'

'Police ...' she starts.

'You're making a habit of this, Mr Balkan.'

A large face sporting a thick handlebar moustache looms into view. Eliot recognises Havering.

'You have to ... he's the boy's father. Please.' Eliot tries to sit up but is firmly pushed back by Havering who is having none of it.

'OK, son. It's OK, nobody's being left behind.'

Another exchange of gunfire. Eliot sees a body tumble out of the trees and roll with a splash into the river. Two doberman hounds appear close to where the body fell.

'Covering fire so we can bring the last one in,' Havering shouts above the engines. 'Prepare to take her up.'

Moments later, Dudu is rolled onto the floor of the cabin and the helicopter lurches into the air. Two police officers tumble in and the sliding door slams shut. As they climb vertically, the pilot spins the helicopter round and throws the machine forwards to get out of range of the men on the ground. In seconds they are out of the valley and coccooned in the snowstorm.

'She's only built to carry seven,' the pilot says, 'but these babies are better than the crap we had in the Balkans. As good as money can buy.'

'That makes a bloody change,' Havering retorts.

A small hand reaches out and grips Eliot's own.

'Sarge, what's that below? At six o'clock.'

'He's right. Down there,' another voice says. 'Look, running up the hill.'

BENEATH THE BITTERCREST

Havering peers at the ground as the pilot allows the chopper to lose some altitude. The searchbeam is still on, floodlighting the snowscape below.

'Yes, I see it.

'A woman running. And another one. Is that a woman?'

'Is it safe to put down?' Havering asks the pilot.

'I can land but we're way over the weight limit.'

'Understood.'

Havering quickly considers the options.

'Are we out of range of the gunmen?'

The pilot glances down at the ground. 'It'll take them a good five or six minutes to reach us, even if they're fit and kitted out to run in this snow.'

Havering nods. 'All righty, put her down.' He turns to his officers. 'I hope you're all wearing your thermals.'

Nobody answers. Two of his team look decidedly white about the gills as the helicopter plunges downwards.

'When we touch down, I want whoever's down there rescued and brought aboard.' Havering points at the pilot, 'He'll take as many of you as he can, the rest of us will have to make our own way out. Understood?'

They aren't exactly enthusiastic, but they understand.

forty three

Having watched the hit squad race across the back lawn, over the wall and into the trees, Draper orders the two remaining men to guard the entrance to the administration block.

Grigston and Lawson stand sullenly behind the reception desk, surplus to requirements. Across the hall two men with automatic weapons, square jaws, crew cuts, and a swaggering casual confidence, guard the entrance. They are everything Grigston and Lawson have never been or could ever be.

'Do we have to ...' Lawson starts.

'You stay here until I say otherwise,' Draper barks, heading for the door to the sub-levels.

Back on Sub-level Three, Draper walks briskly towards room 315. The radio in his pocket crackles.

'We've spotted them below us through the trees. Three of them, we think. There's a river to our left. Maybe thirty metres away. Over.'

Draper fiddles with the buttons on the radio, trying to find the one that will enable him to reply.

'Do we bring them in or deal with them here? Over.'

Behind the crackling squelchy compressed sound of the voice, Draper hears barking dogs and a clearer cleaner sound like an opening door. He presses another button. The radio dies.

'Shit.'

He keeps on pushing the buttons but the radio stays dead. He will have to hope the men are as professional as they appear.

Why has it taken a crisis to finally be given the professional support he has been asking for? For three years they have procrastinated, obliged him to hire social misfits and ex-nightclub bouncers, leaving security at the mercy of barely sentient louts.

310 ... 311 ... 312 ... He counts the room numbers ...

Infrared goggles, weapons, physically fit, plainly used to working as a team; where has Goodlife found them? How much do they cost? Could the minister be persuaded to ...

... 315.

Draper stops and pulls a key from his pocket. There is a faint crackling sound, which he takes to be the radio in his pocket coming

BENEATH THE BITTERCREST 377

back to life, too bad they will just have to wait. He pushes the key into the lock.

The smack across the back of the head fells him before he even has a chance to register it.

To make space for new arrivals, two of the officers have lifted Eliot into a sitting position on the floor of the helicopter. Eliot rests his back against the row of seats on which Dudu has been laid out. His head is spinning, or rather the world is spinning, from left to right. Closing his eyes makes no difference, the swimming sensation carries on in the self-imposed darkness behind his eyelids. He clings to the blanket that has been wrapped around him and does his utmost to control his breathing and remain calm. Around him Havering and his team debate how to persuade whoever is out there to approach the helicopter.

'If they've heard the shooting, they'll not be coming out into the open.'

'Give me positives not negatives, Officer,' Havering replies.

'Maybe the boy can shout out to them,' a woman's voice says.

'Try it.'

Eliot hears Cissé's voice protesting. Eliot opens his eyes. Two police officers are trying to pull Cissé away from his father. The boy is hanging onto his father's arm, threatening to pull him off the seat. Dudu is unconscious.

'We think your mum is out there,' says Thorne, the more statuesque of the two women officers, in as gentle a voice as she can muster.

'No, no, my Papa. Let go.'

'You must help us now,' Thorne insists.

Eliot tries to speak and is surprised at how quiet his voice is, he simply has no energy left. He lifts his left arm from under the blanket and waves it about, trying to catch someone's attention. The scene rotates slowly in front of his barely focusing eyes.

'Hey,' Eliot grunts inaudibly.

Why doesn't the helicopter shut the fuck up? He is so tired.

'Hey.' A little louder this time. Try again. 'Hey.'

Finally the boy turns towards Eliot.

Eliot reaches out his hand. The boy grabs it. The officers let go of the boy and Cissé moves towards Eliot.

'Listen, Cissé. It's OK. Your dad ...' Eliot closes his eyes briefly. He feels Cissé squeeze his hand. 'It's OK. Your papa is safe. They think your mama is out there.' Eliot opens his eyes. 'They're out there and they're frightened. Like we were. You have to call them. I'll look after your dad.'

'And I'll help Mr Balkan,' Faulkner reassures the boy.

Eliot cannot remember when he last said something so stupid, he can barely open his eyes, how he proposes to look after Cissé's father is anyone's guess. His words satisfy the boy however.

Eliot watches him climb out of the helicopter. Out in the snow, Havering puts his hands on the boy's shoulders and speaks to him. The words are drowned in the roar of the helicopter blades. As the aging policeman and the small African child walk away from the helicopter towards the trees some fifteen metres away, Eliot notices the megaphone in Havering's left hand.

Cissé shouts into the megaphone that Havering holds in front of his mouth and, while individual words cannot be made out, the high pitch of the boy's voice is just audible within the helicopter. Eliot scans the treeline for signs of life. The other police officers stand by, their hands in open view to show they aren't carrying weapons.

A minute passes. No sign of life. In the cockpit the pilot checks his watch.

The world has stopped spinning. Through the swirling snow Eliot sees that the light from the chopper's searchlights only penetrates a few metres into the trees.

They have put down near the top of a hill. The intensity of the snow storm means that he cannot be sure where land ends and sky begins. It is like sitting inside the static cloud of a detuned television, waiting for normal programming to resume. He shivers and pulls the blanket tighter around him, wishing the danger and the cold had passed, that the door were closed and the helicopter were in the air.

The pilot revs the engine. Havering raises a hand to let the pilot know he understands. He steers the boy round the front of the helicopter towards the trees on the other side. This time Eliot hears nothing but he can see from Cissé's shaking shoulders, and the huge lungfuls of air he is taking, that the boy is shouting for all he is worth into the megaphone.

Still the darkness keeps its secrets.

'Ninety seconds,' the pilot shouts to the officers standing outside by the open door.

'I'll tell him,' Faulkner says.

She clambers out and runs through the snow toward Havering and the boy.

Eliot sees her shout into Havering's ear. Havering nods, lifts the megaphone away from Cissé's mouth and speaks with the boy. Cissé stamps his feet and protests. A hand on the boy's shoulder, Havering steers him back towards the helicopter. The search is over.

Suddenly Cissé slips out from under the hand and steps back, screaming angrily, he isn't abandoning his mum without a fight.

The pilot is building up the revs for take off. One by one the police officers climb back into the helicopter.

Havering makes to grab Cissé but the boy slips away a second time and runs off towards the trees. Havering glances back at the helicopter before racing away after the boy, with Faulkner in pursuit.

The pilot appears increasingly nervous, he has seen these situations before, where someone refuses to accept reality. It usually ends badly. In conflict it is essential to understand when a moment is lost, failure to do that and instead of losing one man, you lose twenty.

They watch as first the boy, then Havering and Faulkner disappear into the trees

'Fucking hell!' someone shouts to Eliot's right. 'What's the old tosser think he's doing?'

'We'll just have to leave them.'

'You can't do that, Peter.'

'Radio him then.'

The pilot lifts his hand. In it he holds Havering's radio, which has been left on the seat beside him.

'Oh, great, fucking great. Well done, Sir.' says the officer to Eliot's right, executing a sarcastic salute as he speaks.

'Get a life, Mullen.'

'Yeah, fuck you too,' Mullen replies pushing his colleague, causing him to fall against Eliot.

'I'm giving them twenty seconds,' the pilot says, lifting the helicopter a couple of feet into the air. 'After that ...'

It is only twenty minutes since Eliot saved the boy's life in the river deep underground. Eliot tries to shout that they cannot abandon him, not now, but his voice is too weak.

The helicopter hovers a few feet off the ground, suspended in space and time, a purgatory of waiting. Eliot stares at the back of the pilot's seat, counting the stitches that ran round the edge, black thread against the navy blue material, praying the boy will re-emerge. Beside him, Dudu continues to sleep, his face calm, his chest rising and falling, the blanket up around his ears.

The pilot shakes his head. The helicopter rises a further two metres into the air and rotates slowly until it is facing back up the hill. Through the open door there is still no sign of the boy or the others.

'Got to go,' the pilot says.

Nobody speaks as the door is closed and the helicopter rises quickly ten, twenty, thirty metres into the air.

The windows in the cockpit curve down allowing passengers and pilot to see partway under the cabin itself. Below them the searchlight set into the underbelly of the helicopter lights up the ground, a blaze of white reflecting back up off the snow. As the helicopter reaches the top of the hill, it banks right.

Eliot reaches forwards and pulls at the pilot's sleeve with all his strength. The helicopter lurches violently. A shout as one of the officers slams his head against the door.

'What the ...'

Eliot points down at the ground.

'Down there, I can see them,' he whispers.

One of the officers leans forwards and lifts the headphones from the pilot's left ear.

'He's right. Look.'

Down in the field, about twenty metres higher up the hill than where they landed are five figures waving frantically.

The pilot lands as close as he dares. The downdraft of the blades sweeps the snow up in a storm that slams against the figures on the ground, covering them from head to toe. In seconds the door has been thrown open and four have clambered aboard, Cissé, Alima, Femi and Faulkner.

'Right, which two of you lucky people are staying here with me?' shouts Havering, who has stayed outside in the snow.

'Where's Roxanne?' Eliot asks Alima, who is kneeling beside her husband.

'He'll be fine,' someone is reassuring Alima.

'Mullen can go with you, Sir. He was complaining of feeling rather hot, Sir.'

'Where's Roxanne?' Eliot asks again, but Alima isn't listening.

'OK, Mullen it is. And ... you, Peter.'

'Ha ha,' Mullen laughs triumphantly.

Mullen and Day climb over Eliot towards the door, pushing Eliot back onto the floor.

'Don't forget your toys, boys,' Faulkner shouts, tossing hand guns out after them.

They don't hear the shot over the noise of the engines. One minute Mullen is sneering at Faulkner, the next his body is thrown against the side of the helicopter where his head smashes against the windscreen before bouncing back. Blood pours from his nose, splattering the windscreen. His face registering surprise, Mullen slumps to his knees in the snow.

'Go, go, go!' Havering shouts, banging the side of the helicopter.

There is a metallic ping as a second shot ricochets off one of the helicopter's blades.

'Put him on,' the pilot shouts. 'Put him on!'

Havering and Day haul Mullen up and into the helicopter beside Eliot. Both men look nervous, the enemy has caught up with them and it is touch and go whether they can escape. They nevertheless step back from the helicopter.

'We'll see you later,' Havering says. 'And I don't want anyone claiming for more overtime than is necessary.'

Another shot crashes into the windscreen, causing a series of concentric circles to appear in the strengthened glass.

'Get on board,' the pilot shouts.

'But the weight?' Havering says.

'Sod the weight.'

The helicopter lurches into the air at an angle.

'Move across, spread the load.'

Havering rolls over Eliot as the helicopter rocks about like a demolition ball on a crane. The helicopter swings round, Day struggling to slide the door shut. A bullet flies in through the gap, bouncing off the walls. Eliot hears a rip close to his right ear. Snapping his head back, he sees a hole in the seat where the bullet has passed through. It is the pilot's seat.

The helicopter surges forwards and upwards, picking up speed.

Alima, as if finally realising she is not on solid ground, stares wildly about her, making an attempt to stand up. D.I. Day pulls her back down.

Eliot reaches out and touches her arm. Seeing Eliot calms her down.

'Alima, where's Roxanne?' he says.

'She didn't come.'

Eliot stares back, awaiting an explanation, but Alima's eyes offer none.

'Where ... what happened? Is she ...'

'She went.'

Eliot turn towards the voice. His head is spinning again. It is Femi, the younger boy.

'She went where?'

'She went back to find my sister.'

forty four

He knows he is in trouble even before he opens his eyes. Has he shot the two Kurds? Tiny flecks of blood cling to his hands like confessions, like betrayals, but the blood of many people cling to his hands. He was turning towards the door. Who was he expecting? His mother? Whispering reproaches about a talent wasted. But his pockets are full of money, millions upon millions. He has done well for himself. Why isn't she proud of him? Make your own way in the world she taunted him. So he has.

Racing up the stairs, so quickly his feet barely touch the floor. The dead men breathing down the back of his neck. Only now the ground floor has become the tenth floor ... and it isn't a building, it is a tree.

They are all there, way below on the emerald green lawn, waiting, shouting, waving.

The flecks of blood are all the redder in the green light beneath the leaf canopy. He steps off a thick branch and feels himself gliding slowly to earth.

In that instant he understands he is lucid dreaming. In the next, he realises he should be awake, that this is not the time for dreaming. A drum is beating.

His consciousness slips out from under his dream's nose. His senses are on full alert. The air carries the faintest trace of industrial cleaning agents, and a distant humming.

He is not in his bed.

There is no banging drum. His blood is thumping in his ears, slopping back and forth like a spring tide slapping against a harbour wall. Muscles tensing, he opens his eyes.

'Slept well?'

Draper whips his head round. Roxanne is standing across the room, arms folded, her face a picture of concern. He notices the bruising and burn marks on the side of her face. Her trousers are ripped. She carries a dirty rucksack.

'Tables turned,' she says simply.

A spasm shakes Draper's body, fight or flight. He can do neither, strapped as he is to a trolley.

'The two men you had locked up in here helped me tie you up, before I showed them how to escape.'

Roxanne grabs one end of the trolley and propels Draper towards the open door.

'They understand a great deal about torture, the Kurds,' she says, matter-of-factly.

She pushes the trolley out into the corridor.

Draper tries to shout, the sound dies in his throat.

'You'll have to speak up, I'm a little concussed,' she says as she wheels him along. 'Oh, I found some masking tape next door. Had a little wander about while you were taking your nap. So you don't really need to say anything at all.'

It takes a great deal to spook Draper, but now he is spooked. Where are the guards? Has she killed them? Where are Eliot and the Africans?

'Your golden haired boy is damaged,' she says, sensing the flow of his thoughts. 'And another guard. And ... was his name Grey? We found some grenades. I can't even tell you their organs are worth keeping. It was all a bit of a mess.'

Draper hears the lift doors open. She pushes the trolley in.

'Second floor,' she says, pushing a button. 'Oh, I took your pass card, I hope you don't mind.'

Draper sees himself, reflected in the mirror ceiling of the lift. He is trussed up like a turkey. Roxanne, sensing what he is doing, lifts her head and gazes up at his reflection.

'You're going to tell me where Mili is. Then I can get out from under your feet,' she smiles.

Suddenly the smile evaporates. Draper sees dark burning anger in her eyes.

'After you've given me the information I need to shut you down, that is.'

He prefers her anger. Anger he can deal with.

'2b.'

In case he hasn't noticed, she calls out the number on the door.

She leaves him in the middle of the room. Moments later a bright light beams down on him.

'Make yourself at home,' she calls out happily.

He has to get her angry.

There is the sound of covers being hauled off and discarded, followed by something heavy being wheeled across the floor. Draper doesn't have to see what she is doing. He knows. He knows only too well.

A second machine is pushed towards the centre of the room. Switches are flicked. The hums of various fans fill the air. Further switches. A machine springs into action and various mechanical arms appear over Draper. A small circular saw spins on the end of one arm above his face.

'I can't pretend to know how these machines work,' Roxanne confesses. 'We'll just have to do it by trial and error.'

She leans into view and rips the masking tape from Draper's mouth.

'Shall I leave you to shout for a couple of minutes? There doesn't appear to be anyone about, but you might want to get it off your chest.'

She is right, he has sent everyone away, cleared all the staff back to the main hospital. He avoids looking at the equipment hovering above his head and keeps his gaze on her. He says nothing.

'Where's the girl?' she asks.

Draper stares back up at her. 'What is it about the girl, Roxanne? Why have you risked your life for a little African child?' He speaks softly and gently.

'Where is she?'

'Did your father beat you? Did you feel abandoned? It can't have been easy growing up in Calais, with no money, a mother on the bottle?'

Roxanne stares down contemptuously. 'I don't have time for this, Neville.'

'That's the problem, isn't it? Your whole life you have been ...'

He is stopped in mid-flow by a viscious slap across the face from the back of her hand. He has to keep talking.

'You're not a killer, Roxanne.'

His cheek is singing, blood drips from where her ring has torn the skin. He hadn't previously noticed that she wears a ring.

'I want you to tell me where you have put the girl.'

'What if she were already dead?'

He sees the anger cloud her eyes. It is curious that he should feel safer with her anger. At least with her anger she is present, her mind is engaged and, presumably, her conscience. The real danger comes from the calm smiling woman, the woman detached from reality.

The anger passes.

'I really don't have time for this,' she apologises.

Her face withdraws to the shadows. Draper counts the passing seconds. Where is she? Maybe he should tell her where the girl is. Will that buy him time? It might. On the other hand it might simply encourage her.

Another machine is wheeled across the floor. He raises his head.

She must be pushing it from behind. It stops close to his feet. Roxanne emerges from behind it and, without saying a word, begins to remove Draper's shoes and socks.

Above his head, the circular blade continues to spin at the end of its mechanical arm.

'It's probably best if we practise at this end,' Roxanne says, bending over the controls.

The third machine springs to life, the mechanical arms flinching like the legs of an upturned spider. As Roxanne fiddles with the control pad a pair of rubber claws lift into view at the end of an extending arm. A second mechanical arm leaps upwards. A scalpel gleams as it catches the light.

'Why don't we discuss a deal?' Draper says quietly.

A blue laser light suddenly shoots out of the front of the machine, almost blinding Draper who lets his head fall back against the trolley.

'I let you have the girl in exchange for ...'

'There we are,' Roxanne says, her voice a singsong, the reassuring tones of an adult removing a splinter from a child's finger.

Draper forces himself to lift his head and see what she is doing. It is hard to see precisely, due to the afterburn on his retina from where the laser landed.

'It's automatic, isn't it?' Roxanne continues, peering at the computer display on the back of the machine. 'I suppose I simply select a programme like ... this.'

Draper feels the rubber clamps grasp his left foot. He sees the arm with the scalpel on the end of it rotate and slowly descend.

'This may hurt a bit,' she says, her voice trembling with concern.

They land right in front of the A & E department, on a patch of lawn covered by thick snow.

Within seconds, the double doors of the hospital fly open and trolleys are rushed out, the staff having been warned of the helicopter's imminent arrival. The warmth in the helicopter has done much to revive Eliot. The cold air as he is transferred on a trolley into the hospital does the rest.

The commotion is considerable as they are swept through the waiting area where several people sit watching twenty four hour news, while they wait to be seen by the duty nurse. It must be five or six in the morning, Eliot thinks to himself. He wonders what day of the week it is. Two of the men in front of the television are plainly drunk. How many hours or days have they been waiting?

He hear Alima asking if her husband is all right.

'You mustn't worry yourself, love. He'll be right as rain, so he will. Please. You must lie back. Your boys are both fine. What weather we're having! It must have been quite a journey up there in the heeliocopter.'

The nurse's gentle Irish brogue waffles on comfortingly as the cortege or convoy travels in single file into the heart of the building. Eliot hears Havering's voice in the background answering questions put to him by a doctor or nurse. How long have the patients been out in the open? How long has it taken to reach the hospital? Has the African gentleman regained consciousness at any point? Is he known or suspected to have suffered a head injury?

They enter a ward. Two nurses step forwards.

'I want him cleaned up. We understand he's been in a river and then out in the snow.'

'So, we've been in the wars, have we?' says a familiar voice.

A face leans into view.

'Bloody hell,' Eliot says. 'Nurse Riggs. Another hospital full of fantastic brunettes and blondes and I still get the bald headed git with a moustache.'

The nurse laughs. 'How do you think I feel? I moved a hundred and fifty miles to a different hospital to get away from you. Anyway, let's get you out of these damp clothes.'

Riggs draws curtains round the trolley. In the background, Eliot hears Alima demanding to know where they are taking her husband. He sits up to remove his jacket, and has it half off, before Riggs realises what he is doing.

'You never learn, do you?' Riggs says, easing Eliot's arms out of the sleeves. 'We don't yet know what kind of state you're in, so lie back and think of England while I get busy with the scissors.'

Eliot does as he is told while Riggs cuts away Eliot's jumper, t-shirt and jeans.

'Buying your clothes at Oxfam? And look at your feet. It's hardly haute couture, Eliot.'

'Spot on,' Eliot confesses.

'Cheap but ... cheap. Can't imagine the ladies going for it. By the way, did you ever find that woman you were looking for?'

'Roxanne.'

'Was that her name?' Riggs says.

Eliot sits bolt upright.

'You've got to help me.'

'Don't start that again.'

'This is serious. I have to get back to the helicopter.'

Eliot stands up.

'You're not going anywhere like that,' Riggs observes. 'If you're not already suffering from hypothermia, running about in the snow in your underpants should do it.'

'Get me some clothes. Please. Please.'

Two minutes later, Eliot is running back down the corridor in a mixture of hospital uniform and a fleece and coat that Riggs has lent him. Riggs has even lent Eliot his trainers. If Riggs doesn't get the sack, Eliot will see to it that the man is promoted to Chief of Staff or Matron of Honour or something.

He finds Havering in reception, drinking coffee and briefing a doctor.

'We have to go back,' Eliot says, rushing up. 'Roxanne. She's still there, rescuing the girl. We have to go back. Where's the pilot?'

'They're dealing with the bullet wound in his thigh,' Havering says. 'Aren't we meant to be in bed?'

'It's a lovely thought,' Eliot retorts, patting Havering gently on the arm, 'and I'm flattered, really I am, but we have more pressing things to do. I'm the only one who knows where she is and how to get there. You have to take me.'

Havering turns to the doctor. 'Is he fit to travel?'

'I can't answer that,' the doctor answers, well aware that no tests have yet been carried out and that, if Eliot collapses, it could be his job on the line.

'All I need is something to eat and a strong coffee,' Eliot insists.

It has cost Draper a couple of toes but Roxanne has extracted the information she needs. If she felt his pain, she did not show it. Her face is the picture of serenity, a veil, a mask, a soundproof door. She has left him on the trolley, he will keep.

She walks effortlessly, as if on a country walk in springtime.

She pushes open the door and enters. The rooms are on sub-level 3 close to the lifts, only five doors down from where she and Eliot first found Alima, Dudu and the boys. The lights are on but the rooms are silent.

She knows exactly how things will be, what state the girl will be in. She only has to revisit her own childhood to understand. And that is what she does now, becoming the saviour she always sought as a child, the gentle saviour who would rescue her, the knight in bright armour who would emerge from the gloom to be her champion. The knight who never came.

This time the knight will come.

'Mili,' she says gently, her voice reverberating against the bare walls.

She opens doors as she goes, peering into the rooms. A small bedroom, a smaller bathroom. No sign of life. She reaches the main living area. A tatty sofa, a dining table and three chairs.

'Mili.'

No reply. The kitchen is empty. Roxanne opens the cupboards. She hid in cupboards when she was a little girl, anything to escape the beatings, the drunken violence that lashed out at anything that moved.

There is a second bedroom leading off from the main living area but that too is empty. Has Draper lied to her? The anger she has fought so hard to control wells up. Anger blurs edges, erodes boundaries. Roxanne forces herself back to the awful calmness, the still, quiet place where nothing matters where brutality is just another option. If he has lied, then he will pay. She will let the machines skin him alive, bring him the living death he has inflicted on others. He will die screaming like the human sacrifices of the Aztecs, his flayed rotting skin worn by others to appease the gods. She will take back the eyes he stole from Didier, put an end to the evil he has visited upon the earth.

'Mili,' she says imploringly, her mind effortlessly dividing Beauty from the Beast, love from hate, the desire to protect from the urge to kill.

Having checked inside the wardrobe, Roxanne re-enters the living area. Her heart is thumping in her chest and the side of her face throbs from where she was thrown against the wall of the tunnel by the force of the grenade blast. One ear drum punctured and tinnitus ringing in the other like an unattended car alarm. She bunches her fists till her nails break the skin of the palms of her hands.

'Mili.' This time she speaks more to herself than to the room. Somewhere in the building a small girl lies trembling with fear. Roxanne wraps her arms around herself, remembering her own terror.

Her eyes drift towards the cheap sixties furniture, the torn red vinyl of the dining chairs, the overweight lumpiness of the sofa, the worn stained surface of the table.

Suddenly it comes to her. She crosses the room and pulls a cushion from the sofa, revealing the torn hessian upon which a handful of ancient coins, a pencil, and various bits of fluff nestled like woodlice and slugs under a stone. A rusting spring pokes through.

Off comes a second cushion. As she tosses it aside she catches a glimpse of a small shoe disappearing beneath the third and final cushion.

'Mili, it's Roxanne.' Her words like silk in a gust of summer air. 'Your mother is safe. And Femi.' She hesitates. 'And your dad, and Cissé, they are all safe.'

The cushion flinches.

'I've come to save you.'

The cushion stays put.

'I'm going to take the cushion away.'

She does so and, as she does so, Mili leaps up in a flurry of tiny fists and kicking feet. Roxanne grabs her and holds her close, absorbing the blows, taking them as a penance.

She is holding herself, holding the child she once was. How many times was she too hauled out, fists flying? Only this time it isn't to be abused. This time she will be safe and they won't touch her. This time the meek will inherit the earth.

After a few moments the hitting and kicking subside and the crying starts. And still Roxanne remains serene and distant. There will be no tears, not yet.

'Come, we must hurry,' she says, smoothing Mili's hair. 'You must be brave.'

Mili's eyes gaze up into hers, dark and deep as a bottomless well, eyes that no longer know who to trust.

As Roxanne lowers Mili to the floor, she notices the girl's clothes

BENEATH THE BITTERCREST 391

have been ripped. She knows what that might mean. She knows what kind of a man Draper is, she has experience of his sexual preferences.

But she remains calm and focused.

In the corridor, she hesitates momentarily. Which way should they go? Have Alima and Femi actually made it through the tunnel? Roxanne's torch has all but died. And what of the alternative? Is it realistic to attempt to walk out through the front door? Mili stands at her side, holding her hand, saying nothing.

Two miles out they spot a couple of police cars, lights flashing, heading along the country road towards the manor. Maybe Store has decided not to abandon Brown and Draper after all, Havering thinks to himself, still unaware of Brown's death.

The snowstorm lashes at the helicopter, smothering its windows, choking its searchlight. Flying only on instruments, the pilot struggles to maintain a heading against the buffetting wind. He eases the craft slowly downwards, wary of relying too heavily on his altimeter. A brief lull in the storm allows them a glimpse of Fairley Manor Hospital away to their right. The pilot banks hard as the snowstorm sweeps them back up in its arms, the embrace of an avenging angel.

'Bring her down there.' Havering points at a patch of ground to the side of Fairley Manor house. 'We may well come under fire so it might ...'

'I know what I'm doing,' the pilot cuts him off in mid-sentence. Painkillers have done nothing to improve his mood.

Havering waves his hand in apology, everyone is on edge.

Of the officers who arrived with Havering on their first visit to Fairley Manor only two remain, Mullen being in an operating theatre hovering between life and death, and Thorne having been left to guard Alima and family at the hospital. Except for Eliot everyone is armed.

As they touch down arclights flood the scene.

'Fucking great,' the pilot snarls.

'If you prefer,' Havering suggests, 'you can go back up and wait there. But don't go too far, we may need you in a hurry.'

'Can't sit here, I'm a sitting duck.'

'Understood.'

They clamber out into the storm with the helicopter between them and the building.

'Day that way,' Havering shouts to make himself heard. 'Faulkner, you're with me. Eliot, I want you where I can see you.'

Havering covers Day as he disappears into the night, racing away from behind the helicopter across open ground towards the side of the building.

'Right,' he says presently. 'Time to go.'

Trudging through the thick snow, Faulkner first, followed by Eliot, and then Havering. When they reach the side of the building the two policemen check their weapons.

'No heroics, Lad,' Havering says, putting his hand on Eliot's shoulder.

Eliot nods his assent.

The plan, such as Eliot understands it, is for a pincer approach on the main entrance. Havering has picked Eliot's brains about access to the lower levels. At first he refused to believe Eliot's assertion that access was via the door just behind the reception desk but, having heard Eliot's description of the door set high up in the wall over stairs that descended into the ground, Havering accepted the explanation. They will take control of the reception area and then work out how to operate the mechanism that moves the floor.

With the car park to their left they inch their way forwards. Faulkner raises her hand.

Havering and Eliot stop behind her. Faulkner produces a scope and uses it to peer round the corner of the building.

'Located the entrance, Sir. Two by the entrance, otherwise OK.'

'The brownies have to be decoys,' Havering says. 'They couldn't hold back tears, never mind a frontal attack.'

'The two I can see are armed, Sir. Automatic weapons of some sort, possibly uzis. Wearing black with balaclavas.'

Havering considers this revelation.

'Just spotted Day, Sir,' Faulkner says. 'Looks a little out of breath.'

Behind them they hear the screeching of tyres.

'The cavalry,' Eliot says.

A burst of automatic gunfire rips the air.

'Jesus!' Faulkner shouts, still peering round the corner with her scope. 'Day's down. There must be someone else in the grounds.'

'Oh shit,' Havering blurts out, realising his mistake, he hasn't calculated for the return of the snipers on the hill. 'What was I thinking?'

BENEATH THE BITTERCREST

Mili sits on one of the office chairs, grabbing at a desk to spin herself round and round, while Roxanne rummages frantically through the filing cabinets that line one wall, looking for something, anything that will prove what is going on at Fairley Manor. Beside her on the floor is her open rucksack.

She stuck her head round the door of room 2b to check on Draper as she walked Mili down the corridor, taking care not to let Mili see into the room. All seemed in order, Draper was still strapped to the table, the blades hovering just above him.

'What's in there?'

'You don't need to know,' Roxanne answered.

There have to be records somewhere. As she finishes with them, Roxanne throws the files over her shoulder. Nothing, Absolutely nothing of any value. Statistics, commercial reports stripped of all but the vaguest forecasts and figures, quotations and specifications for various items of medical equipment.

'Stop spinning,' she orders Mili out of the blue.

The girl stops instantly, detecting the change in tone in Roxanne's voice.

It is no good, there is nothing she can use. Roxanne kicks the filing cabinet violently, without proof they are dead in the water. No-one will give serious credence to a family of refugees.

'Come on,' she says sweetly. 'One more room and we leave, promise.'

She holds out her hand. Mili hesitates before taking it.

'Where is my mum?'

'We'll see her very soon.'

'Where is she?' You said ...'

'I know what I said.'

Within the hand that softly steers the girl back out into the corridor is an iron fist itching to lash out, to smash every obstacle in her path.

Her voice is tight and abrupt. 'You see those doors. Beyond them are some steps. We climb those and we're out. OK?'

Mili nods.

They are halfway to the doors, two breaths away from the stairs.

'Perfect.'

Draper's voice, just behind them.

Roxanne slips the rucksack from her back and plunges her hand into it in one fluid movement.

'Turn round very slowly,' Draper orders.

Roxanne leans towards Mili's upturned face and whispers. 'When I say now, you run to the doors, open them and run up the stairs. There will be someone waiting for you.'

'Will my mum be there?'

Roxanne nods and smiles. 'Yes, your mum will be there. And remember to cover your ears.'

'Turn round now or we'll shoot,' Draper says behind her.

Roxanne winks at Mili, swallows hard and turns.

Draper isn't alone. Beside him stands the tousled blond-haired guard. Both men are pointing guns. Roxanne is taken aback, having been convinced that the blond guard died in the explosion down in the tunnel. His hair is matted with blood, his right arm hangs limply by his side. His smile is off-centre and unnatural.

'You are going to take your hand out of that bag very slowly,' Draper is saying. 'Understood?'

Roxanne feels calm and in control. No-one is going to bully her ever again. She takes her hand slowly out of the rucksack.

When you hear a pin drop ...

She stands there, rucksack in one hand, live grenade in the other, her fingers gripping the lever tightly. She feels the rum she liberated earlier in the wartime store room, sloshing about in its bottle at the bottom of her rucksack. It will be a waste to use it as a combustant but the best parties always go with a bang.

'Shoot me and we all go up,' she says, matter of factly.

Draper is barefoot, blood oozing through a makeshift bandage. She returns his gaze, feels his hatred, draws strength from it. Draper doesn't want her dead, he wants more, he wants her pain, that is his weakness. To her left a door is open, as she left it when rummaging for masking tape earlier. Maybe, just maybe. She catches herself thinking of Eliot, he turned out all right after all. Her assessment on the train missed the mark, or maybe events have changed him.

'Now!' she hisses.

Mili charges towards the doors, Roxanne keeping her body between Draper and the guard and the racing girl, blocking off the angles, denying them a shot. Please God, let the girl reach the handle. Please God, let the door be open.

She hears the door slam against the wall and is content.

Mili reaches the stairs running so fast she can barely keep from falling over. Almost at the top she remembers that she should be covering her ears. She looks over her shoulders. She can just see Roxanne's shoes.

She sees the blast before she hears it. A blinding flash, followed by a massive boom, even through her hands which are firmly clamped over her ears. The force of the explosion picks her up and throws her against the door at the top of the stairs.

She is still lying by the door when it flies open moments later and two men dressed in black and wearing masks run past her into the smoke. Mili doesn't wait to be told. She races through to the reception hall, smoke billowing behind her.

'I've seen the girl,' Faulkner shouts.

Eliot doesn't wait. Charging past Faulkner and Havering, he charges towards the entrance. A flash of searing pain brushes his thigh. Vaguely aware of gunfire over his shoulder, he throws himself forwards into the building. Ahead of him the glass inner doors hiss apart. An alarm is ringing furiously. Acrid black smoke pours into the reception area.

And there she is.

Eliot scoops Mili up in his arms and clings to her as if she were his own child.

A second explosion rocks the building. Plaster falls in huge chunks from the ceiling.

'Where's Roxanne?' Eliot asks Mili.

Mili doesn't answer. Her body shakes against his chest as she weeps into his lapels.

At the sound of the second explosion, two police cars in the car park slowly reverse and disappear into the night, there is no reason to stay and risk being caught up in the fallout.

The helicopter touches down at the far end of the car park as the first flames start to lick the ground floor windows of Fairley Manor. Eliot, wrapped in a blanket, still holding Mili in his arms, wonders if dawn will ever come.

forty five

epilogue

Eliot sits at the back of the church. Outside, birds are singing and every lull in the service twitters with the sounds of nest building and territorial disputes.

His physical wounds have all but healed, his sideburns have grown back and his haircut feels more comfortable. His mental scars, on the other hand, are still all too raw, he sleeps badly and has yet to spend an evening in the company of others without becoming overwhelmed by a deep sorrow that obliges him to make his excuses and leave. The decision to attend the service has been a difficult one.

He doesn't follow the proceedings particularly, his French being limited. The words waft by, their cadences sufficiently like those he heard in church as a child for the whole experience to feel familiar. As the organ strikes up at the end of the service, he remains seated and waits as the other mourners file past on their way out of the cool gloom of the church into the warm sunlight.

Through the open doors he sees the village square with its pollarded trees, their knobbled branches like upturned octupuses, arms all tied in knots.

'Mr Balkan, merci d'être venu. It is a long way.'

'Madame Lepage, I had to come,' Eliot replies. 'Je ... devoir ... um'

'I understand a little bit English,' she reassures him. She turns to the man standing beside her. 'Chéri, c'est Eliot Balkan, l'ami de Roxanne.'

The two men exchange smiles.

'I was just a friend,' Eliot finds himself saying.

Madame Lepage waves away his concern. 'Please, it isn't ... you do not have to explain.'

A brief uncomfortable silence.

'I am sorry I did not meet your son,' Eliot says.

'You have not come to talk about Didier, monsieur Balkan, but about Roxanne,' madame Lepage answers. 'Come, we will talk.'

Leaving monsieur Lepage talking with the priest, Eliot and madame Lepage find a bench beneath the trees. Behind them a stream bubbles happily, trout blurring the waters, an early neon dragonfly hovering above the watercress.

'I will tell you what I know and then you will tell me what happened.' Madame Lepage clasps his hands in her own. 'I have only learnt much of this in the past few weeks. You know about Calais?'

'When we met, I understood that you were Roxanne's mother,' Eliot says. 'Draper said something about Calais, about Roxanne being half-English. Her mother was a waitress, her father a sailor?'

'Her mother was a whore, monsieur Balkan. And the man who beat her was not her real father. Her mother changed men like you or I change shoes. Twice her real father came over from Hastings and kidnapped her. Then her mother would persuade a man to find her and bring her back to France. Roxanne was beaten, bullied and ...' she struggles to find the right word. 'Yes, abused.' She looks to Eliot for confirmation of her pronunciation. 'I'm sorry, my English...'

'Your English is better than mine,' he reassures her.

'She had a shitty life, Monsieur ...'

'Call me Eliot. Please.'

'You know that Roxanne was not her real name?'

'No, but it doesn't matter.'

'When she met my son, she must have seen her chance. She created a new past for herself. She was very clever, you understand? I am not angry with her, I would have done the same. Her family was abroad, on business she told us. In America, in Africa, in Japan. She would show us cartes postales sometimes. Postcards.'

'She had a head for business, learnt very quickly. My family's export business was easy for her. She and Didier fell in love and they married.'

'Did you meet her mother?' Eliot asks.

'Of course not. At the wedding her family, the one she had invented, sent letters apologising that they could not come. Letters from Japan. I don't know how she did it. But she loved my son, monsieur .. Eliot. They made a beautiful couple.' She glances away. 'No children. I think she was unable to have children.'

Eliot finds himself wondering if this is true or if madame Lepage is simply protecting her dead son.

A trout leaps out of the water causing them both to turn.

'To lose a son is horrible.' Madame Lepage stares at the fish holding position in the current, barely visible through the bright reflections of the sky. 'To lose him and Roxanne is unimaginable.'

The water's surface ripples and buckles.

'She tried so hard to find him,' Eliot says eventually.

He no longer sees the stream but the burning Fairley Manor, windows cracking in the heat, flames lashing out at the falling snow, tiles tumbling from the roof. He and Mili stayed for hours, watching, waiting, desperately daring to hope that Roxanne would emerge through the smoke. The miracle that never happened.

He thinks of the moment he carried Mili in his arms into the hospital and found Alima, with her two sons, by Dudu's bed. The joy slap up against the grief, the emotional rollercoaster almost tearing him apart.

He thinks of his own children. Alexandra and Toby waved him off at Waterloo station a few hours ago. Sue isn't promising anything but they are both making an effort, Eliot's experiences have brought a new sense of perspective.

'It was a miracle any of you survived,' madame Lepage murmurs.

Eliot revisits the horror for the thousandth time, moments flashing in his head like shards of bloodied glass. Those who did not survive. Gwen and Timothy Wesley, the crematorium employee and his wife, him murdered in his office, her shot dead in the family car waiting for Eliot and Roxanne to emerge from Fairley Manor hospital. What if Gwen had been unable to contact Detective Inspector Havering? What if Havering had been off duty that night? What if he had dismissed Gwen's pleas as the delusions of a grieving widow? What if he had been in Draper's employ, like D.S. Store and several of the Swindon police?

Eliot thinks of Han, the investigator, his wrecked cottage standing empty on a hill. The cottage must be surrounded by daffodils now. He remembers the two policemen shot when they had returned to Fairley Manor to mount the rescue.

Did they have families?

The day after the fire, Serina Falcon vanished, leaving Office Solutions in a predicament as she still owns half the company. Stephen, twice interviewed by Scotland Yard, has pleaded ignorance but, humiliated and unable to look Eliot in the eye, he mopes about the office while Serina's protegés drift away one by one and the business crumbles. Eliot has started looking for a new job.

Eliot thinks of the corpse on the wasteland, still without a name, the body in the trunk, the hundreds of refugees who have died, butchered as a result of the negligence, connivance or corruption of

BENEATH THE BITTERCREST

dozens of officials who could have intervened, who should have intervened. Harbour officers, policemen, doctors, security officers, even ministers, for God's sake.

Madame Lepage takes Eliot's shaking hand and sits there quietly beside him, staring into the water. The sun disappears behind a huge bank of dark clouds.

Eliot thinks of Didier Lepage, tries to imagine his last hours, tries not to imagine his last hours. It has been impossible to hold a funeral, no body has yet been found. His parents have to be content with a memorial service.

And who is there to mourn Roxanne?

Somehow Eliot can't see himself contacting her mother nor any of the men who, through the years, have found themselves listed temporarily as her father.

A tear meanders slowly down his cheek.

'Will there be a trial?' madame Lepage asks softly.

'You know what frightens me?' Eliot speaks as much to himself as to Madame Lepage. 'Those DNA databases kept by the police. They took a swab from me after I reported the dead body. They even take them from kids, without explaining what they're doing, or informing the parents. Tens of thousands of people indexed right down to their nucleic acids. What if someone stole the database, or sold it? To a bastard like Draper it would be worth millions. Imagine, children killed to order, disappearing from the streets, to provide a heart or a kidney to someone who could pay.'

Madame Lepage nods and repeats her question. 'Will there be a trial?'

Eliot shrugs. 'An enquiry. There's always an enquiry. Ten years of meaningless paper shuffling until they think everyone has forgotten.' He reaches into his jacket pocket as the sun drifts behind a huge bank of dark cloud. 'Here, I thought you might want to see this.' He hands her a card. 'She went back inside to save Mili, the little girl,' he says by way of explanation.

The card is homemade. Stiff white card on which a photograph has been glued. The Bondembe family are gathered around a hospital bed in which Dudu lies, propped up on pillows. Everyone is smiling, Dudu's arm is around Mili's shoulders.

'It was taken before they knew the government had decided to send them back to Cameroon, on the basis that they had broken their terms of their asylum,' Eliot says. 'They were meant to report in to the police station, once a month or something. Being kidnapped is, apparently, not a valid excuse.'

Madame Lepage opens the card.

The card is covered in hearts and kisses, scrawled and scribbled in coloured pens. A cartoon dinosaur with orange wings sprawls across the bottom of one page. There is a short message.

Eliot, from the bottom of our hearts we thank you.
As you see, Dudu is much improved.
God bless you and Roxanne.

Alima

Madame Lepage looks up at Eliot.

'They know she's dead,' he answers her unspoken question.

'They found the body of the man who killed my son?'

'The fire was so intense that there was almost nothing left for the forensic team to go on but, from what Mili described, they believe Draper died in the initial explosion, along with Roxanne and a second man, possibly a security guard.'

A cold wind sweeps madame Lepage's hair into her eyes and quite suddenly the air is full of swirling snowflakes.